Past the tip of her spear Adira stared into round eyes that glowed an eerie amber-green. The face was a riot of orange, black, and white stripes, and white whiskers jutted from the blunt muzzle. A fourth color was smears of red blood. The eyes were slitted, Adira realized, for the tiger was still furious, eager to spring and rend and kill given half a chance.

"Jedit Ojanen?" Doubting everything, Adira tipped the spear against the prisoner's throat, one strong hand on the haft ready to thrust.

MAGIC
The Gathering®

Experience the Magic

MAGIC
The Gathering®

JEDIT

LEGENDS CYCLE · BOOK II

Clayton Emery

Jedit
Legends Cycle
©2001 Wizards of the Coast, Inc.

Distributed in the United States by Holtzbrinck Publishing. Distributed in Canada by Fenn Ltd.

Distributed to the hobby, toy, and comic trade in the United States and Canada by regional distributors.

Distributed worldwide by Wizards of the Coast, Inc. and regional distributors.

Cover art by Michael Sutfin
First Printing: December 2001
Library of Congress Catalog Card Number: 00-191041

9 8 7 6 5 4 3 2 1

ISBN: 0-7869-1907-8
UK ISBN: 0-7869-2679-1
620-T21907-001

U.S., CANADA,
ASIA, PACIFIC, & LATIN AMERICA
Wizards of the Coast, Inc.
P.O. Box 707
Renton, WA 98057-0707
+1-800-324-6496

EUROPEAN HEADQUARTERS
Wizards of the Coast, Belgium
P.B. 2031
2600 Berchem
Belgium
+32-70-23-32-77

Visit our web site at **www.wizards.com**

Dedicated to
My Hero
Hunter T. Emery
Guardian of the Seas

Chapter 1

Something fluttered, flittered, dipped, and bobbed in the clear desert sky like an addled bat driven into sunshine.

Amber eyes tracked the ragged shape struggling to stay aloft. A curious voice purred, "Keep up, flyer! Keep up, or you're dead!"

The watcher lurked under a canopy of green leaves, for a lush jungle and parched desert lay side by side, their dividing line cut clean as if by a knife. The flyer was a drake, a small, bony dragon clad in fine scales the color of dried blood. Perched atop the drake hunched an equally bony man in dull robes who urged the exhausted beast onward.

No doubt, thought the watcher, the dragon rider wished to reach the safety of the jungle. For to touch the rolling bosom of the Sukurvia was to die.

The drake would never make it. Beyond exhaustion, the creature's wings flailed like rotten cloth. Wracked by fatigue, the dragon steadily sank toward the scorching yellow sand. After flying valiantly too many miles on the hot desert winds, the rider and flyer would fall short of safety by a scant mile.

"Don't!" urged the watcher from the cool jungle depths. "The sands never surrender—*Ach!*"

The last was a cat's spit of disgust as the watcher took

action. Vaulting from a spur of red rock in a long graceful bound, the jungle warrior landed in a high-canted saddle astride a lumbering monox. Big as a hill, the monox still grunted under the weight of the rider, nine hundred pounds or more.

Catching the reins from the pommel with clawed hands, the warrior called, "Get up, Questing Lip! A flyer's about to crash on the Sukurvia! Not my father, drat it, but he might know of him! Hie!"

Rider and beast bulled through the jungle, a fantastic sight towering tall as the big-fronded trees. The rider was a cat man, an upright tiger with limbs like a human's and a curving tail with a mind of its own. Splintered sunlight flashed over an orange-black hide and shone on his snow-white breast and belly. The warrior wore only a goat hide loincloth with a crude bronze dagger bobbing at his back. Clearly the weapon was unneeded, for the tiger sported black claws like chips of chert and white fangs that gleamed under the shortened muzzle. Curiously, the eyes were the most startling feature, a vivid glowing amber with vertical green slits. The eyes of this cat brimmed with a man's intelligence.

The monox was an ungainly brute half the size of an elephant with the ugliest features of camel and horse. Its only beauty came from the saddle and harness decorations, fat glyphs embossed and painted in bright colors like an arcane alphabet. The mount stank like burning garbage in the hot jungle air, a stench so bad the tiger's sensitive nose always rebelled. But goaded, the monox could eat up the ground, its thick legs and feet managing a stiff trot that broke brush with a steady crashing and thrashing.

Another advantage of the monox, the rider knew, would be its usefulness on the hot desert sands. The monox wouldn't survive the short journey, likely, but by then the cat warrior would have reached his goal. He hoped.

In a flash, a last wall of greenery burst before the monox's bearded chin and breast. Shreds of leaves spattered mount and rider, then dropped onto hot yellow sand and withered. Just like that, the tiger had invaded the desert, an arena of unseen death.

The failing drake would be the next to touch down. It struggled valiantly to stay aloft, urged onward by its bony rider, but the bird-thing spiraled like a dying leaf toward the scorching sand.

"Hy-aah! Go, Questing Lip!"

If the oncoming cat warrior worried about the dangerous sands, he didn't show it but kept the monox lumbering on like a wooden-legged ship. When he'd jogged within shouting distance, he craned in the tilted saddle, swaying side to side, and called on the thin desert air, "Make ready to scramble for your life, friend! This demon desert is rife with—"

Probably the rider didn't hear, for the fire drake gave a last gasp and flopped to the desert floor like an arrow-shot duck. Its blood-red scales plowed a furrow of powdery sand as it skidded to a halt. So spent was the creature, it didn't even tuck its leathery wings or coil its graceful swan's neck. It just let its hooked beak and wings drop to the sand for a blissful rest.

The cat warrior astride the thumping monox saw clearly what happened next. The robed rider skipped off the tiny saddle as if it burned his bottom, landed on scorching sands in bare feet, and immediately legged away from the drake. Just in time.

The sand directly underneath the drake suddenly spawned a hole as if a giant plug had been pulled. Disturbed, the drake squawked once as its belly and legs tilted awkwardly on a skittering slope of sand. The hole sported rippling teeth like jagged glass. In the next instant, the rising ring of teeth clashed in a hideous circle on the drake's body. The drake's long-jawed head flipped one way and its spear-tipped tail the other as its body was gnashed to bits. Blood squirted a dozen feet, dark-red drops landing like bizarre rain on the parched desert. The cat warrior, and the running man looking past his shoulder, saw two leather wings fold like torn sails then disappear with the crushed body below the sands.

"Terrent Amese bless us!" called the cat warrior. "Run, man, and give me your hand!"

The tiger flicked its agile claws to nip the monox's side. As the monox charged, the warrior leaned far from the high saddle to snatch the runner's hand.

The monox had other ideas. Its brain was dim and slow, but it had clearly seen death and smelled blood on the wind. It knew menace lurked unseen. The brute swerved in an ungainly circle that almost tipped it over sideways, partially stumbling over its own feet as it swiveled back toward the jungle and safety. Feet big as barrels pedaled shifting sand in a wind-driven blur.

The abrupt swerve nearly unseated the rider as his foot jerked from the stirrup. Nimble and fast, the cat man hooked clawed toes into the monox's hide, saving himself from pitching out of the saddle but raking the beast, so it jolted and jumped worse than before. The tiger spat and cursed as he struggled to stay mounted. The cat had risked his life to rescue this running stranger, and he refused to surrender him to an underground monster.

Time ran out.

The runner was still thirty feet from the monox, and both were still a mile from the cool jungle, when the sands exploded in three places. A perfect triangle of death boxed in the refugees.

The fiends that burst from the desert's depths might have been geysers of steam, but they were solid as gray-barked trees. The soaring columns were topped by round mouths ringed with fangs and writhing tentacles like obscene fingers. Pink-gray fringes like bat wings backed the tentacles or perhaps shaded tiny blind eyes, if the creatures had any. All three living columns coiled unerringly to pounce upon man, man-tiger, and monox.

Prepared for the onslaught, at least mentally, the cat warrior didn't hesitate. Abandoning the reins, the tiger leaped from the saddle in a long shallow dive. He hit on both hands, rolled on a shoulder, and vaulted upright, already running, claws flicking sand in long plumes behind. Before the running man could even blink, the charging tiger was upon him. A black-clawed hand curled around the stranger's biceps and hoisted him off his feet. When the man's bare toes touched down, he was nine feet closer to the distant jungle.

The inhumanly strong tiger didn't waste breath. "*Run!*"

A slobbering groan throbbed as the monox was struck by three hammer blows from the sky. One wurm slammed its ringed mouth onto the monox's broad flank. Hide tore as the mouth clamped like a lamprey's. Jagged teeth punctured the beast's hide, then curled inward to shear away a swath of muscle. As the monox gurgled and squealed, recoiling in pain, another wurm nipped its front leg, clipping the limb off at the breast. Down tumbled the monox onto one bleeding flank, its front leg spurting blood. The third monster, larger than the others, opened a yawning ringed mouth and clapped it over the monox's head, swallowing it entirely. With a jerk of the immense columnlike body, the wurm wrenched backward. Hide, bone, and muscle sheared as the brutish monox was beheaded. Already the other two wurms had consumed most of the bleeding body, ripping away buckets of muscle and bone in single bites. Within a minute, all that remained of the monox was a gory smear on the desert.

With that morsel eaten, the wurms immediately quested for more. The drumming of four feet brought the wurms charging.

The tiger and the man ran headlong without glancing back. A huge shadow curled over them where no shadow should be. The cat warrior shouted and shouldered the man sideways.

From the sky crashed a wurm like a meteor striking. Fastest, the biggest wurm had coiled its titanic body in the air, arching like some fantastic stone bridge, then slammed its ring of teeth right in front of the runners. The shock of the creature's strike nearly flicked both men off their feet. Their only luck was that the wurm drove itself ten feet or more into the sand, so the deadly teeth were temporarily buried. Yet they were cut off by a huge stony body, and two lesser wurms plowed up sand in pursuit.

"Run! That way!" panted the tiger.

Without quibbling, the robed man dashed on bare feet around the buried end of the wurm. The cat watched him go, hoping he'd make it. One shrug would free the deadly mouth from the sand.

The tiger, meanwhile, took a shortcut toward safety. Leaping high, the cat man snagged claws into the scaly hide and scrambled upward like a squirrel. The monster was so massive he felt the heat of its body in waves, felt the desert floor quiver from pulsations within its body, even heard gurglings and creakings from inside its gut. Wurms were decadent dragons, so the legends said. Once mighty, long-ago elder wurms had, for cowardice or sloth, been stripped of their wings and memories and magic and cursed to live underground where no one would see them. To escape even a degraded dragon was an impossibility, went the wisdom, but the cat hoped to get lucky. Reaching the ridge of the great back, he flexed his toes to leap—

—and tumbled as the wurm ripped its head free of the sand. Flicked off like a fly, the cat instinctively twisted to land on his feet, but the distance was too short. With a grunt, the tiger slammed shoulder-first onto sand and gravel and bounced painfully. Still, the warrior rolled instantly to four feet.

Not in time. Fast as a cobra, the wurm punched its round mouth at the tiger-man. He ducked the onrushing blast of hot stinking air but was clipped across the scalp by flesh hard as a millstone. Stunned, the cat flopped flat as the ominous shadow loomed across the brassy sky.

Sand spattered in the tiger's eyes as the human stranger skidded to a halt just as the wurm buckled low to scoop the staggered cat man into its mouth. Cursing at the hurry, the man dipped a long bony arm and scooped up a fist-sized rock on the run. Chanting *"Ain-desh, ain-fore!"* he set the rock ablaze as if it were straw and lobbed the flaming wad into the monster's open jaw—an easy target eight feet across.

White-hot, the rock immediately charred flesh. Scorched, the wurm flinched, arching skyward from the searing pain. Not far and not for long, but long enough.

Too stunned to move, the cat man felt bony hands, surprisingly cold and strong, snag his arm.

The magician hissed, "Come! Quickly! Or we're lost!"

Dazed but energized, the tiger dug in clawed toes and sprinted. Groggily he saw the jungle less than a quarter-mile off.

The cat mumbled, "You saved my—"

"Don't talk! Run!"

"No, split!" countered the cat warrior.

Instantly the two fugitives sprang apart, and between them zoomed a stony column as big as a galloping horse. A smaller wurm, only six feet thick, had squirmed past its bigger cousin. The writhing body thumped and thudded along the sand, fifty feet long. It thrashed like a giant inchworm, and as the men split, it rolled completely over like a sausage, rather than turning.

With the vitality of youth and the added incentive of

panic, the cat had regained his senses in a flash. Now he lashed out with the only weapon handy. Four black claws, sharp as flint, slashed the wurm's hide. Purple goo welled in the gash, but the wurm only twisted closer to assault the cat man, taking the touch as a promise of living food. The cat man hopped like a frog rather than lose a leg to rippling knife-like teeth.

The smaller wurm was crushed as if by an avalanche. The biggest wurm had rejoined the chase, striking at the biggest target. The tiger and the magician redoubled their running as the huge monster chopped its smaller cousin in half. Wurm blood spattered in an arc like purple rain. The two severed halves of the dying creature twitched, coiled, writhed, and spun in aimless circles. The killer wurm's teeth curved inward to shred and swallow flesh in chunks big as an ox. Gore littered the desert as the dead was consumed by its elder. From jungle treetops, vultures soared upward on long-fingered wings to study their chances of getting food.

Tiger-man and magician, meanwhile, pelting headlong, finally quit the fearsome desert and plunged amidst greenery. A hundred feet into the leafy depths they bulled until they were sure of safety, then both collapsed like puppets with cut strings. On hands and knees in a patch of bright mimosa they hunkered, sobbing for air, drooling with mouths open, thirsty enough to drink a river dry. But safe.

"Jedit Ojanen!"

Furry striped legs surrounded the refugees. Craning back, still panting, the tiger and stranger beheld three more cat warriors.

Tribal scouts, they wore blue-painted loincloths and blue headbands entwined around their ears to dangle by their whiskers. Each scout bore a stout stabbing spear tipped with a jagged wurm tooth.

Ruko, chief of scouts, pointed his wicked spear for emphasis.

"Jedit, you know our laws! Man-strangers are not allowed in Efrava! You and he are under arrest!"

* * * * *

The two prisoners were marched along at spear point. The path twisted past white-flowered bushes and shingled trunks of palms and teak trees. Sunlight came and went, filtered by the high green canopy. The air was hot but dry. A blue butterfly flitted past. A beetle bored by their ears, busy at some insect task. Underbrush rustled.

"I'll give you credit, Jedit Ojanen," said the chief scout. "I've never seen anyone stand snout to snout with a sand wurm and survive."

"This is a hero's welcome, Ruko?" returned Jedit.

"You know the laws," Ruko insisted. "Best you'd left this smooth-skin ape to be eaten. He's not worth a monox turd, let alone a whole beast and a warrior's life."

"I disagree," said the stranger mildly, and to Jedit, "I'll thank you, hero, for saving my life."

"Did you know of the danger?" asked Jedit. "The sands of the Sukurvia look placid as a pond but prove a busy place to any who dare step there."

"I've seen sand wurms at close range before."

The man's face and voice remained devoid of emotion, seemingly fearless at being captured by armed animal savages. As he walked the jungle path, the magician pulled a milky crystal from a pocket and idly turned it in his bony hands.

Jedit found the man's manner cold and queer, but then he'd never met a human before. Nor had any of his tribe.

Mildly irritated by the man's insolence, young and hotheaded, Jedit said, "You know, for a stranger in dire straits—"

Something clicked in Jedit's mind. To his eyes, the magician suddenly seemed small and frail, harmless as a tiger cub, even in need of protection. The tiger had no way of knowing

9

he'd fallen under the spell of the crystal in the mage's grasp. The three scouts felt the change too and abruptly flipped their spears to their shoulders, as if it were ridiculous to mistrust so scrawny a captive.

Jedit Ojanen shook his head, which felt muzzy. Perhaps the letdown of battle madness made him sleepy. Still, Jedit was cursed with curiosity that more often than not landed him in hot water.

Stifling a yawn, he asked, "So. Whence have you come? And how? And why?"

"I came from the west. On the drake." The man's eyes roved over the jungle, studying, learning.

Jedit recognized the signs: The man totted up observations like a scout sent to spy out the enemy. Yet so feeble, surely he was no threat.

Jedit snorted, "Your answers tell me naught I didn't know."

"I'm sorry." Yet the man didn't expand. "Where are we bound?"

"The village. This is Efrava." Even with his mind muddied by the crystal's subtle charm, Jedit still burned with questions. "Are there many men like you in the west? How many? How far off?"

"Efrava . . ." The magician frowned as if irked. "How far does this oasis extend?"

"Some thirty leagues east to west, not so many north to south." Jedit backhanded a green snake hanging over the trail. "How large is your land?"

Continuing to ignore questions, the man asked, "Your spears are tipped with wurm teeth, yet your daggers are bronze. Are your people skilled at metallurgy?"

"At what?"

Jedit touched the empty scabbard at the small of his back. Ruko had lifted his dagger. One of the scouts cocked an ear at the prisoners, silently asking if they should be gagged. Ruko shrugged a negative.

Jedit went on, "You mean, can we forge? Yes. Our smith pours daggers in a stone mold. Puddling, she calls it. Tricky work, and the daggers still need days of honing with stones. Why do you ask?"

"How many tigerfolk inhabit this land?" The bony man ducked his head to peer up the trail.

"There are nine clans." Idly Jedit wondered why he felt so talkative. "The Dull Tooth Clan, the Red Rock Clan—"

"Hush! I asked how many *people,* you—" The man bit his tongue, barely civil, then tried again. "I mean . . . My fine host, I appreciate your enlightening me about your homeland."

Jedit gazed into the alien's black eyes, "And I asked where lay your homeland. You have yet to say."

With his face shadowed by greenery overhead, the man conceded, "My land is Tirras, where the mountains meet the plains, north by northwest. A goodly distance. The drake flew for four days to arrive here."

"Four days?" Jedit wrinkled his muzzle. "How can a flying lizard stay aloft that long? Certainly a bird can't."

"Some birds fly a thousand leagues without lighting on land or sea. But I aided my mount with magic."

"Ah. That was a good trick, sparking that rock alight."

"Lucky it worked. That was about my most powerful spell."

Feeling chatty, Jedit made idle conversation. "My mother works magic. She is clan shaman."

"Is she?" For the first time, the black eyes almost sparkled. "And her name?"

"Musata." Jedit narrowed amber eyes. Why did he play cat-and-mouse with this queer man? Were all men so reticent, so jealous of their knowledge? "Yours?"

"Johan. And your father's name?"

"My sire is Jaeger Ojanen." Jedit watched the man closely. "He traveled to the west. Did you ever hear of him?"

"Never," said the magician. "I'd remember a tiger-man."

"No doubt." Unease stirred in Jedit's mind like a coral snake. "Johan is an odd name."

"One to remember," said the bony man enigmatically.

"Jedit, stifle your jabber!" A scout pricked both prisoners in the kidneys with a wurm tooth. "You'll spill all our secrets to this chicken-stinking flat-snout!"

"Let them talk," said Ruko, the leader. "What little the manling learns he can tell his gods at moonset."

Calm as ice, Johan glanced back at the towering tiger scout. "Do you threaten my life?"

"Life is a gift from the gods, stranger," said Ruko. "Yet how long a man keeps it is up to him."

Jedit growled, purring low in his throat, an unvoiced warning for Ruko to back off. Wondering if he'd get any square facts from this twisty visitor, he still persisted, for only by asking questions could he learn of the world his father had gone to explore.

Jedit continued his conversation. "Our legends claim men are a lost race."

"Send your storytellers back to school. Men inhabit the west in countless droves. Do your people inhabit only jungle, and are these your westernmost reaches?"

"Yes. We've moved steadily west since the last days of Terrent Amese."

"Who?" The man's ears pricked. "Why the last days?"

Before he answered, Jedit studied the man like some exotic animal, as indeed he was. He wore a drab brown robe and went barefoot. His head was tanned and hairless, his chin pointed, his eyes flat as a snake's. The mage idly rubbed his brow with the milky crystal—why, Jedit couldn't guess. Despite the close heat under the trees, Johan didn't sweat. All in all, he seemed as helpless as a boar piglet. Especially compared to the tigerfolk, who were all near seven feet tall and weighed up to nine hundred pounds. Jedit Ojanen was the largest. Like men, the jungle warriors had a flattened muzzle, upright stance, and paws elongated into almost-fingers and -toes with dark claws. But they were more tiger than man.

"I asked," Johan repeated, "why the last days?"

"Eh?" With questions buzzing in his brain like a hive of bees and this infernal sleepiness, Jedit was distracted. "Uh, the legends are not clear. My mother can recite the stanzas, but disaster struck the Ancients, so they spread out from our homeland."

"Your tribe halts here," reasoned Johan, "because you can go no farther. That desert heat would kill man or tiger in a trice, if sand wurms didn't snap them up first."

"True. Yet my father dared to venture—"

"Jaeger Ojanen." A crocodile's smile. "I listen well."

Jedit was not reassured by sudden friendliness. "Yes. My father left to explore westward to seek other speaking races. A brave warrior I wish to imitate. I've watched for him these many months. Your fluttering drake seemed an omen."

"I am glad you spotted me," said Johan, "else I'd be food for sand wurms."

"Better the wurms caught you than us," Ruko hinted darkly from behind. "Now shush, both of you. We don't want this skinned pig frightening the cubs."

The trail gave way to a clearing illuminated by golden-green light from the forest canopy. Jedit frowned, for though the village spread for miles, it constricted him. He watched the stranger Johan study the community with black eyes that gleamed like oiled obsidian. A river rippled through a valley bottom, a glittering expanse sixty feet wide but only a few feet deep, which whispered off into dense vegetation to the southwest. Solitary creatures, tigers liked elbow room, so their huts were strung along both sides of the river and stippled up the gentle slopes under trees and brush. Most were separated by a hundred paces. Little more than poles and thatch, the huts were just crawlspaces for sleeping. Two monoxes could be seen cropping brush with their questing lips. Stout ropes of hemp hobbled one massive leg. The village center was only a square of packed earth before a long, ramshackle common house.

As if compiling some mental list, the stranger murmured, "No . . . firepits?"

"Fur and fire don't mix." Jedit looked up as a flock of yellow-headed parrots flapped overhead, all squawking at once. Tigerfolk, singly or in pairs, trickled into the village square. The warrior wondered if they scented the man's wet-chicken odor on the wind or if some other premonition drew them like an oncoming storm. Certainly this manling, a thing never seen by this generation, a race thought extinct, would bring changes to the tribe. And changes, Jedit knew, were an abomination, an insult to tradition, a violation of the sedate sense of foreverness his people smugly enjoyed. This day, for good or ill, would be more than a jotted line in the history of the tribe, and here stood Jedit, dead center in the circle. A troublemaker, they'd say, just like his father.

As Johan and Jedit were paraded by the scouts, fifty or more tigers gathered. No one spoke, not even the cubs.

"Jedit!" A voice piped from the doorway of the common hut. "Jedit! What have you wrought?"

"Mother," said the towering warrior.

The tigers looked much alike, though some were more tawny than orange. Older ones were gray about the head and muzzle. Males wore loincloths of goat hide or pigskin painted with bright angular designs. Females wore halters that covered their flattish breasts and loins, though no one knew why. Some were decorated with armbands of parrot feathers and beads of painted bone. Everyone carried a bronze dagger, a tool used for eating, rarely for fighting.

Jedit's mother, Musata, was tribal shaman. She lived in the

common hut and wore a collar hung with many strands of bone beads that clattered and clacked. A girdle of bronze disks set with rubies circled her waist over her halter. Her eyes were sharp pools of amber and green. Like her son's, they missed little.

Now the shaman peered at Johan, coming so close her white whiskers brushed his face. Sniffing, she circled and studied him, as if buying a monox.

"So it's true. Men live. He came from the west? How?"

Briefly Jedit told of the sailing drake and the double rescue from the sand wurms, with Johan and Jedit toiling together.

Musata nodded. "Does he know any news of your father, my husband?"

"I can speak, madam." Johan was civil but neutral. Again he toyed with the milky crystal. "Your son spoke of Jaeger Ojanen, whom I know not."

"No? Methinks I smell traces of Jaeger upon you." The shaman's amber-green eyes drilled into the prisoner. "Jaeger and more, for you stink of carrion and corruption and cruelty, or else I'm no seer."

Coolly the stranger rubbed his forehead with the ensorcelled stone, which the tigers couldn't know was an aid to projecting harmlessness.

He told the shaman, "Perhaps your son's scent and the wurms' lingers about me, madam. We two grappled repeatedly in escaping the desert raptors."

"Perhaps."

Musata sniffed, but Jedit knew his mother was still suspicious, same as was he.

"Our only real question is—What shall our tribe do with a man-stranger in our midst?"

"No question at all," rumbled Ruko. "He dies at moonset."

"He does not!" rapped Jedit.

All eyes fell on the two tigers. The tribe murmured, and

many shook their heads, fully expecting trouble.

"Who are you, whelp, to oppose tradition?" demanded the scout chief.

"How can you invoke tradition against a being not thought to exist?" countered Jedit.

Tigerfolk perked their ears. A hundred or more had gathered by now. From the corner of his eye, Jedit watched the stranger he was defending. Not surprisingly, the man asked a queer and oblique question.

"May I fetch a drink from the river?"

Ruko blinked at the request, then nodded to the scouts, warning them to be wary lest the man escape. Johan padded on bare feet to the river, knelt, cupped water, and drank. Jedit watched him closely, bubbling with curiosity about this odd stranger. Yet the man seemed simply satisfied with the cool draft and sat back on his heels gazing at the water in both directions.

"Men are evil!" resumed Ruko. "Treacherous, back stabbing, skulking. You know the legends. Your own mother recites them. Have you never attended?"

The last was a sneer, for Ruko and Jedit had disagreed on everything since cubhood.

"Your ancient legends lose ground to present facts," retorted Jedit. "Your source of wisdom is a cracked gourd that won't hold water any more than your head. Behold! A living, breathing *man* comes among us, and you can only crush him like an adder?"

"*Ach!*" Ruko spat on the dirt. "I'm smart enough to heed the legends, which warn us to *beware* men. T'was men drove us from our homeland! We mustn't—"

"We mustn't cast away a chance to learn of the outside world!" roared Jedit. His black claws flexed as Ruko shifted his stabbing spear from hand to hand. Instinctively tigers gave them room. "My father journeyed west to see if men existed! For if so, he argued, some must possess good hearts—"

"Jaeger is lost to wurms!" interrupted Ruko. "He pursued a fool's errand, and like a fool—"

"Watch out!" bellowed an onlooker.

With a roar, claws hooked to slash and kill, Jedit attacked.

Chapter 2

Jedit's screaming attack caught Ruko flat-footed.

The scout's spear was knocked aside as Jedit shot a punch like a catapult stone at Ruko's throat. The scout twisted to dodge, caught the blow on his shoulder, and was bowled into two spectators. They caught and propped Ruko but otherwise stayed out of the fight. Explosive rough-and-tumble brawls were no surprise among the tigerfolk, with so many high-strung young warriors eager to prove their prowess.

A running scout called only, "Recall the rules! No claws!" No one heard over the caterwauls and coughing screams of the combatants.

Despite the swift assault, Ruko lost no time replying. Stamping one foot to regain his balance, he stepped inside Jedit's defenses while the cat man's arms were still extended and slammed an elbow to Jedit's belly, then to his jaw. Jedit's fangs clacked shut. Whirling and dipping, Ruko scooted under Jedit's arm to attack his blind side.

Just as fast, Jedit hooked an arm like an oak club. A knotty fist mashed Ruko's ear and drew blood. Raging, for a tiger's temper was never far submerged, Ruko spun the wrong way to attack more quickly. For a second his back was presented to Jedit.

Toppling sideways, Jedit slapped a clawed hand to the hard-packed dirt and threw both legs in the air. Black-taloned feet rammed Ruko's spine almost hard enough to snap it. Onlookers grunted as Ruko cannoned into a gray-scaled tree. In seconds, Jedit flipped back on his feet, squatted, and jumped—but in haste. Ruko was savvy enough to duck alongside the tree trunk. Sailing through the air, Jedit couldn't stop. Flinging out both hands, he spanked off the tree. Crouched, waiting, Ruko balled both fists and slammed Jedit's brisket like twin sledgehammers. The cat man crashed full length in the dust, momentarily winded.

"You'd assault . . . me for . . . speaking plain truth?" Ruko raged as he punished Jedit's gut with fists like a berserk windmill. "Your father deserted our tribe to enter a wasteland! He's dead! So will you be if you don't abandon foolish notions!"

Berating his enemy while fighting distracted Ruko, and he paid for his neglect. Tough as a monox, Jedit was pained but took little damage. Now, as Ruko swung both fists, Jedit snagged his wrists and pulled. Adding his strength to Ruko's, he drove the chief scout face first onto the dirt with a bone-jarring crunch. Yet Ruko broke free by rolling in a somersault that let him spin to a crouch—

—Right into Jedit's next attack.

The tiger flashed two balled fists in a sweeping circle. Ruko deflected the first blow by shooting an arm high and shunting it aside, but the next blow hammered his shoulder and numbed his arm. Rather than retreat, Ruko lunged with his good arm and slammed his forearm across Jedit's throat. As Jedit recoiled, Ruko whirled and jigged behind his foe. Grasping his own wrist, Ruko yanked backward to half-throttle Jedit and hoist him to tiptoes, off-balance. Muffled snarls, coughs, and curses turned the air blue but were barely heard for the shouting of the tiger tribe.

Ruko's quick-laid scheme failed. Taller and heavier, Jedit stayed planted, tucked his chin to trap Ruko's arm, and dropped to a squat, dragging his full weight on Ruko's arm. As the chief scout was tugged forward, himself now off-balance, Jedit hooked a massive shoulder under Ruko's gut. Before the scout could jerk free, he spilled head over heels and crashed full-length, this time in the river. The tremendous splash spewed water in all directions.

Ruko flung out his arms and legs to gain ground and rise, but water and a soft sandy bottom confounded him. Water filled his sensitive nose and mouth, so he snorted and sputtered. Jedit gave him no relief. Hurling himself from the riverbank, the bigger warrior landed elbows and knees on Ruko and smashed him flat underwater and halfway into the sandy bottom.

For a moment all was confusion, with water boiling like a piranha attack and two tiger tails whipping spray, then Ruko shot into sight, his balance regained, perched on one leg like a crane. Onlookers paused in their cheering to wonder what might happen. All grunted in unison as Jedit's head and torso boiled up from the shallow bottom. With a savage snarl, Ruko kicked his cocked foot and banged Jedit boldly under his jaw. Muddy water flew in a spray as Jedit's head whipped back.

Howling with laughter, Ruko jumped—straight into Jedit's out-thrust arm. A hand like a spear rammed Ruko's belly and cost him his breath. The chief scout sagged around the arm, and Jedit was ready. With a roundhouse swing from far behind, Jedit punched Ruko's jaw so hard two teeth cracked. The scout still hung on Jedit's forearm, sagging, fighting for wind and footing. Jedit gave him neither. Yanking his arm close, Jedit slammed the scout again and laid him on the riverbank.

Pouncing like an eagle, Jedit blasted another fist into Ruko's belly, half-crippling the scout and probably splitting his liver. Growling like a windstorm, Jedit rammed claws into Ruko's shoulder to pin him in place. Whipping his free hand in the air, Jedit extended five fearsome razor claws like flaked chert.

"I'll tear your throat out! I'll—"

A hard-swung spear haft walloped Jedit's skull just below the ear. A second haft from the opposite direction caught him on the rebound. Smacked nearly senseless, the tiger-man collapsed like a fallen leaf onto the muddy bank beside his enemy. Ruko's twin scouts kept their spears aloft like clubs.

One pronounced, "No claws!"

Head spinning in a star-spangled swirl, Jedit barely heard a scout ask an elder, "What shall we do, milord?"

"Hang him and let him ripen?" asked the other.

"He's Musata's cub," rasped the elder.

Dimly, Jedit heard his mother heave a great sigh over her wayward child's antics. "Yes, that's best. Hang him up."

Jedit heard a great roar like the river running wild, then no more.

* * * * *

Hours later, crickets chirruped and nightjars cooed as evening stippled the jungle canopy with scattershot stars.

A lovely sight, thought Jedit, except the stars were framed by wooden bars. He'd awoken with a crashing headache that forced him to lie still or else vomit.

Wooden bars pressed against his spine and rump. One striped leg hung between the bottom bars, so his toes dangled in cool air. "The Birdcage" was a stout cell made of green saplings suspended forty feet high between two leafy teak trees. The bars extended past the cell's six corners, so a prisoner couldn't slash the rope bindings. A determined tiger could have chewed through the green wood and clambered down a tree, but most miscreants didn't bother. The Birdcage imposed public humiliation and cramped confinement, two things that free-roaming tigers hated, but by common law they could suffer only a single day. Jedit could endure twenty-four hours. He'd perched here a dozen times in cubhood and youth.

With naught to do, Jedit watched the tribal meeting on the village square forty feet down and two hundred feet off. Hundreds of tawny tigers crouched on their haunches, tails twirling and twitching as they swapped opinions in low voices like buzzing bees. As news had spread, all afternoon and evening far-flung tigers had trooped in. All gawked at the alien man who'd stepped from misty legend square into their midst.

Johan sat cross-legged in a cage not high in a tree but rather balanced on eight poles driven into the ground, a mere nine feet in the air. Deeming him helpless without claws, the tribal council had ordered him kept close to satisfy the tribe's curiosity. The prison was tucked behind the rambling common hut where the council debated. Two of Ruko's scouts paced underneath the cage. From above, Jedit concluded that if Johan worried about his fate at the hands of savage tigers, he gave no sign. He sat immobile with eyes closed. Occasionally his head swayed as if he tossed in a dream.

Hanging high in the air, Jedit Ojanen whipped his tail and felt the cage swing in response. He wished for a stone to lob at Johan's cage. Young, impulsive, and rash, Jedit resented the queer stranger and blamed him for his troubles. The warrior had argued passionately for Johan's life, yet the man hardly seemed to care if he were executed at moonset or not. Even a rabbit fought for its life, Jedit knew, so why not this skinned rabbit of a man? The jailbird heaved a great sigh, unconsciously imitating his mother.

"Jedit!" A carrying whisper.

Jedit's ears swiveled. He knew that voice.

On a stout branch thirty feet off crouched Hestia. Small and lithe, to a human she would be invisible in darkness, her tawny hide and black stripes matching the silvered moonlight. To Jedit's keen vision, she might as well have been outlined in fire. Before he could answer her call, Hestia wriggled her haunches and leaped.

The wooden cage bobbed and swayed sickeningly as Hestia pounced atop. For a stomach-lurching instant Jedit thought the whole contraption would plummet and shatter on the jungle floor. Slowly the erratic swinging stilled. Jedit squinted through a headache at the she-cat's round face. Hestia's face stripes were a lighter hue than most tiger's, almost tan like a lion's, and her eyes glowed gold like distant fires. She wore a halter of red painted with brown diamonds down the breast-bone. A necklace of brown and red beads swung at her jabot of white fur.

Hestia's flaring gold eyes peered at Jedit through the wooden bars. Mischievously, she swiveled her hips and clawed feet to set the birdcage swinging again. Jedit jolted and bleated at her to stop. She giggled.

"Serves you right." Hestia's sibilant purr did not carry. "I should slash the ties and let you crash. Broken bones would keep you abed, and then I could nurse you back to health. The only time I see you is when you're in strife."

She cocked a hip to rock the cage again. Jedit jolted, but as a feint. Uncoiling, he shot a big paw through the bars and snagged her foot. Hestia chirped as her leg was dragged between the bars, and her rump thumped on wood.

"*Ow!* Bully!"

"Bully?" Jedit released her ankle. "How shall I show my affection? Bite your neck? Drag home a water buffalo? Or bring you Ruko's head as a trophy to hang from your doorway?"

"It would stink and draw flies." The tigress rocked gently, making the cage sway, lulling as a cradle. "Why must our people make war all the time? If we can't fight the Khyyiani or the Hooraree or the Sulaki, we Efravans war among ourselves."

"It's traditional. What else can occupy us in paradise? Food and water are plentiful, the weather is pleasant, and there's no one else to bother." Jedit leaned back, mildly queasy. His head throbbed viciously. "What say the elders?"

"I shan't tell you—and don't!" Crouched atop the cage, Hestia flicked her foot as Jedit reached. "Why should I? You don't care about anyone but yourself."

"I care about my father," Jedit corrected in a whisper, "and my mother . . . and our tribe's past and future."

"Not that again," sighed Hestia. Idly she peeled bark with a claw.

"Yes, that again. Do you know that manling—he's a magician—hit the target first shot when I mentioned why my father journeyed west? He recognized immediately that we tigerfolk have reached the end of our trail. That our people have expanded westward since forever but can't go farther because the desert blocks our way!"

"What matter?" Hestia gazed up at the stars, giving Jedit a silhouette of her lovely muzzle and delicate ears. "Your father didn't need to strike into the desert! Legends say there's nothing but sand forever—"

"Our legends are wrong, as the manling's presence proves." Jedit gazed down at the village. The tribe's gossip and arguing masked their conversation. "There's a whole world of men! Hardly extinct! It would benefit our tribe to meet them and learn from them. We might even take our place among them. Our tribe was great once and accomplished miracles, to hear the legends. Why not again? Think how crowded we grow in this valley. We can't expand forever! If the tribe split, half could journey west . . ."

"Yes, yes." Only half-listening, Hestia noted the pause. "What?"

Jedit tapped a claw on a wooden bar. "I *swear* that magician knows something about my father. His eyes lit up when I mentioned Jaeger. Otherwise he's cold as a toad in winter."

"Bosh," said Hestia. "Why should he know Jaeger? Think, silly! A whole world of men can't all know each other."

"Ah, right." Jedit pondered, suddenly overwhelmed by the idea of hundreds, even thousands, of men. He shook his head, making his headache flare. "Ugh! Either way, I must keep that magician close if I'm to find my father in that wide world."

Hestia didn't say, If he's alive.

"He's alive." Jedit watched a shooting star wink out and hoped it wasn't an omen. "I should be with him."

"Ach!" spat Hestia. "Your mother is right. As keeper of our lore, she knew it was jinxy to also name you 'Ojanen.' A legendary name is too large a legacy to pile on a mortal's back. You'll end up sacrificing yourself somehow, same as the first Ojanen sacrificed himself to save Terrent Amese and all the tigerfolk."

"I can think of worse legends to live up to," said Jedit. "I'm already becoming famous. No one's been banished from our valley in generations, but if anyone can manage, it's I, Jedit Ojanen, headstrong son of the headstrong Jaeger and Musata."

"I just wish you were happy. For yourself, and your parents' sake and mine."

The young tigress shivered. Her slim paw descended through the bars. This time, Jedit held it gently as if cradling a butterfly. For a while the two hung in space in silent communion, but both wondered what their futures held.

Hestia said, "Do you really believe your future is tied to this hairless manling?"

"It must be," said Jedit. "Else why did the gods send him right into my paws?"

Hestia didn't contest that. "We'll see what transpires."

"What? Where are you going?"

"Trust me!" Scooting on long lithe legs, the she-cat vaulted for a nearby tree branch and vanished in the silver-splintered night.

Bored again, and now lonely, Jedit Ojanen watched the meeting below. Tigers milled and murmured. After a while heads turned toward the common hut. Many tigers clustered near the door. As Jedit wondered what was going on, his aerial prison gave a lurch and descended. Jedit was standing when his wooden cage thumped on dirt and thick tree roots. A score of tigerfolk had gathered. Jedit chafed as the guards flicked dark claws to sever the corner ropes.

"What do you want with me now?" he demanded.

Ruko snuffed through his nostrils. "I want nothing of you, Jedit the Jinx Ojanen, but the elders demand your presence."

Bemused, Jedit stalked toward the large hut as tigers fell away at both sides. The inside of the hut was dark, but cat's eyes let him see the nine village elders, one his mother, sitting in a circle. At the center stood the stranger Johan, free of his prison and unfettered. Beside him stood, oddly, Hestia. Outwardly calm, her whiskers twitched from nerves.

Jedit's mother gave the news. Bone beads clicking, Musata said, "Jedit, my son. Our council has debated long. We have weighed both tradition and . . . newer ideas, and come to a compromise. Remember—a compromise is a decision no one wanted."

Musata wore the hint of a smile. Frowns of elders overshadowed her words. Jedit ignored them, having no use for outmoded thinking.

"Our decision is, in part, to heed your words. Our laws state that men are evil and should be exterminated, yet clearly this manling's arrival is a sign from the gods. Or a test. Whatever it be, such a message we cannot ignore, nor can we act in haste. Thus, for the time being, Johan is set free to roam our valley—but no farther—with one stipulation."

Struggling to absorb the news, and minor victory, Jedit asked, "And that is?"

"Johan must be watched day and night. You, Jedit Ojanen, can hardly serve as an impartial guard, so another has volunteered." Musata nodded.

"Hestia?" asked Jedit.

The she-cat bowed her striped head, embarrassed by the attention. Jedit made the connection: By sticking to Johan, Hestia stuck to Jedit.

"Uh, I thank the council for their wise decision. We can learn much from this man of the outside world. Such knowledge will benefit—"

"The outside world does not concern us!" He who interrupted was old Noddel, a tiger nearly white with age, eyes clouded by cataracts. "Your father was cursed with curiosity about the world beyond Efrava, Jedit Ojanen. Yet we tigerfolk are content and see no need to quit the jungle. Your father, Musata's husband, I'm afraid, paid a fatal price for questioning. Mend your recalcitrant ways lest you be seduced to your death!"

Rather than discourage him, Noddel's close-minded pronouncement only reinforced Jedit's desire to explore, but for once he bit his tongue.

"At least we hold off a death sentence until wisdom can be shared," he finally commented.

"See who speaks of wisdom?" Musata smiled. "A cub who makes the wild warthog seem the soul of reason. Go, Jedit. The council must ponder. And Hestia, lead your charge thither."

Without another word, the two tigers and lone human departed.

Outside, a few hundred tigers stared at the trio in puzzlement. Raising his voice, Jedit said, "The council has set Johan free to explore our valley. You may all bespeak him and, it is hoped, learn. Hestia is his guardian."

Belatedly, Jedit asked Johan, "Does that suit you?"

"Kind of you to ask." The man's voice dripped sarcasm. "A guest of your people is afforded the same courtesy as a cow. Yes, it suits me to explore this valley. Let us do so immediately."

"Uh, Hestia, does that suit?" asked Jedit. "We can begin on the morrow—"

"Now," said Johan.

Jedit regarded the man's black eyes, which glittered even by starlight. Pointed chin, bald brow, and slit mouth seemed aimed at Jedit like weapons. Were all men this fearsome and unfriendly?

While the tiger wondered, Johan stepped out, bare feet treading silently on hard-packed dirt, brown robes swishing against his skinny legs. Hestia blinked and jumped to catch up, then Jedit. The tiger crowd parted as from a leper, while Johan crossed the small square for the path that wended along the riverbank. Johan went surefooted as a cat in the darkness, and Jedit and Hestia padded behind.

"Where do we go?" hissed Hestia.

"To explore, I guess," said Jedit.

"Is this what you wanted?"

Jedit swiped a huge paw across his nose. "I'm not sure, but best we quit the village for a while."

"Best for whom?" she asked.

* * * * *

They walked for weeks.

With the tigers tagging along, Johan explored the valley, walking steadily as a millstone fifteen miles a day or more. He stopped only when the tigers asked to sleep or soak during the heat of the day. In the course of several weeks, the odd trio traversed the oasis valley from west to east, then crisscrossed it north and south, until Jedit and Hestia knew every square mile and figured Johan must know it too.

Jedit was confused the entire time, and Hestia admitted the same. To the tigers' eyes, Johan seemed to take no pleasure in exploring but treated it like a job, surveying the valley as if he'd buy it—or conquer it. Jedit enjoyed the chance to escape the confining village and to question Johan as much as possible. Hestia said little, but when asked, admitted she was happy just to be near Jedit.

For days they followed the river, which the tigerfolk had never named, there being only one. It wended steadily upward, for the valley rose as it trickled east. Pacing alongside its placid bubbling, Jedit realized for the first time that his village in Efrava was the lowest point of the valley.

Once, prodded by Jedit amid his studies, Johan conceded, "Yes. The river flows from the east, then sinks into the bosom of the world and is not seen again. Much of the Sukurvia is undershot by a sunken ocean, a secret sea. The water eventually reaches the southern sea at Bryce." He spat the last name, though the tigers didn't notice.

One day they reached the end of Efrava's oasis. The jungle shriveled to gorse and thornbush and stunted trees with only a few graceful acacias like tall fans. The river became a sprawling swamp stitched by sawgrass and weeds. Johan departed the river and plodded on, the tigers trailing behind, until they reached a tall headland. Standing on a brow of parched grass, they gazed east and saw only rising desert.

Jedit gazed back at the coarse, impassable swamp. "How is this possible?"

Gazing eastward, Johan answered only because Jedit would persist. "Obviously, somewhere farther east, the river runs aboveground but then sinks into the soil. It percolates out here, pooling as this swamp, then continues on down the valley. As you said, Efrava is thirty leagues long, just the length of the river, its nurturing mother. What lies yonder?"

The eastern sun was fierce, and Jedit squinted in glare. "Four days' walk lie more oases. East by north lies the land of the Khyyiani. East by south, the Sulaki and the Hooraree."

"Rivals?" asked Johan.

"We kill each other on sight. Most of the time." Jedit frowned, puzzled. "It's tradition to fight them all, but every six years we meet on neutral territory and exchange the cubs below three years. Otherwise we'd become inbred and die out. More often we sally against them, warring to keep them in line. The Khyyiani are cruel, loving to torture captives with lingering deaths, and the Sulaki sacrifice captives and even their own people to a bloody god named Ergerborg."

Johan squinted in concentration. Over weeks he'd tuned his ear to the tiger's antique accent. Now he fixed the twisty tribal names in his mind. "There's no hope of reconciliation, then?"

"Oh, none. We'd sooner nest with mud imps than those bastards."

Johan nodded, seeming satisfied, leaving Jedit and Hestia as puzzled as ever. Abruptly the magician turned. "We've walked one end of Efrava to the other. Now let us venture south, then north."

"What do you seek?" asked Hestia.

Johan's teeth showed a shark's grin. "Knowledge."

Skirting the matted swamp, Jedit warned of mud imps. Johan didn't seem to care.

On their second day circling south, amidst clouds of annoying mosquitoes, Hestia gave a sudden bleat. Her foot had tangled in a snare. Rather than rush to her rescue, Jedit Ojanen unsheathed his black claws and spun a quick circle. Well he did. From both sides in tall bushes popped a dozen evil faces with bamboo blowguns. Johan, in the lead as always, muttered some enchantment and waved a languid hand, invoking an aura of protection. Jedit flicked a paw at a zipping wasp and spanked a poisoned dart aside, then another. A third struck his neck but lodged in his short mane, not penetrating the skin. Two darts shot at Johan stopped a foot away to hang in midair, then slowly sank to the ground. Hestia had slashed the snare from her ankle. Crouching low, she leaped into a slot in the brush, giving a keening cry that set nerves on edge. Jedit bulled into brush after the biggest clutch of imps.

Squawling mud imps scattered through the brush. Belt-high, covered in reddish fur clotted with mud, they had devils' faces with black rams' horns, pug snouts, yellow fangs, and scruffy dark manes. Jedit caught two. One he killed with a swipe of his huge paw, claws splitting the creature's skull. The other he stabbed from behind, severing its spine. A third he tried to kick to death, but it dove into a bush and vanished. Jedit ripped the bush out by the roots only to uncover a gopher hole. Disgusted, he trotted back to the trail. Hestia, her stripes dusty and leaf-strewn, carried an imp's head by one horn. Showing it to Jedit, she pitched it into the brush.

Obviously protected by some magic aura, Johan hadn't moved a pace. He asked only, "Are these common?"

"As mosquitoes in some spots," said Jedit. He rubbed his own black nose, which was drilled with bumps. "Pests. They avoid us in large groups. They live on rats and hogs and ducks, mostly."

Soon they entered the jungle proper again, nurtured by southward-trending trickles from the river. A herd of tiny yellow deer bounded away from a pool. Everywhere ran game in plenty: water buffalo, deer, wild pigs, red monkeys. Even parrots and giant anacondas and tortoises were food to tigers. Jedit and Hestia ganged up to encircle and kill an animal when hungry. They would gorge, eating flesh, organs, even brains and eyes, then needn't eat for four or five days. Johan seldom ate, subsisting on water and roots and now and then a nest of eggs.

Everywhere, the tigers noted, Johan absorbed the lay of the oasis, until he must know it better than any native. He studied the sky, asked about the year-round weather, memorized hillocks and swamps and open glades, noted the types of trees and how they clustered, tasted the water, sifted the soil for minerals or clay. Whenever the tigers asked why, Johan gave vague answers about "wanting to know everything there is to know."

One time, pacing a sun-dappled trail, he asked abruptly, "Do your people have any legends about flying?"

"You mean," asked Jedit, "about tigers flying like birds?"

Hestia put in, "No, not as such."

"No true talk of magic carpets or winged shoes or soaring boats?"

Numbly the two tigers shook whiskered heads, and Johan marched on.

Over four months, they scoured all of Efrava, until the only place left unexplored was the village itself. Camping by night without a fire under three teak trees, Johan sat against a trunk, hands in his long sleeves and feet drawn up under his robe. Jedit lay sprawled on the ground. Hestia lay nuzzled against his broad back, one arm around him, as they always slept of late. The tigers were nodding when Johan startled them both.

"I have a confession to make," said the mage. "I did know your father."

Chapter 3

The shaman dreamed.

Alone in the large common hut, in the dead of night, Musata, shaman of Efrava and mother to Jedit Ojanen, had hung the burlap mat to close the doorway, then banked a low fire of coals with handfuls of herbs. Among her tribe, only shamans knew how to kindle fire, for only they dared risk it. Into the fire had gone mystic herbs: rue for keen sight, fennel for memory, toadwort to draw strength from the earth, hyssop for purity, teak bark for inner vision, and many other herbs gathered in secret from the forest of Efrava, for only by imbibing native plants with native strength could a native remain anchored to this plane while sending her mind questing to unseen worlds.

Sitting cross-legged, clawed hands on her knees, striped muzzle drooping on her bosom, Musata inhaled deeply and dreamed. Jedit Ojanen, her wayward son, had been much on her mind lately, indeed on everyone's mind, and Musata kept his face centered in the arena of her mind. Yet before her inner eyes, Jedit's head began to spin, and suddenly she beheld—on the back of his skull—the face of the strange man called Johan. Another spin, and Musata saw Jedit's face again. No, Jaeger's, older, broader, with white sprinkled among the black fur. A triad, she knew, for magic always happened in threes. No surprise, for the three beings were linked.

She cast her net wider. More faces, a sea of them. Hestia's. Her own, Musata's. Faces of humans, strangers. A young woman with wild chestnut hair and a devilish eye. A bearded man, the face of a saint. More people ranged behind them. How many humans were there in the world? Ironically, Musata had never glimpsed humans before, even in the spirit world, yet here trouped a veritable parade. People tied to Johan's legacy, no doubt. He carried remnants of their spirits, or even their ghosts, with him. So who exactly was Johan?

Sinking deeper into a trance, Musata's brain swam in uncharted waters. Tricky business, and dangerous. A shaman who strayed too far risked being lost, her spirit irrevocably cleaved from the corpus. Many a shaman had been found dead, his body shriveled to a husk, the soul unchained. Yet Musata knew her search was important. She could sift truth, if only she could *see*.

Farther afield fled her astral mind. High, high as the moons, until she shivered in chill upper air. The myriad faces receded, until she beheld the throng occupied a desert far below. Surrounding the desert . . . She strained, mentally squinting, for her eyes were no longer sharp. Surrounding the horde were three—what?

To the south, where must lie an ocean, loomed a vast black gap. To the north, a single tall mountain smooth as a cone of sugar. To the east and west, smaller mountains in pairs. What meant they?

Smoke filled the hut now, so thick it leaked through the walls, though Musata didn't see it. Her nostrils twitched, rebelling against alien fumes. Yet she bore on, breathing to fill herself with the mystical combined essence.

Hanging in not-air up high, Musata breathed fire and fought to understand the vision. Below lay the black gap, a single mount, and twin mountains, all framing a vast horde of unknown humans. Somehow the picture hung on the stranger Johan, for he was central to this vision, same as her son and husband. Three threes, she realized. Magic trebled. Powerful stuff.

Straining, Musata's head began to spin. The people below were shouting, she realized. Calling a name? Crying for justice? Leaning, tilting until she felt nauseated, Musata began to descend in a sickening spiral. She must get closer to the crowd. Their words, their cause, were vital to her tiny tribe, though she couldn't imagine how the affairs of humans might impinge upon Efrava. Faster she fell, in great swooping circles like a stricken vulture.

A black gap, a lone mount, twin mountains.

None, One, and Two.

The knowledge came as a shock. Suddenly Musata was spiraling out of control. She'd die when she struck the ground. Lurching, flailing her arms, crying out, she fought for balance, for a return to safety, but plunged helplessly toward the horde, where burned a fire—

"Musata! Musata, wake up!"

Strong paws caught the shaman, dragged so her feet and tail trailed in dirt. More paws whapped her body painfully, rolled her in dirt, beat her.

Groggily she complained, "Leave me be! Stop hitting—Oh!"

The shaman's eyes pried open with difficulty, as if gummed shut. Bright yellow flames leaped and surged against a black night. Her sensitive nostrils smelled charred dust and green leaves and old burlap. Rubbing her face made her eyes sting. Her paws were sooty black. She hurt, the fur of her neck and muzzle scorched.

"What—?"

"That cursed fire." A young tigress named Zellig and others propped Musata up. Other tigers brought water in curled leaves and gently swabbed her charred fur. Now Musata realized the long common hut blazed from end to end. Flames licked at the night and withered green leaves in teak trees overhead. The glare was painful to watch.

Zellig explained, "The night watch heard you cry out, inside. We know not to disturb you when the door flap is down, but all that smoke worried us. Good thing we peeked. You fell facedown in your own fire!"

"Ah. Terrent Amese bless me!" Oddly, though burned so badly her pink skin leaked fluid, Musata was unafraid. Burning to death was another risk shamans took. This effort had been worthwhile, for she'd seen—

Like a thunderbolt, she remembered her dream.

"None, One, and Two! The coming of prophecy!"

"What?" asked several tigers.

"Ancient prophecy. I know, it's one of many, but I saw this from high above. A black gap for None, and mountains for One and Two. 'When None, One, and Two clash, only Two will remain to usher in a new age.' "

Bewildered striped faces stared. Musata didn't see them. She looked inward, at her son, and the mysterious stranger Johan, the eye of a hurricane. . . .

* * * * *

"What?" Instantly awake, Jedit roared, "You knew my father all along? You *lied*?"

"A tiny lie." Johan didn't shift where he sat against a tree in the dark night. He didn't even raise his hands. Instead he drew from an inner pocket the calming crystal to toy with it. "Once I sniffed the wind, I thought it best not to mention Jaeger's name in the village. You seemed in enough trouble already."

Johan watched Jedit's anger evaporate as if he'd been doused with a bucket of water. The tiger even looked as if he'd doze off again. The cat mumbled thickly, "You didn't . . . All right, I see the sense of curbing your tongue. But you've had months of travel to tell me, us, before tonight!"

Johan flipped the milky stone to his forehead and rubbed furiously, as if cooling his brow with ice. These half-human tigers had skulls thick as oxen. Enchanting them was hard work.

"Be calm, my friend. Let's talk like reasonable beings. . . . That's better. You're right. I failed to mention your father before tonight. To speak of Jaeger is difficult for me."

"How so?" Again calm as a snake, Jedit sank to his haunches to listen. Hestia hovered over him, one soft paw clutching his thick shoulder.

"I met Jaeger only briefly." Johan's voice was a soothing balm. "I was a minor magician in the army of, uh, Lance Truthseeker of Tirras. Lord Lance assembled a mighty army and journeyed down the River Toloron. Of all the northern lords, only he dared wage war against the evil armies led by Hazezon Tamar and Adira Strongheart."

Johan talked at length, garbling facts, spinning pure lies. He was careful to steer toward a goal, though.

Jedit and Hestia listened, rapt, but the tiger warrior finally snarled, "Enough history! Where walks my father in all this human fumbling?"

"Your father was a magnificent creature," pontificated Johan. "I was proud to meet him. When he learned of strife in the Sukurvia, he knew instinctively who was right and joined Lord Lance's army. As said, I was a minor mage. Naturally I wanted to question a talking tiger never seen before. We talked briefly of his homeland here in Efrava. He spoke of you, Jedit, with the utmost pride."

"Hmmm." Mollified and flattered, charmed without knowing it, Jedit preened. Hestia, however, squeezed Jedit's shoulder so hard her claws drew blood. Jedit flicked her hand away.

"Came the last battle." Johan spun more lies in the night as mosquitoes droned. "I can't say what happened. Jaeger was always at the forefront of our army, battling savagely, giving heart to our lads and lasses. Some said he *was* the heart of our army! But sometimes heart isn't enough. We were outnumbered and betrayed. Hazezon and Adira knew every dirty trick of war and were pitiless with helpless prisoners. They stacked skulls to the sky and pitched dead babies atop! They broke soldiers at the wheel and set them afire to scare their own troops into battle!" Johan listed more atrocities, some actually committed by his own troops. "Yet our campaign was doomed. I don't know if your father survived. I believe nothing could still his fine ferocious heart, but I never learned the outcome. As a humble apprentice mage, I rode a drake above our freedom fighters. I was chased by some of Adira's flying contraptions and fled east. Once aloft, my drake panicked, so I kept onward, blown by the breath of the gods. Then I realized whither I steered, toward the homeland of the incomparable Jaeger Ojanen. Perhaps, I thought, this was a heaven-sent opportunity to help our cause. Could I but find Jaeger's people and appeal for help, we might defeat the hellish hordes of Hazezon and Adira."

"My father . . ." Jedit stared unseeing at darkness. "At the forefront, charging a superior force. . . . Imagine!"

While Jedit and Hestia pondered, Johan plied his conjuring crystal like a spider plucking the strands of its web. Johan, Tyrant of Tirras, Emperor of the Northern Reaches, and Would-Be Conqueror of All Jamuraa, had indeed met Jaeger, but always in combat. The tiger warrior and a dozen other stalwarts had opposed his march of tyranny from mountainous Tirras into the southlands. Johan had assembled an army of thousands of humans, dwarves, barbarians, fairykin and others, and they carved a swathe of blood. Yet Johan had run afoul of a creaky alliance cobbled together by Hazezon Tamar, governor of Bryce; other coastal cities; and Adira Strongheart, chief of the Robaran Mercenaries and mayor of Palmyra.

More than any, Adira and her accursed bodyguards, the Circle of Seven, had balked Johan at every step. And among the Circle had loomed Jaeger Ojanen, the mysterious tiger-man who'd crawled from the desert and eventually died attacking Johan, falling victim to a sand wurm.

So had fate served Johan. Fleeing the final battlefield, Jaeger's blood warm on his hands, Johan had flown west, following his karma, and had crashed almost into the maw of another sand wurm, only to be rescued by Jaeger's son. How the gods favored him, Johan thought smugly. True, his initial assault had failed, but only for lack of preparation. Huge losses had only hardened Johan's determination to punish his enemies and seat himself upon a throne of immovable granite, Emperor of All Jamuraa.

Yet, if the gods bestowed favors, so might they rescind them. Johan bore many thorns in his side, and the tigerfolk were the worst, though he didn't understand why.

Jaeger's final words had been, "Even if I fail, there will come another." Who but his son Jedit? While this young warrior was brash and inexperienced, he would learn. In addition, Johan was haunted by the prophecy of None, One, and Two, another mystery that vexed him sorely. Yet he knew these cat warriors were somehow key. To master the prophecy, Johan had to master these striped savages.

The she-cat Hestia spoke. "Why now, Minor Mage Johan? For months you've surveyed our land from root to branch. Why tell us this night of Jaeger's glory?"

"Because I'm afraid." Johan sounded so meek that, despite her suspicions, Hestia wanted to cuddle him for comfort. "I'm not a brave man. Tomorrow we enter your village. I fear for my life, or at least my liberty. If your tribe demands I remain a prisoner, or even be executed—"

"They won't." Jedit cut him off. "We're going west, you and I. No one will stop us."

* * * * *

The attack was cold, calculated, and effective.

One minute Jedit, Johan, and Hestia threaded a game trail descending a thicket, and the next, rope nets whisked to box them in. Striped bodies hurtled from bushes and dropped from trees. Jedit was slammed in the back by two tigers and driven muzzle-first into the quivering net. The warrior snarled and slung fangs and claws, but within seconds he was cocooned in layers of rope.

Johan was shoved hard by furry hands and dumped to the ground. Inwardly the tyrant seethed to be touched by commoners, and animals at that, but he was wary of their feral tempers, so sat meek and unmoving while they clumsily tied his hands and feet.

Hestia was left unbound, braced by two scouts, as Ruko ordered, "Stand fast, Hestia, daughter of Grapter! Interfere not in tribal justice!"

"Justice!" Jedit Ojanen raged and thrashed in the enveloping net, almost incoherent. "What kind of justice—*Aargh!*—do you call ambush!"

"Scream your lungs out, Jaeger's son." Ruko settled his blue turban and picked up his wurm-tooth spear. "Your mother also cast a vote to capture you."

That fact silenced the fighter. The two prisoners, with Hestia under guard, were toted back into the village slung on long poles like dead deer. The entire populace awaited them, scores of tigers waiting with the council before the scorched ruins of the common hut. Jedit and Johan were laid on the hardpack of the village square. Ruko and his scouts stood back respectfully but watched the prisoners.

Johan tucked his feet and sat up. He had no fear for his life and was curious to see this new interaction. Anything he could learn about these cats, especially their decision making, would aid him later.

"Mother," snarled Jedit, twists of net snagging his muzzle and whiskers, "why this betrayal?"

"No betrayal, my son." Musata's voice was calm and cold, a village elder fulfilling an unpleasant duty. Only the quaver of a mother's tears underlay her words. "We act for the good of the tribe. While you wandered with the manling Johan, we searched our hearts and beseeched Terrent Amese for an answer. I was granted a vision, a glimpse of prophecy—"

"None, One, and Two?" Despite himself, Johan blurted the question.

Glowing amber-green eyes fixed on the man. "Yes. 'When None, One, and Two clash, only Two shall remain to usher in a new age.' "

What? thought Johan, but kept his face blank. In his stronghold far away, he'd heard the prophecy differently, put more simply. Now, closer to the source, he learned additional information. Two shall clash? And Two usher in a new age? The same Two? How so? Stunned by the news, Johan's mind reeled, so he barely caught the next news, a threat.

"Little matter." The crowd stirred as Musata went on. "You shall not see that fabled day, manling. We sense your discontent. Eventually you would depart to tell other men of our secret homeland. We heed the warnings of ancient history, of law, even of prophecy. All tell how the workings of men bring evil to our people. Thus will you be executed at moonset. Neither my son nor Hestia will interfere."

Jedit's answer was a howl so horrific the elders jumped back. Some tigers glanced around, wondering if their representatives had made the right decision. Yet no one spoke up. Still raging, Jedit was hauled away.

Johan remained icy calm but again smoldered with anger as he was hoisted like a prize pig and lugged to his wooden cage perched on stilts. Stripped of his bonds, he was clapped inside. The lock was a stout green stick too strong for a man to pull free. Standing on wooden bars nine feet off the ground, Johan ground his teeth. Ever since arriving in this uncharted valley, he'd been treated like an animal. As Tyrant of Tirras, he had treated every living thing like an animal, as if they existed only to serve him, and he'd snuffed out anyone who opposed or displeased him. To be treated the same way galled him.

No matter. He knew almost everything about this valley, about its savage striped inhabitants, their exact numbers and weaponry and customs. He'd even gleaned more of the benighted prophecy. He had enough. Time to leave, so he might return and conquer. That the mage was imprisoned in a stout cage and watched by twin guards didn't matter.

The cage stood in a small clearing not far behind the common hut, which had somehow burned. Before, curious tigers had been allowed to gawk, but now two guards shooed them away, even piled slash and brush to hide the man from sight. Showing respect for a condemned criminal, no doubt. Two scouts paced in a curious rhythm, one circling thirty feet out, the other marching back and forth under Johan's feet. Other scouts had gone elsewhere, likely to patrol near the berserker Jedit.

All to the good, thought Johan. Rubbing his charming crystal against his forehead to appear humble and harmless, the mage struck.

"Guards."

Pacing tigers glanced upward.

"Both of you come close," said the magician evenly. "I have something to say."

Unworried, the scouts in blue headbands and loincloths and carrying wurm-toothed spears approached the wooden cage, their heads almost level with Johan's bare feet.

In that curious antique accent, one scout asked, "What say you, manling?"

Johan squatted as if to whisper. Tigers leaned closer. The mage flicked a hand as if brushing a fly. "Die."

The scouts recoiled too late. Johan could have killed them

in a dozen ways, but this method both rendered them harmless and silenced them instantly. Both scouts clutched their throats and gargled a whimper. Their necks ceased to exist. Two heads were drawn into bodies like turtles until chins rested on chests. Too, the tigers' heads spread sideways, melting like candles. Clawed paws elongated and fused into two fingers that turned into dark spikes. Their bodies bloated, swelling like ticks full of blood, until their loincloths split off. Orange stripes on their sleek hides grew dark and merged with black stripes, then turned shiny and iridescent. Both guards gasped in pain and fell as their sides split to disgorge extra legs, while their existing limbs curled and withered and darkened like tree branches.

Johan too was changing. He hissed in agony as his form expanded and split and shriveled all at once. When, half-crazed by pain, he toppled to the barred floor of the cage, he clattered like a coin dropping on a table. Feebly he kicked stick-legs and thrashed as a white-hot searing burned his body like firebrands. Valiantly Johan struggled to maintain his sanity and wits, for he must escape once fully transformed.

Slowly, after seeming weeks of prickly pain, Johan's wracking subsided. Opening his eyes, he found the world reproduced a hundred times in tiny facets like a diamond. Images of jungle and wooden bars swirled, a hundred pictures moving in unison, a dizzying sensation. Experimenting, Johan moved three arms and found he could stand, then crawl. Poised on six legs, he tried to turn his head but could not, for he had no neck, just a gleaming black skull jointed to a glistening carapace.

Johan had become a beetle. A giant insect five feet long. Good. That suited.

Scuttling awkwardly, crawling on thin but strong legs braced on wooden bars, Johan scooted until his mandibles bumped wood. His beetle's jaws were almost a foot long and hard as blacksmith's tongs. Swinging his bulky head back and forth, Johan attacked the first wooden bar. Squeezing his jaw, he snipped green wood as easily as cutting a daisy. Shuffling sideways, he plied his crushing mandibles to snip the next bar and the next. A few more and—

—With a lurch, drop, and thud, Johan was free, dumped on the dirt beneath the prison cage. Tucking his legs close, Johan reached into his mental library and, mandibles wiggling, recited a disenchantment. Immediately he was wracked by more pain, but this agony was offset by the delicious sense of relief that the spell worked. The odds were small but real that, transformed into a non-speaking creature, he could never utter the reversal spell.

Since he was returning to his original form, the transformation went quicker. Within minutes Johan could sit up, roll to all fours, and stand, whole but shaken. Blinking, glad for normal vision and not a hundred refracted images, the sorcerer cast about to see if anyone witnessed his escape.

All was quiet except for the wasp-buzz of the tigers on the square. Both transformations had taken only a few minutes.

Johan looked for his twin guards. One huge beetle, black with only the vaguest stripes for decoration, twirled aimless circles not far away. Another beetle had driven itself into a thick bush as if to hide. Six legs scrambled stupidly to push deeper. Coolly, the mage picked up a fallen wurm-tooth spear and stabbed the circling beetle at the joint of head and carapace. Stricken, the insect collapsed then died as Johan twisted. Stepping, Johan drove the gory spear into the other beetle's soft hind end, ramming the shaft forward until the wurm tooth lodged in the head. That beetle twitched and stopped digging, then lay quietly.

Dusting his hands, Johan strode into the jungle along a rude path faintly outlined by tiger hair at the tips of branches. Once the village was left behind, so only darkness and the cool night air accompanied him, Johan turned.

West.

* * * * *

"What's happened?"

Faint cries carried on the night air. Two scouts guarded Jedit Ojanen, bound to a tree a mile from the village. He'd remain isolated, they'd said, until the moon was fully set and Johan properly executed and buried.

Yet more cries and a hideous wail of a tiger grieving set them all twitching.

"Terrent Amese!" rumbled one guard. "Could it be an attack?"

"You mean the Khyyiani?" asked the other.

"It's not the season." Jedit growled, still angry at his impotence. His hands and arms were swaddled in rope.

"Bite your tongue, Jedit!" One guard shook his spear in the prisoner's face. "We've had naught but trouble since you found that manling! Likely when you and he traipsed all over Efrava, you led a war party of Khyyiani straight to us!"

More cries from the village, more sobbing than fighting. Finally one guard said, "Go. I'll watch his highness."

The guard departed at a trot. The other paced, shifting his spear from hand to hand. Jedit looked at the moon just risen.

"If there's a raid," he said, "you should free me. The execution of the manling can wait—"

He jumped as something brushed his back, then realized it was a paw, small and soft. Unmoving, he blithered, "Uh, that is . . . Ruko would let me go."

One by one the ropes binding Jedit were severed by a razor claw. Jedit flexed his wrists. "They'll need every warrior in the village—"

"Will you belt up?" Torn between duties, the guard whirled on Jedit and was knocked cold by a fist like a sledgehammer.

"Hestia."

The small she-tiger stepped from shadows. "Jedit. I slipped

away from my family. I had to see you. Something's gone horribly wrong in the village. People panic and wail."

Not knowing the problem, Jedit didn't know how to proceed, especially given his prisoner status. "I'll . . . circle around and keep out of sight."

"Go." Hestia's large eyes were moist by moonlight. "I fear I shan't see you again."

"You will," said Jedit. "I promise. Terrent Amese be my witness, I'll return."

For a moment, electricity crackled with a thousand things unsaid. Then Hestia grabbed Jedit's huge shoulders, pulled him close, and pressed her muzzle to his. To exchange breath was a tiger's kiss. She pushed him away. To not say goodbye was another custom.

Jedit loped off, veering west to circle the village and its queer, spine-chilling wails. Dashing through the jungle, eyes alert for bare footprints, Jedit covered miles in minutes. Yet his target was ridiculously easy to find. Of all things, Jedit heard three voices in the middle of nowhere.

At a wide spot in the trail, Johan faced Ruko and another tiger scout. Jedit assumed Johan had been led from the village to be executed by the two designated scouts. Yet the three conversed as calmly as neighbors gossiping in the marketplace. Slowing to a jog, Jedit advanced until all three turned his way.

The tiger-man rubbed his nose, mightily puzzled. The lone man showed no fear or apprehension of the scouts. By starlight, the man's bony face was luminous as a bleached skull, completely placid. Why didn't Ruko move to intercept Jedit?

"Johan. Ruko." Unsure of his mission or stance, Jedit blurted, "What of the execution?"

Ruko's face was blank. "Execution? Oh, it's been stayed. Johan and I are talking instead."

"Talk?"

In the darkness, Johan's black eyes were invisible, so his bone-white face seemed blind. He toyed with his enchanting stone. "Yes, we talk. People should be allowed to go where they will. No one should stop them. Isn't that true?"

"What?" asked Jedit. "What nonsense is this?"

"I wished to leave and did." Johan stared. "I met this patrol, and no one should be restrained against their will. Isn't that true?"

"True," echoed Ruko and the guard.

"Wait! Why the wailing in the village?" Jedit shook his head, whiskers shivering. His skull buzzed as if full of bees, making him dizzy.

"Oh," said Ruko, "someone died."

"No one important," added Johan.

The mage's brow began to ooze sweat. These tigerfolk had alien minds not easily subdued. Lucky there were only three, or Johan would fry his brain controlling them. Gasping, concentrating, he rattled to sink the hook.

"I go my way, and you go yours. Back to the village. That's reasonable, isn't it? Sensible? I gain my home, yours. I go. Won't you agree?"

"Agreed," said Ruko.

"And I?" Jedit blinked amber-green eyes as a fog floated in. Queer on such a starry night.

"You?" Johan sucked wind for energy. "You go with me, by your own choice. To find your father. Jaeger will be glad. You come with me. All right?"

"Yes." Having decided, or so he thought, Jedit said to Ruko. "I go with Johan. You return to the village."

Abruptly the two scouts whirled. Johan recalled that this race never said goodbye, thinking it bad luck. Winded, exhausted, he blurted, "Wait!"

The scouts whirled, amazingly fast, and for a second Johan thought they'd shed his spell, but he put out a hand and gingerly brushed the hafts of their stabbing spears. "I only wanted to say, your spears are impressive weapons. Fine workmanship. Lovely rich-grained wood. Now go."

Wrinkling noses at the odd comment, without further ado Ruko and the scout turned east. Immediately Johan jogged west.

Jedit trotted to catch up. "What's the hurry?"

"Uh, to gain the desert before dawn." Johan cursed, tired of fabricating lies for cretins. "We've a long way to go. To see your father."

"Oh, yes." Still squinting against the fog in his mind, Jedit loped alongside the barefoot mage.

Meanwhile, Ruko and the other scout had paced a hundred yards, eager to return to their village and—what? They couldn't remember their mission. A furious buzzing filled their heads, but Ruko marked it down to fatigue. In the village they could rest. Except . . .

Ruko stopped short and snuffled his black nostrils. "I smell smoke."

"Queer," said the scout. "My spear feels—"

Fwash! With a whisper and whoop, their thick spears suddenly ignited. The tiger scouts dropped the burning shafts immediately, crying in pain and surprise, but the magical immolation had already spread. Flames surged up their arms, across their chests, down their bellies, and around their necks until their shaggy heads were wreathed in flames. Acrid smoke spiraled from their fur, sizzling so hot leaves on bushes shriveled and caught fire. The tigers howled as hair and flesh charred. Yowling, they dropped to the forest floor and thrashed and kicked, but the flames would not be quenched. As their flesh blackened and split into raw seeping wounds, the tigers' wild scrambling stopped. Finally they lay still and died. Flames continued to flicker awhile, as leaves and dirt crackled and burned, then even those small fires extinguished.

Far off, Jedit pricked his rounded ears and asked, "Did you hear a yell?"

"No," said Johan, for once truthful. "Come, the desert awaits."

"Ah, yes, the desert. And my father."

Rather, his ghost, thought Johan. And yours, soon.

Chapter 4

Without a sound, Jedit Ojanen collapsed facefirst on the desert sand.

His muzzle banged gravel so hard that blood jetted from his black nose. Even slumped, he struggled to keep his green-gold eyes open to ward off danger, but his senses had fled under the scorching sun. He lay full-length like a toppled tree and didn't stir except for shallow breathing with blood bubbling in one nostril.

Johan stifled a curse. He cast about, but rolling dunes of sand and pebbles and nothing else filled this portion of the Sukurvia. High up, nine Osai vultures rode the air currents. Squinting against the searing sun, Johan mused on these wastes. A dead land, thought the dictator, and another barrier to his conquest of Jamuraa, for ordinary mortals couldn't cross it, unless he found some way for men to fly like vultures.

Grinding his teeth, Johan chafed at delay. He needed no rest. Hundreds of years old, sustained by arcane magics, Johan seldom slept or ate, having transcended bodily needs. Looking at the helpless tiger, with no way of moving him, Johan pondered slitting Jedit's throat and ripping off his skin or carving his skull from his hide, so later he might commune with his essence. If the cat man couldn't serve Johan alive, he'd serve dead.

"Cat warriors. Tigerfolk." Johan talked to the still desert air, venting his spleen. "Why do the gods punish me with these half-man half-cat bastards? Why must I endure when they buzz around like horseflies, distracting my purposes and contributing nothing?"

Johan knew why, if indeed any man could correctly interpret the whims of the gods. Because of None, One, and Two. Too many times in his campaign of conquest had Johan stubbed his toes on this prophecy. "When None and One clash, only Two shall remain to usher in a new age." The tigress shaman had unknowingly added a snippet to Johan's tiny understanding. Piffle, he thought, but he feared it rang true. He'd heard this ancient wisdom or curse before. It was as common as moonlight, spilling from Citanul Druids, from desert nomads, from Palmyran spies, from advisors, from tortured prisoners, from a dying cat man. Whispers from the past swirled around Johan and ensnared his schemes like spider webs. He had to grasp the prophecy's import like a handful of nettles. He had no choice.

Yet who was None? What was One? Which Two would survive and prosper? At first, Johan had taken the prophecy literally. None could be anything. One might be Tirras, his homeland, or himself. Two remaining might be his homeland and his empire ushering in a new age, the dynasty of Johan the First. Or None could be a cat man, a two-in-one creature, neither one race nor another. Yet half a tiger and half a man might make One. None, if they were freaks of nature not part of any grand scheme, too far outside humanity to affect its history. Yet shouldn't Johan be One, triumphant, inviolate?

"The eternal problem of prophecy," growled Johan. "What does it *mean,* and *how* do I bend it to my will?"

Who knew? Maybe None was this accursed desert, a notland for no living thing. One cat man had clashed with it and collapsed. Predictably. Tigers were like humans in the desert. A jungle suited only if they could bathe in water during the sun's peak. This young idiot had lost his first battle. Johan should spike his spine and feed the vultures.

Yet even an emperor had to accept what the gods dished out, and they'd dumped this tiger in his lap. Somehow tigers were his personal demons. He must conquer them to conquer Jamuraa, or so he guessed. Johan damned the gods and himself and his own superstition. He would obey, for now, and someday push the very gods off their celestial thrones.

"Get up!" snarled the mage.

Jedit gasped.

"Get up, or I'll leave you for wurms!"

So far they'd seen no wurms. Jedit had guessed they simply walked softly and stretched their luck. Johan knew better. A magical combination of shielding aura and a deluding glyph that displaced their trail four feet in the air let them safely plod across the endless sands.

We should have brought water, thought Johan, and robes against the sun. Now, after six days with only a sip of water from a rain puddle, Jedit had crumpled like an empty waterskin. Johan admired his stamina and wondered how his father Jaeger had crossed the desert without sorcery.

Fascinated by the question, Johan cast about the pebbly dunes. Eventually he'd need some way for his army to cross the desert. Legends spoke of mages who could shift themselves and any load across myriad planes and mystic realms, but Johan had not yet attained such a lofty level, nor had any mage in Jamuraa, to his knowledge. Right now, he just needed a way to get this half-cooked cat out of the desert.

For hours Johan searched in man-killing heat for a way out. He still wore his traveling disguise, appearing a bony, bald, tanned man in a brown robe. Once he'd adopted a disguise, it was easier to keep it rather than drop it momentarily and risk detection. In the shade of a curling dune like an ocean wave he found what he was looking for—a patch of sand smooth as if broomed. Gingerly Johan approached. A dozen feet away, he ran and jumped square on the patch.

Sand geysered in a cloud as the living patch rebelled. Wings curled at two corners as the creature fought to rise, but Johan pinned it to the ground with a spell. Helpless, the desert beast flailed and flopped but went nowhere, kicking off its sand covering. Cousins to manta rays of southern seas, desert rays not only skimmed the sands but could instantly burrow underneath, either to rest or to await prey. Big as a collapsed tent, the ray was a mottled tan that, even as Johan watched, changed hue to a dark rust-red. Perhaps the color startled predators.

No matter. Johan was master. He crept to the ray's head. Like a toad, its eyes could retract into the head or else bulge to see a complete circle. Some of Johan's cavalrymen and nomads had tamed and harnessed big rays, but the mage had never examined one. Given time, he would dissect one and wrench out its desert-dwelling secrets.

Wary of the mouth with tiny sharp teeth, Johan dug a long-nailed thumb into the ray's eye socket and hopped off. Goaded by pain, the ray flapped and flopped while towed across the burning sands. Johan hoped the tiger-man hadn't been plucked clean by vultures.

In a short while Johan had settled Jedit Ojanen facedown atop the captured ray. Johan sat astride the tiger's back to balance their weight and, borrowing Jedit's bronze dagger, pricked the ray's flesh. Instantly the creature hopped into the air. Another jab made it bank right, north-northwest. The ride was jerky, as much up and down as forward, but they soon attained a steady gait like a horse's canter. They'd cover miles in no time, Johan was sure.

Always curious, the mage wondered why the rays weren't consumed by sand wurms. He could only conclude they were too tough and unappetizing. He must experiment. Desert-ray blood smeared on chariot wheels might keep sand wurms at bay. Horse hooves might be wrapped in green ray hide.

A croak sounded above the creak of leather wings.

"You . . . saved my . . . life," Jedit gasped with eyes shut.

"Yes," said Johan. "It becomes a habit, our rescuing one another. We share a bond. Now, rest. We've much to do when we reach my homeland."

"Home . . ." whispered Jedit and sank into oblivion.

* * * * *

Jedit Ojanen splashed into water that closed over his head and threatened to drown him.

Floundering, clawing for air, the weakened tiger felt his head grabbed and tugged into the air. Snorting, the cat man caught a stone lip with his claws, then leaned back and soaked in delicious blissful coolness.

"Don't drown." Johan walked off to talk to some dun-robed herdsmen.

Recalled to life, Jedit slurped gallons and let his parched body soak. His watering trough had been laboriously carved from a single piece of dark gray stone. The well was the centerpiece of a low valley between shale outcroppings. The ground was littered with shale flakes like autumn leaves. Jittery sheep huddled under the protection of a boy shepherd. No doubt the flock was terrified by the scent of a giant cat and bleeding desert ray. Johan turned as nomads pointed northwest. The natives wore double folds of robes, for in early autumn the nights froze solid.

"We . . . we crossed the desert!" Amazed to have survived, Jedit clambered from the trough. His clumped fur streamed water.

Johan grunted. "Palmyra is another eight days' walk. There are wells along the way, say the erg dwellers."

"Fine." Jedit tossed his head and whiskers, whipping water

on Johan's robe. "I can walk to the moons if I have water, but can we buy a sheep? It's been six or seven days since I ate."

Rolling dark eyes, Johan dug in his pockets for a worn coin. After some ritual haggling, the nomads dragged out a balky ram with horns so curled they obscured its eyes. Jedit thanked the shepherds, raised a paw big as an axe, and slashed. One swipe severed the ram's head. Jedit lifted the carcass by its back legs to drink blood spurting from the gory neck. Nomads skittered away like a flock of starlings. Johan started walking. Northwest.

For days the odd couple trekked from well to well. They slept under the stars, awaking under frost thick as blankets. Jedit subsisted on jerboas, a big-eared fox, a dead vulture, a hyena, a covey of hedgehogs, dead sheep, snakes, and any other creature that crossed his path. Johan ate nothing but cactus pulp and water.

Once, topping a rise, Jedit saw long furrows of dark sand. Something had stirred the ground from below. Curious as ever about this new world, he asked, "Is there danger of sand wurms?"

"There may be." Johan walked steady and unhurried. "The wurms never ventured this far east before, for they can't burrow easily through the pebble desert. But in past months a titanic sandstorm smothered the region and gave the wurms new inlets. The wind blows, as always, so sand sifts back east and south, but some stretches linger. As must some wurms."

Once before dusk, as their shadows stretched like skinny giants, Johan mounted a pebbly hill with a short stone tower, obviously a lookout post, now deserted. At the summit, setting sun glared in their eyes. Johan nodded at distant cubes on a knoll. Silver winked and flashed as the sun dropped.

"Palmyra." Johan ground his teeth.

"Palmyra?" asked Jedit. "Ah, the village waystation! Didn't they oppose the army of your lord, Lance Truthseeker? And my father?"

"That's correct," lied Johan. "A city of degenerates, thieves, and traitors. But we must swim amid the sewage, for I need supplies."

"Supplies?" Jedit glanced at the bony mage who for weeks had subsisted in the desert with no more equipment than a tortoise.

"And other things," hedged Johan. "Come."

Jedit Ojanen tripped along, eager as a cub after weeks of boring desert. Even in an enemy city, he might learn about his father.

So dusk claimed the desert, and stars came to life while the odd couple marched on, over the cooling sands.

* * * * *

"Stand still. I must disguise you."

"Why?" asked Jedit.

The towering tiger and the bony mage stood in darkness behind rambling stone corrals on the outskirts of Palmyra. Midnight was past.

"How would townspeople react if a tiger strode into their midst?" Johan worked as he talked, pacing around the cat man and sketching in the air.

"Oh, yes. I forgot my father would have been a celebrity, always in the forefront of the battle against Palmyra. None of those goatherds feared me. Will you adopt a disguise?"

"My face is unremarkable." Johan didn't explain he already wore a guise and had for months. "Now hush."

Shapeshifting and transmutation were out of the question, for such drastic spells would warp the tiger's body cruelly and cause immense pain. Picturing what he wished to project, Johan laid bony hands on the tiger's tufted mane. Running his hands out and down, over rounded ears, then whiskers, then the thick neck and down the soft pelt, Johan chanted softly under his breath, "*Dru-in-bolik, dru-in-va-te. Dru-in-bolik . . .* "

Taking care to stroke every inch, Johan finished between the tiger's furry toes, making the cat dance from tickling. Carefully, as if poising an egg on end, Johan drew away his fingers.

He almost smiled.

Standing before him was not a tiger but a hulking barbarian from Jamuraa's far north. Ugly as a broken rock was the creature, but Johan was pleased. The clever disguise mimicked the tiger's natural height and weight, those hardest features to mask, leaving only skin to be cloaked. Barbarians even bore broad noses and short tusks that matched the tiger's snub muzzle and fangs. Standing under starlight, Jedit loomed like a suntanned giant of a man with red-blonde haystack hair and long dangling arms roped with muscle. Johan had even tricked the skimpy goathide loincloth to mimic a leather vest and kilt, though they were stretched tight over the massive frame.

"T'will do."

Bemused, Jedit held up his hands, staring with the dull eyes of a barbarian at human skin and fingernails. "It's foul ugly. How long must I wear this sham?"

Johan frowned. The voice was still a tiger's, a droning purr in a queer antique accent. "Don't talk. The spell will cling until I disenchant you. It shan't be for long. Now come."

Yet the new man's first step made Johan curse under his breath. Jedit's natural tread was the lithe loping glide of a tiger, not the brutish stumping of a barbarian. Still, night should cloak the flaw, and the tiger was just a tool to be used and discarded anyway. Though Johan was plagued by superstition, he nonetheless possessed the keen mind of a general who always planned conquests at two levels. Thus, while Johan hatched long-range plans with a thousand tiny components, he could still diverge from a plan to snap up promising opportunities that popped up.

He muttered, "He who thinks both longest and quickest prospers first and last."

"Eh?" The barbarian turned beady dark eyes on the mage. "Nothing. Don't talk."

Leaving desert and corrals behind, the pair took the dusty road that led to twin watchtowers and the city wall of Palmyra.

For four centuries since the Ice Age glaciers vanished overnight, Palmyra had occupied an oxbow bend in the River Toloron. Originally tiny, the village clung to a shelf of bedrock the river could not erode so instead partly circled. The hostile Sukurvia resented permanent dwellings, but Palmyra stuck because the river protected and nourished it. It was the only real town within the vast desert. Far to the north, where the river rushed from the mountains, crouched a craggy city like a condor. Tirras was the dark heart of rich and fertile northlands where wealth and populace had exploded of late. Its iron-fisted ruler was Johan, Tyrant of Tirras and Emperor of the Northern Realms. Far to the south, where the river lost itself in the Sea of Serenity, sat the seaport Bryce. The River Toloron spanned the desert and linked the two cities, and it was down this river that Johan had launched his invasion of the southlands.

His invasion foundered on the rock called Palmyra. Adira Strongheart, erstwhile mayor of Palmyra and leader of the cutthroat Robaran Mercenaries, called Palmyra home and defended it tooth and nail. To Palmyra's defense had come an alliance of southern city-states led by the governor of Bryce, Hazezon Tamar. Johan's invasion ran square into a new-built dam blocking the river, then a newly fortified village, then a nimble and unflagging patchwork army, and finally hearty doses of magic. The river itself had been magically spirited away by merfolk. Weeks of thirsty fighting ground Johan's forces down. Finally had come phalanxes of ensorcelled sandmen and a withering sandstorm that smothered the invading army. Only remnants had escaped to crawl back to Tirras.

Thus Johan's face was slashed by a frown deep as a knife wound as he padded into Palmyra with a hulking barbarian alongside. Everything in Palmyra seemed calculated to gall the would-be conqueror. Palmyra's town wall was again strong, showing no traces of the Tirran siege. The twin towers were manned by militia soldiers with spears and horns ready to sound an alert. Guards demanded the strangers state their business, but Johan's powers of persuasion got them past. The town had never been much more than adobe huts, dusty wells, and a few scraggly trees, but the citizens had taken new pride in digging out from under the fabulous sandstorm six months past. Though some cellar holes were still choked with sand, many flat-roofed houses were freshly painted. Wells were dredged and dressed with stone, for suffering without water for weeks had reminded townsfolk of the precious commodity's worth.

Sleeping away the afternoon heat, Palmyra came awake at night. The swirling populace sang and laughed and called to friends. The town felt festive, the air still sweet with victory. A chain of giggling girls danced and wove through columns framing one street. A man played a flute, and his dog yipped along. Two women shared gossip and grapes leaning from the second stories of their homes. Young lovers cooed and kissed in shadows where starlight didn't fall.

Fuming, Johan strode along, the only busy man in the village, but time and again he had to catch Jedit's hand and tow him along. Wearing the barbarian mask, the tiger-man gawked at every sight and smell as they mounted ancient steps cut in stone. Palmyrans seemed as varied as birds in the jungle. As they reached the highest point, the town square where people drifted, the visitors saw dark-bearded nomads, gaudy pirates, soldiers from Yerkoy and Enez, plump Brycer merchants, lean desert elves like knives in black robes, Keepers of the Faith, red-rouged prostitutes, elephant handlers, Aisling leprechauns, and doughty dwarves clutching foaming tankards. Mixed in, Johan noted coldly, were many north-blood Tirrans, likely deserters from his shattered army.

The strangers slowed as the crowd piled up. Johan jerked to a halt, hooked like a trout by a hated name.

"Adira said this lad could join us?" bawled a lusty voice in mock horror. "What's the Circle of Seven sunk to that we need a beardless youth to keep us hale and hearty?"

"I told you, Badger," corrected a woman primly. "Murdoch was a sergeant in Yerkoy. That's a rank of responsibility—"

"He's rank, I'll warrant," interrupted the rogue named Badger. "His fighting style stinks—Avast!"

The towering Jedit pushed forward to see, and the crowd parted like tall grass. Johan slipped behind to peek, seeing but not seen.

Sword practice in the cool of evening had become a spectacle for townsfolk. One side of the square was formed by the town hall, a long adobe building that served as headquarters for Adira Strongheart when not at sea. Adira's personal body-guard were the infamous Circle of Seven, the quickest, most canny, and most loyal fighters, thieves, and pirates culled from her three hundred-odd Robaran Mercenaries. Members of the Circle were popular and famous as the mayor herself, and their wild antics were often the talk of the tables. Tonight would add to their reputation.

Johan wished them all dead and rotten in their graves.

Inside a circle ringed by four torches on poles stood the older sailor named Badger for his white-striped hair and beard, and opposite him stood a new recruit to the Circle, a sturdy sergeant still in the green and gold tabard of Yerkoy. Watch-ing were several of the Seven, especially Sister Wilemina in blonde braids and blue cowl, a Calerian archer, skinny but with arms like rawhide. Johan hissed, for her arrow had once nicked his ear.

Sister Wilemina chirped, "You must give Murdoch a chance! Please, Badger! It's only fair!"

"Fair's a funny word from a pirate, pretty thing." Playing to the crowd, Badger made them laugh. "Even a fair wind's nothing to bank on. Come on, Murdoch, pick up that pigsticker! A cask of Brycer stout goes to the winner, and it's thirsty work watching you fall down!"

Though Murdoch was in his prime, barely past twenty and sturdy as an ox, and Badger's best days had ended three decades back, it was the older man who skipped and dodged while the younger man charged like a blind bull, panting with his tongue out. Murdoch lugged a spear with a wicked barbed head. Badger had only a small round shield and a cutlass. The sergeant should have stabbed the sailor a dozen times, but Badger was only dusty while Murdoch was bloody.

Sucking wind, Murdoch lowered the spear and rushed. The old pirate seemed to stumble, and the crowd gasped, then Badger kicked backward with one foot. Suddenly he was side-on as Murdoch blundered past too fast to stop. Badger could have split his spine with the cutlass but settled for spanking the sergeant's bum. The crowd roared. Still game, Murdoch dropped the spear point to dig in dirt and whirl half-round. He whipped the spear butt back to ram Badger's gut. The pirate was gone. Gasping, Murdoch snapped his head to one side—

—and slammed his face flat into Badger's upright shield.

Stunned, Murdoch grabbed his aching forehead. Grinning, Badger blew a mighty puff and, with one finger, shoved the sergeant over. Murdoch raised dust when he flopped, and the crowd cheered with delight as he was dragged from the circle.

"Pitiful." Badger shook his salt-and-pepper head in mock sorrow. "If Johan fetches down another army, we'd best arm the children and our spryer dames. What say you, citizens of Palmyrans? Could our eldest crones send an army of Tirrans fleeing in terror with naught but brooms?"

"Aye!" laughed a hundred. "We'll spit Johan's head on a pike yet!"

Behind Jedit Ojanen, the disguised emperor's eyes flashed so bright he expected sparks to set fire to the tiger's fur.

"Badger, you spout wind like a split spinnaker!" called a voice. It was Simone the Siren, a buxom black woman lounging against the wall, another Sevener. "If you're done dancing with dainty Murdoch, 'haps you'd care to fight Wilemina! I've a double-eagle crown from Kalin says she dumps you!"

"Yes, yes!" shouted the crowd. "Fight! Fight!"

Always ready to show off, Badger laughed agreement. Sister Wilemina shook her twin braids but consented. Accepting an oblong shield, she drew a leaf-blade archer's sword and saluted.

People cheered and hooted and hissed in good fun as the fighters circled. Simone accepted a quick bet from a grizzled man with an unshaven jaw.

Badger and Wilemina scuffed, skipped, tagged shields, clashed cutlass and sword, all while pacing a circle like two gamecocks.

Badger, puffing now, finally waved his blade and asked, "Here, daughter, did you come to dance or—"

Quick as a cobra, Sister Wilemina threw her sword. Not at the man, but straight down between his feet. The blade bit dirt and vibrated, and Badger's eyes flew wide.

The oldest trick in the book. As the pirate was distracted, the archer coiled an arm like an oak branch. Her knotty fist slammed Badger's broad brisket and nearly dented his spine. He lost all his wind in a tremendous "Oooof!" Sister Wilemina ducked and snagged his ankle. Badger flipped over backward and banged dirt so hard his belt buckle broke.

"That'll teach you to bash a friend of mine!" snapped Sister Wilemina. No one heard for the cheering.

"Come," ordered Johan and towed the disguised tiger away. The emperor's revenge couldn't start soon enough.

Crossing the small town, the odd duo descended worn steps cut into stone to finally stand where the town's west wall overlooked the docks. Johan gazed at the silver-gleaming water, which rippled a mere thirty feet across.

Jedit murmured, "Quite a river for so parched a place."

"This puddle? Barely enough water to let a man spit."

Johan stroked his pointed chin and glared as if the river were also his enemy. As expected, the River Toloron had returned. The mighty river rolled from the watershed of the northern mountains, so it couldn't be extinguished. Flushing along its old bed, scouring away smothering sand grain by grain, the Toloron glittered in the light of a crescent moon as it again snaked around the bedrock supporting the village. The narrow channel would swell as spring snowmelt rushed down, but for now, Palmyra's docks stood high and dry fifty feet shy of the water. It might be years before the river was navigable by barges again, thought Johan. He had an army to move—or would have soon.

Turning his back on the traitorous river, Johan gazed at Palmyra under starlight, his ears aching at gay laughter. Venom dripped in his voice.

"You'd think an invasion never occurred. What are you doing?"

Still cloaked as a barbarian, Jedit descended the town wall and walked to the river's edge. He knelt and lapped water like a house cat stealing cream. Johan jerked as a pair of lovers laughed at the country bumpkin.

"Wait!" Johan's bark made the lovers freeze. "You two! Tell me! Is Adira Strongheart in town? And what of Hazezon Tamar? Where stands he?"

"Sir?" The girl's eyes were large and dark in dim starlight. "Uh, yes, sir. Adira still limps from a broken leg, but she surveys the rebuilding from a sedan chair. Lord Hazezon Tamar visits her. To advise, they say." She giggled the last, for Hazezon and Adira were ex-spouses, the two most notorious on-off lovers in all the Sukurvia.

"Hazezon too . . ." mused Johan. "Very good. You may go."

Bemused, but not daring to tease the ragged madman, the couple sidled away into shadows.

"Yes. Oh, yes! We'll strike a treble blow and sink the windswept ship of Palmyra forever!"

"We'll what?" Silently on masked cat feet, the towering Jedit startled Johan.

"Never mind," snapped the mage. "We must see someone who lives here. Someone who knows things worth knowing."

Chapter 5

"Johan! Uh, I mean, milord! You're—"

"Alive, yes," said Johan dryly. "Let us in, quick."

Flustered, the woman fell back from the door. Johan told Jedit to remain outside, then glided into the tiny house.

The woman's voice was a low contralto, husky from breathing incense smoke. Shifting blue clouds threatened to smother a visitor. Johan glanced about. A baby dozed with tiny snores in a cradle. The house had only one room, too small to hide anyone else. The mage bolted the door and sat on the only stool at a rickety table.

"Milord Johan, we thought you'd vanished, swallowed up by the desert."

The witch had the underfed look of a girl, though her mahogany skin was laced with fine wrinkles. Her black hair was raked back in even rows. She wore only a brown felt vest laced across her small bosom and baggy trousers of wrinkled silk. Her eyes were outlined in kohl, and her long nails were red as if dipped in blood. She was clearly nervous confronting her master, for she'd served as one of Johan's spies before the invasion.

"I did vanish, but I've returned," said Johan enigmatically. "I need your skills. Recall you your lessons?"

Back straight, the slim woman said, "Of course. What do you require?"

Johan told her.

The witch gazed at the door with dark-rimmed eyes. "That would be . . . very costly. I'd have to quit Palmyra for good. Very costly indeed."

"In gold or magic?" Johan dug in his many pockets, sifting items with his nimble fingers. He hadn't planned for expenses, having hatched this latest plot on the spot. Irritated at mundane concerns, he dumped trinkets on a tiny table. "This charming crystal disguises guile when rubbed against the forehead. This claw is a petra sphinx's. This psionic whistle will drive men mad as long as you blow it. . . . Gold coins here. Electrum."

He stopped. The witch's eyes were wide in their black circles. Panting, she swept the items and coins into a velvet sack. "T'will do. Bring in the brute."

Stooping under roof beams, still in his barbarian guise, Jedit plunked on the three-legged stool that threatened to shatter under his weight and gazed curiously around. The witch lit new sticks of incense until smoke billowed in lazy curls. She walked around the false barbarian as if considering how to cut his hair. Gingerly she touched Jedit's ear, chin, and nose with a red-nailed finger. The foreigner watched cross-eyed.

The witch frowned. "This is no barbarian."

Johan scowled. To ensorcell someone not in their true skin could make magics conflict, muddying spells like mixing two colors of paint. Too, the witch must wonder why, if Johan were a mage, he didn't enchant the victim himself.

Johan snarled, "It won't matter. Earn your pay."

The witch shrugged but arched an eyebrow in warning.

Opening a small metal box, the witch signaled Jedit to hold out both palms. The disguised tiger did, but asked, "Why are we here?"

"Kismet." The witch draped across both huge brown palms a long white veil. "Do you know the word?"

"No." Jedit began to toy with the dangling veil.

"Be still. Kismet is an old word, one of the oldest in our language. It means fate." The witch tugged the veil from Jedit's hands, then laid it on again. Jedit's nose wrinkled in confusion. She said, "Do you believe in fate?"

"How so?" asked Jedit. "Do you mean, how our fates are engraved beforehand? Scratched in bark before our birth, our every deed?"

"That's kismet." The witch tugged the veil away, then draped it again over Jedit's palms. As she flicked it away, the false barbarian tried to catch it but missed. The veil seemed diaphanous as incense smoke. The more Jedit stared, the more it shifted.

The witch crooned, "In large, our fates are cast in stone when we first draw breath, and nothing can alter the plan. But in small, we can seize control by our actions. A strapping man like you, so handsome and generous, could surely rule himself. Kismet lets us do that."

Johan watched a long while as the woman talked, cooing, flattering, running rings around logic. With every "Kismet" she flicked the veil away. Jedit tried to catch it in vain. He couldn't take his eyes off the cloth but watched it glassy eyed. The witch talked on and on.

"One way to take control is to remove despots who tax us, who rule our lives, who command us willy-nilly. Strong and clever, you could smite the rulers of Palmyra and become a hero. Do you know our rulers? No? Your friend can finger them. One's a strumpet with unruly hair and the manners of a gutter rat, Adira Strongheart. The other is an old goat, a cruel man, Hazezon Tamar. Could you command fate, good sir? Could you embrace kismet and kill those two for the good of all?"

"Yes." Jedit Ojanen stared at nothing. "Easily."

"Good." Raising the veil before Jedit's eyes, the witch shimmied it like a lure before a trout. Gently she steered Jedit toward the door. Ready, Johan guided the tiger into the frosty darkness before dawn. As Johan slunk after the mesmerized Jedit, the witch whispered, "Fret not, milord. I'll tell no one of your return."

"I'm sure you won't." Johan actually smiled, a chilling sight. From a pocket he gave the witch a small lump of coal. "This will buy your silence."

The witch looked indignant but accepted the fragment, so polished it might have been a black jewel. Gently she closed the door and turned to check on her baby.

Jedit and Johan turned a corner of the crooked street when the witch's house exploded with fire. Flames shot from the windows and smoke hole. Yellow hell outlined the door until it charred and crumbled. Neighbors came stumbling and shouting in their nightshirts and blankets but couldn't approach the tiny house for the fearsome heat.

Jedit noticed nothing.

* * * * *

"You're wasting wind, Haz!" snapped Adira Strongheart. "And my time! Your honeyed words might make fat-bottomed merchants roll over and drool, but my people think for themselves, and we've had enough of Brycer bellyaching! So haul anchor and shove off!"

"Sweetheart." Hazezon Tamar tried patience and reason, knowing both were useless. He'd resolved not to shout. "This is your famous shortsightedness. Just because Johan's vanished into the desert doesn't mean he's dead, any more than a smooth sea portends no storms. All I'm asking is for you to lend me a score of your cutthroats to scour the eastern reaches for sign of the plagued tyrant."

"Don't call me sweetheart, Haz." Adira juggled a stoneware

mug ominously. "Or I'll kick your plums so far past your liver your palace eunuchs will call you sister."

"Here we go," said Badger to the air.

"Here we go what?" asked Murdoch, the young soldier bested earlier.

"Knives and curses," said the old sailor.

"Or kisses and cuddles," smirked Simone the Siren.

Without looking, Adira Strongheart hurled the mug. Badger and Simone jerked back their heads as crockery smashed on the wall.

The damage hardly showed in the abandoned inn that served as Palmyra's town hall. The big room had walls of scabby adobe, naked wooden beams, and a dirt floor. Torches at four corners and cheap candles shed a watery, sooty light. Scarred tables and rickety stools and chairs were the only furniture, and many were broken, for fights were common as cockroaches in Palmyra.

Yet the message was clear enough. Chastened, the onlookers shut up and let the unhappy couple squabble.

To see the two glare, it was hard to believe they had ever been married. Adira Strongheart was a stunning beauty with wild chestnut hair barely contained by a green silk headband. She wore tight trousers and a faded shirt that only emphasized her proud bosom. Bangles of gold, silver, and copper jangled at earlobes, wrists, and ankles even over her brown boots.

Hazezon Tamar had also been a pirate and freebooter, but decades ago. Now he looked a governor's part, a man who plied wits and diplomacy, not magic and might, and prospered in his trade. An embroidered vest of satin and a silk shirt met flaring pantaloons above yellow boots. His seamed face and white beard were framed by a nomad's keffiyeh that swished at his broad shoulders. Clearly he was thirty years or more Adira's senior. Yet the divorced pirate queen and prominent governor could still glare with murder in their eyes and hands itching to jerk a brass-hilted scimitar or twin matched daggers.

Adira's Circle of Seven and Hazezon's clerks held their breaths as if awaiting lightning.

It came from the wrong direction.

Roaring loud enough to raise the roof, still clad in his barbarian disguise, the outlander warrior Jedit Ojanen exploded into the room like a thunderbolt.

Chairs and stools upset, papers and mugs flew, and tables tumbled as if a whirlwind struck the town hall. Hazezon, Adira, scribes, soldiers, and pirates vaulted from their seats and ripped weapons from scabbards, blades glittering in torchlight.

"Who in the seas is this squid?" roared Badger.

"Who cares?" shrieked Simone. "Kill him!"

"Adira, get down!" shouted Hazezon.

"Fend for yourself, puffer fish!" Adira hoisted an overturned table for a makeshift shield. Twin daggers appeared as if by magic in her right hand. She hobbled stiffly, for in months past she'd broken a leg and arm battling Johan's troops, and now another skirmish came calling.

Masked as a barbarian, with his brain befuddled by sorcery, Jedit Ojanen charged blindly at Hazezon and Adira. He'd never seen them before, had only glimpsed them through a window, pointed out by Johan. It was unlikely he even noticed the dozen other people in the room. With the bestial fury of a berserk jungle warrior, Jedit plunged headlong, mindless as a ballista bolt. A fairykin and swordsman were hurled aside like rag dolls. Jedit kicked a table aside, knocked down two others, trampled a trio of stools. Both hands were out straight as he raced in magic-mad rage at Adira.

When the monster closed to six feet, the pirate queen pegged both daggers at his head. Jedit flicked a great hand and the daggers cartwheeled, one bouncing into a corner, the other sticking in a ceiling beam.

"I don't believe it!" gasped Adira. "No one could—"

Jedit the juggernaut smashed into the table she held aloft. The wooden legs shattered, boards broke. Only a crazy leap over another table kept Adira from being crushed.

She shouted, "Pitch me a cutlass, someone!"

Mindlessly, Jedit bashed the wall, cracking adobe in great flakes, then rebounded for another target. Hazezon Tamar stood with his mouth hanging open. Many people had tried to kill him of late, but nothing matched this fury.

"It must be magic!" the desert mage blurted, then plied his own attack. "Blast of winters past!"

Hazezon blew across his hand at the barbarian. Instantly frost rimed Jedit's thatched hair and broad, stupid face. Ice crystals clotted his eyebrows and pug nose, even made his huffing breath blow like steam. The man-killing cold didn't slow him. Roaring like a tiger, Jedit charged the mage.

Old he might be, but Hazezon had long ago learned a pirate's habits. Rather than bobble another spell, the mage flung a heavy candlestick while ripping his scimitar from his sash.

Too late. Jedit smashed into Hazezon with a bone-breaking crunch. The mage toppled across spindly furniture that crumbled underneath him. The barbarian clutched Hazezon by the throat with two hands and shook him like a terrier shakes a rat.

"Love of Lustra, stop him!" Simone the Siren was buxom in clothes brilliant as a tapestry. She slung a round iron-rimmed shield that bounced off Jedit's back.

"He'll snap Haz's spine!"

"Stand aside!" Murdoch, the brawny ex-sergeant in green and gold, snatched a spear from the corner. A boar spear, it had a diamond-shaped head and stout crossbar meant for stabbing, not throwing. Yet the soldier made do. Slinging it past his shoulder, he skipped twice to gain momentum, then hurled the wicked lance. The shaft whistled in the close hot room, and every watcher flinched as it struck.

Yet it didn't. Alerted by inhuman jungle senses, Jedit dropped Hazezon with a thump and squatted, cocking an elbow so the flying spear spanked off the wall.

Murdoch barked, "Impossible!"

More attacks came thick and fast. A small, dark-skinned nomadic woman named Echo, formerly a clerk of Hazezon's, drew her sword and dashed behind Jedit to jab his spine. One flick of a hand like a ham, and she caromed off a wall to tumble in a tangle. A woman in a purple-blue tunic and skirt flicked open a sling, plopped in a round knot of hardwood, whipped the weapon twice, and let fly at the barbarian's head. That too the brute dodged.

The druid sang, "Mask of Makou! That's no northman! He's too fast!"

"Children!" Badger carped and lobbed whatever came to hand at the invader: stools, a book, a candlestick, two redware jugs that slopped red wine in artful spirals. Simone the Siren cocked a crossbow and fumbled a quarrel to the nock, but her sizzling bolt only thudded into a chair someone else pitched. A female fairykin no taller than a fawn drew a rapier and slithered under two tables. Skidding behind the barbarian, she whisked her blade at the back of his knee to hamstring him. Dodging, she was still clipped by a foot kicking backward, a foot she'd supposedly crippled forever. She was stamped underfoot to howl like a banshee.

In the whirlwind of flying feet and fists and furniture, the battle was difficult to follow, for two torches had been wrenched from the walls and many candles spilled, and dust swirled as the brawl raged. A hardwood sling ball cracked adobe by Jedit's head, but more objects hurled his way failed to hit, for the barbarian launched his own offensive.

"Adira," shrieked Simone, "look out!"

Adira Strongheart ruled her mercenaries with her heart, head, and fists, but her game leg slowed her down. Terrifying as a tiger, the towering barbarian snagged Adira's sore leg, his hammy hand encasing ankle to calf. The pirate queen was hoisted in the air, so her chestnut hair dangled on the dirty floor. Anyone else might have panicked, but even upside down, Adira snatched a table leg from the floor and rapped the stranger's knee and ankle with fearsome cracks. When she tried to slam his crotch, he dropped her with a shoulder-crunching jolt. Bravely she bounced and rolled and grabbed for any kind of weapon while keeping one eye on her enemy.

"Adira!" croaked Hazezon Tamar, still half-strangled by his earlier throttling. Choking and spitting, he lurched to rescue Adira with scimitar raised. Simone the Siren rushed with her cutlass, as did Badger and the new crew member Murdoch. Four converging blades threatened Jedit, but he charged anyway with hands outspread. Roaring, he swiped left and right with his fingers, raking the adventurers across the heads, shoulders, and chests. Badger was stunned and knocked spinning, and Simone had her vest ripped clean off, but otherwise no one was hurt, which some onlookers found strange.

"What kind of attack is that?" Scrambling to her feet, cursing her stiff leg, Adira Strongheart still could observe the fight coolly. She asked aloud, "Why does he slash like a sawfish in a school of mackerel?"

No one heard. The barbarian's stiff fingers swatted Murdoch's nose and made it spurt blood. The sergeant lashed out with a straight-arm sword jab that skidded off the barbarian's ribs and punctured the wall. Badger, sprawled on the floor, whisked his cutlass in one hand and pegged it like a throwing knife. The blade pinked Jedit's knee. Yet Badger frowned.

"This's one queer sea-wight! It's like he's there and not there!"

Slower, Hazezon Tamar rushed from the side. He gasped with pain from cracked ribs as he threw his weight behind a stroke to lop off the barbarian's head. The shaggy assassin sliced at Hazezon with stiff fingertips that only ticked his embroidered vest. The curious attack fuddled the mage, then he tumbled backward as fearsome hands tried to rake his face.

"That's a tiger's attack!" Adira's shout rose above the havoc. "He's slicing with claws! *He's Jaeger!*"

Even bewitched, the name of Jedit's beloved father made the disguised cat man whip his head around. Jedit hesitated, hands in the air, while the cogent part of his brain warred with the spellbound portion. For the briefest instant the room was silent, hung in a lull like that between lightning and thunder.

A rapid pattering resounded as two more of Adira's Circle of Seven made a concerted attack. The glum Virgil and the iron-armed archer Wilemina charged, huffing, lugging a heavy oak table. Jedit turned from Adira's astonishing pronouncement just as the table rammed his midriff at a full run. Jedit smashed into the back wall so hard chunks of adobe cascaded from the ceiling and wall. Winded, he slashed feebly as Virgil and Wilemina rammed him again with the table. Jedit crumpled, skidded, and sat down hard, dragging table and pirates on top of him.

"Quick!" bleated the fairykin. "Slit his throat!"

"No!" Adira shouted as if hailing from the quarterdeck in a hurricane. "Anyone touches him gets keelhauled! That's Jaeger, I tell you!"

In the hush, people canted weapons and sobbed for air and cast about in total confusion. Questions spilled.

"Why's he look like a barbarian?"

"Why's Jaeger attacking *us?*"

"Why don't he speak?"

"If he's bewitched, who did it?"

Badger, canny veteran, jumped quickest on the truth. "Someone sicced him on us!"

In a wink, the mariner, Wilemina, and Simone bolted for the door. Jamming in the doorway, the three looked both ways down the nighttime street. Simone gasped, "Whoever 'witched him might've run—"

The sharp-eyed archer pointed. "There he goes!"

"Johan!" barked all three and took off running.

"Wait!" cried Adira but too late. Cursing a blue streak, she limped on her sore leg to tend Echo, who'd dented plaster with her skull. Bidding the ex-clerk to stay seated, Adira saw the rest of her crew was equally battered. Murdoch's nose streamed blood, Hazezon huddled against the wall wheezing, the fairykin Whistledove bore a sprained arm. Adira rubbed her upper lip not to sneeze in all the dust. "Give us light, someone!"

Virgil and Murdoch and two clerks knelt on the heavy table pinning the prisoner. Picking up the fallen boar spear, Adira tilted the tip against the table.

"Drag it away. Handsomely!" ordered the pirate chief. "That means slowly, you cockeyed codfish! Brace up to gaff him if—Ten thousand virgins! It *is* Jaeger!"

"No. Jedit. Ojanen."

A hulking northman had fallen, but under the table and four people lay a living, breathing tiger. Past the tip of her spear Adira stared into round eyes that glowed an eerie amber-green. The face was a riot of orange, black, and white stripes, and white whiskers jutted from the blunt muzzle. A fourth color was smears of red blood. The eyes were slitted, Adira realized, for the tiger was still furious, eager to spring and rend and kill given half a chance.

"*Jedit* Ojanen?" Doubting everything, Adira tipped the spear against the prisoner's throat, one strong hand on the haft ready to thrust. "Same name, so what relation?"

"My father was Jaeger."

A dangerous rumbling growl. The yowling accent was barbaric and old-fashioned, with words twisted out of shape. Only by concentrating could Adira understand him.

Jedit said, "You should know the name well, being his most dire enemy."

A confused murmur arose from Seveners and clerks.

Murdoch blew blood from his nose. "Someone's cockeyed."

"Shut up." Not retracting the spear, Adira fought to think this mess through. "You've been gulled, tiger-boy. If you've tramped around with Johan, I can swear to it, for that devils' tool never spoke a true word in his life."

"Johan's back?" Still crouched on the table, the scruffy Virgil huffed. "Is that what Badger yelled? Our troubles are starting all over?"

"I said, belt up, you lot!" Adira whapped Virgil on the head, he being nearest. If she read an enemy rightly, the tiger was only resting up for another attack. She had to talk fast but should also rouse her Robaran Mercenaries to ferret out Johan. But one menace at a time.

Whipping sweaty auburn curls from her face, Adira snarled, "Listen to me, Jedit son of Jaeger! Your father fought on *our* side against Johan! That red-striped fiend and his followers marched down from Tirras to stamp over Palmyra and seize Bryce! It's no secret he hopes to conquer all Jamuraa! We fought like furies just to stay alive, and Jaeger braced us in every battle, never flagging, always faithful! *You* disgrace his memory to side with Johan, the most treacherous snake that ever crawled out of a dung heap!"

Seconds ticked away. The room might have been frozen but for the flicker of torches. Jedit Ojanen continued to glare, his thoughts unknowable. Once he squirmed, half-crushed by the table and crouching pirates, and Adira stifled him with a pinprick under his white-whiskered chin. Eventually, Jedit snorted through his black nostrils. Near panic, Adira thought. He doesn't believe me. I'll have to kill him!

"If I might say a word."

Eyes shifted to Hazezon Tamar, hunched over and clutching his ribs. Hovering near Jedit, but not too close, he plied years of political persuasion through clenched teeth.

"Adira speaks the truth, tiger-son. I found your father in the desert and drove away vultures and hyenas. For my rescue, he returned the favor a hundred times. He saved me and Bryce and Palmyra and a thousand others. You needn't take our word for it. I propose to let you go—"

"Haz!" chirped Adira, leaning the spear. "Have you fractured your skull?"

"Hush, Dira." Hazezon had no breath for argument. "Forgive her, friend tiger. Adira would contradict me if I said the sun arose each morn. I propose we back away. You'll be free to go. Leave this room and ask anyone in Palmyra whether Jaeger was our savior and champion. Even the dullest porter or smallest child will sing his praises. Then ask about Johan and sift the answers, if not a fist or spittle. See for yourself."

As Jedit ruminated, suspicious and sullen, Hazezon added, "Before you go, tell me something. I recognize certain symptoms. You are lucid now but were befuddled before. Your thoughts swam in a fog within your mind, true? Johan cloaked you in sorcery, arguing Jaeger was unloved here, but then he laid on another spell, did he not?"

"No!" Jedit frowned in concentration. "No. He brought me to the house of a woman. She . . . she . . . I can't remember!"

"That enchantment was knocked out of you." Hazezon waved for a clerk to bring a stool. Painfully he sank onto it. "If it consoles you, young Jedit, many are bewitched by the Tyrant of Tirras, whom we call Johan. Let him up, you fellows and girl. Adira, put up your spear. I'll not see the son of Jaeger Ojanen, the fiercest warrior and finest friend I ever knew, mistreated a second longer."

Carefully, with weapons poised, pirates and clerks backed away. The table dumped over. Framed in flaring torchlight so he glowed orange and black as a stormy sunset, Jedit Ojanen stood up, and up, until he towered over Adira Strongheart, Hazezon Tamar, and their astonished retainers. Black-clawed paws smoothed the tiger's whiskers and tufted mane. Amber-green eyes peered as the muzzle wrinkled. A pink tongue passed over white fangs. Still, the tiger had to lean against the cracked wall for dizziness.

Glaring about, he demanded, "I am free to go?"

Hazezon Tamar waved expansively toward the door but winced as ribs squeaked. Everyone watched the tiger warily.

A step to one side, a coiling of haunches, then in a flash Jedit Ojanen sprang to the door and vanished into predawn darkness.

Pirates and clerks gaped, astonished by the tiger's lithe speed. They jumped as Adira cracked the spear haft on a table.

"What're you gawking for, you wall-eyed mothers of moonfish! Find Johan! Rouse the militia! *Move!*"

As people jammed in the doorway, Adira slumped on a chair and raked chestnut curls off her face. Her arm ached, and her throbbing leg wouldn't support her. She tried to spit but only sighed.

"Dratted weakness! Some freebooter I be!"

"Don't blame yourself. Blame Johan for running his army over you." Hazezon clutched both arms around his ribs. "Now another tiger's arrived, bigger, faster, and far more powerful than Jaeger, and more impulsive. Whiskers of Wullab, why do the spirits of the sands mock us so in times of strife?"

"Who can say?" For once, Adira didn't argue with her ex-husband. "Life is struggle and suffering."

"Speaking of suffering," groaned Hazezon, "might you fetch a leech? And stretcher bearers?"

"Make it two. Echo's blacked out." The pirate queen dragged off her chair. "You know, it's just as well Johan showed up. This town's been palling dull lately. But oh, I almost feel sorry for that murderous mage when this tiger-lad pounces."

* * * * *

The Tyrant of Tirras and Emperor of the Northern Realms was doing two things unusual: running headlong and cursing outright. His brown robe flapped around his skinny shanks as he dashed with bare feet through dusty alleys and crosswalks. He couldn't believe the fell luck that dogged him. Siccing Jedit on Adira and Hazezon, old friends of Jaeger's, seemed too outlandish a joke not to succeed. But contradictory spells, one to deceive others and one to deceive the self, had conflicted and sputtered out. Now instead of Jedit rending Tamar and Strongheart into bloody gobbets, they'd ceased fighting and dispatched pursuers. Thus Johan ran for his life. He'd been too clever. Better he'd killed Jedit outright and assassinated the twin rulers later.

Craning his neck, pelting along, Johan glimpsed Adira's lackeys hot on his trail. Skidding to a halt at a corner, the mage scooped up a loose stone and rubbed it vigorously between his palms.

He panted, "No matter. Once free of these clattering clods, I'll order my spies to smuggle me out of town. I can reach Tirras in a fortnight. No matter. Let us end this nonsense!"

Down the alley rushed Adira's pirates, as unalike as comrades could be. A sailor rife with gray streaks that earned him the nickname Badger. A devotee of Lady Caleria, Sister Wilemina, in a blue cloak and blonde braids like a girl's, and in her knotty hand her talisman, an ornate bow of horn and ivory. A buxom woman in every color of clothing, skin black as a cauldron, grinning at the chase, almost singing with joy, who'd earned the name Simone the Siren. Such an odd trio could spring only from Adira's Robaran Mercenaries, whose only credo was a craving for adventure. Heedless and headlong they rushed after Johan, arguably the most dangerous man on Jamuraa.

Johan leaned past the corner. The alley ran straight forty feet between adobe walls. Johan rubbed the stone more briskly, then flicked it into the air.

"Die, gutter trash!"

A flash answered. In mid-air, the stone exploded into a pulsing yellow light too bright to behold. Light sparkled from the sphere like the crackling rays of a shooting star. The light-spiked globe sizzled down the alley toward the pirates, soaring fast as a ball of burning pitch hurled from a catapult.

Forced to avert their eyes, squinting for a way out, Sister Wilemina chirped, "Call of Caleria! We're trapped!"

Chapter 6

"Dive!"

"Jump!"

The fireball screaming toward them fired reflexes honed in a hundred battles and brawls. Simone, lithe as a panther, bunched her legs and leaped in the air. Skinny Wilemina flopped flat, face in the dust. Only Badger hesitated, panting and fretting. He'd nearly drowned a few months past, and his lungs creaked from all this dratted running. Too, being older, he kept a fatherly eye on Adira's hotheaded youngbloods. So, when he should have leaped or dodged to save himself, instead he flung out both hands, one to knock Wilemina flatter and another to boost Simone higher, assistance neither woman needed.

In a second's fatal hesitation, the spiked force-sphere caught him. Badger had barely twitched aside when the sizzling death clipped his brisket and hurled him against the wall. The ball of ectoplasm streaked out of the alley and smashed a house front across the street, punching a hole big as a bushel basket and instantly igniting paint, lathes, and timbers. The householders dashed outside as someone yelled to form a bucket brigade.

Badger was down, feebly thrashing and slapping at his

clothes. His shirt and vest burned and smoked, his formerly hairy chest was seared pink, and now his hands and even beard were scorched from licking flames. He could scarcely breathe. Simone and Wilemina whisked out the flames, then tried to stretch Badger flat to check his wounds.

Angry, sobbing, his hard hands beat them away. "Never mind me! I'll live! Get after Johan! Don't let him escape!"

Both women objected, but a sturdy kick sent them scampering in pursuit. The sailor crawled painfully to his knees and scrubbed his face with gritty hands. Sticky fluid gummed his eyes, and rubbing his wounds made them flare in agony, but he forced his eyelids open. Thank the stars, he wasn't blind. The pre-dawn world was dim and hazy.

A rumble like thunder over the horizon asked, "Are you all right?"

"Eh?" The sailor squinted painfully. The blurry figure wore some red- or orange-striped robes. Whoever he was, he was tall as a monox and seemed to steam in the chilly air. Badger was glad this was no enemy.

"Uh, yes. The women went after Johan."

Like a whisper in the night, the stranger was gone.

"Fish and follies," Badger asked himself, "who was that?"

* * * * *

At the mouth of the alley, Simone and Wilemina peeked around for their prey when a rapid padding rang behind. Nerves taut, they spun—and almost fell down. A whirlwind of orange and black stripes charged down the alley like a juggernaut. They barely jumped aside as the tiger-man blew past.

Both yelped, "Jaeger!"

Jedit didn't contradict them or explain. He'd leave it to Johan to answer a thousand questions, even if Jedit had to skin the man alive.

Dawn cracked the eastern horizon. There were only two

ways to go. To the left, the street joined a wider thoroughfare. To the right, it jinked—for no street in Palmyra ran straight—then widened and rose toward the marketplace.

"Likely he went that way, Jaeger! Into the market!" said Simone. "The other way offers little shelter!"

In a crashing hurry, Jedit leaped to all fours as if pouncing on a rabbit. His flat black nose and whiskers snuffled dirt. Launching into space, he landed ten feet farther and sniffed again, then took off running, with the women hard-put to keep up.

In the early morning market, shepherds and melon farmers and leatherworkers greeted neighbors, sipped mint tea, stacked wares, propped awnings, cooed to chickens and lambs, and warmed up singsong calls.

Every eye turned as someone blurted, "It's Jaeger!"

"Jaeger!" echoed a hundred voices. Palmyrans gawked at the towering figure who appeared as if by magic in the street. "Look! It's Jaeger! Hurrah!"

Intent on the hunt, Jedit Ojanen jolted to a halt. The chorus of calls and cheers confused him utterly.

Simone and Wilemina crept up beside the tiger-man. Gently the blonde archer touched his furry elbow. "Jaeger, what's wrong?"

"These people . . ." murmured the tiger, gazing at the cheering crowd. "They chant his name like a hero's."

"Eh?" Simone gazed at her companion, equally fuddled. "Of course. You're a hero to everyone in Palmyra."

Jedit's mind reeled. It was true. As that older mage had urged, ask anyone in Palmyra and learn Jaeger was revered. Arrested by new evidence, Jedit fought to work it out. If Jaeger were a hero to Palmyra, he must have been an enemy to—

"Johan!" The tiger roared the name like thunder crashing. People stumbled back in fear. "Where are you, you lying monkey?"

No answer. Frustrated, Jedit gazed at the gathering crowd, a hundred people or more of all sizes and colors: dark-bearded nomads, sleepy-looking barbarians, tiny brown-clad leprechauns, goose girls, solemn Keepers of the Faith, Palmyran city guards in yellow smocks painted with red crescents, black-skinned freighters, hawk-nosed desert elves, dusty dwarves, and more. All jammed around a maze of wares stacked in heaps, piled on carts, hung from racks. Somewhere among them was Johan.

"Impossible! Impossible for the eyes! And the ears!" Jedit Ojanen hissed to himself like a kettle boiling. Coming from the sheltered valley of Efrava, he'd barely adjusted to one human being, then small groups, before he was catapulted into a goggling, gabbling mass of humanity. Furthermore, his rage, never far submerged, had built steadily at the man who'd lied, who must know his father's fate, who might have killed his father.

Ignoring all else, Jedit again dropped to all fours. Snuffling a wide circle, eyes closed, Jedit sifted a thousand scents, old and new in his mind, and concentrated to find the smell he'd known in weeks of crossing the desert. Whiskers to the ground, dust tweaking his nostrils, Jedit smelled dogs, elephants, cats, rats, goats, and people, hundreds of them.

There. The snake-dry musky tang of Johan leaped into his nostrils, fresh and strong.

Eyes closed, still on all fours, Jedit charged.

Palmyrans screamed and scattered as the tiger careened into the crowd like a raging bull. People newly arrived to the marketplace were bowled over by slung blankets and saddles, or else they turned to run and careened into more arrivals coming to see the ruckus. Havoc hit the marketplace as Jedit Ojanen plowed a furrow like a tornado with his nose glued to the ground.

Behind Jedit clattered Simone and Wilemina, one dark, the other fair, both panting.

Wilemina gasped, "I never saw Jaeger bull past citizens before!"

"I'm not sure that *is* Jaeger!" rasped Simone. "Does he look bigger? And more orange?"

"Orange?" asked the archer and promptly tripped over a watermelon for not watching her feet.

On the tiger pressed, now in five- and eight-foot bounds like a wolf spider that bowled aside people and wares. The marketplace only got thicker, more crowded, more frenzied as people rushed in every direction. In seconds, Jedit had covered fifty feet of the marketplace, sifting and discarding a thousand smells to follow Johan's. Palmyrans jabbered and hurled insults and questions as the tiger raised his head from the invisible trail in the dirt. He sneezed hard enough to snap a man's neck.

"Can you sniff him out?" asked Simone. She and Wilemina had caught up. The tiger gave off heat in palpable waves. As the sun topped buildings, the two pirates scanned the marketplace.

Jedit's eyes were slits of amber-green. Ignoring yells and curses, scampering livestock and spilled fruit, he growled, "His scent is close, yet I don't see him! Is this more human witchery?"

"With Johan, damned likely," agreed Simone.

"He must be disguised!" chirped Wilemina. "He's notorious for that!"

"Disguised?" Yes, Jedit had forgotten in the heat of the chase. Diving once more, snuffling a circle with quivering whiskers, Jedit suddenly bunched his legs to pounce. People shrilled and split like a covey of quail.

All but one.

Directly before Jedit stooped an old woman in once-red robes. Unkempt white hair straggled over her hunched back, her rheumy brown eyes were buried in wrinkles, and her lips crawled over toothless gums. She carried a frayed basket woven of palm leaves. Despite her foreknowledge, Sister Wilemina shrieked for the crone to move or be killed. Simone the Siren, however, ripped her cutlass from its scabbard.

Roaring like a windstorm, the tiger-man leaped full-length and soared through the air. Like a great striped bird, near a thousand pounds of destruction hurtled at the crone. Claws flicked from massive paws to tear the woman to shreds. Jedit never even noticed that he burst two poles supporting an awning, or that his whipping tail upset a stack of dried gourds, or that a small cart of watermelons collapsed as one foot brushed it like a hammer blow. The tiger saw only his enemy, and he clawed the air to do or die.

At the same time, the old woman seemed to melt like a candle, blurring as if seen through water. Her form flowed upward like volcanic smoke issuing from a fissure. The basket fell to earth and rolled away. White hair blew away like dandelion fluff. Faded red robes flushed a vivid plum-purple. The crone's mottled brown skin turned ruddy red and was immediately covered with black stripes like a tiger's pelt. Tall reared the figure, no longer ascetic and bony like some desert hermit but lean and dangerous as a bloodied knife blade.

In Palmyra's marketplace stood the real Johan, Tyrant of Tirras, Emperor of the Northern Realms, foremost wizard of all Jamuraa. A travesty of a human, he was twisted by the marks of arcane sorcery: red skin, black tattoo stripes, a dark V between hairless brows, and living horns jutting from his chin and downturning from his temples. He was clad in a slithery robe of iridescent purple like the skin of some giant lizard.

Worst, his eyes glistened coal black, mercilessly prepared to kill. Johan hissed an arcane spell as he whisked together red-black hands to warm a small stone plucked from the ground. Between his palms suddenly crackled a ball of lightning.

"Beware, Jaeger!" shouted Sister Wilemina.

Too late, for the great cat had already leaped in the air. Jedit Ojanen heard a brief snort, the only laugh Johan would allow himself, then the sizzling rock struck him with a blow to cripple an elephant.

Simone and Wilemina had suffered from the same spell earlier, so both flinched as the scorching sphere walloped Jedit in mid-air. Punished by magic, Jedit yelped. Yet the tiger managed to twist in the air faster than a human eye could follow. The crackling sphere smacked Jedit on his striped shoulder. Hair frizzled and caught fire, skin charred and curled. Jedit was seared across his shoulder and down his back, then the glowing miniature sun spanked off his lean hip and burned the tip of his thrashing tail. The sizzling spike sailed on to punch an adobe wall.

At the vicious stroke, enough power to kill a dozen men, Jedit Ojanen was blown from the sky. Knocked spinning, the tiger crashed on a heap of rugs. So hot did his fur burn that sparks set fire to red- and blue-patterned rugs that smoked with a dusty odor. Rolling, almost panicked by an animal's instinctive fear of fire, Jedit rolled over and over, smashing into a cart, bowling over a table, crushing baskets in a tangle of split wicker.

Running, Simone and Wilemina both chirped "Jaeger!" Still clutching swords, they plied callused hands to flip baskets and rugs and awnings aside. Revealed were orange-black stripes smeared red with bright blood.

Wilemina wailed, "He must be dead! He took the full force—"

"Get after Johan!" Simone pointed her cutlass at the purple-robed man who again fled. "He mustn't—whoa!"

A roar like a hurricane made the woman recoil. Jedit Ojanen exploded from the wreckage like a phoenix from a funeral pyre. The tiger bled freely from a long hideous slash down his beautiful hide, but he was hale and hearty—and fighting mad.

As the tiger launched past the two pirates, Sister Wilemina bleated, "Lady Caleria protect us all!"

* * * * *

The archer's amazed cry made Johan turn in his flight. Glancing over a shoulder, the ruddy mage glimpsed a vast expanse of snow-white belly and throat, white fangs long as his fingers, and black claws curving like a condor's talons, all not ten feet behind.

Johan gulped. "Impossible! It can't be."

Only a lurch and wild leap saved Johan's life. Claws swept by his scalp and shoulder, ticking his robe and skin and pricking bright drops of blood. A fold of lizard-skin robe was sheared away like lamb's wool by five razor talons. In one stroke, Johan stumbled half-stripped, so his bony red ribs and one arm were exposed to the rising desert sun. The mage actually shuddered, for that blow had come as close as the kiss of death, the closest chance ever of destroying Johan's mortality. Staggering against a shelf of leather purses and vests, Johan fumbled at shreds of clothing, his mind temporarily rattled past all reasoning. The tiger should be dead! Yet the creature raised a fearsome right paw to tear off Johan's horned head—

—and halted. Johan hardly dared breathe in case some unseen spell had been cast upon the cat. Blind with battle lust, the tiger should have torn Johan apart, for he cowered small and helpless as a blind monkey. Black claws were upraised to slash the mage's red skin from his bones. Yet clearly, Johan could see, some strange sight had frozen Jedit's hand in mid-air. Jungle rage warred with a human's keen mind in the tiger's skull as he stared at Johan's shoulder.

Flustered, the sorcerer glanced down to find his robe in shreds. Amid rags gleamed a round buckle or medallion. Big as a man's palm, the half-circle of twisted white metal formed a double-spiraled emblem like a stylized ram's head and horns.

A broken sigil. Any mystic power the emblem had contained must have dissipated, for Johan recalled how he himself had driven a dagger through the buckle and into Jaeger's hide. That, he hoped, would put an end to the cursed cat who dogged his trail and haunted his dreams. Yet here was another such animal-man poised to take his life.

"My father's emblem," rumbled the cat man, still with one hand curled to strike.

Johan flinched as realization struck in the tiger's mind. Quivering all over, like a geyser set to explode, Jedit muttered, "You could gain that symbol in only one way! You did kill my father!"

"Kill *him!*" screamed Simone, not ten feet behind.

Blind with rage, Jedit lashed out with both paws.

Fear gave Johan wings. Wrenching backward in desperation, the magician lost more robe as sweeping paws ripped the air before his nose and chest. Johan crashed to the ground painfully and kicked backward like a crab. His shoulders bunched in cloth and table legs as market items clattered and clinked on his bare chest and legs. Still the battle-mad tiger lurched to rip him apart, and Johan had no place left to retreat.

Better die than surrender, thought the mage. With no other hope, he reached into distant memory and plucked forth a spell once glimpsed in an arcane book so horrid he'd suffered nightmares for months. There were many places among the infinite planes of Dominaria so frightening that even to imagine them drove seasoned mages insane with horror. One land was so volatile that even to breathe its air would blister a man to ashes. Yet desperate times called for desperate measures.

"Unleash," Johan gasped, already recoiling from horrors to come, "the beasts of Bogardan!"

* * * * *

Flaming hell descended on Palmyra's marketplace.

Chest-high, the creatures were part goat, part hellhound, and part dragon with twin rows of scales down their spines. They carried part of Bogardan with them, for flames licked at their nostrils. One second Johan was crawling like a half-naked crab through the dust of the marketplace, about to be torn to flinders by a raging man-tiger, and the next instant thirty-odd beasts appeared in a circle around the mage and stampeded toward anything that moved. Nor were the goat-beasts the only creatures to escape Bogardan, for a flock of long-winged bats circled and peeped and dove at folks' heads with ivory teeth seeking blood. Most fearsome were two black beasts like great apes. Tentacles whipped the air behind their shoulders, and red flame shone in mad eyes.

As dawn lit the Palmyran marketplace, panic followed on the heels of war. People cannoned into one another and ran headlong for cover as the beasts of Bogardan ripped into them like wolves into sheep. An urchin carrying candlewood was attacked by two goat-dogs. Flaming fanged jaws snapped off a foot and hand before the child could even scream for help. A milkmaid was grabbed by a tentacled ape and squeezed so hard her back broke and ribs punctured her lungs. She died with blood bubbling from her lips. An old cobbler was knocked flat by three stampeding beasts, then had his liver ripped out before he died. Flittering and squeaking, bat-things flocked over two rug merchants, smothering them in smoking-hot flesh, so their screams were drowned out as razor teeth slashed skin and rasping tongues lapped up spurting crimson. Many more people were attacked from all sides, as well as from the sky. Running, screaming, or standing their ground, a score were immediately pulled down and savaged by coal-black beasts from an infernal pit.

Johan was saved by the onslaught of the hellish beasts. Jedit Ojanen, Sister Wilemina, and Simone the Siren found the fight of their lives.

The women jumped back to back and filled their fists with steel, Wilemina with an archer's leaf-blade sword and her ornate bow, Simone with a cutlass and dagger jutting point down. Immediately they were attacked, for the beasts showed no fear of weaponry. As a pair of beasts lunged for Wilemina's legs, the oaken-armed archer rammed her blade straight into one flaming mouth and rapped her stout bow atop another beast's skull. The throat-pierced beast died in blood, but not before it leaped higher on the blade and snapped at the archer's fingers, skinning them to bone. For the other, Wilemina yanked upward to tangle the beast's bearded chin between string and ivory while she ripped her bloody sword free of the dying beast's mouth. Whirling in a frenzy, she slashed at the attacking beast's eyes. The orbs also flamed, and oddly the archer wondered how the fiend could see. The goat-dogs stank of burned metal. Her sword blow knocked the beast sprawling, but it scrambled on four crooked legs and leaped again. Flaming breath licked at Wilemina's bare legs hot enough to raise blisters.

She wailed, "They're hard as Arcades's armor and hot besides! What shall we do?"

"Fight or die!" snapped Simone, busy with her own troubles. "And hope the other Seven pick up their feet!"

A flame-mouthed goat-dog jumped and snapped at Simone. The black pirate punched straight-armed with her sword to spear its nose, then chopped diagonally to cut the thing's foreleg out from under it. She scored, slashing the beast above the hock, so the blade lodged in bone, but if she expected the Bogardan denizen to whimper or cave in, she was disappointed. It ignored its wound and attacked anew. A belch of fire gushed from its nostrils and set fire to the sleeve of Simone's blue silk shirt. Mad as the place that spawned it and unmindful of pain, it clamped flaming teeth on Simone's dagger blade. The pirate cursed and grunted as she beat the thing to the ground with hard sword blows. Meanwhile a dozen more beasts cavorted nearby, as eager to attack armed fighters as screaming townsfolk.

Jedit Ojanen saw no one else's plight. Closest to the fallen Johan, the tiger was swarmed by five coal-black brute-dogs. Toothed mouths brimming flame latched onto his striped tail, onto his thighs, his belly ruff, his forearm. A thousand pounds of forge-hot fury hung on the tiger's mighty frame even as sharklike teeth tore furrows in his bright orange-black hide. Yet Jedit proved just as savage and heedless of pain. A beast clinging to his right thigh, the tiger-man hammered straight down with a fist like a sledgehammer. With a sound like a tree splitting, the beast's neck broke. Only reluctantly, dying, did the goat-dog slacken its jaw. Another creature latching onto Jedit's forearm like a leech received a slash from black claws, so half its neck was shorn away. Blood sprayed from a severed throat where red froth bubbled. Even then Jedit had to dig claws into the beast's snout and pry open jaws like a steel trap. Some of his orange fur stayed lodged between the wicked incisors of the dead goat-dog.

Hung with dog flesh, Jedit half-turned and lashed out with a big clawed foot, for another creature gnawed on his thigh. The first kick, hampered as the tiger was, bounced off the beast's brisket. Crouching, snarling in berserker rage, Jedit kicked hard enough to break down a temple door. Four claws like flint spearpoints rammed into the goat-dog's belly, so blood welled onto the dust of the marketplace. Growling, Jedit kicked outward, straightening his leg with the power of a battering ram. Sinew and tendons parted, yet the Bogardan fiend refused to lose its hold on Jedit's thigh, and finally it was torn in half, hips ripped away from its spine. Jedit flicked his leg, bloody to the knee, and sent the lower half flopping to the dirt. He caught the goat-dog's head, where the flame in its eyes smoldered and flickered out, and wrenched a half-circle to pry loose the beast's jaws.

Infuriated at twin goat-dogs still chewing on his foot and

tail, Jedit joined two fists, slung them in the air, and brought them whistling down while squatting to add weight to the blow. With a fearsome crunch, the skull of the beast on Jedit's foot pulped like an egg. Slinging his backside and hips, Jedit whisked the creature gnawing his tail in a swooping circle. The wretch tumbled atop its comrade, still growling furiously. The tiger raised both fists and dived like a cormorant. Missiles of flesh and bone hammered the beast's chest, ribs, and lungs into mush.

Yet the tiger wasn't spared a moment's rest, for the tentacled gorillas, fresh-bathed in the blood of innocents, singled out the battle-weary tiger-man as a challenger. With guttering roars like an avalanche, eyes and lips flaming, the coal-black fiends leaped upon Jedit with sloping arms and lashing tentacles. With a roar just as fierce, the wounded cat accepted the challenge.

Ungodly howls made the whole marketplace wince, but no one paid attention to the grappling man-tiger and hell-apes. From the far end of the marketplace came wild curses that smoked the air blue. Adira Strongheart had arrived to scream at townsfolk and pirates alike.

"Belay there, you skulking bottom-feeders! Drop anchor and pick up that wagon tongue! Virgil, beat that goat-thing to death, and be quick, or I'll scourge you bloody! You there! Smash those things with that jug! Don't stand gawking! Murdoch, lend a hand there, you worthless scalawag!"

With snappy orders and sparkling curses, Adira Strongheart hurled herself, her Circle of Seven, and anyone still alive into the battle of Palmyra's marketplace.

Where the market ran down both sides of the wide street, kiosks and awnings and carts had been upset, rent, chucked underfoot, and trampled. Fires springing from the Bogardan beasts burned canvas and wool awnings, nomadic robes, and more. Scattered about were saddles, bottles, melons, chickens, wooden serving bowls, and other detritus. More than a dozen townsfolk had been killed, dragged down and torn asunder by the terrible black goat-beasts, and a dozen monsters still tussled with fighters and savaged innocents. At the far end of the rambling melee, the tiger-man Jedit, more scarlet than orange, grappled with two monstrous apes whose backs sprouted lashing tentacles. A heap of dead goat-dogs encircled them, shedding blood, making even the dry dust slippery as ice. Nearby, Simone the Siren had momentarily lost her balance, tilted on one knee. Gamely she jabbed her cutlass to fend off three marauders. Sister Wilemina, so bloody even her short blonde braids looked dipped in red ink, straddled her companion and flailed sword and bow to keep them both alive. Elsewhere townsmen and women wrestled with dogs, crimson to the elbows from bites of the fiery jaws and stickle backs. Women sobbed, men cursed, children shrilled as a blacksmith and a farmer tried to brain a beast with a wooden stool and a manure fork. A mother with a child strapped on her back struggled with a beast whose throat she'd rammed with a wooden cart tongue. Two men punched a beast that wouldn't release a child's belly. Two town guards in yellow smocks painted with a red crescent labored to kill goat-dogs. More fights just as furious raged up and down.

Counting noses and looking to the worst scraps, Adira sent Virgil to drive a long-toothed spear through a goat-dog's side. The grizzled pirate shoved so hard and fast the struggling beast was rammed into a wall and the spear shaft snapped off in Virgil's hand. Grousing as usual, Virgil swung the broken haft like a club to belabor the brute's blazing head.

At Adira's order, Murdoch, the former sergeant turned mercenary, flung himself into the fray to prove his mettle to his new commander. Dark-tanned and ruggedly handsome, Murdoch fought with an iron-rimmed buckler strapped to his left arm, a fighting knife in his left fist, and a broadsword in his brawny right. With a battlecry "For Yerkoy!" he split a goat-dog in half through the spine.

Adira's two other recruits hung back, appalled by the carnage and unsure where to jump in. One was a brownie or halfling named Whistledove Kithkin, another refugee rescued from the fabulous sandstorm that smothered Johan's army. With smooth red hair and a billowy shirt and pantaloons in pink and purple, she resembled a child dressed for court, yet her rapier stung like a cobra. The other was Jasmine Boreal, a druid with red-blonde curls who wore linen and wool leggings, earrings of polished bone, and a wide leather belt hung with pouches and charms.

Shoving both women at the enemy, the pirate queen snarled, "Four bells, you two! Get the lead out! We're not playing at any Circle initiation! We're at war! Whistledove, fly or whatever you do! Get to Wilemina and stick something with that hairpin! Druid, waggle your fingers, and smoke some hides!"

Leaning back, Adira Strongheart whisked a dagger to hand and sent it spinning into the sky to skewer a bat. She caught the pommel in one hand without looking and flicked a dying Bogardan horror off the blade.

"All hands! Stand fast and earn your grog! Cut 'em down, fire their sails, and send these bastards to the bottom of the sea!"

Chapter 7

Under the hard-handed leadership of Adira Strongheart, the Circle of Seven flung themselves at the beasts of Bogardan until blood puddled underfoot.

Needing only orders, Whistledove Kithkin skipped along a row of jugs still upright and in one long leap seemed to glide like a hummingbird over a savage dogfight between townsfolk and monsters. The brownie kicked off an arching lintel and landed light as thistledown beside Wilemina, just in time to jab her rapier up through a goat-dog's jaw and into its brain, dropping the fiend in its tracks. Even Adira grunted approval at the feat.

Jasmine Boreal, meanwhile, had squeezed past the nearby dogfight to peer down a public well. Adira, limping on one stiff leg, readied a filthy epithet to bark at the feather-brained druid, but she stopped as Jasmine extracted some glittery powder like mica from a pouch and sprinkled it down the well. Instantly a column of water, hundreds of gallons, vomited out of the well into the sky. Snapping her callused hand, Jasmine pointed at some townsfolk harried by goat-dogs. Obedient as a spellbound water elemental, the column of water arced across the marketplace and doused the dogfight like a tidal wave.

Cannily, the druid had reckoned the fiery makeup of the beasts of Bogardan would shun water. She was right, for they were knocked silly. Stumbling and shambling as if poisoned, the coal-black fiends banged into one another and snapped at thin air as if demented. Flames around their eyes and mouths extinguished, and smoke and steam billowed around their heads. As the brutes staggered, angry Palmyrans belabored the dog-monsters with knives, butcher's cleavers, crockery, brooms, tent poles, and anything else that came to hand. Six beasts of Bogardan were beaten down and snuffed out.

"Drop the anchor and drag out the gangplank!" marveled Adira and threw Jasmine a mock salute. Smug, but moving on, Jasmine fiddled in a pouch and tucked dry leaves between her fingers. Tripping over dead goat-dogs and puddles, she caught up with Virgil and Murdoch.

Side by side, the two men plied swords in rhythm to hack at another clutch of beasts that stood their ground. The pirates tried to reach Wilemina and the downed Simone, but the dog-monsters punished the men with nips, bites, and flame breath even as they skipped and skittered away from sword blows.

Coming up behind, Jasmine slapped both men on the back with her herb-charmed fingers. Virgil and Murdoch jumped as if struck by lightning—or energized by it. Their arms suddenly swung swords so fast the action blurred. Flashing steel hacked alien beasts a dozen times in seconds, then a dozen times more, so fast and hard the beasts couldn't dodge. Within a heartbeat the infernal fiends lost a dozen legs cut out from under them. Virgil and Murdoch collapsed gasping and wheezing as if they'd run ten miles.

Impressed, Adira scanned the marketplace to see who else needed help. The long-winged bats, keening like seagulls, were evidently smarter than they looked, for three had jittered from the sky and latched onto a little girl's hair. As her mother shrieked and yanked on the girl's legs, the bats tried to get airborne with their prey. Cursing, Adira grabbed the nearest thing at hand, a melon, and hurled it overhand. It smacked into two bats, smashing them against the wall and breaking their wings. The girl fell into her weeping mother's arms. Adira saw more bats fluttering over a crowd and wished for archers with bird arrows.

For that matter, she wondered, where in the seven seas were all her infamous mercenaries? Surely some of them must have heard the commotion. Yet their chief fought on with what resources she had.

Wilemina, Simone, and Whistledove dispatched more hellhounds with deft blades. The women marched in lock step and actually made a pack give ground. Adira shouted a warning too late. The trio went too far, pressing so the goat-dogs' rumps hit a low wall. Instantly, thinking themselves trapped, the fiery fiends rebounded to the attack. Adira saw Whistledove go under a set of cruel paws and began to run that way—until Simone kicked mightily with a boot, bowled dogs off the brownie, and hoisted her to her feet.

Worst off, perhaps, was Jedit Ojanen, who wrestled two tentacled apes. The battle of giants rocked the end of the marketplace. It was impossible to see who won or even gained the top. Carts, stalls, fruit, and crockery went flying as a snarling mass of orange stripes and black backs, white fangs and dark tentacles rolled over and over. Despite the danger of being crushed, Adira trotted that way over smashed bric-a-brac and food. She had to shove past more sensible Palmyrans who fled like rabbits. Yet she halted at blood-chilling shrieks.

Again the long-winged bats had joined forces to smother the market like black ashes. The creatures might have been disconcerted by the bright desert sun, but now they flitted down to tear at women and children shrunk in a corner. Adira looked for Whistledove, who was lightning quick with her rapier. Jasmine took one look, fished in a pouch, drew out a pinch of something and, muttering under her breath, flicked it like a marble at the jittering flock.

The white glob spun in the air and expanded into a gossamer web that entangled most of the toothy bats. Their wings gummed, the bats flopped to earth and were quickly stamped to death. The few bats who escaped fluttered into the sky and out of sight.

Stumping past trash and bodies to aid Jedit, tracking scuffles and still counting noses, Adira Strongheart for the first time missed Badger and worried. Surely he'd fallen in pursuing Johan, for the faithful sailor would never miss a fight. Heath, her Radjan archer, was out of town, and Echo nursed a broken head back in the town hall, but reinforcements finally arrived. More than a hundred of her Robaran Mercenaries lived in Palmyra, after all, and the screams could be heard all over town.

"About time you got here, Canute! And you, Gerda!" Adira snarled at the tousled two with swords in hand. "Did you get stuck hiding under your bunks?"

"What?" Canute, a burly redhead, squinted about at the carnage. "Whips and wheels, Adira, I came soon's the noise woke me! What orders?"

Disgusted with herself, Adira didn't answer. Of course. This battle wasn't ten minutes old and had started before dawn.

Everyone in the sullied marketplace froze as tremendous roars rebounded from the walls. The coal-black apes adorned with tentacles shrieked in outrage, for they'd met their match in Jedit Ojanen.

One flame-eyed ape pinned the tiger's wrists above his head with massive paws. It snapped its back tentacles like six whips to blind Jedit or else slice his throat, for each tentacle was edged with horny callous as sharp as turtle shell. The other gorilla clung like a leech to Jedit's back. Black hands like pickaxes were lodged deep in the tiger's jabot, steadily throttling. Jedit Ojanen fought back all the harder.

Bucking, twisting, straining, Jedit dragged down his and the ape's mighty arms. Inch by inch he hauled the ape's face close. Flame-red eyes widened as it saw Jedit's yawning mouth lined with gleaming white fangs. Long strings of saliva had been champed to foam, for Jedit was being strangled from behind. Powerless, now pinned itself, the gorilla began to gibber. With the power of a battering ram, Jedit wrenched the ape close and clamped bone-breaking jaws on its muzzle.

Arriving almost too close, Adira Strongheart shivered as the tormented fiend squealed in terror. Slowly, despite being throttled, Jedit cocked his wrists to trap the ape's paws against his lean hips. Flexing his back, Jedit set clawed toes in the dirt of the marketplace and craned his neck upward. Even Adira, veteran of a hundred battles, felt her stomach churn as Jedit tilted his chin, wrenched the ape's skull out of joint, then broke its neck with a gut-wrenching snap. The ape collapsed like a black rug at the man-tiger's feet. Dark tentacles on its back drooped and died like obscene flowers.

Spitting blood and flexing his paws, Jedit Ojanen fought without even turning around. Adira saw his strategy. Rather than claw to dislodge the strangling hands from his throat, Jedit used them to attack the attacker. Reaching by his rounded ears, the tiger clasped the ape's forearms with mighty paws. Squatting, Jedit tugged the ape forward and off-balance. The hellish creature whipped its tentacles in a pelting storm at the cat's face, but Jedit ignored the stinging, slicing blows. Even Adira could see that for all its fearsome strength, the ape was tiring just trying to strangle Jedit, for the tiger's neck was tough as an oak tree. Now it was too late.

Sinking to his hams, Jedit coiled in a ball. Levering against the ape's forearms, he kicked with sinewy legs. Immediately the ape flipped over the tiger's head. Sucking tentacles ripped fur and flesh from Jedit's head and neck, leaving bloody puckers tufted with fur. The ape's back struck the marketplace. Adira clearly felt the dirt jump under her boots.

Roaring in rage, free of the clutching black talons, Jedit Ojanen sent a fist big as a kettle into the sky and brought it down on the ape's muzzle. Adira grunted as bone and teeth shattered. Tentacles shot straight out as in disbelief. Jedit brought down the other paw and smashed bone again. Probably the ape was dead by then, but the tiger continued to pound the ape into a shapeless mass. Still the cat vented its fury, now slapping with claws that raked furrows in the battered body. The carcass was more a red hash than black, and Adira had to turn away.

Another roar made her flinch. Jedit Ojanen had risen, seared by fire and drenched in blood, amber-green eyes glowing wildly with battlelust. He roared defiance at the world as he cast about for another foe, and just for a second Adira felt like a mouse about to be pounced upon.

She blurted, "Slack your sails, tiger shark! We've won! It's over."

Somberly the pirate and panting tiger scanned the shattered marketplace. The reek was awful, a compound of smashed vegetables, spilled wine, fresh blood, broken cheeses, and the sour, scorched stink of the beasts of Bogardan. Yet only townsfolk and a score of Robaran Mercenaries were standing. Many tended the fallen, covering them in rugs or blankets, laying them on broken carts as stretchers, stanching and binding wounds, or pinning bodies flat to wrench broken limbs aright. Simone the Siren was on her feet, as were all her Seveners. Worst hurt, Adira realized, was Jedit Ojanen, unless Badger lay dead in some alley.

"Johan escaped." The tiger spat blood off his muzzle, both his own and his enemy's. Both ears bled, as did a dozen other rips and tears. "Give me your best scouts to track him."

"My best scouts?" Used to giving orders, not taking them, Adira was both flustered and irked. "My best scout is Heath, but he recuperates in Bryce. Wilemina can track a trail, and so can Jasmine, she claims—"

"Wilemina! Jasmine!" Jedit's coughing bark made everyone in the marketplace jump. "Come! We hunt Johan!"

"Heave to!" snapped Adira. "No one crimps my crew without—"

Adira froze as Jedit's bloody, scarred, fire-singed muzzle bobbed an inch from hers. The tiger's growl chilled her blood.

"Don't refuse me revenge."

Blood-flecked tail swishing, limping on a chewed foot, the tiger trotted down the street, bearing west. Wilemina and Jasmine tripped up to Adira, breathless, asking questions with arched eyebrows.

"Go," said Adira. "Keep an eye out. We'll need him and more now that Johan's returned, damn his ornery hide. Damn both of them."

* * * * *

"Enemies beset me, yet I escape unharmed. Such is my destiny. Yet again I am cursed by cat warriors!"

Alone, Johan complained as he marched barefooted into a wasteland. Tatters of his purple lizard-skin robe trailed, ragged and wet and collecting sand. His red-black tattooed skin shone like fresh blood on agates.

"Forced to brawl in a marketplace like a common thug, and I've squandered the secret of my return, forfeited the element of surprise to the enemy! Still, perhaps this is best. Adira Simpleminded Strongheart and Hazezon Hamhanded Tamar will lose sleep knowing I plot against them, knowing doom dogs their every step!"

Had he been lucid, Johan might have worried that he sputtered and fumed like a village idiot and stooped to childish insults. Yet he blithered on, more exhausted than he realized. Careless of eating and sleeping, Johan had spent weeks crossing a deadly desert before reaching Palmyra, months before that exploring Efrava, and a year or more before that waging war. The furious battle in the marketplace had spent his resources, both mystic and physical, yet he was unaware and plowed on in a mental fog. Fleeing the fight, he'd waded the River Toloron and struck west, for no other reason than that his enemies would expect him to push north. Shaking his horned head, he'd walked for hours, barefoot, without hat or waterskin, no possessions but the shredded purple robe and a few spellcasting oddments in his pockets. Magic sustained his body but took a toll on his mind.

No one heard the half-mad sorcerer mutter, not even an errant shepherd. The land was inhospitable. A few miles from the life-giving river, the terrain reverted to broken shale, crumbled arroyos of orange sand, and scanty bush. Neither sheep nor goats could graze out here. A desert by a different name, these Western Wastes. Few entered these barrens. Nomads shunned the area, considering it unlucky, believing from ancient legends that unscalable cliffs blocked the way west. There was no water, no greenery, no iron nor gems, no animals—nothing to serve as a lure.

"Tigers. Tiger-men. Man-tigers. Why?" Befuddled without knowing it, Johan talked as he blundered on west. "The cat warriors are too great a force to ignore, so I must control them. Conquer them. But how? Killing them seems too easy. Yet to break them to harness, render them docile, exploit them . . . What do we know of them? Nothing. What's their secret? How to decipher animal minds? Fabulous knowledge could be had. Yet so much was lost, smothered and crushed by the Ice Ages or swept away by the glacial floods. Somewhere must be preserved the ancient key to subduing the cats—Hunh!"

Johan halted as if poleaxed. Before him, silhouetted against a flaming desert sunset, wavered a mirage—or a vision.

A beautiful woman in blue layered robes, with startling black hair and golden skin, stood with one small hand poised as if to ask a stranger a question.

Hideous in red skin and black stripes and horns like a dragon's, Johan squinted to make the vision freeze, but the woman rippled and shimmered like smoke on water.

Not wishing to appear ignorant, he stated, "I know you!"

"Perhaps." The vision didn't argue. The woman's eyes slanted upward at the corners. A foreigner to Jamuraa. "I am Shauku. I reside in the west."

"You have a library in a palace." Johan nodded like an angry bull. "Hundreds of volumes collected from the far corners of Dominaria. I read of it long ago but only now recalled."

The woman nodded. Johan could clearly see a chipped rock on the horizon through her head. "It's true. All you might wish to learn would lie at your fingertips, were you here."

"Knowledge of the catfolk?" blurted Johan, and could have bitten his tongue for giving up a secret.

"Catfolk? Talking tigers, do you mean? Yes, they are chronicled. A thick book is bound in orange-black hide. Everything to know of cat warriors lies therein."

"Such a book exists?" Johan jerked forward as if yanked on a leash. "To see that—"

He stopped himself rather than reveal a desire, a weakness, but anything that could give him power over the cat warriors he wanted. They were his personal curse conjured by the spirits of the sky, he was sure.

Shauku gestured with a ghostly hand, and from the desert sands seemed to spring the sketchy outlines of a massive palace that just as quickly blew away on the breeze.

She trilled, "My abode is not far for one who can shift body and essence through the planes."

Johan didn't answer, for he could not. To shift, to conjure a spell that whisked one's self immeasurable distances in an eye blink, was a power denied him. Shifting was the first step toward true planeswalking, a feat of true sorcerers who'd grasped the most fundamental secrets of the cosmos. Johan had striven for years to shift but had always failed. So had every other mage in Jamuraa, he knew, even the hated Haze-zon Tamar. Perhaps no one in Dominaria could shift. In ancient times drenched in magic, wizards had snapped their fingers and flown to the stars, but it seemed the Ice Ages had first frozen and then diluted all magics. A curse on the current generation, Johan feared.

Lacking an answer, Johan lied. "I'd need an entourage to pay proper respect at your court. It's too much bother to shift weaklings, a strain upon them. I'll come over land."

A smile creased the woman's ghostly cheeks. "I understand. We shall prepare for your visit. It's been too long since so distinguished a guest graced our halls. Until then."

Shauku tipped her chin or perhaps blew an imaginary kiss. Johan wasn't sure, because her visage had already faded. He was left squinting at a chipped rock framed by molten sun.

"Shauku," he muttered. "The ageless librarian, guardian of all the wisdom accumulated by men. Yes, there I must go! And see? I embarked westward before even knowing my journey! No one is more clever than Johan except Johan!"

Pausing, Johan noted his surroundings for the first time. The sun dropped below the western horizon. A cool breeze blew against his right ear, a wind from the north, as always. Already he spoke in imperious tones.

"Very well. We must send word to Tirras for lackeys. Make ready to journey. We strike west! Toward knowledge and greater conquest!"

* * * * *

The far-roaming scouts limped into the town hall just after dawn. Jedit flopped on the floor like an overfed housecat and instantly nodded off.

For a while, people stared at the tiger-man, plainly awed. He sprawled on the floor like a colorful rug, more than seven feet long from toes to nose, with an armspan a fathom wide and a chest like a hogshead barrel. The striped tail, big as a king cobra, stirred and squirmed, never resting. The cat bore scars and scabs from combat that would have killed a man. Ferocious bites marred his muzzle, neck, and shoulder. Some wept fluid, some were swollen and infected and already in danger of breeding maggots. The gruesome burn down his back continued down one leg, and to scorched skin had been added sunburn and rash. All four paws bore bloody scabs from sharp desert shale. He was ticked and dinged and scratched in a dozen other places. Yet despite the homey purring noises, Jedit Ojanen looked deadly as a dozing dragon, and people lowered their voices rather than wake him.

Nursing wounds, yawns, and tankards of beer lounged Adira's Circle of Seven. The governor of Bryce, Hazezon Tamar, was not present, for he roomed in other quarters when forced to visit Palmyra.

Adira sent Virgil to fetch him, adding, "Insist that Haz come right away, for he's been bred to luxury. If he's hurried at his toilet and denied his morning figs and wine, he'll be grumpy, and that's always a treat. On your way back, fetch a leech to heal our cat friend here. Or a horse doctor. Your choice."

Exhausted and parched, Sister Wilemina accepted a mug of beer and drained it, then another, before she could talk. Laying her cloak and bow on the table, she shucked her boots. Murdoch massaged her blistered feet. The druid Jasmine Boreal flung off a poncho, slugged half a jug of wine, laid her head on a table, and slept.

Rasping, the archer explained, "We tracked Johan into the Western Wastes. Feet of the efreet, but that tiger sets a fierce pace! We jogged leagues with him, dropping and sniffing every long bowshot. Johan's spoor went straight west. Cursed queer, that. We kept expecting he'd veer north, but he never did. Where he's bound we can't imagine, nor how he survives without water and sunshade. Those rocks would bake a basilisk! After a while, Master Stripes and his hot temper cooled some, and those wounds of his must have ached! They'd cripple a war-horse! Jasmine and I pleaded to turn back. Finally he did, though I'll not deny his courage. He left blood in every footprint. Pawprint. Oh, I hope never again to see such a blighted land! May I eat? Please?"

"Of course. Do." Adira had ordered a sturdy repast because the day promised to be busy. Gracing the table were bacon, cold cock, flat bread, dates, honeyed yogurt, goat cheese, and more. Wilemina wolfed while Adira summed up her crew's state.

"We found Badger in an alley, kicking like a beached grouper and half-blind, but he'll live. The Keepers tend his burns. Heath, our favorite fifth wheel, arrived by packet boat late yesterday, just in time to miss the fun. The marketplace is a shambles. The dead we buried. I attended their gravesides since I'm mayor of this illustrious rat hole. Jasmine and Whistledove and Murdoch have proved official Seveners, so I suppose they'll want higher pay."

Adira Strongheart sipped beer and wiped foam off her upper lip. Staring at the wall, she dandled one booted foot, and finally said, "West? Why would Johan run west and not north toward Tirras? I should think he'd head home to flay his subjects and eat babies. But west? A hundred leagues or more of nothing . . ."

"That's our biggest setback in brawling with Johan," said the sensible Simone. "You can't outguess a madman."

"Johan's not mad."

Everyone startled as Jedit Ojanen uncoiled from the floor, evidently refreshed by his nap. Scabs on burns and wounds cracked and wept anew, but he scarcely noticed. "That shaman's canny as a wounded fox, but he's not mad."

The Circle of Seven craned their necks. The tiger-man's rounded ears brushed the ceiling beams. Except for a painted green loincloth supported by a thin shoulder strap, he went naked, his body a riot of orange, black, and white stripes, with an astonishing expanse of white chest. Scarred, burned, and wounded, he was still a magnificent creature.

"But you're not Jaeger." Adira thought aloud. "Jaeger was older, steadier. Quick into combat but a thinker. Even a brooder. You're just a cub, albeit a mighty big one. You think with your fists. Claws."

"Tell me of my father," said the tiger. "Please. We know nothing from the time he left Efrava."

"Efrava?" asked Adira.

"Our homeland. An oasis in the eastern desert. The heat and sand wurms prevent our people from journeying west, but my father braved it to gain knowledge. Tell me first, please."

"Very well." Adira tapped another cask to wet her throat. "Though it was Hazezon who found him almost dead north of Bryce. . . ."

Listening, but licking his fangs with a raspy pink tongue, the tiger-man strode to a bench and plunked down, making sturdy pine creak in protest. Without asking, he hooked a roast hen with one hand and bit off half, bones and all. He devoured three more hens, half a ham, a wheel of cheese, a slab of smoked bacon, four loaves of flat bread—everything on the table, including licking clean a pot of honey.

The while, Adira talked about Jaeger, the first cat warrior ever seen in the central desert of Jamuraa, the first tiger-man ever heard of. She spoke of their comradeship and Jaeger's valiant skills, both at fighting and diplomacy, and recounted without emotion the months-long battles and uncounted skirmishes to stop Johan's invasion of the southlands.

The story ran long in the telling, for Simone chimed in with other accounts of Jaeger's valor. "He saved Heath's life once by ripping a fire drake out of the sky. Badger's too, and mine a few times. Everyone loved him. Even those crotchety merfolk liked Jaeger."

Virgil returned with word that Hazezon Tamar was on the way. Coming too was a witch who knew herbs. After those announcements, a long pause hung in the air. All the Circle of Seven watched their leader.

Suddenly weary, Adira Strongheart rushed the story's end. "When we dug out after the sandstorm, Johan's army was dead and buried, though most of Palmyra was too. Yet first thing, Jaeger announced he must quest south. He sensed Johan had survived—how I can't say. His duty and destiny to kill Johan, he said, was cast by prophecy."

"The prophecy of None, One, and Two?" asked Jedit, amber-green eyes glowing.

"Aye." Adira scratched her head vigorously. "It made my brain ache to hear Haz and Jaeger blither about it. They'd spend hours arguing about which was None and which One, and so on, round and round, but Jaeger believed the prophecy implicitly, and . . ."

"And it killed him?" asked Jedit.

"Perhaps," sighed Adira. "No one knows. Your father never returned. Once we'd gained our sea legs, I sent out scouts and nomads. They scoured the desert for leagues east, but all that new-blown sand made avenues for wurms. They could burrow this far west for the first time, you see. We lost near a score of people to the crawling scourges. That may've been your father's fate, deep-sixed in an ocean of sand. Or Johan may've killed him, though it seems impossible that any mortal could put out that flame. Jaeger Ojanen was a—a living legend." Surprised at her own depth of feeling, Adira fell silent.

After a meal, a tiger would normally sleep, but Jedit picked up a chunk of fallen plaster and filed his claws razor-sharp with a harsh grating noise. In morning sun slanting through the door, his eyes sparkled like cold emeralds. Filing, concentrating, Jedit told his own story, as Hazezon Tamar arrived with clerks and palace guards in tow, of how Johan arrived on an exhausted drake and crashed in the desert only to be rescued by Jaeger's son. How Johan toured Efrava and assessed every feature as if to buy the oasis, or conquer it. Winding up, Jedit asked a score of questions that showed his keen mind had absorbed every detail of Adira's story. The humans' estimation of the tiger's mental prowess rose considerably. Finally, Jedit spoke.

"I believe Johan killed my father. Elsewise Jaeger would have returned to you, his friends. That egg-sucking sorcerer wears my father's medallion like a trophy of the kill. Now Johan's wreaked havoc on Palmyra again. Likely he's a slave to prophecy also. Those few words seem to gang we tigerfolk to Johan like a yoke of oxen. Now to fulfill prophecy and finish my father's work falls to me. No doubt Johan plans new grief for these southlands, as you call them. Surely only death will quell his misdeeds.

"Efrava . . . Johan must have designs on Efrava too, if only because it's part of Jamuraa, as you call our motherland."

"An oasis in the eastern desert?" Hazezon Tamar spoke for the first time, white beard wagging. "So far? How could such a site aid Johan in conquering the southlands, if that's his goal this time? His army couldn't deviate even ten miles from the River Toloron without perishing. Never could they cross the eastern sands of Sukurvia. No one can, not even nomads."

"One thing bubbles from this muddle." Adira Strongheart shook her head of tousled curls. "Johan's off the leash, and someone must bring him to heel."

"True." Jedit surveyed the room and the Circle of Seven as if ready to take command. "Terrent Amese makes our path shine clear as moonlight. The sooner we hunt down Johan and kill him, the better for all our peoples. Are we avowed? You know what such an endeavor entails."

"Suffering and death," said Adira without self-pity. She rubbed her game leg. "We've done it before. Yet what must be, must be. We mount an expedition westward into the wastes. For justice, and finally, we hope, for a lasting peace."

Chapter 8

"Unbelievable!"

"It's not a cliff?" asked Sister Wilemina.

"Nay," said Hazezon, "it's a wall. Built by hand and magic, but I can't imagine how."

Adira Strongheart and her Circle of Seven—Virgil, Whistledove, Murdoch, Simone the Siren, Heath and Wilemina the archers, and the woods witch Jasmine Boreal—sat on horseback and stared. Traveling with them were Hazezon Tamar, an entourage of servants, and four palace guards. Sixteen people and a talking tiger, gaping awestruck at the legendary cliffs that boxed off the Western Wastes. Except the looming monstrosity was not a natural-hewn cliff but a hand-laid wall hundreds of feet high.

"I'd never have believed it had my own eyes not beheld it," murmured Hazezon.

Kneeing his horse onto a small rise, Hazezon scanned from south to north. The Western Wastes were just that, a dreary expanse of pebbly hills and crooked draws with little vegetation and no water. A single charmed jug of ever-flowing water was all that allowed the adventurers to enter these barrens. Hazezon had paid dearly for that jug, and with every sip every member held his breath and hoped its magic didn't fizzle and die, or they surely would. Three weeks it had taken to cross the wastelands on horseback, though Jedit walked every step because no horse would have him and no lumbering monoxes had been available. Often, too, he must drop to all fours to snuffle the sands, for he tracked his enemy.

From Palmyra, Johan's barefoot trail had wended due west into the desert, then, abruptly, diverted north. Twelve days later he'd rendezvoused with twenty people descending from Tirras. Tyrant and entourage had marched west, straight toward the towering wall barring their way. Why Johan had entered the wastelands, why he changed course, how he'd summoned servants across empty miles, how he'd surmounted the wall—these were mysteries.

Always curious, Hazezon Tamar had accompanied Adira's crew simply because he'd never journeyed here before. Now, after three mind-dulling weeks, he wished to never see them again. Yet he was unexpectedly rewarded by this engineering phenomenon of titanic proportions. Shading his eyes, the mage saw the wall ran for miles, far out of sight to the south and north, though not compass-true. Perhaps it curved inward. So immense it was, Hazezon couldn't be sure. The construction reared more than two hundred feet, not quite sheer, with each layer of stone set back a small interval. Even godlike engineers, the wizard supposed, hesitated to push their luck and fudged the slope back a hair.

Turning, Hazezon called, "Heath, how far to the wall, do you reckon?"

Nickering to his horse, the pale archer clopped forward. Hazezon had known Heath for decades, yet he remained an enigma. The quiet man never aged. His hair was bone-white, his face thin, his eyes melancholy as if harboring a secret sorrow. He wore a linen tunic of no color with a deer-hide vest and carried a bow of glossy ebony. His eyes were sharp as a hawk's.

With a glance, Heath pronounced, "Five miles and nine rods, I make it."

"Amazing." Hazezon's eyes were weak from forty years of

pirating on bright water and glaring deserts. Yet he could see the wall was made of rough stones carefully stacked and chinked with smaller rocks. No single stone looked hewn by a hammer. "So, a single boulder must be . . ."

Heath scratched his nose and pointed with a string-callused finger. "That granite stone with the black streak is nineteen armspans or more across."

The others stirred in their saddles. Jedit Ojanen stood with arms folded as he studied the cliff, high as an oncoming cloud bank. Someone whistled.

Simone the Siren asked, "Who can shift rocks fifty feet across?"

"Gods," said Jasmine, "and a few magic-makers. But not many."

"What's that tuft of greenery near the top?" Wilemina pointed.

"A birch grove," answered Heath.

Another whistle. The "tuft" spread like moss along a cottage roof. Heath pointed to a twig and pronounced it a wolf pine growing sideways. Its roots were seated amid rocks bigger than houses.

Jedit pointed a black claw. "What's that white stuff dusting the rocks?"

"Snow," said Heath. To the tiger-man's fuddled look, he added, "Soft ice that sifts from the sky."

A frown creased Jedit's striped face. Obviously he was unsure if the humans joked.

"I don't understand." Simone pouted, lips red and luscious in her oiled-ebony face. "Glaciers covered all these lands in the Ice Ages, then melted overnight and flooded everything before them, or so legends say. How could this giant wall have been built since? By whom?"

Hazezon shook his white head. "The wall predates the glaciers. It could be tens of thousands of years old. As to who built it, who can say?"

"And who cares?" Adira cut off discussion. "It doesn't matter if the wall is made of rocks or wood or green cheese. We can't scale it, that's certain. So—"

"I could scale it," interjected Jedit.

Adira Strongheart glared, for she disliked being contradicted, as Hazezon well knew. Yet Jedit Ojanen was at least talking again. He'd been quiet these three weeks, asking again and again for stories of his father's exploits, then silently absorbing them. Day by day, with every step Jedit Ojanen seemed to sink into the earth, as if weighed down by the burden of punishing his father's killer.

Sniffing away Jedit's boast, Adira stated, "We're beached. I didn't believe the cliffs existed, or if they did, they'd be puny and surmountable. Now that we've shoaled . . ."

"I can lift you up the cliff face," Hazezon jibed his ex-wife.

"How?" sparked Adira. "You're an old and surefooted goat, it's true, if not a randy one, but you couldn't hoist that lardbelly up a coaster's companionway, let alone a stone cliff."

Stung, Hazezon glared from under white eyebrows. "You'll see. Before nightfall. Unless we lose the day arguing."

Calling to their mounts, the troop clattered down a shingle slope, ever westward. Echo was absent, for she'd suffered dizzy spells from her head blow. Missing too was Badger, still recovering from burns. Lacking the old mariner's leadership and light humor, Simone the Siren had adopted the dual roles of lieutenant and court jester.

Now she quipped, "It happens every time. Adira and Hazezon get thrown together by politics, and first they're polite, then they spit, and finally they flay each other with words sharper than an enemy's sword. Makes me glad I wore my old shirt. We'll all be spattered by blood before their love-making is done."

"Shut up," said both Adira and Hazezon.

The party rode into the shadow of the cliffs, which stretched for miles across the desert floor as the sun sank, and no one spoke, struck silent by awe. Up close their necks tired from craning upward. Far, far toward the heavens, thin clouds spilled past the lip of rough rocks and misty greenery. The majestic heights and autumnal chill made the party shiver after weeks of austere, scorched desert.

As the riders slid stiffly from saddles and watered and tended their mounts, Jedit Ojanen squatted over tufts of green and brown that sprinkled the stony soil.

To the tiger's obvious confusion, Heath explained, "Pine needles. Like cactus thorns, only soft."

Frowning, Jedit Ojanen touched a black claw to an invisible spot on the soil. "Johan's last footstep. The trail ends here."

In silence, the party stared upward, thinking but not asking the same question.

"Then we'll stop here too." Hazezon Tamar made his voice flippant, for the atmosphere was chilled and gloomy in the wall's shadow. He opened a saddlebag and unwrapped a squat, square jug. With jug in hands, he asked, "Who goes, and who stays?"

"Goes where?" As always, Adira was suspicious of Hazezon's magic, which had a tendency to run riot once unleashed. "Atop the wall?"

"Where else? It's why we came!" Refusing to be sucked into another endless argument, Hazezon explained patiently. "We shan't all go, uh, aloft. I'm staying here in Sukurvia."

"You'll what?" barked Adira. "You whiskery walrus! Why did you waste three weeks trekking a wasteland just to sheer about and haul for home?"

"I came," Hazezon spat through gritted teeth, "to boost you, you ungrateful minx, up to the top of the cliffs!"

Adira raked back her auburn curls, always a danger sign. "Oh, so? Us and eight horses, near five tons of deadweight, flung into the air like a flock of flamingos? How did you know there even were cliffs, O Master of the All-Seeing Eye? You're so bat-blind you've pitched down a privy hole just lifting your skirts!"

"I wear *robes* as befit a civilized gentlemen!" retorted Hazezon. "Unlike some hell-bound hussies who dress in men's garb because they can't decide which side of the bed to sleep in!"

"I slept in your bed too many nights," shrilled Adira, "and suffered one damned disappointment after another."

Some pirates chuckled as the squabble rattled on. Others grimaced in embarrassment. Simone the Siren clutched hands over her heart and simpered as if love-struck. Jedit Ojanen studied the wall as if measuring the best route to climb.

" . . . leave it to Hamhanded Trembler to concoct some addle-pated scheme built on untried magic!" Adira Strongheart didn't mention that she practiced small magics herself. She jabbed a callused finger at the bottle in her ex-husband's hand. "What stinkpot trick this time? Will you stuff me and my crew in that jug like imps and *hurl* us up high?"

"No, I'll shift you!"

"Like hell!"

A stunned silence fell as the words sank in. Hazezon was aware that both Adira's mercenaries and his own servants and palace guards stared.

Rubbing her nose in agitation, Adira demanded, "Shift? As in, step across the spheres?"

"Nothing so grand," mumbled the elder mage, "but I've practiced and experimented many a long night. Shifting is the first step toward planeswalking, it's true, but likely I won't live long enough to achieve that. Still, I *can* shift. Some things."

"What things?" snapped Adira. "How far?"

"Statues, if you must know!" snarled Hazezon. "And within eyeshot!"

Heads tilted heavenward. Simone said, "Eyeshot?"

Sergeant Murdoch echoed, "Experimented?"

And Heath, "Statues? Not the ones at your villa in Bryce?"

"If we don't land atop the wall," asked Wilemina, "where will we end up?"

Hazezon Tamar held up both hands as if to say, Trust me.

Jedit Ojanen asked, "How did Johan surmount the wall?"

Glad for an interruption, Hazezon lectured. "Oh, likely he just levitated his entourage. That would be no hard feat—"

"Why don't we?" asked Virgil.

"—no hard feat for *some*," Hazezon plowed on. "Or they may've flown. Remember the Tirrans possessed cloth-wing gliders and animated bird carcasses. Or Johan may have shifted them. I can't know his grimoire, but any of a dozen spells might suffice, and what one magician can conjure, another can replicate. Sometimes."

"Drag your anchor, Haz," sighed Adira Strongheart. "We're beached, so any harbor looks homey. What needs doing?"

Smug at a small victory, Hazezon beamed. "Link hands. Quickly, before we lose the light. And stop grumbling. Hold tight. Don't drop hands, or you'll break the ring—Eh?"

"Milord Tamar."

For the first time, the captain of Hazezon's bodyguard spoke up. Lieutenant Peregrine was tall with fair hair cropped square to her turban-wrapped pointed helmet. She wore the ocean-blue tunic with gold wave that represented Bryce's wealth, come from the sea, and over it a blue cloak. A pirate's scimitar was jammed in a sash, and like all the guards, she carried a lance with a fluttering blue pennant, but now she put that aside. Speaking out of turn on a personal matter, her cheeks flushed rose under a southern tan.

"If you'll permit, sir, I wish to accompany Her Ladyship's party, if Her Ladyship will allow it."

"What?" Mentally rehearsing a spell, Hazezon was taken aback. "Peregrine, why this sudden decision to quit my service?"

"Milord." The woman stood soldier-straight while squirming

inside. "My ancestors are said to come from Buzzard's Bay. I request a leave of absence to visit the region. I promised it to my—my mother. And I suspect Her Ladyship Strongheart would welcome an extra right arm."

"Not if you hail me as 'Her Ladyship' the livelong day," said Adira. "You bespeak me like some whaleboned brine hag. Aye, you're welcome to ship aboard. I'd give my right arm for one soul who can follow orders! And we mustn't disappoint your mother."

Teasing made the proud lieutenant blush deeper.

"Yes, go, Peregrine." Worried about his spell, Hazezon didn't care. "No need to dock your pay. Consider it detached duty. Guard Adira as you would me. The stars and moons know she attracts trouble like a lightning rod. Now, all join hands and hush, children! Remember, don't let go your grasp!"

Formally passing command to her second, Lieutenant Peregrine joined the circle with Adira Strongheart, Sergeant Murdoch, Sister Wilemina, Whistledove Kithkin, Jasmine Boreal, Simone the Siren, Heath, Virgil, and Jedit Ojanen. They joined hands, facing outward in a ring that corralled nine nervous horses. Jedit's big furry paws enfolded Wilemina's and Simone's hands halfway to the elbow.

Hazezon Tamar pried the wax stopper from his jug and dipped his finger in a bluish gel like berry juice with an eye-watering reek like vinegar. Touching a gooey blue finger to Adira's left hand, he traced up Adira's arm to her neck, crossed her throat gently, and striped down to her right hand. Adira protested "slime," but Hazezon carried on, dipping and smearing the liniment across Lieutenant Peregrine's chest, careful to keep the azure thread intact. Around the circle he plodded, smearing goo across leather and cloth and skin and tiger hide, all the while incanting under his breath, until he returned to his ex-wife. The desert mage's brow dripped sweat, which made the travelers cringe, but they kept silent.

Looking at the bulky horses and towering cliff wall, Hazezon gritted his teeth as he wound up the incantation.

". . . on the wings of Wullab Fountain-Spitter, on the hooves of Gybo the Galloper, with the speed of the Firestorm Phoenix, upon the breath of Phanal-Unorg, I bid you, all joined as one, be gone!"

A great wind swept from nowhere to sizzle about the adventurers. Hair and skirts and mustaches billowed. Capes flipped over quivers and shoulders. Dust spattered faces, making people squeeze their eyes shut and snort. Horses whinnied with fright and skipped to break out of the human corral.

Adira gasped above the howl, "Don't let go or the magic—"

Gone.

Hazezon's servants and guards chirped. One second, Adira's crew swayed in a gale, the next they vanished, and the air fell still. Ears rang in the silence. The heroes hadn't faded away like sunlight nor been whisked upward like birds. They just ceased to exist.

A guard walked to the circle and gingerly toed a boot print.

A cook squeaked, "Did the charm work, Milord?"

In the shadow of the cliff, Hazezon Tamar leaned back and squinted at the distant blurred cliff top. The others peered upward.

Then a guard shouted a laugh. "Look!"

Arcing from the cliff, bright against a darkening sky, fizzled a fire arrow. It soared far out, high overhead, and gradually dropped to disappear in the desert.

Hazezon Tamar laughed with relief. "I knew it would work! I just dislike to boast and tempt fate. Our desert gods are fickle. Silly of me not to have arranged a signal beforehand. Live and learn, live and learn."

He wiped his face and shivered.

"Don't stand gawking, children. Tighten your cinches and mount up! Let's quit the shade of this fell cliff!"

* * * * *

Atop the cliff wall, Heath watched his fire arrow wink out far below. He had no fear of the bluff's sheer drop, but everyone else staggered back from the awful precipice. Wilemina sank onto shaking knees and gasped for breath, frightened both by magic and heights. Whistledove Kithkin crept on all fours to peek over the edge, then changed her mind and crabbed backward. Murdoch and Simone grabbed reins and cooed to nervous horses. Others straightened tackle or tended weapons to soothe shaking hands. Only Adira Strongheart turned to the business at hand, to explore a new-found world.

What she saw were pine trees, hundreds of them.

Marching almost to the cliff's edge, the trees reared straight and tall a hundred feet or more. Their uppermost branches swayed together, murmuring quietly like surf surging. The ground was soft black loam thickly carpeted with brown needles that hushed footfalls. Jots of unseasonable snow were dotted in hollows like flowers. A heady spice of turpentine and moss and water enveloped the party, the breath of the forest. Up here the sun was still high but was already eclipsed by towering trees. The adventurers could see past scaly gray-brown trunks for a hundred, in some places two hundred, feet, but past that light was defeated, and the forest lay still and dark, quiet and cool.

Adira blinked. An orange-black form glided between trunks then vanished. Spinning in place, Adira realized Jedit had slunk into the forest without a sound. At the roots of one tree, the tiger crouched to sift a handful of snow, totally amazed.

Marveling, Adira Strongheart kicked her boot heel and only disturbed more dirt. She wondered how far down it sank, since somewhere below must begin the massive stones of the giant hand-laid wall. Then she shrugged and retied her head-band, dropping concerns of tigers and titans.

People startled as she asked, "Who's been here before? Heath? Jasmine?"

The part-elf shook his pale head. "Other pinelands, yes, but not these."

Jasmine Boreal was most local, hailing from a clan that lived beyond Buzzard's Bay, but she, too, shook her head. "This is Arboria, they call it, or the Pinelands. Near a hundred fifty leagues to the Goat's Walk and Buzzard's Bay, methinks. None cross this forest. Rather they trek the heath to reach the Northern Realm."

"Had we sailed the Storm Coast, we'd ride in luxury instead of tramping in mud and rain," groused Adira, "but we must follow Johan and see whither he wanders."

"Why," asked Whistledove, "does no one enter this forest?"

Jasmine shook her head, irritated by a lack of knowledge. "This forest was once home to pine dwellers who hunted and trapped and traded at Buzzard's Bay. Pixies too, t'was said, though none were ever seen or caught. They left. Driven out, perhaps."

The heroes gazed at the mysterious and green-misted beauty of the land. The forest seemed to wait, but for what? A red squirrel scrabbled down from a branch and crossly chattered a challenge. Simone the Siren chucked a pinecone, and the defender scampered up and away. People laughed, and the spell was broken.

Adira nudged Sister Wilemina, still shaking from the magical shift, gazing back the way they'd come.

"Close your trap, Wil, before a swallow builds a nest in your jaw."

"Look," whispered the archer. "Down there lies sere desert and up here lush forest! A division sharp as beach and sea! Because of this giants' wall! Surely we must wade knee-deep in ancient magics, and what can protect us?"

"I'll protect you, sweetheart," laughed Murdoch and swatted Wilemina's rump, so she jumped a foot. His laughter died as the blonde archer cracked a horny fist on his jaw that toppled him to the turf.

"There's magic for you," chuckled Simone. "Woman magic!"

Fretful and wary and heartened and excited, the party tightened cinches and swung into saddles.

They goggled as Jedit Ojanen stepped from behind a tree, silent as a ghost, to report, "No scent of our enemy."

"None?" asked Adira. "How can that be?"

"If Johan levitated his party," put in Jasmine, "they may've alighted miles within the forest."

"Or anywhere," said Virgil, always glum.

"Or nowhere," admitted Adira, "but we'll flush him out. Jedit, Heath, take point. Murdoch, Peregrine, the vanguard. And don't 'Yes, milady' me, Peregrine, or I'll kick you off this cliff top. 'Adira' suffices. We're brigands, thank the stars, not soldiers."

Perched in a basket atop a packhorse, Whistledove Kithkin held her rapier in one hand, so looked like a child playing pirate.

Peering big-eyed under flat red hair, she asked, "Why would native peoples abandon such a beautiful forest?"

"Only one way to find out," said the pirate chief. "Hi-ho and go."

Strung single file on skittish horses, led by a talking tiger, Adira Strongheart's Robaran Mercenaries penetrated the deep woods.

The leader added in a hush, "Besides, if someone does live here, we shouldn't fret. We've done naught to aggravate them. So far."

* * * * *

Miles ahead, in the depths of the forest . . .

"Halt and speak! Where are you bound?"

Johan, Emperor of Tirras and the Northern Realms, again disguised as a drab monk, sat bald and unblinking as his sedan chair settled. His entourage gaped at strangers who'd materialized like shadows from pine scrub, a prime spot for ambush.

Four dull-witted barbarians lugged their master's chair. A Tirran captain and four pikemen in gray linen tunics painted with Johan's four-pointed star carried spears. Tagging along were a scribe, a lesser mage, a seer, five porters lugging chests and sacks, and a huntsman, cook, and helper. The tyrant kept the party small to move quickly and attract less attention.

Yet they were surrounded by forest denizens. Thin to the point of emaciation, the men and women had fair skin and auburn hair, sharp cheekbones, and slanted eyes, as if part fox. They wore leather kilts or skirts and leggings and jerkins, though a few had shirts of rough cloth obviously traded from the outside world. Everyone was trimmed with a king's ransom in furs: brown, black, ermine, sable, spotted. Most wore the faces of their prey framing their faces, so Johan's entourage seemed doubly surrounded by people and animals: beavers, bears, red and silver foxes, wolverines, wolves, and wildcats. In their hands hung iron spikes, mauls, and axes, and at their backs bows and arrows. Nine warriors, Johan counted.

"We ask, where are you bound?" The spokesman's wispy beard and flat coyote headpiece accentuated his thinness. But rippling knots in his arms suggested a greyhound. "Our people war with an invader. We must know your allegiance or else turn you back."

"Oh, pray, never let us be strangers." Deceptively mild, Johan tugged his brown robe at the knee and stepped onto brown needles in bare feet. The pine folk exchanged glances, wondering how a poverty-clad hermit rated such an entourage. They frowned, bewildered, as Johan picked up a fallen twig still fresh with green needles.

124

"Who are you," asked the wizard, "besides my future subjects?"

"Subjects?" blurted the thin leader.

A woman in a wildcat cap snarled, "The people of the pines are no one's subjects!"

Toying with the twig, the stranger replied, "I am Johan, Tyrant of Tirras and Emperor of the Northern Realms, soon emperor of all Jamuraa. Thus, you peasants of the pines, will become my subjects and pay homage to me—if you survive."

Nine warriors recoiled from malice or madness, weapons poised, then shouted as Johan let slip his disguise.

The homely bald monk polymorphed into a demon from legend. Fire-red skin glowed with black stripes. Downturned horns sprouted from his chin and forehead. The drab robe curdled into a loathsome purple hide that squirmed with life. As the natives stood stunned by the horrific vision, Johan snapped the twig between long black nails.

Immediately came a thrashing as a dozen pine limbs overhead broke and fell. Plummeting, thick branches like giants' spears thundered around Johan's party. A woodsman was lanced in the neck and fell, spurting blood. A dodging woman was impaled through the skull. A lad was crushed by a branch big as his waist, so he squirmed and twitched under a hundredweight of deadfall. Bark chips, splintered heartwood, and pine needles rained. One of Johan's porters flinched backward into the deadly hail and was clipped across the brow by a branch.

Only two woods warriors remained standing. Shrieking, vaulting deadwood, one swung an iron hatchet but was speared in the belly by Johan's pikeman. The other shouted and dived in a crouch but was slashed across the throat. Both fell dead. One guard snatched a wildcat cap as booty, and the other looted a wolf pelt.

Just like that, except for groaning wounded, the attack was done. Without a word, Johan stepped to his sedan.

Color drained from his skin and robe like fading twilight. Again a drab monk, the mage brushed pine needles off his chair.

"Dispatch the wounded, milord?" asked the Tirran captain.

"If you like. Leave a few to tell the tale."

Frightened survivors would spread more terror than plague. Johan ordered his shaggy bearers to rise.

"This porter is hurt." The captain nudged the fallen man with his toe. Another northern barbarian, one of many tribes conquered by Johan, he'd joined the army to see the world. "Sling him across the poles, your worship?"

"No. Divide his goods among the others." An invader left behind could spread terror too, singing songs of Johan's conquests, under torture if need be. "Come. The day wanes. Which way, seer?"

The seer, a gray-haired woman with no teeth and bad eyes, knelt on the pine sward, set down an open-weave pentacle of poured brass, mumbled an incantation, and threw a handful of bones, wood chips, river stones, and other bracken. Leaning close like a hound, the seer studied into which arms of the pentacle the oddments had fallen, then rocked back and pointed west of north.

* * * * *

"Blood. Human. And Johan's stink, like snake musk."

Rising from all fours, the great talking tiger Jedit Ojanen peered about the forest. Granite broke the surface, so hemlock and laurel scrub abounded. Off a ways, wild turkeys strutted and pecked and watched the intruders with beady eyes.

Jedit pointed a black claw. "This fight took place just yesterday."

Adira Strongheart surveyed the scene. Brown pine needles were churned, so black loam showed like open wounds.

Smashed branches and greenery bore jots of blood and scraps of leather and fur. The pirate craned her neck and saw, high up, that a circle of pine trees showed stark white breaks.

"What happened? Did Johan call down a meteor on someone's head?"

"There'd be scorch marks," said Heath. "A good spot for an ambush."

Jasmine the druid dabbed a finger in blood and tasted it. "Meat eaters. Pine dwellers must have run afoul of Johan."

"You said the pine people quit this forest," objected Adira. Jasmine only shrugged, and the party pressed on.

"Is it good luck or bad we cut Johan's trail?" asked Virgil.

"Good," said Adira. "He steers for Buzzard's Bay, our goal."

Over the dull thud of hooves, Lieutenant Peregrine called, "I've a question. Why is yon port called Buzzard's Bay?"

"Ask rather why it's called the Storm Coast." Simone the Siren rode with her cutlass handy in a saddle scabbard, and now she tugged the blade free to test it.

"All right," Peregrine played along, "why?"

"Because storms wrack it six months out of nine." Simone's voice lost its mirth. "Anyone who ventures past the headlands consigns his soul to the sea and to squalls. So many ships wreck on the rocks, the buzzards can't fly from gorging on smashed corpses that wash ashore."

On that note, the party wended after Johan, bearing west of north.

As the last switching horsetail passed out of sight, a jittering was heard like locust wings. From the scrub flitted a tiny feather-thin figure dressed in rabbit fur. Buzzing on wings a yard wide, the pixie droned through the forest like a bumblebee, wary of hawks and owls that might prowl by day. Miles on, the pixie alighted beside a slender man in leather and wolf skin. Panting, she piped a message in a jerky voice like a chickadee's.

"West of north, eh. On horseback?" The scout pondered. "We can't spare hands for an ambush. Still, stay awake. We'll await their return, and make them pay in blood."

Chapter 9

"I seek the library," said Johan without preamble.

"Library?" The woman had once been tall and robust, like most of the coastal folk, but middle age and many children had softened her. Her hair was more gray than blonde, and her robes were patched, puckered, and peppered with burn holes and stains.

"I own the only library in Buzzard's Bay. Forty-two books, I'm proud. See for yourself. I am Hebe, a sea sage, by the way. You are . . . ?"

Disguised as the drab monk, Johan gave no name as he glanced around the room. Tilting shelves were jammed with bric-a-brac. A stuffed seagull perched atop a conch shell. Strings of dried starfish dangled from the low ceiling. A horseshoe crab shell served as a dish for smaller shells. Tables were heaped with dried seaweed and blowfish, and nets bulging with oddments hung in corners. A slovenly bed and stool were all the furniture. In the corner hearth, a driftwood fire burned blue and green. The room reeked of sea salt and spoiled fish, for it occupied a loft above a fishmonger's market.

A clever, ruthless man, Johan could be pleasant when it served, yet politeness got him nothing. He studied the clutter as the sage fiddled, sizing similar shells on a board propped between tables. Alone most of the day, she blathered at her company.

"You've the look of a scholar, poor and thin like me, ha ha. You're welcome to read my books, but only here. They were hard-won, hard as plucking a drowning man from storm surf. Three, I confess, I wrote myself. I track sightings of sea monsters, you see, and other odd things the fishermen report. Fairy lights, ghosts who walk on water, tritons, giant turtles. If it floats above or below the waves, I hear the tales. The ocean harbors a thousand secrets."

Sliding edgeways past stacks and heaps of objects, Johan laid a hand on a crooked shelf of books. "The library I seek belongs to another. Not this trash."

The tyrant hurled the bookshelf over. Volumes thumped and skittered on tables and the filthy floor. Shells and sponges and skate purses were smashed and scattered. Johan shoved over a table with his bare foot and wrenched strings of starfish from the ceiling.

"You . . . you barbarian!" Horrified, Hebe shrilled curses as she grabbed a gaff studded with a rusty shark hook. Johan scooped a heavy book from a table and slung it backhanded. The volume smacked Hebe in the face and bowled her against yet another table. Johan picked up a shark's jaw and slashed the woman across the forehead. As blood ran in her eyes, he hooked a foot to dump her on the floor.

Stamping one foot on Hebe's flabby neck, Johan pressed hard enough to strangle her, then let up a bit. "I ask you, where is the library?"

Wedged amid debris, suffocating, Hebe gasped, "You'll—never—"

"I always," corrected Johan.

Sticking two fingers in his mouth, he flicked them at the ceiling. Instantly there whispered down a fine mist all about the room. Droplets hissed louder as they settled on spilled books and seawrack. As the mild rain touched Hebe's face, she screamed as if burned and struggled valiantly. The evil mage only shifted his stance and mashed her throat harder. Smoke began to fizzle from tables and parchment. The old librarian struggled and writhed.

"It burns savagely, does it not, Hebe?" Johan's gleaming pate sported glistening raindrops at a half-inch removed, for his invisible aura shielded him. "Don't open your eyes, else you'll be blinded. Tell me, quickly, and I'll release you. Where lies the fabled library?"

"You'll s-suffer!" Shuddering, the tough old woman tried to protect her face with her elbows. "The t-townsfolk will f-find you—"

"You waste breath." Exasperated, Johan picked up the gaff with the rusty shark hook. He snagged the point through Hebe's scalp and began to pull, twisting. Blood flowed. "The library is where?"

"Ar-Arboria! *Aghh!*" Helplessly Hebe flailed her arms as iron tore and acid ate her flesh. Squirming in pain, she babbled, "D-deep in the forest! Fol-follow the coast south to Fulmar's Fort! Wh-where the river spills to the sea, follow its b-banks into the depths! But you'll never survive Shauku! Oh, p-please, release m-me! I'm dying!"

"True, but too slowly." Still pinning the sage, Johan picked up a thick book no bigger than his hand. Stooping, he struck the sages nose, making her yelp, then shoved the book in her mouth and stamped with his free foot. Choking, the sage bucked and shuddered but couldn't squirm free. Johan added, "I'll release you dead, I'm afraid. I couldn't bear you babbling my destination to others."

Patiently Johan pressed on the old woman's face until finally, with a chest-breaking sigh, she fell limp. Climbing off his murder victim, Johan uttered a single word to dispel the rain of death. Puddled with poison, parchments were curled and browned, shells had turned dark, seaweed and oddments had shriveled.

Johan stepped to the hearth fire. He planned to strew live coals to fire the room and cover his tracks but halted. Just as he'd left cripples behind in the pine forest to spread tales of terror, here too the sage's body might rattle his pursuers.

"Even better," murmured the murderous mage, "her death might aid my cause immeasurably."

Nodding grimly, Johan left clutter and corpse lying, then passed out the door and pulled it shut. Tracing a line around the doorframe, he sealed the portal with a simple binding spell. The spell would remain until magically dispelled, which he doubted any in Buzzard's Bay could do. Mortals would need to batter down the door.

Descending the narrow stairs, Johan passed through the echoing fish house on the ground floor and outside into the narrow twisted street. As always, the sky was overcast, the buildings drear, and the streets a welter of mud and crushed seashells.

Buzzard's Bay was a huge bite in the eternally battered Storm Coast, one of very few safe harbors, and hardly safe at that. The bay was riddled with jagged rocks, many lurking just below the churning surface. Seamounts of scoured granite thrust from the water to encircle this southern arm of the bay, called the Witch's Weir, where squatted this port. Hunkered on a long ragged spit, the town was lashed steadily by the western wind as it swirled around the weir. Even the landward retreat climbed a fierce slope of stone before meeting a green plateau that verged on Arboria, the endless pine forest to the south.

Curious, thought Johan. He'd held pinefolk in his grasp yet had neglected to question them about the location of Shauku's fabled library—an unfortunate oversight. Yet he consoled himself while striding the mucky streets.

"No matter. Destiny led me here. It will lead me to win over Shauku."

Built to withstand wind and shed snow, the town's

dwellings consisted mostly of first stories of rough stone and second stories of pine boards or slabs, all roofed with cedar shakes green with moss and white from salt spray. In places the town elders had strewn clam and oyster shells tamped into hardpack, but most streets were mires of black mud studded with ankle-twisting stones. Behind every shop and house ran rickety drying racks hung with fillets of split cod, herring, and hake that jittered and fluttered in the wind and gave the town a distinct odor. Johan's party had taken refuge from the wind in a tavern called the Dandysprat, and to this hostel the mage plodded, sinking in muck at every step.

As the day waned, the tavern grew rowdy with fishermen and loggers celebrating the day's end with ale. Johan had no use for frivolity but stuck to business. Luckily, as ordered, Johan's huntsman waited at an alley, then slunk into it. Johan joined him.

Funneled by nearby buildings, the wind whistled furiously behind the tavern but not enough to carry away the stink of privies and fish. Johan's huntsman pointed out two men lurking under a drying rack in sunset shadows.

No names were exchanged. The men might have been brothers but were not. Everyone in Buzzard's Bay was descended from the same stock: tall, blond, thick-limbed, slow of speech but keen of mind, for the sea didn't forgive fools. Careless clods sank beneath the brine, leaving the clever alive and cautious. These two wore thick quilted jackets and fur hats and vests. The only difference showed in their footwear—the one covered with silver mackerel scales wore sea boots, while the other wore knee-high riding boots. Both their mustaches blew in the breeze.

Muzzy from ale, the huntsman said, "These are the blokes you want, milord. One is feared on land and one on sea."

Johan studied the men as if buying cattle. The locals stared back.

Johan asked, "You shan't shrink from an odious task? I can

133

reward smart agents who do a good job but make it look like another's work."

The two coasters nodded. The scale-speckled corsair said, "If you can pay, milord, we can deliver. We're not men to shirk or question. The *Drumfish* is ready to sail at your whim."

"And my gang's armed and awaiting orders," added the highwayman.

Nodding, the bony mage fished in his pockets and doled out a handful of gold and electrum that made eyes bulge. Immeasurably wealthy, Johan seldom dealt with money, so he never knew its value. He'd only asked his scribe for "enough coin to buy two crews." Hurriedly the assassins split the haul.

Johan also gave a puffy leather pouch to the highwayman. Light as thistledown, it was stoppered with a wooden peg sealed with beeswax.

The mage warned, "It's full, so don't peek until it's needed. Let the contents float downwind into a crowd to rile them."

To the pirate, Johan gave a small nautilus shell lacquered black. The mouth was also stoppered with wax. "If you engage in a sea battle, break the seal and pitch it overside. T'will help you win."

Johan lifted his eagle's beak eastward. "Your prey are a roving pack of mercenaries and a talking tiger. They will arrive within days. Adira Strongheart is their leader."

"I've heard tell o' her," said the corsair. "Sovereign of the Sea of Serenity, some fancy. I doubt she wrestles sharks for supper."

"So spake many a man whose bones are coral," chided Johan. "Don't underestimate her, nor the tiger. His brain is keener than yours, I'll warrant, and he can sow slaughter like no man. Just do as you're paid. Kill whom you can of Adira's crowd and loot their carcasses. I'll add a further reward for their scalps."

"Where'll we collect that?" asked the brigand, but Johan ignored him and turned away to enter the tavern.

Having gotten what he needed from Buzzard's Bay, Johan would roust his entourage and shake this town's muck from his feet. No need to linger and risk running into Strongheart and Ojanen. Lesser men could scotch those annoyances. Johan had a continent to conquer.

* * * * *

In four centuries, Buzzard's Bay had seen many strange sights wash from the sea and descend from the mountains, but none so strange as a tame tiger walking on two legs, calm as if going to market.

As the sun set three days later, Adira's troupe plodded into town on horses weary from crabbing down the switchback road from the mountains. Fishermen and loggers, foaming jacks in hand, stepped from taverns and shops to see the tiger-man. Many locals and children trailed the party just to watch what happened.

Having sailed here before, Adira steered straight for Seafarer's Quay, famous all over Dominaria for its deep bottom and welcoming Adventurers' Guildhall. While the humans straggled on horses sinking hock-deep in mud, Jedit Ojanen padded alongside, watching everywhere, learning as he went. Murdoch and Simone and Virgil licked their lips to see brimming mugs in local hands. By the time the party reached the guildhall at the quayside, half a hundred coasters formed an impromptu audience.

The tavern was huge, built like a lord's mead hall, stout stone on the first floor able to withstand a battering ram, with beams and stucco for the second and third floors. Up there, separated by sexes, weary travelers could stretch out on thin pallets and sleep in safety.

Sliding off her mount on stiff legs, Adira signaled Heath to accompany her and the rest to stay with the horses. Ignoring her newfound audience, the irate chief pushed into the hall.

Fifty Buzzard's Baymen faced nine pirates, and all studied Jedit Ojanen to see what he'd do. The tiger stood stock-still, whiskers shivering in the wind, and studied the town, only the second big human enclave he'd seen since leaving Efrava.

Locals sipped beer while Adira's pirates drooled. The pirates were amused at how the locals all looked alike, like one big family. Indeed, they all resembled Lieutenant Peregrine, whose ancestors hailed from here. Adira's pirates, on the other hand, were of all sizes and colors and dress, though the bay folk were used to seeing every race descend a gangplank. But the upright tiger provoked curiosity too hot to hold in.

Clearing his throat, a red-faced man asked, "Where're ye from?"

He'd asked Murdoch, who still wore remnants of his green-gold uniform, now tattered. The sergeant scratched his jaw and replied, loud enough for the whole crowd to hear, "Yerkoy."

"Ye're all from Yerkoy?" asked the man in amazement. That seaport lay halfway across Jamuraa.

"No, just me," said Murdoch.

"Well, I didn't mean just you!" chided the man. "I meant all of ye!"

"Oh." Murdoch's face was wooden, and even his comrades wondered if he teased or not. "We're from all over."

"I can see that!" snapped the local. "Y'er every color from sun-baked to half-dead! What I meant was—"

"Where'd we catch the tiger?" Murdoch grinned, and people relaxed.

"Aye, that's it!" Glad to gain ground, the local asked, "Aye. Where'd you get this big cat?"

"Palmyra," said the sergeant. "We found him in an alley. The rats in Palmyra grow big, you see, big as dogs. So the cats that eat the rats grow big too. You wouldn't believe it, but when this one was born, he was not but a ball of fluff you could cup in your palm."

"No," said the local, not smiling, "I wouldn't believe it."

"Oh." Murdoch pretended to think. His comrades stared, and Simone beamed, glad to see another joker. "Well, you could always ask him."

"Ask who?" asked the local. Townsfolk watching the exchange were bewildered or bemused, but all were entertained.

"Ask the tiger."

Sister Wilemina rolled her eyes and huffed in disgust at Murdoch's lack of manners. Jasmine snorted. Lieutenant Peregrine drummed her fingers on her saddle and shook her helmeted head at the sergeant's puckish sense of humor. Drawn by the crowd, more locals wandered up to hear the strange conversation.

The bayman sipped beer for time to think. Finally he said, "The tiger talks?"

"I think so." Murdoch looked dim, then asked Jedit, "Do you talk?"

Having listened the while, the tiger turned baleful green eyes on the former sergeant. "No."

"Oh." Murdoch turned back to the local. "Sorry."

"What?" asked the local. "No, wait. The tiger does so talk!" To Jedit, he asked, "You. Where d'ya hail from?"

Jedit Ojanen stood unmoving except for his tail, always with a mind of its own, that swished and lashed, betraying his agitation at unwanted attention. The tail tip spanked a horse's flank and made it jump.

Finally, with hundreds of eyes watching, Jedit conceded, "Efrava."

"E-far-va?" asked the man. "Where under the stars is *that*?"

"Near Yerkoy," rumbled the tiger.

"What?" It was Murdoch's turn to be surprised. "It is not! I'd know if a herd of talking tigers lived nearby!"

"Perhaps you're not really from Yerkoy," countered Jedit.

"I am so!" Hoisted by his own petard, Murdoch grew indignant. Locals hooted, chuckled, giggled, and buzzed. One man said to the red-faced spokesman, "Want us to chuck him in the bay, Cefus?"

"Eh?" The local snorted and killed his beer. "No, he's all right. For a bloke from Yerkoy. *If* so."

"Hey, you—" sputtered Murdoch.

The big door swung open, and Adira Strongheart tramped out with Heath in tow. "That's set! We can spend the night." She stopped. "What sort of trouble have you been up to?"

"Nothing," said Murdoch.

Suspicious, Adira told her crew, "We'll bunk here the night. Haul your kits up the stairs, men on the second floor, women on top. You can eat here or elsewhere. We'll ask after you-know-who on the morrow. We know he's in town."

"No, we don't." Jedit's announcement made everyone look up. "His spoor leads into town, it's true, for I sniffed it out. Nor does it lead back out the mountain road. Yet the one we seek may have departed by another route, or even on a boat."

If Jedit expected a reward for his canny observation, he was disappointed. Adira glared. "Don't contradict your captain, sailor, or I'll have you lashed to the grating and given a new coat of stripes. Clear?"

"Aye aye, cap'n." Simone joked to break the tension. "But there's something else we should do first."

"What?" snapped Adira.

"Pitch Murdoch in the bay!" crowed Simone with a laugh. "What say, you all?"

"Aye!" shouted near two hundred people.

Murdoch yelped uselessly as, grabbed and hoisted over a hundred heads by locals and pirates alike, he was ferried to the edge of the quay and lobbed at the scummy water to land with a tremendous splash.

Adira Strongheart stood by her horse, saddlebags in hand, flabbergasted by the queer action. Turning to her straight-faced crew and one bland tiger, she fixed on Peregrine, someone with sense.

"What was *that* all about?"

The lieutenant bobbed her head. "Would you believe they're all drunk?"

"The locals?" carped Adira. "Yes! But my crew, no! We just got here!"

Wilemina said, "Murdoch makes friends wherever he goes."

Adira gave up. Slinging her saddlebags over her shoulder, she sighed, "I was going to warn you to steer clear of the locals, but never mind."

* * * * *

"Plains of plenty, what's that wretched stink?"

"Arrgh! It's putrid! Only one thing can smell that dratted rotten, and that's a fishgut-gobbling cat!"

The insults came from down the dark street in hoarse nasal tones not quite human. Sergeant Murdoch, in dry clothes, Virgil, and Jedit Ojanen paced in semi-darkness under the stars. The men wore their weapons, a sword and boarding axe, not so much for protection as to keep them from being stolen back in the guildhall. Boots plodded in gooey mud while the tiger padded silently.

"Something tells me those jabs are aimed at you, Jedit." Murdoch didn't turn around to see who blustered.

"Oh so?" asked Jedit. He towered a full head above the two men, who were not small. "Am I the only cat in Buzzard's Bay?"

"Let's not start that again." Murdoch thumped the side of his head. "I'm still daubing sea water out of my ears."

The scruffy Virgil, always expecting trouble, cast a glance over his shoulder. "It's cavalry."

"Cavalry? That don't make sense." Murdoch turned to squint into darkness.

The only light came from slits through house or shop

shutters, for the town was buttoned for bad weather. The sky was solidly overcast, with no moon or starlight. The trio had been strolling toward the next pool of light, the next tavern. They'd been sampling local brews and, after fourteen mugs, had yet to be satisfied. Murdoch insisted they test every pub in Buzzard's Bay if need be, though pubs numbered in the scores. The going was slow, for the men wove, and the mud was gluey.

"Ahoy, cat!" called the coarse voice, closer. "Your kind ain't welcome in this port! You're liable to get your tail tied in a knot or your fur set afire! You hear me, meat breath?"

Jedit waited in the street, apparently without worry. Virgil peered at the huge tiger, at the distant light and sanctuary, then at a seagull croaking overhead, for he was drunk. Murdoch put out a hand toward a building to steady himself, but the building was five feet away, and he missed. Then he saw what approached them.

"Polish my toenails! It is cavalry! Or—no, it's not! Hoy, what be you loudmouths?"

"Loudmouths? We be centaurs, manling, of the Oyster River clan, and the heartiest soldiers to ever strap on a sword!" The booming voice filled the narrow twisting street. "And we be enemies of any cat warriors foolish enough to show their twitching tails among decent folk!"

"Ah," agreed Murdoch. "I see why."

Immense, dark-faced and dark-bearded, with shaggy coats and stiff manes, the centaurs wore only coarse shirts overlaid by leather straps and tall helmets with forward-pointing fins. Lethal cutlery jingled from their harnesses, but they scarcely seemed to need weapons. Between four thudding hooves like mallets and brawny bare arms like gorillas, the man-horses looked capable of tearing down a tavern or kicking it flat.

Halting in mud on eight stout legs, they glared down long noses at Jedit Ojanen, who for once had to look up to meet another's eyes. Despite the street-blocking pair, Jedit stood with striped arms folded across his furry white chest. A night breeze whiffled his whiskers, but in no other way did he move.

Caught between a tiger and two horses, who could only be mortal enemies, Murdoch and Virgil wished they were sober, if only to scramble clear.

The sergeant gulped, "Uh, gentlemen. Gentlebeings. Our friend, the cat here, means no harm—"

"No harm!" interrupted a centaur. His black eyes were invisible in the gloom, but he snorted, or whinnied, down his long nose. "Cats are meat eaters, ain't they? So cat warriors must be too, though they're a bastard mix of two races not half as good as either! Centaurs always war against cat warriors, you know. We just can't stand the ugly sight of 'em or their maggot-gagging stench!"

"Aye!" brayed the other. Both centaurs had been sampling beers themselves, to judge by the fermented cloud swirling about. "I've killed half a dozen cats meself! Some I stomped to death on the battlefield as they fled squawling! The others I just ran down like chickens, then laid a noose around their necks and dragged 'em to death! Thirsty work, that! Cats weigh too much from all that meat eatin'!"

One of the centaurs jigged to one side and clopped forward. Casually, Jedit was braced on two sides. One centaur seemed to scratch himself, but in fact his hand brushed a brass-hilted sword nearly six feet long. The other also scratched, giant hands lingering on a rope or bullwhip coiled at his harness.

"Men," blurted Murdoch, and hoped that wasn't an insult. "We're all fellow soldiers here, all comrades at liberty for a night on the town. What say we go into that tavern—uh, over there—and I'll buy the first round."

"I've drunk enough beer for one night," said Jedit Ojanen suddenly. "I fancy something thicker. Horse blood, say."

Murdoch and Virgil threw themselves flat in mud as all hell broke loose.

A tiger's coughing scream and two harsh brays split the night. A sword slithered from a scabbard like a cobra spitting. A bolo rope spun a sizzling circle, so leaded ends smacked the eaves of a house. The two men cowering in mud waited to hear the sinister strike of steel or lead on furred flesh, then lifted their heads as both centaurs neighed in dismay.

A homeowner had unwisely thrown open a door to see what the noise might be, casting a shaft of candlelight. Thus Murdoch and Virgil saw a sight to thrill their alcohol-drenched blood.

Jedit Ojanen, screaming and slavering with long white fangs, had bunched corded thighs and shot straight into the air as if launched from a catapult. The tiger-man touched down briefly on the salt-streaked shingles of the cottage, then vaulted into the air at the two enraged centaurs. Dodging a whirling bolo and thrusting sword blade, Jedit crashed full-length on the shoulders of the first centaur, a thousand pounds of feline muscle and bone. The massive man-horse was rocked off all four hooves. Bashed sideways, he fetched into his comrade.

Murdoch almost had a hand crushed by a hoof, then the two humans scuttled free like mud-caked hermit crabs. Flopping on their butts, trying not heave up their guts, they watched the breathtaking battle.

Far better able to see by night than the big-eyed horsemen, and not hampered by mud sucking at his feet, Jedit had all the advantage in the air. He hooked his claws deep into the shoulder of the first centaur even as he swiped the second. Slashed and surprised, the assailants were knocked together like two toppling trees and almost spilled in a tangle of eight legs. Black claws ripped furrows in the far side of one centaur's head, nearly tearing a pointed ear from a skull. Blood scented the air like seasalt. Yet Jedit had only begun to fight. Using his opponent's weight against them, the tiger hung on grimly with both hands and convulsed the muscles in his massive chest. Two long-nosed heads crashed together, and the centaurs staggered.

Still, the horse-men were accomplished soldiers and could attack while being attacked. Jedit was forced to leap upward or feel six feet of steel lance in his belly. As it was, the second centaur, bleeding from one ear like a harvest pig, nearly decapitated his partner by thrusting blindly with the long sword. The first centaur snapped his bolo. Three leaded weights whipped the air dangerously. One snagged Jedit's ankle as he leaped into the sky.

Laughing harshly, the centaur wrenched on his bolo to yank the tiger down under punishing hooves. Yet Jedit was barely discommoded. As he dropped, he twisted as only a cat can and flicked a massive paw that severed the cord. In the same moment, rather than land on the ground where he was vulnerable, Jedit pounced on the second centaur's haunches.

The horse-man shrieked as claws rent his hide with long gashes. He stabbed wildly behind his head to kill the cat, but Jedit was already gone, having squatted, flexed, and leaped, all as silent as a butterfly.

Landing on all fours atop the cottage roof opposite, Jedit scrambled up wooden shingles like a monkey. Two weights of a snapped bolo whickered after him but missed. Then a six-foot sword was flung his way like an arrow. Yet Jedit could watch one way while dashing another, and he swerved his hips to let the sword flash by. Jedit chuckled, further enraging his foe.

"Come back and fight, coward!" called one of the centaurs, grabbing for a throwing knife at his harness.

"Stand like a man, you yellow-bellied fiend!" called the other illogically. "Drop back down, and we'll trounce you!"

Whatever the centaurs expected, they got more than they bargained for. Jedit Ojanen had reached the peak of the cottage. Doubtless the man-horses thought the cat warrior fled. Instead he paused by a small chimney of battered brick that emitted a savory smell of fish stew and biscuits.

"Fight, you say?" called Jedit with a fang-creased leer. "Very well! Catch!"

So saying, the tiger laid powerful mitts on the brick chimney, grunted and twisted, ripped it loose from the house, then lobbed the chimney to crown the centaurs.

The two attackers raised arms before faces just in time. Dozens of disintegrating bricks bashed their forearms against their long, dark faces. Blood started as foreheads were banged and scraped and noses mashed. Bricks rapped the centaurs' breasts, tender legs, dancing hooves, flanks, and every other part, all to a horrific clatter and jingle of steel harness.

Fear of broken bones and further attack while half-blinded gave wing to instinct. The two centaurs lowered their chalky heads, lifted dinged and scratched legs, and bolted back the way they'd come in a churning slop of hooves in mud.

Gradually the night grew quiet except for a distant drumming as the centaurs reached hardpack. A few doors creaked open. Local baymen and women gaped in wonder at the tiger who dropped from a roof light as thistledown, then calmly licked his paw to smooth his orange-striped fur.

So fast and furious had the battle been, over in minutes, that Murdoch and Virgil still sat stupidly on wet rumps in chilly mud. Shaking their heads in disbelief, the men unstuck themselves as locals in nightshirts or blanket coats gathered to marvel.

Except one, who declared, "That was the quickest, slickest fighting I ever saw, cat man, but you owe me a new chimney."

"Wait," said Jedit, and he disappeared into the shadows behind the house. In seconds he came back to plant a sword at the homeowner's feet. The leather-wrapped handle stood just even with the man's goggling eyes. The tiger said, "Sell this. It must have value enough to buy you a new—chim-my, did you call it?"

While locals buzzed, Murdoch shook his head and scraped off mud. "Jedit, you're a wonder. Let me buy you a drink. Beer, not horse blood. You could be general of shock troops if you signed on with the army of Yerkoy. Eh? What is it, Virgil?"

"I'm just thinking," said the grizzled man, "we'd best be careful."

"Why?" asked Jedit Ojanen. "Surely you do not think those slue-footed fools will return for a rematch?"

"No," moped Virgil. "I'm thinking we better hole up in a tavern and lie low. Adira told us not to trouble the locals. If word'a this brawl reaches her ears, there'll be *real* hell to pay!"

Chapter 10

"Must everything in this port stink of cold fish?" Jasmine sniffed her arms and a hank of hair. "*I* reek of fish!"

Adira Strongheart, Jasmine Boreal, Simone the Siren, Sister Wilemina, Lieutenant Peregrine, and Whistledove Kithkin descended the wide stairs of the guildhall. Some tripped daintily while others clomped in sea boots. Despite a late night, the pirate chief had kicked all the women awake. Yawning, Wilemina tried to braid her hair and walk, and almost pitched down the stairs.

"What would you rather stink of?" Adira Strongheart scratched her unruly auburn curls and tied her green head-band. In town she wore bangles at ears, wrists, and over her boots, so she jangled like a windchime. "Everyone in Palmyra smells like a camel, but if I've picked up fleas from bunking on the floor, blood'll run out the scuppers."

The Adventurer's Guild main floor was one big room crammed with scarred sturdy tables and benches. For the morning repast, a mix of fifty or more transients and locals slurped, dabbed, and chomped. This being a seaport that served all of Dominaria, every color of mankind was represented, and not all the sailors and travelers were human. A clutch of bearded dwarves gargled in low voices, a brace of barbarians gnawed brown bread with slack jaws, and two hung-over centaurs at the bar quibbled in brays and snorts.

Adira braced the bar and plunked down a thick Brycer danat. "Breakfast for six, whate'er it be. And ale. Who's your guildmaster?"

Like most coasters, the barkeep was big and brawny from a lifetime diet of fresh fish and red meat.

Before answering the barkeep wadded a towel and lobbed it at a kitchen boy. "Go fetch Fedelm, will ye? I've somewhat to tell him." He then lifted a small scale to the bar top and proceeded to weigh Adira's silver and make change. "The guildmaster eats at home because his wife don't trust my kitchen. Speaking of which, have you got a husband in port, sweetie, or are you still footloose?"

Adira ignored the come-on. Everywhere her mane of chestnut hair, striking beauty, and voluptuous curves, two bulging from her old shirt, drew men like bees to honey. She took three "fisheyes" in local coin and plunked on a bench with her female crew.

"What about the men?" asked Wilemina.

"What about them?" asked Adira, peeved.

"I mean, shall we send a boy to summon them?"

"Let the bastards starve."

Breakfast was fish chowder, black bread, wedges of cheese, and dark, foaming ale. The women dug in hungrily.

Lieutenant Peregrine had set her turbaned helmet on the bench. Her fair skin was tanned dark as mahogany from desert campaigning, a stark contrast to her fair, square-cut hair.

She mumbled, "If this is pirating, I can endure it. You lot eat right fine."

"You sound like Murdoch," snorted Adira. "He makes up for years of army chow by clearing the table at every meal. I'd think love of food made him join the Seven, but t'was Wilemina recruited him. Why Murdoch chases a virgin devoted to chastity fuddles me, but many things do."

Women chuckled as the archer blushed. Jasmine Boreal, not usually one to chatter, swallowed cheese and called down the table, "Is that true, Wilemina? You've no plans to drop your bow and don a veil?"

"Jasmine, I thought *you* fancied Heath," teased Peregrine. "While riding, your eyes bore holes in his back."

"Never!" snapped Jasmine, suddenly serious. "Who could fancy a man with a face like a corpse and hands like ice?"

"When have you felt his hands?" asked Whistledove, impishly.

"Take Murdoch or Heath, or both!" laughed Simone. "Wilemina sleeps with her bow!"

"Forswear demeaning gossip, if you please!" Embarrassed, Wilemina grew formal. "Everyone knows the tenets of Lady Caleria. To surrender our greatest treasure to carnal sensuality robs a warrior of skill in the hunt. Murdoch is well aware of my leanings."

"Just see he doesn't lean too far and tip you over," jibed Simone, and everyone laughed.

"Be you Adira Strongheart?" demanded a loud voice.

Calmly, Adira regarded a big-bellied man bearing an oak club. The weapon was substantial, for the thick head was drilled out and weighted with lead. Behind him waited two men just as big and also armed. A sheriff and his deputies.

Lithe and lethal, Adira slid off the bench to set her back against a post. Gently she shifted her cutlass scabbard jammed in her sash. Patrons of the bar watched the exchange, hoping for a fight. Simone nodded to the Seveners to mop their bowls and get clear of the table. When she stripped the bangles from her wrists, they knew a fight was brewing.

"I'm Captain Strongheart. Thirty-six days out of Palmyra, though we came overland. What is it?"

The sheriff's fat face, wreathed with a gray beard and framed by a brimmed leather hat, was stamped in an official frown. "What d'ya know about the death of our sage, a woman named Hebe, three days ago?"

"Not a damned thing," retorted the pirate chief, though she smelled trouble spelled Johan. Casting about for time, she asked, "Who are you?"

"Fedelm. Sheriff." He waggled his club, the badge of office. "Rumor has't you know somewhat of her death."

"Rumor has a big mouth but little brain." Adira was doubly irked that the barkeep had both cozened her and sicced the sheriff on her. The pirate queen watched idlers drift up to listen. So far, no one looked perturbed except the sheriff. To judge by hard looks, Fedelm was not popular.

Still, Adira ordered, "Simone, pipe grog, will you?"

A deputy clamped a hand on Simone's silk shoulder to keep her seated. The black pirate bumped the man back with her generous rump. Sashaying to the foot of the wide stairs, she shoved two fingers in her mouth and whistled "Grog call" loud and shrill.

In less than a minute, the stairwell resounded to clunks and clatters. Into the hall thumped the grizzled Virgil and natty Murdoch, both red-eyed; Heath, the pale archer, always with his ebony bow; and, ducking the lintel, the great orange-black tiger Jedit Ojanen. Many patrons goggled at the last. Once the bleary men saw Adira braced against a post by three bullies, their hands fell to swords and an axe. Onlookers backpedaled out of reach.

As tension crackled in the room, Adira raised a hand. "Back your sails, lubbers. Sheriff, I'm friendly as a fork-tailed mermaid, but if you don't claw off half a cable, we'll tangle spars."

"We'll fare worse than that!" The sheriff flaunted his authority before the audience. "You'll come quiet and answer our questions! Hebe was well-liked in this port, and whoe'er kilt her will sink for't, mark my words!"

"D'you hear your own blather, you slime-whiskered codfish?" Adira might warn her crew to stand easy, but a captain could indulge a temper. "You said this Whatsername was killed three days past! We just broached your headland yestereve! Look yonder! How many talking tigers does this town sport? Think we've waltzed around unnoticed for three days?"

Suddenly a man called from the back of the crowd, "Don't listen to her! Hebe was murdered by a black hand!"

"Magic murder!" called another spectator, very loud. "We had to bash the door to splinters! It was locked tight with magic!"

"Who speaks?" demanded Adira. "Show yourself, flap-lips!"

No one stepped forward. Some in the throng turned in curiosity as the first voice crowed, "Poor Hebe was poisoned and strangled, I heard!"

"And burned with acid or fire!" echoed the second. "Horrible way to die! Some bastard must pay with hands or head!"

"A good woman cut down in her prime!" came yet another voice. "One of our own venerable elders, beloved by everyone!"

"Belay that bilge!" Thinking fast, Adira couldn't decide whether to name Johan or not. Even pursuing him was dangerous, for strangers might condemn his enemies by association, and Adira hadn't yet gauged the town's loyalties. Buzzard's Bay verged on the Northern Realms, so the populace must know of Johan. The locals might loathe the tyrant or else encourage his southward conquest. Northerners had served in Johan's doomed army, and Adira had been instrumental in destroying them.

Now three begrudging loudmouths shifted position behind the crowd while trying to rouse it. Adira's anger evaporated as she smelled a trap. Why stir up trouble, unless . . .

"Round 'em up, Fedelm!" called a disguised voice. "Lock 'em up! We'll help corral 'em!"

"Thump 'em!" urged someone unseen. "Bash their heads in! Make 'em pay for hurting Hebe!"

Adira's Circle of Seven had closed ranks around the table.

With a hand on his belted boarding axe, Virgil growled, "No one's locking me up!"

"Hush, you guppy!" snapped Adira. "Sheriff, let's step outside, free of these hecklers. We're plain innocent, but we can—What's this muck?"

Fluff like dandelion seeds floated above the crowd. People wrinkled noses, and a few sneezed as the thistledown bobbed in the air. Someone laughed.

Then came growls.

"It's not fit," carped a man who'd hitherto kept silent. "Strangers creeping into town and killing our folk!"

"Drive 'em out!" said a fishwife. "Whip 'em out of town!"

"A pox on all foreigners!" rasped a dwarf. "They don't belong in Buzzard's Bay!"

Adira and her Circle turned just as ugly and vulgar. Virgil shouted into a man's face while Simone shrilled blistering curses. Heath curdled his nose at being called "stinking baby-stealing elf-kin" by a fisherman. Peregrine tugged on her helmet only to have it slapped off. Sister Wilemina was grabbed by a braid.

The storm broke. Yelling "For Yerkoy!" Murdoch drew his broadsword and punched a man aside the head. Wilemina whipcracked her knuckles into a woman's nose. The knee-high Whistledove, fearful of being trodden, scaled a post like a monkey but was knocked off by a hurled beer mug. Simone the Siren snarled and flung mugs off the table, full or not, one, two, three. The air grew thick with flying furniture, mugs, weapons, fists, and a few people.

Adira Strongheart fought more fiercely than anyone. Gargling epithets, the pirate queen tilted on one leg like a stork and rammed her boot into the sheriff's fat gut. The man whooshed and collapsed like a punctured bladder, but his deputies waded in to swing leaded clubs at Adira. She snatched behind her back to grab her matched daggers but clutched them pommels down with the blades laid along her forearms. Quick as a cobra, she jumped at one deputy, landing inside his defenses, and hammered a dagger pommel between his eyes. Stunned and blinded, the man reeled backward, until someone jostled him into Adira. Tangled, she couldn't strike the other deputy, so instead she caught and propped the drooping deputy just as the second deputy swung. With a fearsome *crunch,* he walloped his companion's head. Adira leaned around the staggered man and shot out her right arm. A silver pommel bashed the deputy's jaw and clacked his teeth shut.

Yet despite her magically induced battle fury and so much noise it was impossible to think, Adira knew she'd been tricked somehow. These locals were not real enemies. Swearing, ducking to avoid flailing fists and knives, she shouted in her hurricane-besting bawl, "Seveners! Don't kill—uhh!— don't kill anyone! We're all bewitched!"

"What?" Furious but fuddled, Virgil knew enough to drop his fighting axe lest he split a skull. A blond bruiser with a doubly braided beard charged. The scruffy pirate snatched both braids and pulled as he raised his knee. Knee smashed nose, so blood gushed. Splashed with crimson, Virgil let go the squawling man and sought another victim. He found two who swung meaty fists and only dodged one. The other fist bowled him clean over a table, so he clattered amid fallen benches.

Lieutenant Peregrine had been trained to disperse crowds of surly citizens without doing harm, but since some of these bayfolk were kin, a family fight meant no holds barred. Mobbed from all sides, the officer hopped and caught a beam overhead, then drove both boots into faces. Landing in a cleared pocket, Peregrine rammed her thumbs into throats and eyes. Tipping a table, she tried to drag together a makeshift shield for Adira's crew to gather behind.

With everyone mad as wild bulls, Wilemina found her

braids grabbed again and again, once so hard her neck popped with a white-hot jolt. Vowing to shave her head at first opportunity, the Calerian archer jabbed viciously with her ornate horn-and-ivory bow. She rammed a crotch and a brisket, got her hair free, then jolted the armpit of a grasping man. Braids whipping, she sought her companions and spotted Heath dodging and jabbing. Backing, she bumped rumps with the part-elf.

"Wait! It's Wilemina! I hope Adira has a plan to get us loose of these cretins!"

Heath grunted, too busy to answer.

Heeding Adira's orders, Simone whacked coastal heads with the battered cup guard of her cutlass. Two dull-witted barbarians bulled into her belly. The pirate was rammed rearward until her spine smacked the bar. Aching, with her kidneys crushed, pinned by a mountain of muscle, Simone hammered both hands on the duo to no effect. An iron-hard hand caught her wrist and cutlass and bent both cruelly against the bar to break or dislocate her arm. Cursing through gritted teeth, helpless, Simone gave up and relaxed, momentarily confusing her attacker, who fell back a hair. Instantly Simone jackknifed her knees into the air. Squirming a lopsided somersault, she skittered across the bar and tumbled behind it, wrenching her arm loose but losing her cutlass. Still, she was free. Seizing a keg slopping with ale, she hoisted it overhead, sousing herself with beer, then smashed the keg into staves and hoops over two blocky heads.

Jedit Ojanen saved Whistledove's life by brushing half a dozen coasters aside and scooping the brownie from the floor where she was in danger of being crushed under churning feet. The feisty fighter had tears of rage in her big eyes and her rapier out ready to sting. Jedit took it away and stuck it into a ceiling beam like a needle.

Above the noise, while flicking aside fists and daggers,

Jedit said, "Adira desires we not kill. Do you know why we fight at all?"

"Eh? Let me go! I want to hurt the bigfoots!"

Whistledove leaned from Jedit's arms and snagged a woman's ear to bite it. Jedit jostled her loose.

Whistledove panted, "What's wrong with you?"

Jedit asked himself the same question, not realizing he was immune to the prejudice-invoking charm blown about the room by Johan's hired agent. In fact, the tiger-man was the only being in the room not outraged. With wry bemusement he watched humans shout and mill and brawl, unsure if this was normal behavior. He decided to ask Adira for guidance, so flipped the brownie across his shoulders like a sheep, then waded through the mob.

A double drumming pricked Jedit's ears. The two centaurs galloped headlong down the room, heads ducked below the beams and heedless that they trampled fallen coasters. The dark-furred horse-men bore bruises and gashes from their scrap with the tiger not twelve hours past. Whether they were ensorcelled by the prejudice charm or just hung over didn't matter much, for they raced at Jedit with murder rimming their round black eyes. Weapons jingled from their harnesses, but they rushed with giant, four-fingered hands outstretched as if to tear the tiger between them like a chicken.

One bellowed as he charged, "Meat eater! This time we'll break your back and stomp your limbs to pulp!"

Whistledove bleated and leaped onto a ceiling beam. Jedit made no move except to push some coasters aside, then lazily half-turned and dropped one paw behind his hip.

As the centaurs thundered within arm's length, the tiger drawled, "Pull dung carts, you cud cutters." He swung.

A fist big as a smoked ham whistled through the air and walloped the first centaur alongside his long jaw. Bones shattered as the horse-man was hoisted off all four hooves to crash into his partner. The building shook like an earthquake as tons of horse-human flesh crashed to the floor. Jedit overstepped the kicking, groaning tangle to again seek Adira Strongheart.

Swamped by brawling bodies, Jasmine the druid, never comfortable indoors, found herself stranded as a fish out of water. Desperately she ran down her mental list of spells. Nothing seemed useful. Cowering between the howling Murdoch and Virgil, Jasmine noted the Circle was being overrun by baymen with more spilling in the door. On such a bright morning, she thought, half the town might attack them . . .

"But we sit by the ocean!" she caroled alone.

Casting amid surging bodies, Jasmine ducked under Virgil's arms as he throttled a dwarf and splashed her hands in beer spilled on the floor. Rising to a crouch, Jasmine flicked her wet fingers at the ceiling three times, each time chanting, "*Sav-be-gol, lav-be-nol, tel-be-tolloh!*"

Nothing happened. The druid strained her eyes and wracked her brain, wondering how she'd flubbed the incantation. Then, slowly, the wooden ceiling was obscured. A cloud grew, mushrooming across the ceiling, then billowing downward. Jasmine grinned when the first wetness kissed her face. Already she couldn't see the tavern door. A few coasters noticed too. One shrieked in fright. Some raced out the mist-filled doorway.

Adira Strongheart wondered if she'd been thumped and rendered half-blind. Fog clung about her head. Even her own crew seemed ghostly just a few feet off. Cool air soothed her fiery brow and flushed away the last of the prejudice-invoking charm. The pirate queen could think clearly. Funny, though, that a fog should roll in at mid-morning.

A pair of beefy coasters still pressed Adira, one fencing with a long knife and the other plying a stool. Tired of fighting, Adira feared she must kill the coasters to stop them. Feigning a stumble, she lured the stool wielder close, then flicked her blade past the wood to pink his arm. As he yelped and dropped the stool, Adira caught and reversed it just in time to block the other's dagger. As the point thunked in wood, Adira twisted and plucked the weapon away. Two quick thumps with the stool laid the coasters at her feet.

Fog blanketed the room from end to end. Adira's breath frosted, and the clammy touch chilled her heated bosom. Only a dozen people were even in sight.

Huffing, dappled with dew, Adira called, "What a pea soup! Robars! Make ready to break free!"

"How?" called someone.

"Follow me," came a growl.

An orange-black nightmare loomed from the fog like a sea serpent. Jedit Ojanen laid gentle paws on two brawny coasters and heaved them a dozen feet to clatter amid spilled stools and benches. Between fog and fights sparked just among coasters, the pirates enjoyed a tiny respite.

"Follow you?" Adira's bosom heaved as anger surged anew. "Who in blazes elected you captain?"

"I only seek to help," rumbled the tiger. "Is that wrong?"

"Damn right it is!" rapped the pirate queen. "I give the orders, you numb furball! Step on my toes, and I'll carve out your liver! Robars, brace up! Jedit, grab a table and clear a path to the door!"

"Very well." Looking up, Jedit put out a paw and caught someone lurking in the dense fog. Whistledove Kithkin had skipped along ceiling beams to retrieve her rapier and find the pirates. Tucking the brownie on one shoulder, the tigerman hefted a scarred table big as a coffin and marched for the door. Caught in swirling fog, Buzzard's Baymen and women were bowled aside like tenpins as the tiger bore down like a barge.

Cursing, Adira tugged her crew by sleeves, belts, and collars. Murdoch and Heath had to drag Virgil off the floor, for he'd been hammered from behind. Wilemina bit a man who'd slid his hand down the bodice of her leather vest. Jasmine broke a stoneware mug on his skull. Lagging and lurching like a batch of balky children, the Robaran Mercenaries blundered after the tiger's broad back and swinging tail.

Fourteen paces in blinding fog spilled them through a doorway into open air. Gasping, tugging clothes and tackle aright, mopping off blood and sweat and beer, the pirates blinked about, for even an overcast morning seemed eye-squintingly bright.

Adira cursed. Outside would prove as dangerous as inside. Dozens of bay folk had spilled outdoors to see the fracas. Bewitchments notwithstanding, their friends had been thumped by Adira's crew. Already some coasters pointed at the disheveled pirates.

"Have we a plan?" lisped Simone around a split lip.

"Aye!" blurted Adira. "Run like nine devils!"

* * * * *

"What in Stangg's benighted name happened back there?"

Murdoch puffed as he and Heath lugged Virgil, whose toes trailed furrows in mud. Jedit, still wearing Whistledove on his shoulders, picked up Virgil like a kitten. Trotting, they made better time as the crowd behind shouted.

"It was deuced strange!" chirped Wilemina. "One minute everyone's talking polite as you please, and the next we're all shouting and fighting!"

In a pack, Adira's crew jogged into narrow alleys between warehouses and boathouses. The high buildings gave them momentary cover, but Jasmine fretted, "We'll be trapped against the water!"

"That's what we want!" said Simone but shivered in the keen wind, for she was doused to the skin with beer.

Bangles at her booted ankles jangling, Adira Strongheart chivvied her underlings with a hard hand. Fortunately, only Virgil was knocked groggy, and they all had weapons.

"Hush, all! Let me think!" Adira blocked a mucky alley, cutlass at the ready. At the far end, fishermen and laborers pointed her way. She panted. "The room was hexed. Johan must've left agents behind to muddy waters against us. If we don't get a chance to talk, we might be lynched first and questioned later. These locals share more than a drop of berserker blood. Sheer aport!"

Past the warehouses they ran out of street. A corduroy wharf of pine slabs on mud gave way to ramshackle docks and piers in a ring. At midday, the fishing fleet was out, all the nearby slips bare. Farther out were moored deep-water vessels: south-sea luggers, carracks, and caravels like upturned shoes. A few nets lay idle, for fishermen repairing them had wandered up the street to see the fuss.

"Give me Palmyra," rasped Adira, "where citizens mind their own business! We need a boat, damn it!"

"There!" Sharp-eyed Heath pointed along the line of warehouses.

Adira ducked and glimpsed a rudder past big open doors. "That'll do! Get it! Fight if need be, but for love of Lustra don't kill anybody! I'm hoping we can talk our way off this lee shore!"

The tall buildings were of unpainted wood silvered by seasons of salt and rain. Adira's crew veered into the fourth. Larger than its neighbors, the combined warehouse and boathouse sported tall doors on the street but also a rear entrance that jutted over the water. The pirates clattered for it. Shouts behind gave them wings. Chestnut hair flying, cutlass flashing, Adira charged first.

The echoing space smelt of salt, fish, tar, hemp, and seaweed. A fishing smack with a lateen sail furled was dogged to bollards. One old sailor guarded a cargo of wall-eyed cod.

He goggled like the fish as the pirates stampeded toward him.

Adira hooked a callused thumb.

"Git."

He got, and Adira barred the streetside door.

The pirate queen's cutlass pointed around her Circle of Seven. "Heath, Murdoch, brace the door. Simone, Wil, cast off this pig-boat. Peregrine, Jasmine, pitch the cod overside."

Jedit still wore Whistledove on his shoulders while Virgil hung in his big paws like a dead skunk.

"Jedit, wrap Virg in a tarp to keep him warm, then hang back as reserves. Whistledove, watch Virgil. Weigh anchor!"

People scurried to posts.

"Wait! I'm sick of being jerked in circles like a cow!" Pausing for a moment, Wilemina whipped a knife from her belt, tugged her flaxen braids out straight, hacked them off just above her ears, then tossed them in the greasy water. Belatedly she chirped, "How do I look?"

"Your head looks like a dog's hind end!" called Murdoch from the door.

The archer clapped both hands to her ragged scalp. "Call of Caleria, that bad?"

"I'll cut off your head!" Adira booted the skinny archer onto a heap of slimy cod. "Fish or chop bait!"

Simone whacked lines short with her cutlass rather than untie them. Beside her, Peregrine grimaced and chucked fish overboard with her bare hands.

The desert soldier asked, "What use is such a small boat?"

"It gains us the harbor!" snapped Simone.

"And then?" insisted Peregrine.

"We steal a ship! We're pirates, remember?" Adira hopped into the boat and popped an aft hatch. Needing light, she stroked one hand and barked, *"Ah-shist!"* Her skin glowed with cold light like a firefly's. She stuck her head into the stinking bilge to see if the craft needed pumping.

Hollowly, she called, "Out there we'll have our pick of the fleet. I can sail anything with a keel below and rags aloft."

"What about our horses?" asked Jasmine. "Our blankets and saddlebags are still at the tavern!"

"If this town doesn't crucify us," Adira clapped shut the hatch, "I'll buy you new ones!"

"*Ram!*" Murdoch backpedaled from the door, sword in hand.

"Ram?" asked half a dozen voices.

BOOM! The building rocked as the big wooden doors creaked inward. Coasters had fetched a timber log for a ram. At another bash, the pirates saw daylight peek through. The shouting of townies rose higher.

"You'd think folk could find other entertainment in a port this size." Simone the Siren slotted the rudder into its greased iron socket. "Why don't they take up dancing?"

"I can't cast half my spells without my potions and oddments!" Jasmine complained as she caught cod by their red gaping gills. "And druids don't go to sea!"

Adira dropped her cutlass and picked up an oar to lever against the dock. The smack eased from the dock, black water gapping. "First thing you learn in the Robars is to keep anything precious in your pockets. I've lost ten fortunes ten times from having to cut and run. Up gangplank!"

"Wait for me!" As the ram smashed the doors and the bar tore loose from its brackets, Murdoch jumped the intervening five feet and crashed atop Simone. Frantically pirates grabbed oars to paddle out of the boathouse into open water.

"Adira!" Whistledove again perched on Jedit's shoulders. The brownie pointed at the harbor. "Boats are coming our way!"

"What?" In two lithe bounds Adira leaped atop the furled yards, balanced as a tern. Just past two docks sculled two long whaleboats, rapid as water beetles. Evidently the fishermen had been signaled from shore by the crowd to block the outer passage.

Too busy to curse, Adira thought aloud. "And us back-asswards as a beached whale. Better afloat than marooned ashore. We'll ram and cut free with cutlasses. Make way! Out oars!"

"Adira." Useless on a boat, Jedit Ojanen stood in the bow out of the way. He crinkled his muzzle of orange, black, and white stripes, exposing long lethal fangs. Sniffing the air, he called, "You should know—"

VA-BOOM! With a hearty roar, the coasters shattered the big warehouse bar and doors with their ram. Rugged blond men and women spilled on their hands and knees. Others, some worse for drink, climbed over them to be heroes at the forefront of battle.

"Jedit, Murdoch, knock boarders into the water! The rest'a you, ply hooks and oars against the boats!"

The fishing smack had barely backed her stern into open water before an incoming whaleboat bumped noses. The jolt shocked the landlubbers to their knees. Seasoned sailors like Simone and Wilemina rammed boathooks into the bellies of careless fishermen, fending the wiser ones back. Meanwhile citizens of Buzzard's Bay surged along the wharf, looming over the pirates in the trapped smack. In the whaleboat, men shouted comrades to move aside. They hoisted rusty shark hook gaffs and tomahawks, then perched on whaleboat thwarts and gunnels, ready to jump aboard.

Boxed in at both ends, Adira Strongheart lifted her cutlass for all to see. "Avast! First one steps foot aboard my craft loses his lights! Hear me! We didn't come begging trouble, but we're ready to deal death unless you sheer off! Will you let me speak or stop steel with your guts?"

A tense silence strained the air. Men and women muttered, unwilling to take the first step. Some townsfolk whispered questions, trying to recall what started the trouble. Virgil came to, moaning and clutching his head.

In the stillness, Jedit's growly purr set hair tingling on arms and necks. "Adira, I wished to tell you, there's fire in the next building."

"Fire?" The bleat was immediately echoed in the street. "Fire! Fire on the docks! *Fire!*"

Chapter 11

With homes and shops and ships in danger, the coasters quit the riot and surged out the door yelling. Two drunkards tumbled into the drink. Men in the whaleboats, with sailors' instinctive terror of fire, fumbled oars to row free of the warehouse.

Shouts rocketed up and down the docks. "Fire in Noah's warehouse! And Heta's loft! Call out the bucket brigade!"

Adira cocked an ear and immediately heard a spine-chilling crackling and muffled roar. She imagined heat licking at her neck and stifled a panicked urge to leap from the boat, even into the bay, to get clear. Docks, boats, and chandlers' supplies, layered with paint and varnish and tar and dried years in the sun, burned more brightly than any forest.

"Adira!" Simone pointed toward the bay. With the whaleboats gone, the way was clear. "Shall we scull out?"

Adira Strongheart bit her lip for just a second. Years of pirating and captaining had honed her wits razor-sharp. She could shift course like a jackrabbit when needed, and she did so now.

"Belay! Dock us! Aye, and be quick! Dump your weapons and tail on! And fish out those two drunken fools before they drown!"

Within seconds, and without understanding, Adira's crew found themselves dashing into a smoky street toward the very crowd that had pursued them. Teams of townsmen had formed a bucket brigade while others fetched giant firehooks: long poles with iron ends used to pull down burning buildings before the fire spread. They attacked the warehouse next door. Engulfed in flames, three walls were etched in stark yellow. Curling smoke vomited from ragged holes in the roof. Cedar shakes broke free to rain like autumn leaves or else skid into the water with hisses like snakes. Sparks spat and danced and flitted on an on-shore breeze. Already the warehouse Adira had commandeered was charred on one side and roof. As flaming debris spun into the bay, dinghies and smacks, piles of cordage and lobster traps, nets and sails strung to dry, all were dappled with hungry orange flames.

"They'll lose half the town!" cried Sister Wilemina.

"Someone set that fire to cook *us!*" gasped Murdoch.

"Best grab our horses and go!" yelled Simone. "We shan't get another chance!"

"Nay." Skidding to a halt on boot heels, Adira tolled off. "Virgil, you're hurt. Sit and stay put. Jedit, accompany me. The rest of you, help fight the fire. Make sure the locals see you do it. Tell 'em you're pirates, even. This is our chance to mend fences and learn a thing or two."

"Or fry!" countered Simone, her black face shining with sweat from the fierce heat.

"That too. Go!" Taking her own advice, Adira got busy with Jedit trotting after her like an overgrown puppy.

Pirates lurched from crisis to crisis on land and sea. Acting on Adira's daring orders, the Circle of Seven split up and plunged into firefighting, jostling elbow-deep amid locals who only moments before had been hot to hang them.

With a hunter's stealth, Heath slithered into a crowd grappling a twenty-foot firehook. People skidded in mud trying to manhandle the long hook through the air and let it fall amidst the burning rafters of a boathouse. Jumping high and grabbing the sooty shaft, Heath whirled off his cloak and flipped it underfoot for traction.

He yelled, "Come, friends! Doff your jackets! That's it! All together, set your feet! Prop the butt! Ready? Then let fall and *pull!*" With a few coordinated yanks, charred rafters broke. Fiery debris cascaded into the building in gouts of sparks. Townsfolk grinned as the grimy Heath called and joked and helped them work together. Within fifteen minutes, the fire-hook shaft had burned through, but the boathouse was a pile of burning rubble safely collapsed into its cellar.

Reckless as a rooster, Simone the Siren dashed through a crowd and ran what looked like the wrong way. Over her shoulder she asked if Jasmine Boreal could swim. Of course, the druid replied, and before she knew it she was bounding along a springy floating wharf where dinghies, prams, and pinnaces were jammed thick as cockleshells. Fishermen and sailors shouted as they shoved the boats clear before the pier could burn. Stealing oars from a rack, Simone and Jasmine hopped into a rain-washed pram and rowed furiously. Now Jasmine saw what busy others had missed. Freak eddies of wind had carried sparks to one of three fishing smacks moored together. A sail left drooping to dry had ignited. Ugly black rings ate into faded canvas. Bumping the boat's side, Simone boosted the lean strawberry-blonde aboard just as the sail caught fire. Drawing cutlass and knife, Simone slashed furiously at burning canvas.

Adira's lieutenant ordered the druid, "Draw aft the staysail sheet and cast off the port running rigging!"

The terms were gibberish to the woods-lover, but between them they severed the proper lines. Freed, the burning sail flapped once like a dragon's tongue, then flopped into the harbor and sizzled to extinction. Simone bowed theatrically to sailors sculling out in prams, making sure they knew who'd saved their vessels. She clapped the druid's shoulder with a sooty hand.

"Kiss the wind, Jasmine! You're a sailor!"

Despite valiant teamwork, the warehouse fires spread as the afternoon wind freshened. Sparks fanned across the seaport. Boats, shops, and cottages were in danger. Everyone turned out for the alarm. Men formed bucket brigades and scooped water from the bay. Crews jogged hither and yon with firehooks to rip flat flaming buildings. Mothers bearing babies strapped to their backs directed children with wet brooms to swat sparks. Two sober centaurs, one with a bandaged jaw, manhandled cauldrons to pitch gallons of water at burning houses. In the harbor, barbarians were given axes and mallets to smash the planks of burning boats, so they sank in great geysers of steam. Dwarves scaled rooftops to stamp out fires or rip loose burning shingles with axes and mattocks.

Through the long chaotic day, Adira's crew worked hardest both to fight the fire and to be seen fighting it. Used to high rigging, Virgil teetered atop a ladder to pour bucket after bucket through a charred hole in the tavern roof. Lieutenant Peregrine barked orders in parade-ground tones, shepherding volunteers to break doors and make sure no one was trapped in dead-end alleys or between buildings while flames skipped from roof to roof.

Throughout, Captain Adira Strongheart watched people as much as the fires, so she often spotted potential disaster first. Late in the day, Jedit Ojanen labored to upend a hogshead to pour water into the first floor of a burning house. Whistledove helped by scaling a hot roof like a squirrel and spying through eye-smarting smoke with her superior vision. She jolted as Adira shouted to descend while snagging Jedit's elbow.

"Forget that! Someone's trapped on the docks!"

Racing past people running every which way, Adira led brownie and tiger near a warehouse that burned so furiously it distorted the overcast sky in wavy ripples. Skidding to a halt, Adira squatted and pointed below the smoke. Through squirming haze the mismatched pair saw shapes dance at the end of a distant pier.

"See 'em?" demanded Adira. "These blokes attacked the fire from the harbor end but flubbed it. Their boat's adrift, and they're trapped, and the building's an inferno. We must— Where are you bound?"

Leaving humans dizzy with his power and speed, Jedit Ojanen made three mighty bounds and arced into the harbor. A geyser blew as the tiger crashed underwater, then greasy waves churned as he swam for the pier. Firelight from the flaming warehouse glistened on his orange-black hide until he seemed some elemental composed of living flames and roiling water. Sparks and flaming chips spattered around him, hissing like vipers. Adira and Whistledove and some coasters watched, helpless and awed, as Jedit Ojanen cut the water like a shark, reached the tarry pilings, and climbed from the deep streaming water like a sea monster or sea god.

Through rippling smoke, Adira saw the tiger address the four trapped townies, three men and a woman.

Whistledove asked, "Why don't they swim?"

"Many can't," said Adira. "Probably the others won't desert him or her."

A fat man and woman obviously couldn't swim, for both protested with upraised hands, hoping for a boat rescue. Jedit Ojanen solved the problem handily. Grabbing with claw-sheathed paws, the tiger-man hoisted the tubby man and lobbed him shrieking into the harbor. He said something to the woman, and she gamely jumped after, as did the other two. Last to leap, Jedit dived and burst free of the water like a tiger shark with the spluttering fat man and woman in tow. Jedit let them lock arms around his neck. Still treading water despite their weight, Jedit beckoned the last two swimmers to latch onto the fat man, for the water was paralyzingly cold. Then, with inhuman strength and despite the deathgrips throttling him, Jedit twisted like an eel and stroked outward toward open water, away from the dire flames. Soon he reached a sturdy fishing boat. Paddling, clinging with iron claws, Jedit hung slack while the humans climbed his huge frame to get aboard. When all were safe, Jedit clambered aboard, shed gallons of water by shaking like a dog, then turned toward shore. Spotting Adira and Whistledove, the tiger saluted, grinning so white fangs shone.

Laughing, the two pirates waved back.

Adira crowed, "Love of Lustra! Had I a hundred tigerfolk in my crew, I'd usurp Johan's throne and become empress of Jamuraa myself!"

* * * * *

". . . So, humbly, we thank you for most dire-needed aid. Know you carry the gratitude of all the good citizens of Buzzard's Bay in your bosom."

Night was full on. The dark sky loomed without stars or moons, so rings of torches illuminated the impromptu ceremony. Plenty of scrap wood lay about to be kindled. The wind off the bay was brisk, but none of the locals seemed to notice.

The speaker was a lean man in oyster-white robes with an enameled blue medallion of stars hanging on his breast. His white wreath of hair and beard accentuated his angelic appearance, an oddity in a town of burly fishermen and loggers, but one callused hand sported four crooked fingers broken long-ago in some mishap. He was Bardolph, a cleric of the Holy Nimbus, acting spokesman for Buzzard's Bay, for the sheriff was incapacitated, and their only other authority was a once-a-summer folkmoot.

"You're welcome. We were glad to help." Adira's hair and face and clothes were smudged with ashes, and she reeked like a campfire, but she was happy because her charges had fought the fire bravely and won over the townsfolk, and a daring captain loved to see a crazy scheme succeed. Her Circle of Seven attended her, some proud, some embarrassed. All chugged beer handed 'round by a tavernkeeper who'd rolled up a keg on a barrow. Throats were parched from eating smoke.

Adira slurped and said, "We never sought trouble. Rather we hunt Johan, Tyrant of Tirras, who is our enemy."

Adira let the name hang in the air. She'd thrown all her dice on this calculated gamble. Sooner or later Buzzard's Bay would learn why the pirates had come. Best get it out while half the town was assembled and grateful.

"Johan is Emperor of the Northern Realms, as you must know," announced Adira. "What you don't know is that we hail from Palmyra, the first obstacle crushed under his boot on the march into the sands of the Sukurvia. Our alliance of southerners opposed him until a sandstorm smothered them. Yet Johan crawled out of some hole and escaped, and he still sows mischief. We want to stop him. For that, we need your help."

Buzzing murmurs. Adira watched faces closely. Anger and regret glowered, but none was directed at her.

"We know Johan," said the priest. He pitched his voice high as if preaching. "He enslaves our mountain kinsmen. We saw signs of the great sandstorm. Even here the sky was dark for days. Sand rained on the Blue Mountains to the east, an event never witnessed. Though many of our cousins died, we blame not you, but Johan. He is evil incarnate. Destruction follows in his wake as death and despair trail a dragon."

"This is Johan's work." Adira nodded at the charred and ruined warehouses and ships. "Or that of his agents."

The crowd rustled at the word "agents."

Virgil muttered to the Circle, "Destruction follows in our wake, too."

Simone jabbed his ribs.

With half a town listening raptly, Adira told how Johan had escaped east and found "this child of the forest," meaning

Jedit, which drew a laugh. Laughter died as Palmyra's mayor recounted the savagery that ravaged her marketplace.

Throat raspy and seared, Adira finished, "We tracked Johan here, only to learn he killed a kindly old sage named Hebe."

"We imagine it was he," corrected Bardolph the cleric. "No one witnessed his crime. Among our kind, only a confession or two witnesses can sink a criminal."

"Johan killed her, Bardolph." A broad-chested man with a yellow-gray beard had eyes and face red from fighting fires. "We all know it, even if we can't prove it. No one else had reason. Hebe was poor as a mouse and harmless and well liked. Ofttimes she tended ailments for no pay when the fishing was poor. The murderer had to be Johan, a stranger wreaking havoc and hate. But I want to know *why* he killed her."

"I can't say for certain," returned Adira, "except Johan dislikes leaving witnesses alive. Most likely Johan asked Hebe some questions, since she's local, and he doesn't know the region. We don't know what the tyrant seeks or where he goes, but both must link to magic. Hebe was a spellcaster, but only a small sage, you say, so it's unlikely Johan needed sorcery. That leaves only local knowledge. What might be Johan's destination that relates to magic?"

"Which way did he go?" asked a woman in a thick, soot-stained shawl. "Someone had to see the tyrant leave town. He rode in a sedan chair, and we don't see many of them! And he had that big crowd to feed!"

Murmurs drifted through the crowd. Heads were scratched. With Bardolph moderating, people came forward to offer facts. A vintner sold Johan's scribe three casks of wine. Johan's dotty old seer bought new shoes. The barbarian bearers had purchased a peck of oysters. As hours of testimony and debate dragged, Adira Strongheart gritted her teeth and stifled the urge to scream over dreary details. She was relieved that Johan had not booked passage or bought a ship. If the cruel tyrant sailed into the sunset, he might as well visit the Mist Moon for all Adira could find him.

Then someone mumbled that Johan's party vanished.

"Vanished?" blurted Adira. "How so?"

"Dunno." A blond, beardless lad was reluctant to speak. "I saw them quit the Dandysprat. The barbarians scooched, so the master might mount the chair. I thought it a powerful queer time to be departin', for t'was after midnight. Where could they walk by night? But the bald man waved a hand and off they trotted. South. Johan craned his head around like a vulture, but he didn't see me in the shadows. Lucky, I was, I know now! Then he twinkled his fingers, an' the whole party disappeared!"

"Invisible," said Adira, who possessed that trick herself.

"Yes, cap'n. Must'a been."

"South, they turned?" Musing, Adira faced that way. Night cloaked the coast, but Adira had seen that a rugged rise verged on a high plain, then trees.

She asked, "Are there roads along the coast through the forest?"

"We only venture south in ships," said a dark-tanned woman. "Precious little beachhead exists along the Storm Coast. Not till you round Sheep's Head."

Past that bald knob, the shore veered east to become the Craggy Coast on the way to Bryce.

"There's ox-paths for logging, but they dead-end," said a logger. "They don't like us venturing too deep."

"'They'?" Adira wished she could throttle these slow-speaking folk and shake out quicker answers.

"The people of the pines," said a lithe woman in furs with the look of a scout. "They don't welcome trespassers. They allow some logging, for they like coin to buy our iron and brassware. Too, they barter furs. But they ain't friendly about it."

"Arboria," put in Bardolph, "so they name the pinelands.

A mysterious clan. They've reappeared these past three years. For decades before they were gone."

"Where?" asked Jasmine Boreal, a wanderer of the woods. "Why disappear for decades, then come back?"

"And what," asked Adira, "could Johan seek in the depths of a dismal forest?"

Fear skittered on the night wind. People stared at the ground. Puzzled, Adira repeated the question.

With a pained sigh, the cleric Bardolph admitted, "Legend speaks of . . . an undying mage who inhabits a castle in the forest."

"Name?" prompted Adira.

More gloom. Bardolph shook his head. "We dare not invoke her name. The less said, the better. But be warned. She's capable of greater evil than Johan can conceive."

"She?" Adira waited, but no one sullied the silence. Finally she sighed and rubbed her smudged nose. She craved a solid meal, a bath, and a day's sleep, but likely she'd get none. Pondering the sparse news, she mentally shrugged. Many mages were undying or very old. Johan was centuries old, by all accounts. Yet he'd been bested by a ragtag army and Hazezon Tamar's sorcery.

For just a moment, the pirate queen's thoughts drifted to her ex-husband. She wondered what Haz was doing now and how he might have aided her quest. Mostly she wondered how two people so in love couldn't live together. Their marriage had had to end peaceably before it erupted in blood. Still . . .

"Dira?" Simone the Siren touched her chief's elbow.

"What? Oh. Bless me, I'm luffing." Adira's apology made the Circle glance about in amazement. "It makes sense. Johan would visit a local mage to learn about another mage living in the nearby forest, then he'd kill the informant to cover his tracks. He hired agents to slow us further."

"Oh, yes," said Bardolph. "You mentioned agents before. Do you suspect someone in Buzzard's Bay stirred up strife?"

"I know it," said the pirate chief. "Meaning no offense, but one minute I was talking to your sheriff civil as I might, and the next some fluff sparkled in the air. Everyone turned ugly and riotous, including my crew, and here we be."

"Oy, I remember!" A lean man in the crowd rose on tiptoe to peer around. "It was Darswin and his gang shouting you down. Queer, them talking like patriots being offended. None of them wastrels was ever civic-minded. The whole bunch needs a good hanging."

A woman bleated, "I saw Darswin and one of his brigands duck into Noah's warehouse just before the fire! I thought they was pilfering."

"They must'a fired Noah's warehouse to kill the strangers!" bawled a man. "That arsonous son of a—"

"Find the bastards!" rose a chorus. "Find Darswin and his cronies! Scour the town! Find 'em!"

Roaring, coasters fanned out through dark streets. They left no door closed, no barrel standing, no shed unexplored. In the meantime Adira and her crew accepted Bardolph's invitation to sup in his small rectory. Slabs of coarse black bread and cheese were washed down with more beer. While Adira questioned Bardolph about forest lore, Jasmine Boreal and Whistledove Kithkin sat rapt. Virgil and Wilemina and others dozed off, Murdoch actually standing upright. The halloo of the hunt, like a pack of dogs chasing a scent, seemed to echo off the surrounding mountains.

Adira and Bardolph halted as halloos turned to cheers. Bardolph sighed. "Our quarry is treed. I must preside at their last sunset."

With pirates tagging along, the cleric paced sedately to the far end of Seafarers' Quay where most of the town congregated. Big men stood over three quailing suspects who had been shoved to their knees with hands bound behind. The criminals bore black eyes and bloody noses. Adira's pirates felt no pity, having fought fires that claimed half the shorefront.

Unfolding hands from his sleeves, Bardolph asked mildly, "Have they confessed?"

"They have," boomed a man. "They wanted to unchain their souls before they died. Darswin was recruited by Johan's huntsman and instructed by the high lord himself. They was to stir up strife and get these newcomers killed. They squealed like rats in the bilges."

Bardolph nodded. "It's a shameful life you've led, Darswin, and doubly a crime for roping your friends into assassination. We are all born free under the skies, masters of our fate. You three chose the twisted path to the end of this dock."

The ominous words hushed the crowd. Adira's pirates wished they were elsewhere, but they burned with curiosity. The crowd parted. Sailors bore rolls of canvas like rugs. Darswin began to curse and another thug to sob. The criminals' bonds were cut, but a dozen strong hands mashed each flat on an unfurled canvas: an ancient linen sail. Still pinned, the felons were rolled over and over, swaddled so tight only their heads and feet stuck out. A sailmaker ripped a scrap from the edge and tied a stout knot around the wrapped men. All in silence.

"By the light of the Holy Nimbus," intoned Bardolph, "the ever-shining star that guides us home, I charge you three to change your ways and return better beings. Now go, washed free of all sorrows."

"Return from where?" whispered Virgil, but was shushed.

Solemnly three men hefted each swaddled offender, swung them thrice without counting aloud, and pitched them off the docks. Darswin shrieked as he hit the water with a great splash that scared cormorants and gulls off the water. The trio sank in a light froth of bubbles.

One big-bearded man dusted his hands. Gruff, to cover emotion, he said, "That's that. No use dallying here. Let's get those burnt timbers cleared away." Quietly the crowd trickled into the night.

Adira Strongheart and her crew stood gawking at the bay and the grisly execution.

Gently Bardolph explained, "Thus is always our way. Offenders are cast into the sea to begin life anew. Thus we speak of their future return."

"In the meantime," said Simone in a hushed voice, "they feed crabs and lobsters."

Bardolph nodded sadly. "The current is swift. Things on the bottom are swept out to sea. But you're right. No one in Buzzard's Bay eats shellfish. We chuck those to hogs."

* * * * *

"We sail on the tide. Our ship's the *Conch of Cortis,* wherever that is. The master seems to know his stuff."

On the third floor of the Adventurers' Guildhall, Adira Strongheart and her crew packed bags and tied blanket rolls. Sister Wilemina, lacking her butchered braids, sat on a stool while Jasmine used borrowed scissors to trim her hair by her ears. Whistledove Kithkin stitched armholes in a newly bought sheepskin vest. Other preparations bustled.

Adira aired new knowledge and future plans to her lieutenant, Simone. "Just as well we hoist anchor. Our honeymoon as heroes will end soon. Some loudmouths will tar us with the same brush as Johan, claiming half the docks were burnt because of us. My, how fish blow bubbles! Never mind. I spent the night with Bardolph —"

"We know," interjected Simone with a grin.

"—trading tales over mugs. The man's closed as a clam, but I oiled his hinges with brandy. We seek Fulmar's Fort, which is a jumble of rocks above a swift river sixteen leagues south. Follow that inland to find the castle. Some folk visit the place, it might be. According to Bardolph, four times in the last three years a ship from the far west debarked men with a yellow cast to their faces. They don't say much and always march south at first light. Dock workers think they're foreign mercenaries. Where they go is a guess, but most reckon it's the castle."

"Can we beach at this pile of rocks?" As Adira's lieutenant, Simone often had to carry out impossible orders. "What of these pine people? Will they let us pass? Will they demand a tariff? How much?"

Adira flicked a callused hand. "None knows for sure. The pine people were gone for decades, then suddenly were back, lurking in the forest and taking trade goods for timber rights. Elders remembered their claim to the forest and respected it—mostly. One rough-cut logger said he'd be damned if he'd pay for trees and went in cutting where he willed. His whole crew was lost."

"Bonny." Simone the Siren lashed her oilskin jacket over her leather rucksack. "If we get past these murderous tree-toads, what then? Waltz up to this hag-mage's door and demand she hand Johan over for punishment?"

"Cheer up." Adira slung her saddlebags over her shoulder. "We might drown in a storm."

"Better than being ensorcelled into swine." Simone hefted her bag to go. "Did you pry out the name of our new enemy-to-be?"

"Oh, aye, but not till very late." Adira lowered her voice, for some of Bardolph's trepidation had carried with the name. "It's—Shauku."

*　*　*　*　*

"Hire a horse and ride 'round. Gather a crew. Have 'em fetch enough gear for a fortnight and bring all their cutting tools."

Captain Rimon, with a forked blond beard, was a big man who looked bigger in a quilted coat that stretched to his knees and a vest of mink with the fur turned inward. His vest was smattered with mackerel scales, but now he picked up a chip of cordwood to scrape them off. His audience was a fisherman with a crooked nose, sometimes his sailing master. This tiny cottage perched on rocks at the north of Buzzard's Bay, where many fisherman made their homes. A fishwife stood by her hearth not speaking, nor did she offer Rimon refreshment.

"Thank the Sea King that bald outlander washed up at our shore," Rimon went on. "No more fishin' for us. Once we sink Adira Strongheart, we'll split a goodly treasure, for she won't travel without one. With her breathing on the bottom, we'll be famous up and down the Storm Coast as folks to fear and can stick to corsairin' year round." He used the local polite term for pirating.

"If," said the sailing master.

"We'll sink her," insisted Rimon. "It's folks spreading stories that make her out a bold sea captain. She don't know nothin' about broaching the Storm Coast. We'll snare her like a duckhawk takes a duck. 'Sides, I got this."

The captain displayed a small nautilus shell hardly bigger than a walnut painted with black lacquer. The opening was sealed with wax.

"What's it do?" asked Crooked-Nose.

Rimon didn't know, so hedged. "It's powerful magic, be sure o' that. Now get gone. I'll see *Drumfish* outfitted. Tell the crew to be aboard by dawn."

Rimon tromped out in sea boots, letting in a gust of wind. The corsair with the crooked nose opened a chest to pack his spare shirts and stockings.

He asked his wife, "Where's Matty? It's time that boy learned real sailing. Sharin' treasure will see us through the winter."

"You'll not take Matty on this voyage." The fishwife's tight lips suggested no compromise. "Goin' to corsair is bad enough, but goin' after the woman Strongheart is plain foolish."

Crooked-Nose frowned. "It's just made-up stories they tell 'bout her. I never believe a tenth what I hear 'bout anyone."

"Neither do I," retorted the wife, "but if even a tenth of what's touted about Strongheart is true, she'll break *Drumfish* in half and hang Rimon's head from her spritchains—and yours too."

Chapter 12

"Is that a smile?" called Simone above a keening wind. High aloft, she and Adira toed a thin rope and leaned over a thick yard to furl a balky sail.

"I'm just glad to be at sea!" called Adira. "Even in this bath-tub of a bay!"

"We have to make landfall some time!"

"Don't spoil my fun!" Yet Adira glanced at the distant coast called the Goat's Walk. Jagged rocks and cliffs were topped by dark pines. Surf exploded on hidden rocks, a deathtrap for any careless ship that careened too close. Yet despite an angry ocean and gloomy skies, Adira Strongheart laughed to feel a sturdy ship reel under her feet and wind blow in her hair, even if she weren't the ship's master.

The *Conch of Cortis* was a sturdy caravel like an upturned shoe with high castles fore and aft, buoyant as a cork and easy to maneuver, though it lost miles of steerage way to leeward. The ship carried four stubby masts, acres of gray-brown linen sails, and miles of yellow- and black-tar rigging. Low and stable, she was packed with timber, hides, and raw copper to be sold in Garaboss on the Cape of Hope at the bay's south-ern end, or else wrestled round the cape to southern cities like Kalan and Enez and Bryce.

Yet always the threatening coast trickled by to port, until secretly Adira cursed the benighted mission that would take them inland. Initially she had discounted local sailors' tales and hoped to land in a jolly boat at Fulmar's Fort. But unless the clashing surf and ugly rocks eased, beaching was impossible. Adira's Circle might have to stick with the ship and debark at Garaboss, then buy fresh mounts and backtrack eastward. Meanwhile, somewhere Johan's sedan train threaded that unrelenting forest, and only the gods knew what mischief he pursued.

Still, two days out of Buzzard's Bay, Adira Strongheart shrugged cares away and enjoyed a holiday. Her Circle of Seven had rated bargain passage because they could make sail—most, anyway. Sergeant Murdoch, late of Yerkoy's land-hugging infantry, hung head down over the gunwale strangling.

As the wind picked up, the sailing master had called to shorten sail, so Adira and Simone furled damp canvas. They'd shucked sea boots and climbed barefoot to better grip the toe rope, their only suspension sixty feet aloft.

Simone's large brown eyes turned westward. "This coast is fey. That horizon brims with dirty weather."

"Your eye is jaundiced," countered her captain, temporarily her mate. "This coast blows foul year 'round. Kiss a fish! I've lost the hang of reefing!"

The job got done, and the topsailmen slid down the ratlines. All except Adira, who climbed the futtock shrouds another six feet and rapped on the crow's nest like a door.

"Hello, Adira!" Peeking over the rim of the tub, with big eyes green under a crown of flat red hair, Whistledove Kithkin looked like a child playing hide-and-seek. The brownie was too small for most shipboard tasks but proved eagle-eyed at lookout, so now bunked in the mainmast crow's nest. At the far end of the mast's enormous lever, the nest rose and dipped while yawing a dizzying circle, but Whistledove liked the sensation and seldom came down.

"Shall I send up Heath to help keep watch?" asked Adira. "Two can see twice as far as one."

"Really?" Unused to the pirates' straight-faced jokes, the brownie was often puzzled. "That doesn't—"

"Forget I spoke," said Adira. "I'm just making the rounds. Are you content?"

The brownie had no complaint, though even the pirate chief found her iron-hard stomach bubbling in the wild pitch and swing. She peered to windward, eyes watering, to study the waves and sky, then slid down the lines to thump on the quarterdeck.

Big blond Edsen was master of the caravel, not captain, for on Jamuraan seas only pirate chiefs and naval officers rated that title.

Adira reported to the Buzzard's Bayman, "Sir, windward grows foul. The waves run gray with whitecaps whipping to spume."

"Is that so?" Like most seafarers on this coast, Master Edsen wore a faded quilt jacket with a bearskin vest and hat. "I wouldn't fret, bosun. We're used to slop such as you southerners seldom see. But d'ya mind hustling Gack-Guts below? He's puked up so many dinners sharks're gnashing our rudder."

"He's—yes, sir." Adira swallowed her temper. It irked her that a mere merchant master dismissed her keen observations with lubberly gibes. Yet Edsen must assert rank, for Adira was just another hand to the four officers and twenty-one crewmen. Adira commanded only her own Circle of Seven as a bosun.

Duckwalking to the rail, Adira levered the seasick Murdoch over one arm and half-dragged him down the aft companionway.

White-faced and shaking, the soldier groaned, "Mother of the Erg, why does anyone go to sea?"

"No flies nor mosquitoes, for one thing, and it's seldom hot. It beats walking or riding."

Below in cramped passageways and pitch darkness, Adira groped to Murdoch's bunk, rolled him in, and flipped a dusty blanket over him. In the bunk above, she prodded ribs until someone grunted. A female.

"Jasmine?" asked Adira, for it was black. "I thought this was Heath's billet."

"It is." Groggy, Jasmine poked someone deeper in the bunk, then flopped back to sleep. Heath slithered forth, warm as a sun-soaked cat. Adira recognized his scent, an earthy odor of campfires, greenery, and resin from his bowstring.

"Get aloft," said Adira. "See if a leviathan stalks our wake."

"What?" The part-elf reared and banged his head on a beam.

"I jest. Go, but don your jerkin." Finding her own bunk, Adira fished out her leather jerkin, which was heavily oiled to shed sea spray, and laced it over her thick gray-cabled sweater. She'd bought both items for each of her crew, for this coast sent man-killing cold even in autumn.

Stepping on deck, wind snarled Adira's chestnut hair, making her retie her green headband. The air smelt thick with salt, and Adira had the satisfaction of seeing Master Edsen and his sailing master argue about clawing to windward and dragging a sea anchor. Why fret, Adira wondered, unless a storm threatened to drive them ashore?

The sailing master picked up his trumpet and bawled, "Starboard your helm! Closer to the wind, you codfish, or I'll flay you to bones! Hands aloft to shorten sail!" So up the ratlines again went Adira and Simone.

When the sails were reefed once more, Adira trekked through the ship to check the rest of her crew. Forward in the forecastle, Virgil and Wilemina slept soundly, for they had night watch. Peregrine, a lubber, trimmed beef in the galley amidships, not happy but not complaining. Finally Adira squeezed down slimy companionways to the bilges to relieve Jedit. The fearsome warrior had been dubbed the ship's cat by

Master Edsen and ordered to kill rats. Adira grinned but saw no rats. Jedit was glad to seek fresh air.

On deck, Adira felt wind kiss her cheek with wetness. She plunked on a bucket where Simone unraveled old rope to make oakum.

Picking at hemp, Adira said, "You may be right about the weather."

Simone didn't gloat. Even speaking the word "storm" tempted trouble. Impishly she asked, "Get everyone tucked in their bunks!"

"Ach!" Adira spat. "I should deep-six the lot. Their romantic foolishness makes me spew. Murdoch chases Wilemina's tail, but the devout virgin hoards her greatest treasure. So Jasmine makes eyes at Murdoch, except he's yellow-dog sick. So now when I rouse Heath, I discover Jasmine sharing his blankets!"

"Go easy on poor Jasmine. Her pride's hurt that a druid must chop onions in the galley."

Adira snorted. "It explains why Wil's nose is out of joint. The silly bitch is jealous of something she can't have!"

"You're jealous," Simone teased.

"Me?"

"Aye." Simone grinned, teeth white in her black face. "You miss the fun. You've gone too long without loving, Dira. Order a man or two to warm your bunk, and forget your troubles."

"For three minutes, maybe," groused Adira. Inexplicably she thought of Hazezon Tamar. "Love's not worth tying up your heart and head."

"Too bad Jedit's a tiger." Simone watched the great cat gaze westward. Raised in a landlocked jungle, the enormity of the ocean perpetually fascinated him. "He'd make a fine man. Maybe we can pay some sage to shape-change him again."

"Into what? A furry seven-foot fathead with red hair and big teeth?"

"Perhaps we'd keep the stripes."

"And the tail? And you claim *I'm* never satisfied?" Both women giggled, but then Adira sobered. "That's another thing. I must bespeak Jedit. I'm a captain, and you're lieutenant, but he thinks he's king."

Rising, duckwalking the deck, Adira hooked a tarred mainstay and parked her hip against a rail. "Jedit Ojanen, we must have words."

The tiger-man regarded her silently. His eyes were slit against the wind so looked to have three parts, green, amber, and green, an unnerving display. Further, Adira was peeved the tiger could stand on a pitching deck without any handhold. Possessing perfect balance, he never stumbled, never blundered, making humans feel spraddle-footed and awkward and stoking Adira's famous temper.

"Jedit, I don't like you striking out on your own hook. It happened half a dozen times in Buzzard's Bay." Adira fumed at the huge tiger. "If you pocket my coin, you obey *my* orders! *Don't* order my crew about, no matter how nasty our crisis! If you want to seize command, you'll fight me with matched daggers, elsewise you carry your hat in your hand! Is that clear?"

"Aye, aye," the tiger purred above the shrill of the wind. "If I give offense, I'm sorry. I'm new to human ways and still learning. I appreciate that you let me join your band. Such kind generosity I can never fully repay."

"Oh." Adira's temper sputtered as if doused with ice water. Expecting an argument, Jedit's sincere apology and gratitude flummoxed her. Gruff, she snapped, "Just bear it in mind, Stripes, or blood'll be spilt between us."

Stalking back to Simone, Adira plunked on her bucket and savagely unraveled rope.

"My, my," murmured Simone, "see his fuzzy round ears smoke."

"Shut up."

Jedit

"Sail!" A cry from Heath in the crow's nest. "*Six points abaft the starboard beam!*"

Immediately everyone dropped chores to cluster in the ratlines. Simone the Siren scurried a dozen feet above deck to see the new vessel, a stumpy carrack straining under all sail. Some Buzzard's Baymen clucked their tongues.

The pirate lieutenant said, "So we're not the only lunatics to brave the blustery deep!"

"All hands!" came Master Edsen's sudden cry. "Prepare to repel boarders! Crack the cutlass locker! Fetch the spare canvas and netting! Lively, lads! You, Strongheart! Front and center!"

As coasters jumped, suddenly in a hurry, Adira swallowed her temper at being summoned like the rankest cabin boy.

Striding to the deck, she grated, "Sir?"

"What's this about?" Edsen glanced astern as if a tidal wave loomed. His teeth were bared, but his eyes flashed fright.

"What?" asked Adira. "Yon ship chases us?"

"You know damn well it does!" Edsen glared. "This is your infernal trouble-making again, ain't it? Buzzardmen don't attack Buzzards. Even Rimon sticks to that rule. So if *Drumfish* chases us like a hound after a hen, it's your fault! I've a mind to dump you and your patchwork pirates into a longboat without oars and let Rimon snap you up!"

Already fuming, Adira let slip her temper. "You'd never maroon us in this life, you hamhanded mucker! My crew'd split you brown-water bastards from gills to gullet and chuck your heads to bob in our wake! *Jedit! Whistledove! Simone, pipe up the Seven!*"

Edsen's crew, busy breaking out boarding pikes, axes, netting, and spare canvas, stopped to goggle. One second Adira Strongheart argued with the master, and the next she was surrounded by her half-mad bodyguard. Even the brownie clinging in the rigging clutched a rapier in her fist.

In command, calm again, Adira asked, "What are your orders, Captain?"

Edsen gulped and looked to officers for support, but they steered clear of mutiny and massacre.

Finally the bayman husked, "Uh, stand by to repel boarders. And get . . . off my quarterdeck."

Nose in the air, Adira skipped to the main deck with her Circle of Seven in tow. Other shipmates shied away to cluster on quarterdeck and forecastle.

Simone asked with a grin, "Your orders, Captain?"

Glancing about, Adira said, "Looks like these crawfish want us to defend the waist alone. So we shall. Make ready to repel boarders, but watch your backs. One by one, slip below and fill your pockets with anything precious. We might have to quit the ship on short notice."

Adira's pirates nodded, used to crises striking like lightning. The lubbers looked at the angry gray ocean and wondered how cold the water might be, but, shepherded by the lieutenant Simone, they fell to tasks with a will. Adira perched on the ship's gunwale to study the sea, the sky, the ominous lee shore, and the oncoming *Drumfish*.

The corsairs' ship was a carrack, built like a box to carry diverse loads, with three masts. The versatile sails and lack of a load made the pursuing boat fast but awkward. She skittered sideways as much as punched ahead, her crew tacking endlessly. At this distance, Adira could see her rigging was black with corsairs like spiders in a web. Pirate ships typically carried three or four times the crew of a merchant vessel.

"Edsen's rats'll likely roll over and squeal for their lives. So . . . eighty-odd fighters oppose my Circle of Seven, or nine, and all the time Edsen's eager to stab us in the back." Adira juggled odds and options and her meager resources. Her eye fell upon, of all things, the druid looking lost as a fish in a forest. "Hoy, Jasmine! Here, woman! Tell me. A ship's built of wood, but dead wood, true? Still, could you . . . ?"

Jedit

* * * * *

Two frantic hours had passed, and the sun had cracked the western sky just before setting, when *Drumfish* crept to windward within hailing distance. Both ships pitched and rolled on a steepening sea. Rising wind, harder to fight by the minute, blew toward the forbidding coast and its gnashing rocks a mere five miles away.

The corsairs from Buzzard's Bay were ready. Not as many as Adira had reckoned, some sixty fishermen-turned-raiders were poised with swords and pikes to slam alongside *Conch* and swarm aboard. Under Edsen, the merchant ship had made only token efforts to arm. Her twenty-odd crewmates carried sharp cutlasses and had lined the ship's sides with a wall of netting and spare canvas, but all the baymen and women hoped Edsen could cave in quickly. More than their cousin corsairs, the sailors feared the coming storm and threatening shore. Only Adira's Circle of Seven expected a fight.

"Ahoy, *Conch*!" Captain Rimon of the *Drumfish* bellowed through a leather speaking trumpet. "Give us Adira Strongheart, and you can sail on free!"

"Drink bilge and drown!" came a cry, not from the quarterdeck, but from the waist. Adira Strongheart didn't need a trumpet to bawl above the wind. "Think ye'll take Johan's blood money with one hand and the Circle of Seven with the other? You yellow hagfish! Earn your pay or eat dung like a dog!"

"Don't listen to her, Rimon!" shouted Master Edsen from the quarterdeck. "She don't speak—"

"Edsen's a coward!" Adira drowned out the quavering master. Oddly, she was the only person in sight in *Conch*'s waist, standing beside the midmast with a cutlass upraised. "An eye-picking, gut-eating, bottom-feeding crab! He won't lift a claw to save his own ship! But you're worse, Rimon!

Turning against your own kind to kiss Johan's backside! He killed your kinfolk, yet you skulk the sea lanes at his bidding and break the only truce you ever knew!"

The pirate queen went on to curse Rimon's mother, father, ancestors, and crew in filthy tones. The waiting corsairs fairly chipped their teeth sputtering in anger.

"Die in the deep, Strongheart!" roared Rimon from his quarterdeck. "You're our meat dead or alive! *Helmsman, hard a' port!*"

Roaring a war cry, Rimon's corsairs braced their feet as the helmsman spun the wheel. Shoved by rudder and wind, the corsairs' carrack jumped through the water and pounced on the *Conch*, slamming her so hard sailors were jolted off their feet. Two corsair officers called "Loose!" and a cloud of crossbow quarrels flew from *Drumfish* to stipple the wood and a few Conchers. In the corsair's waist, Drumfishers shoved for elbowroom to lay out grapnels and chains that would bind the two ships for boarding.

Yet a curious sight gave the raiders pause. For along the amidships of *Conch* suddenly rose a yellowed sail like a theater curtain in reverse. Cleated to a spare yardarm and jerry-rigged blocks-and-tackle, the sail zipped upward and was quickly lashed in place by Adira's crew.

Furious and fuddled, the Buzzard's Bay corsairs, male and female, collectively scratched their heads. The entire midsection of the merchant ship was hidden behind that queer curtain. Granted, it was only old canvas and they could easily peg crossbow bolts and arrows through it, yet the marauders hesitated to attack victims they couldn't see.

"What on the briny deep—" On the quarterdeck, Captain Rimon cursed and wondered if Adira Strongheart had gone crazy. Yet the two ships clashed hulls with an awful racket, so the time to attack was now. Making his decision, Rimon bawled, "Never mind that bed sheet! We'll cut it to shreds in seconds! Hurl the grapnels! Hurry aboard, and fetch me Strongheart's head!"

A *whisk!* and *whap!* seemed to answer. Rimon whirled to see his helmsman shot through the chest by a long-fletched arrow. Lacking a guiding hand, the rudder instantly straightened so the ship lost way. A gap of green water churned between the vessels. Shouting for the bosun to grab the wheel, Rimon grunted with satisfaction as iron grapnels on chains soared jingling across the gap to snag *Conch's* wooden gunwales. Two hooks bounced off the taut curtain-sail and splashed in the water, but corsairs were quick to haul them back inboard.

Rimon bellowed, "Now *heave* on those lines, you bastards, and bring us alongside! A bonus to the man who cuts Adira down."

Another *whicker* and *whap.* Rimon blinked as the bosun who'd gained the wheel slowly keeled over. A black arrow jutted from his liver. Rimon screamed for the sailing master to seize the helm, but the officer balked. Rimon sputtered curses and stepped to grab the wheel, but even he quailed. To touch the wheel was to die. Rimon squinted aloft. Two archers were crammed hip to hip in *Conch's* crow's nest. They'd kicked a slat out of the wooden tub and hunkered inside, hiding from crossbow bolts while peeking for a chance to kill a helmsman.

Snarling, Rimon raged, "We'll steer by trimming the sails! Jump aboard, lads and lasses!"

"Whoa! What's *that* thing?" called a voice. Puzzled corsairs pointed overhead and were confused anew.

Something round swung on the end of a rope from below *Conch's* midmast. It was a barrel, a big one called a hogshead, wrapped with a cradle of rope. Cut loose at just the right moment, the hogshead swung a looping arc, curved through the air as the ship dipped, then hung, poised, not three feet below *Drumfish's* own crow's nest. Before it could swing back, a vision of orange and black spilled from the barrel.

Immediately Rimon thought of infernal fire, the flaming liquid so often used against castles.

But the barrel spilled a tiger.

Braced by black claws sunk inside the barrel, Jedit Ojanen leaned out with long arms and snagged *Drumfish*'s rigging. For a few seconds, Jedit made a living bridge connecting one ship to the other. Several things happened.

The brownie Whistledove Kithkin scampered like a monkey up Jedit's great frame, hopped onto tarred rigging with a rapier in her fist, and lanced the blade through the eye of the lookout leaning from the crow's nest. Immediately after, Jasmine Boreal, less nimble but game, slithered from the barrel. Grabbing hanks of tiger fur, she scrambled hand-over-hand until she caught hold in the ropeworks. Jedit Ojanen gave a roar, obviously a signal, for the line holding the barrel to *Conch* was chopped free. The tiger relaxed his foothold, and the barrel plummeted. It bounced off a stay, collided with the midmast, then struck the deck with a splintering crash.

Gallons of rancid fishy liquid squirted from broken staves and hoops to splash the raider crew, a longboat, sails, and ropes. A few corsairs recognized the smell and shouted.

High above, clinging to rigging by one hand, Jasmine Boreal jerked a wad of resin-soaked rags from her bodice and gabbled, "Spark of life, bringer of strife!"

As the rags erupted into crackling flames, she dropped them squarely into the shattered spilled mess below.

Whale oil ignited and flared. Flames rippled like fire sprites set free. Shouting corsairs dropped their weapons and yanked off their vests to beat the flames or else snatched buckets to scoop seawater.

Though the fire burned fiercely, the ship could spare a score of sailors to combat it. The rest of the raiders, incensed by this daring and clever attack, rallied to kill the *Conch* and its quarrelsome crew. Grapnels and chains were sheeted home, so the two ships chafed and thumped like butting whales. Roaring to spur their courage, and ignoring the queer curtain amidships, a score of corsairs leaped the churning gap onto *Conch's* gunwales and ratlines. Several even took advantage of the taut curtain and flopped against it as a cushion.

Those clever killers died instantly.

Waiting just behind the upraised curtain were Adira, Virgil, Peregrine, Murdoch, and Simone the Siren. The misplaced sail obscured their view of *Drumfish*, but they clearly saw silhouettes of boarding corsairs etched against canvas by setting sun behind. Hollering like fiends, Adira's crew shoved boarding pikes into bellies and groins right through the canvas. Drumfishers died as their blood stained the yellow curtain.

Nor was that the only attack. At either end of the taut sheet were poised Adira and Simone, the ablest fighters. Each gripped a cutlass and dagger, and as corsairs thumped on the sides or slithered around the canvas, they stabbed and chopped at heads, hands, and feet. Adira cursed and shouted as she swung wildly with both blades, and she prayed her delaying tactics would work. Dozens of corsairs could easily evade her weird curtain and bloodthirsty crew by swarming aboard at the ship's stern and bow, but *Conch's* crew would have to deal with those raiders, for even Adira Strongheart couldn't do everything.

High in the sky, Jedit, Whistledove, and Jasmine had carried the assault back aboard *Drumfish*. Her lookout in the crow's nest died as he peered over the wooden side, for Whistledove's blade rammed into his brain. Jedit Ojanen caught the man's arm and tugged him from the crow's nest to topple to the deck. He shooed Jasmine and the brownie up into the tiny tub as sizzling crossbow bolts came soaring at them from below. The ship's midmast was still two feet thick even at this height, filling much of the tiny shelter, so the three Seveners were jammed cheek to cheek.

The tiger called, "Jasmine, time for your trick!"

"Hush! I don't perform 'tricks!' " Shooting her blue-dyed sleeves, the strawberry-blonde druid plucked an acorn from a pouch on her wide belt and mashed it against the mast with her thumb, chanting, "Soul of the tree, return unto thee!"

Drumfish shivered as if rocked by a wind gust. Jedit and Whistledove grunted as the mast's varnish curdled and cracked, flaking yellow peelings. Smooth wood grew corrugated and crazed, taking on the appearance of live bark. The brownie squeaked as a tiny branch popped out and unfurled a green leaf no bigger than her fingernail.

The ship quivered so much that Jasmine's teeth rattled. An enormous groaning and creaking sounded below. The shouting of corsairs, very loud as they fought both fire and Adira's cutthroats, became a frenzied wail. Jedit nodded as the tiny branch unfurled more leaves.

"Impressive, but if the mast is recalled to life, and sprouts leaves up here . . ."

"That's right." The druid was smug, almost laughing. "Down below it grows a full set of roots. Where the butt of the mast is stepped on the keel."

Whistledove's big eyes grew round. Jedit Ojanen purred as if to comfort himself. Rising, standing high above the world in the crow's nest, the tiger found no one shooting. The whale-oil fire had scorched a black circle but been knocked down, though a few errant flames crackled up tarred stays. A pitched battle raged along *Conch*'s gunwales until blood painted wood, ropes and canvas, but now corsairs struggled to board *Conch* not to kill and plunder, but to save their lives.

Drumfish was disintegrating. Deck planks buckled and split around the midmast as it swelled in its narrow socket. Water spurted in jets as the hull breached and caved under the monstrous pressure of spreading tree roots. Ropes and yards strained too far snapped like kindling. Corsairs ran hither and yon, some shouting incoherent orders, some just shouting.

No one got help from their officers. The sailing master and others lay dead or dying in glistening pools of blood on the quarterdeck. Only Rimon could move. He'd sheltered behind the binnacle but even then caught a long barbed arrow through his hip. One leg hung lame, and blood ran in a river. Surely he'd die, he thought, while his ship crumbled to flotsam. Yet he might survive and even gain revenge with one last trick. Gasping in agony, the corsair captain dug in a pouch for the black lacquered nautilus shell given him by the mysterious Johan. Rimon had no clue what it might do except "help him win." With nothing to lose, he popped the wax seal with his thumb and flung the seashell overboard.

Swaying high up in *Drumfish's* crow's nest, Jedit and Whistledove and Jasmine stared through a wealth of open air at Sister Wilemina and Heath staring back from *Conch's* nest. From their shocked looks, the two archers reckoned their comrades were in dire straits. Two comrades agreed. Whistledove Kithkin and Jasmine Boreal clutched the tub's edge and peered down into dizzying space. So much rigging had parted, or threatened to snap, they had no trustworthy path to descend. More than a score of corsairs had taken refuge from the churning deck in nearby yards, but even then some were whiplashed into the hungry ocean.

Whistledove asked, "What's the plan to get back aboard?"

"There isn't one," squeaked Jasmine. "Adira said we'd think of it when the time came."

Watching the chaotic fracas below, Jedit Ojanen said, "The time has come, and Adira's busy. I've an idea. Hang on. Better yet, lock arms around the mast."

"Why?" asked both women, but Jedit just slid out of the crow's nest.

New to the sea and sailing, Jedit Ojanen didn't know exactly how ships were held together, but some facts were obvious. From atop the mainmast, he looked around at a dozen tarred ropes called stays that held the tall mast upright. Some of the stays ran all the way to the ship's sides, while others were fastened to the first and third masts. The precise arrangement was bewildering to any landlubber, but Jedit understood one simple fact—cut the stays and the mast would topple.

Starting on the side distant from the *Conch of Cortis*, hanging by one leg and paw, the great man-tiger skittered like a spider over ropework and severed each one either by champing mighty fangs or hooking razor claws. Curious *pungs* and *pings* and *prongs* made weird music, as if a demented giant plucked a harp to pieces. There was an ominous creaking as the magiked mast began to tilt, then screams. Corsairs cowering in the tops howled at the destruction. Marauders on the deck below pointed and yelled. Inside the crow's nest, the brownie and druid hugged the shivering mast until their fingernails drew blood.

Jasmine objected, "This is mad! He'll get us—*Whoaaaa!*"

To the creak of tortured wood and snapping stays, the midmast-turned-tree tipped farther, then farther, then toppled and crashed amid the upperworks of the *Conch*. Whistledove and Jasmine barely had time to scream before the tilted crow's nest snarled and stopped dropping. Great furry striped paws caught their arms and hoisted them from the sideways nest. The women clutched warm fur in stark terror as Jedit pinned them with one arm and, single-handed, descended safely to the solid deck.

"By the balls of Boris!" Murdoch slapped the tiger on the back. "I've never seen an escape half as wild as that! Never seen a keener nor more crazy battle either!"

The Circle of Seven laughed, jubilant at their impossible victory. Adira's crew was spattered with blood and panting with exertion, but aside from cuts and bruises, no one was hurt. Their victory was doubly sweet because they watched from safety while their enemies perished in panic.

The ships were still lashed together by grapnels with iron

chains, and ground together with a nerve-grating racket. The corsair's midmast, now more a living tree than dead mast, stayed fetched among *Conch*'s upperworks. Ropes and sails continued to sheer as the mast sawed back and forth. The guts of *Drumfish* had been torn out by tree roots wrenched awry, so the ship broke up on the angry gray waves, sinking fast. Corsairs shouted for succor while chucking jetsam on the ocean to cling to, knowing they'd never last ten minutes in the frigid water. A few raiders clung to the outer gunwale of the *Conch*, terrified to return to their dying vessel but more terrified of Adira's madmen. Aboard *Drumfish*, flames licked at tarred lines like fireworks, ropes and deadeyes dangled and swayed, and the quarterdeck seemed a charnel house with bodies strewn like oyster shells. Blood streaked sails, decking, and lines, and trickled out the scuppers to dapple the dark water. Captain Edsen bawled for his crew to grab axes and cut away the entangling mast before it dragged them under. Men and women raced to obey, for with the corsair ship almost gone, they recalled the danger of crashing on rocks to the east.

Adira Strongheart commanded her own crew. "Belay the backslapping! Help cut that curtain and this rubbish free! Find a crowbar and wrench loose those grapnels, or *Drumfish* will drag us to the bottom! Whistledove, get aloft and watch for rocks! Jedit, grab what corsairs you can and haul 'em aboard! We need every hand we can spare, and I don't care where they hail from! Virgil, cut loose that curtain—"

"What's that noise?" chirped Sister Wilemina. "It's not the wind, but it howls like a pack of dire wolves!"

"Danger to port!" shrilled a woman from the forecastle. "White water under our keel!"

"What?" Adira Strongheart jumped to the bloody rail and peered overside. White water in a ship's lee could only mean rocks, a spine-chilling notion. Yet they should be safely distant.

Under the stricken *Drumfish*, the ocean boiled. Adira

caught her breath as gray water seemed to sink, a dizzying sight. Two currents ran in opposite directions, one north and one south. The corsair ship lurched as timbers pulled in two directions groaned. The pirate queen cursed in confusion. Conflicting currents meant either a rip or—

"All hands!" bawled Adira. "All hands drop all tasks and make sail! We skirt a whirlpool bound to suck us under!"

Chapter 13

The sucking of the whirlpool was audible even above the howling wind and cries of the wounded. A terrifying sound, it seemed to clutch at sailors' souls and leech away their wills.

Drumfish, more a scatter of spilled firewood than a ship, spun lazily but steadily picked up speed. Water raced around the vessel in an unnatural swirl. Two men threw their hands to the heavens and screamed for the Sea King to save them. Even some of Adira's Seven slowed in hacking free the midmast that was pulling the *Conch* half-over.

"Get aloft!" Adira shouted, whacking people with a hard hand. "Making all sail is our only hope! Move!"

Pushed, prodded, and kicked, sailors and corsairs flew into action. As if by magic, sails began to fall from the tattered rigging as seasoned salts slashed furling strings with knives rather than untie them. Eager hands grabbed sheets and lashed them to anything that didn't move. Immediately the *Conch of Cortis* strained like a hunting hound at the leash. Yet the dead weight of *Drumfish*'s midmast threatened to sink her like an anchor into the widening whirlpool.

Still, thought Adira Strongheart wildly, the tangled mast was the only obstacle that prevented them from fleeing. The iron grapnels had been pried off the gunwales and snarls of rope severed. Now if the ship could only scoot before the wind—and never mind that they raced toward a granite shore—they might win free of the whirlpool and survive another hour on this ship-killing coast.

Bounding to the companionway, Adira vaulted to the quarterdeck and ran squarely into Master Edsen.

"Keep off my quarterdeck!" roared the merchantman hoarsely. He blocked the top of the ladder, glaring down at Adira. "I'm in command! You and your damned mercenaries have cursed us!"

"Belt up and steer three points before the wind!" snarled Adira. "It's the only way."

"*Before* the wind?" bellowed Edsen. Rain slanted now off and on, and silver droplets clung to his bearskin hat and vest. The waning day grew dim as the sky lowered. "We sheer *into* the wind, you damned fool."

With no time to argue, Adira cruelly punched the master in the crotch. As Edsen lost his breath and doubled over, Adira bulled her head into his belly and lurched backward while grabbing the ladder. Edsen pitched over Adira's head to crash painfully in the waist. The pirate queen charged onto the quarterdeck, a cutlass and dagger in her hands.

She bawled at the helmsman, "Steer three points wide, or you're a dead man!"

Eyes bugging, the man spun the wheel through a quarter-turn and let it steady.

A noise like the end of the world grated on the ears and chilled the heart. With a slithering roar, the misplaced midmast of the doomed *Drumfish* tore free of the *Conch*.

Adira Strongheart ran to the quarterdeck rail. Eerily, like some giant sea serpent in reverse, the varnished mast now corrugated like bark slithered along the shattered gunwale. What remained of *Drumfish* churned and bubbled as it sank into the whirlpool. The ocean spun like a potter's wheel, with the center dimpled a full ten feet below the water's surface. *Drumfish*'s torn sails, fractured deck planks, uprooted binnacle and ship's wheel, a broached longboat, and many broken bodies spun thrice in that awful gyre and then disappeared under the dark waves. The corsair's departing midmast whacked her splintered crow's nest against *Conch*'s waist in one last vindictive blow, then plashed full length. Tugged inexorably from below, the mast whipped spray as it stood upright as if in defiance, then sank out of sight.

The danger wasn't over, for the whirlpool continued to grow, though it now sagged only six feet deep at the center. Adira wished she might drop a sea anchor off the starboard side, or else trim the sails to bite the wind, or try any of a dozen sailing tricks to free them from the vortex, but there was no time. Praying to the Sea King herself, Adira didn't even shout at the sailors scattered across the tops, for they worked as hurriedly as possible to free sails, let them drop, and sheet them home.

Slowly, after agonizing minutes, the merchant vessel kicked up her heels and lurched from the maelstrom's pull. Free, the *Conch* took on new life and fairly leaped as wind filled her tattered sails. Adira frowned as seawater gurgled into a rent torn in her side, but the pumps could eject it, if anyone could spare a hand for the pumps. Charting a new course closer to the wind for the helmsman, Adira hopped into the waist.

Simone the Siren, often Adira's navigator, met her captain where cordage and shreds of sails dangled. The waist was a dangerous place, for smashed longboats and pin rails, buckets and spars careened back and forth, easily able to sweep an unwary sailor out the nine-foot gap of missing gunwale.

Simone called above wind and rain, "We only broke free because that whirlpool sucked down *Drumfish*, you know! The jetsam blocked the gyre from catching us!"

"I know!" called Adira, though they stood only two feet apart. She glanced aloft. "Tell the hands to secure. We'll tack on my command."

"There's naught to sheet home to for half the canvas!" Simone cut her off.

"Do your best!" countered Adira. "We need to claw to windward."

"Won't happen!" Simone's dark eyes closed in negation. "We've lost half our backstays! Try to tack, and you'll shiver the timbers down on your head! Best we steer for shore! Lash the lubbers and wounded to a baulk and scout for a soft crop of rocks!"

"Never!" shouted Adira. "I won't surrender a ship! If the coast veers just two points west we'll weather it! Tell the hands we'll tack!"

"Aye aye!" Simone didn't argue. "*All hands! Take care to tack for your lives!*"

"What?" Adira spun as someone tugged her sleeve. No one stood there, and for a second Adira imagined ghosts and selkies and other sea haunts. Then she saw Whistledove Kithkin peeping up from under her cloak hood, the brownie barely taller than a crane.

"Whistledove! Why don't you man the crow's nest!"

"I did, but no one could hear me cry! What fish wears tall stickles on its back and tail?"

"Lots of fish." Adira's heart dropped into her belly. Queer, she thought, how the simplest questions proved so daunting. "What color? How big? Where away?"

"Greenish with brown webbing." The brownie was chagrined by her lame observations, but she stood far from her native hills. Her shivery voice piped above the wind, "The sail fin reaches high as our rail, I think. I don't know the creature's length. It follows in our wake."

Adira's eyes bugged at the ominous news so casually delivered, for Whistledove had no idea of the horrors that lurked in the deep. Hissing, Adira scampered back to the quarter-deck and ten feet up into ratlines. Straining her eyes, Adira saw nothing off the stern but churning waves, dirty gray and steepening. Perhaps, she prayed, the unseasoned brownie had imagined the sight or had just spotted flotsam from *Drumfish*.

She told Whistledove, "Carry on. We don't have time for new worries."

The ragged *Conch of Cortis* no longer climbed and dipped but bucked and juttered through the water like a three-legged horse. With the sails set crossways to the rudder, the two helmsmen tried to force the ship to windward with the tiller alone. Simone and the sailing master had clambered aloft to direct the topmen. Old salts fished together mismatched lines and bypassed missing deadeyes. Acting on Adira's orders, her Seven lubbers and sailors jettisoned smashed boats and other furniture across the tilted deck and out the gap in the gunwale. Losing the junk both lightened the ship and made it safer, since fewer obstacles clattered and skidded underfoot.

Rain pattered. Whitecaps burst over the weather railing. Adira noted spume blew sideways past her nose. Oily clouds like black smoke boiled overhead, seemingly close enough to pierce with an arrow. Adira and her Circle had seized command, and it showed the baymen's agitation that no one objected. Master Edsen, lame from Adira's belly blows, had crawled below to his tiny cabin. Yet Adira couldn't relax for a second, for the oncoming storm still shoved them hard toward granite-studded waters not a mile distant.

Dashing everywhere at once, Adira helped rove new rope through a block, so the crew might hoist the mizzenmast main yard.

"It's bad, ain't it?" asked Virgil, worried but calm.

"Afraid to take your annual bath early?" Adira kept her voice light, refusing to concede the ship was doomed, nor to let the crew fret with idle hands. In her mind's eye their bodies washed up on foreign shores: stark naked, bloated and white, hair straggling like seaweed, skin nibbled by fish and crabs. In this moment, with them gathered round, so loyal and brave and willing, she loved her Circle of Seven as fiercely as if her children, and tears escaped her eyes. She snuffled to mask her emotion.

"Jasmine, if you've any weather-magic in your bag of tricks, now's the time to let it slip."

"I don't ply *tricks!*" corrected the druid.

Murdoch snorted. In rain with wet heads, Adira's pirates looked much alike, for they all wore the long gray sweaters and oiled leather jerkins. Belts were stuffed with cutlasses, short swords, daggers, and axes, though the only enemy was the awesome sea.

Murdoch said, "Hey, Adira. What happened to prize money? You let *Drumfish* slip through our fingers. Where's the profit?"

"Think of a lesson learned, landlubber," countered his captain.

"I wish I were on land. I wish I could swim." Peregrine joked, but her voice shivered. "We don't see waves like these in the Sukurvia."

"Nor the jungle," added Jedit. He told the frightened lieutenant, "You'll gain shore safely, if not dryshod. I promise."

Despite the damp and cold, Adira's temper flickered like a coal. Dare Jedit allude to taking command after she'd blistered his hide earlier? Then she let it go, too busy to be petty.

With a heave ho, the riggers hauled up the yard on wobbly blocks. Adira's Circle gave a hoarse cheer at a small victory. Their captain turned away, a lump in her throat.

Prowling the ship, Adira Strongheart watched sky and shore, gauging their chances. Clawing seaward might let them ride out a squall, but a sustained storm would drive them on the rocks. Adira ordered Murdoch, who was handy, to help the ship's carpenter and sailing master fashion a sea anchor from a broken spar and spare sail. Clumsy on the slippery deck, they managed to shove it overside. As the hoop of canvas sank and bellied, it dragged like a wagon brake to slow *Conch*'s speed. Virgil and Peregrine muscled and hoisted spars. Jedit carried lines as he climbed like a spider. Heath and Wilemina, with clever hands, wove new rigging from dangling ropes.

Indeed, everyone was so busy only Adira saw the monster strike.

As sudden as winter lightning, alongside the ship reared a green-black scaly head and neck high as the mainyard. The skull was elongated like a pike's, the neck sinuous as a snake's, and the mouth lined with white daggers. Fast as Adira could blink, the sea serpent hooked its impossible neck at a man slaving to hold the tiller. The helmsman barely shrieked. Adira was reminded of a bird pecking a worm as the serpent bobbed and bit. Its horny muzzle rapped the deck as razor teeth engulfed the man, snapping so hard one foot sheared off to bounce on pine planks. The serpent flicked its chin high, gnashing and crushing, then gulped and swallowed the broken man whole.

Consternation swept the ship. Howls and screams rang even over the ear-piercing wind.

In the tiny pause while the serpent devoured its victim, the *Conch* raced on. The fearful beast was left a cable's length behind. Yet the ship lost headway as the remaining tillerman deserted her post. Rudderless, pushed by the wind, with sails haphazardly trimmed, the bow came around, so the stern broached the half-gale. Immediately the ship's quivering roll degenerated into a slamming gait like a crippled horse. Men and women slid along wet decks to bang painfully into masts and rails and furniture. From long years of practice, Adira's pirates gripped something, but Jasmine, Peregrine, and Murdoch tumbled headlong until seasoned sailors nabbed them. Instinctively all scuttled toward their captain. Jedit Ojanen hunched as if ready to spring, snuffling the salt air with black nostrils.

Virgil fumbled his axe from his belt and held it up helplessly. "How do we fight that beastie?"

"Don't they coil around ships and crush 'em?" asked Murdoch, totally out of his element.

"Hush! Heath, Wil, nock your bows!"

Adira's keen mind sifted standard defenses but came up short. She'd barely believed sea serpents existed. Squinting into eye-stinging rain, she said, "If we batten the lubbers below—"

"It's back!" screamed Sister Wilemina and loosed a wild arrow into the sky.

Unexpectedly, the sea serpent flung its head above the port side, having swum or slithered under the ship like an eel. Water sluiced from its long green head in buckets. The mouth, a full six feet long, cracked to reveal rows of needle teeth. This time Adira saw the comb of tall spines that jutted from its head and stippled its spine. Shaking its head, perhaps to fling water from its eyes, the creature stabbed at the largest target—Adira's Circle of Seven.

"Back!" Adira slapped one arm wide to brush her crew out of harm's way. In her other fist sprouted her cutlass, though she didn't remember drawing it. Lurching against the unfamiliar lunging of the ship, she stabbed upward as the serpent drove down. A scaly head big as a coffin banged Adira's thigh as her cutlass pierced the thing's chin from underneath. The pirate queen felt the blade split skin like thin leather, then the point jammed in springy fish bone. The serpent waggled its head at the pinprick, ripping the cutlass from Adira's hand and almost breaking her fingers.

In that instant, Jedit Ojanen struck.

Unlike humans, the "ship's cat" kept his footing on careening wet deck by digging claws into pine planks. As the tiger's comrades spilled and skidded and dived to avoid the onrushing serpent, Jedit was free to act. Slinging a long arm behind, he swiped a huge circle. Black claws struck the serpent's head. Four long weals of skin were peeled from the monster's muzzle to hang in shreds flapping in the wind. Surprised and hurt, the serpent whipped its head back and paused, so it was left behind as the *Conch of Cortis* raced on directly for surf-drenched rocks a half-mile distant.

"Bastards!" cursed Adira Strongheart at no one in particular. Her ample breasts heaved as she panted. "Damnation and hellfire! Jedit, Heath, the rest, fight that thing! Simone, Virgil, come! We've got to claw off the rocks!"

Used to obeying blindly in crises, pirates fell to. Murdoch, Jasmine, and Peregrine crabbed to a mast and unlashed eight-foot boarding pikes. Heath and Wilemina nocked their favored weapons, bumped rump to rump, and tried to watch all sides at once.

Following Adira, Simone the Siren and Virgil pulled hand-over-hand across a sloped deck and up to the quarterdeck. It was deserted, the officers having fled below. The tiller snapped back and forth like a dragon's tail, making the ship veer sickeningly. Virgil jumped on the long wooden arm, taking a painful rap in the ribs. Simone dived in, and together they steadied the vessel.

Virgil called to his mate, "What if that fish-beast attacks while we steer?"

"We die!" yelled Simone.

"Can't we just lash the tiller hard over?"

"No. There may be rocks! Belt up and bear down! Uh oh!"

Up the short ladder staggered Master Edsen and three officers. All carried cutlasses and murder in their eyes.

The master shouted, "Strongheart! You've been a jinx since you first stepped aboard! I'm taking command, and I'll kill—"

Far overhead, Whistledove Kithkin keened like a tern. Her tiny finger pointed astern.

The serpent struck where it had found good hunting earlier. Virgil and Simone sprawled on their butts but never let go the tiller. Edsen's officers dived back down the short ladder, leaving the two captains gaping in the open. Adira acted. Heedless of how she landed, she vaulted the low railing overlooking the waist. As she soared, she snagged Edsen's tunic to drag him along to safety. Half-turned, Edsen failed to see the fearsome head swooping. As Adira yanked on his tunic, the serpent sank fangs into Edsen's shoulder. The master howled as cruel teeth sheared muscle and bone. Pulled between Adira and the monster, the captain split apart. Dragged from Adira's fist, what remained fell and flopped like a fish. Blood spurted in a surf-washed cascade across the quarterdeck. Edsen died as the sea serpent tossed its chin and gulped down the master's arm.

An errant gust shoved *Conch* onward as the beast slipped below the waves.

Adira Strongheart earned her name again by hooking her boot toes in the quarterdeck railing. Shouting orders, she seemed to move the ship by her voice alone.

"Simone, Virgil, on your feet! You three, get forward and let slip the capstan! It's shallow enough to drag anchor! Seveners, stand fast to fight the monster! The rest of you ignore it and get aloft to tack! No, I'm not mad! We save the ship or die on the rocks!"

Forward, a woman shrieked as the sea serpent reared again. Jedit, Wilemina, Heath, Jasmine, and Peregrine rushed that way as Sergeant Murdoch slipped and crashed on a coil of rope. Dusk had descended, and footing was tricky in semidarkness. Rain stung faces. Jedit Ojanen slit his eyes and tiptoed on thorny claws to the bow, then waited, watching both ways.

Silver flickered overside.

"That's not—" Jasmine gulped air. "That's its tail!"

Indeed, the tail whisked alongside the ship like a misplaced palm tree. Whip-thin, the tail splayed spines almost like a porcupine's. The curious sight seemed to hypnotize the human Seveners. Yet the warrior Jedit Ojanen whirled and skipped on clicking claws for the opposite beam. He reached the gunwale just as the creature's head leaped over the rail like a horse jumping a fence.

Gaping jaws of razor teeth drove at the orange-black warrior. A man would have died, snapped in two, but Jedit was no man. With a coughing roar, he launched like a stork and landed square on the sea serpent's nose. Four clawed paws gripped tight. Jedit saw two long arrows smack into the scaly head just below his. The serpent pitched and thrashed on a rolling blowing sea to flick off the stinging insect. Jedit plucked free one brawny right arm and stabbed straight as a ballista bolt. Four black claws smashed into the serpent's tiny eye and pulped it like a jellyfish.

Gargling in pain, the serpent snapped its neck back in one gigantic flinch. That mighty whipcracking action even Jedit couldn't overcome. As if flung from a catapult, the tiger splashed in the dark drink a hundred yards from the ship.

"Jedit!" At the quarterdeck, cursing and weeping bitter tears, Adira Strongheart nevertheless tended her command. By shouting herself hoarse at topmen and tillermen, she directed a new strategy to tack the ship. One by one, with heart-stopping thumps and slams, the sails shot home and bellied. Forced onto a new tack, the caravel's nose pointed southward. The wild gut-churning pitch smoothed. At the bow, the anchor had been let go, but there was no indication the iron caught bottom. Adira took small comfort that they rode deep water, yet she could hear surf burst on rocks, always a bad sign. Song of the Sea King, how could she be so thirsty with all this rain running down her bosom? She could have drunk the ocean dry! And how could Jedit be drowned? He'd seemed unkillable!

Sailors howled as the serpent again slung its sharp head over the prow. Water slung in silver wheels as the jaws waggled. The beast seemed torn between suffering a ruptured eye and an empty belly. Half-blind, the sea serpent stabbed at a sailor and missed, biting instead the oak capstan and chipping long teeth. Swinging, unable to gauge distances, it chased a woman with champing jaws but slammed into the foremast. By then Murdoch had crabbed forward to pink the beast with his boarding pike. Snapping in anger, the sea serpent yanked the spear from the sergeant's grasp, then bashed the butt on the deck and splintered the shaft. Murdoch raised both arms as the bloodied spear point barked off his hand. In diving, the addled serpent whacked the hull so hard that Adira felt the blow at the stern.

"It won't be back!" crowed Simone through gritted teeth.

"Neither will Jedit!" Unable to savor victory or trouble, Adira looked west, east, high, low. Booming spume at the east made cold terror squirm in her belly. The half-hidden rocks were perilously close. The sky westward boiled blacker than ever, as if clouds sought to crush them. Wind and rain lashed like whips. Everyone's teeth chattered. Fearing for her crew, Adira despaired. They'd never escape the eastern shore. Perhaps she should run close to shore and abandon ship. Small boats and even flotsam and hatches might survive the grinding surf, though any survivors would likely die of chill.

"Dira, look!" Simone's shout broke the captain's glum thoughts.

An orange-black arm curled over the port gunwale. Slowly, as if carrying the world on his back, Jedit Ojanen crawled over the side and collapsed in a sodden matted heap. Snorting water from his black nostrils, streaming water, the tiger-man looked up as his comrades surrounded him. Amber-green eyes were lit by fiery anger.

He growled above the roar of wind and wave, "Where is it?"

Before anyone could answer, the serpent reared like a waterspout on the opposite beam. Still jigging its head, flinching from pain, the dim-witted sea monster nevertheless recognized the assailant who'd half-blinded it. Hissing, with jaws gaping wide enough to swallow a cow, the serpent launched like a missile for the tiger-man. Jedit too gave in to savage nature and leaped six feet off the deck to claw and rend.

Adira and her pirates goggled at the strangest and fiercest clash ever witnessed. Half-flying across the cramped tilted deck, the enraged sea serpent sliced ratlines, shrouds, and furled sails with wicked teeth in a frenzy to snap Jedit in half. Yet the ship wore a thousand such lines, and with a hideous strangling gasp the sea serpent entangled itself in a giant net. Thrashing only hooked the beast deeper, for its iron scutes snagged a hundred spots and wedged it tighter. Before anyone could blink, thirty feet of furious sea creature was enmeshed in the rigging of the *Conch of Cortis*. Snapping, twisting, hissing, the beast gnashed its dagger teeth against a pine mast.

Jedit pounced.

Yowling, coughing, roaring, the man-tiger landed astride the serpent's twisted neck and sought to rip snaky head from squirming body. Blood geysered and was whipped to froth by storm wind. Jedit gouged a hole big as his arm in the serpent's neck, a gory portal gleaming white with bone, while the bloody head snapped and jigged to catch the tiger's legs. All the while, the berserk tiger roared an ear-wracking caterwaul.

Adira cursed anew at Jedit's battle madness, for endless yards of the serpent's thick body still kicked in the water alongside *Conch*. The wild struggling made the balky caravel impossible to steer. At the tiller, Virgil couldn't keep his feet on the deck. Stays and rigging were sheared anew so sails billowed and flapped.

The pirate captain gasped to Simone, "Fetch axes! Hack

that beast through the body before it drags us under."

With a heart-stopping jolt, the *Conch of Cortis* beached.

Adira and her crew were flung on their faces like drops of water as the ship snagged on rocks. Virgil fared worst. Trapped between tiller arm and taffrail, he was swatted as if by a sledgehammer across the ribs. The tiller yawed, setting him free, but swung and whacked him again as he fell. Crumpling to the wet deck, Virgil didn't even wrap his arms in pain, but fell like the dead.

Upperworks snapped like twigs. Masts, spars, and yards whipped once and broke. Lines parted like arrow strings. Tangled wood and cordage rained from the skies and made a shambles of the deck. A corsair was flicked into the sea like a fly. Heath and Wilemina were hurled together so hard one's arm was broken. Simone slid into the quarterdeck railing, broke through, and tumbled into the waist. Even Jedit Ojanen, busy rending the dying serpent, was knocked off by a mass of falling cordage.

The ship careened as if kicked in the stern, then bobbed on the tide, shifted, dropped, and spun free. Blinded by brutal pain in her hands and knees, Adira sensed instinctively they'd grazed a hidden rock and bounced off. Yet the damage was done. The *Conch* listed to port. Half her bottom must have torn out, Adira knew, and she took on water.

"Abandon ship!" Adira tried to shout, but only wheezed, winded. Grabbing drunkenly for support, she again spilled to the deck, slicing her hand on a jagged splinter. Cold spume scoured her wound and made her whimper in pain. Fear for her crew clutched her guts. This was it, she thought wildly. They'd feed the fish, and none would mark their graves except gulls.

Dizzy and sad, Adira crawled on bruised knees to help Virgil, but bumped into jagged stiles, all that remained of the quarterdeck railing. She'd gone the wrong way. Where was she, anyway? To her blurry rain-swept vision, this queer place resembled a jungle with a giant snake wrapped in tangles like vines. Crabbing around, she reached Virgil and tried to lift him, but her bleeding right hand lacked strength. Chestnut hair soaked by rain and blood stung her eyes.

"Virgil, brace up! Damn you, we need—"

With a horrendous jolt, the ship struck again. This time it stuck fast, but Adira Strongheart didn't know that. She skidded headlong over the shattered rail into the waist. A storm giant clouted her head with a mast, or else she banged her skull. She lay staring at black clouds with rain dappling her eyes, unmoving. Perhaps her back was broken. Under her aching spine she felt the ship grind on rocks, lift, slam again, grind, lift, smash down. A few minutes, she thought, and they'd swim. Drown.

"Adira." The roiling sky was eclipsed by a face of orange, black, and white stripes all dripping crimson blood. Jedit's whiskers were broken on one side. She started to giggle, for the cat man looked so serious.

In his odd antique accent, he purred, "Hold still. Your head is bleeding."

"Leave me alone." Adira croaked. "Help Virgil. I couldn't wake him. Peregrine can't swim. Where's Simone? And Hazezon?"

"Safe, all safe." Shifting a fallen spar, Jedit hooked a brawny arm around Adira's back and lifted her gently, though it still hurt. Even the tiger stumbled as the ship smashed to bits on unforgiving granite. Detached from her body, Adira watched swirls of gray go past.

Distantly she heard Jedit say, "Adira's dazed. Her last command was to abandon ship."

Someone answered. Another argued. Adira didn't care. She tried to say, "Get Virgil," but ran out of air. Cradled in the tiger's mighty arms, with his wet-cat stink filling her nostrils and his body heat glorious as a campfire, Adira listened to people talk, call names, babble. Jedit gave orders in Adira's name to hurl flotsam overside. The tiger was oddly calm, given his berserker rage to kill the sea serpent a few moments ago. But he could swim like a tiger shark, thought the captain idly. He needn't worry.

"Heath! Heath, swim to that hatch!" The tiger yowled through a fog in Adira's mind. "To your left! Left! Keep Wilemina's head above water! Good thing Adira wrapped you in wool, eh, Simone? We'll float. Yes, go. I'll follow. Does anyone see Peregrine? Whistledove, cleave to Jas—"

Wood splintered like a forest rent by a hurricane. Or were such storms called cyclones on this coast, wondered Adira? Someone screamed the ship was giving up the ghost. Adira felt like a ghost herself, airy and floating, beyond pain and care.

"Brace, all!" warned the tiger. Adira's stomach lurched as the cat jumped high and far overside. Water crashed over her: in the face, nose, mouth, ears. She gargled and strangled and sucked down an ocean's worth of water. It filled her lungs, she was certain. There was no air anywhere. Her mind flickered like a dying coal.

So this is drowning, she marveled, then thought no more.

Chapter 14

Johan had glimpsed the fabled castle of Shauku in a vision in the Western Wastes. Granted, he'd been exhausted at the time, perhaps delusional, but the blurry image had shimmered and soared into the desert skies, truly impressive. Such an ancient and revered queen of sorcery could only occupy a shining palace.

What he found proved a shock.

For a fortnight Johan's sedan train had trekked into the forest called Arboria by the natives. Never had Johan seen any people of the pines, though his huntsman reported traces. The forest was a gloomy place, dim under towering trees rearing straight to a dense interwoven canopy. Pine needles carpeted the ground so thickly even footfalls were muffled. Often his party heard their own breath as the only sound. Yet Johan's party was never molested, though they sensed native eyes witnessed every move. The Emperor of Tirras assumed his destruction of the first scouting party quashed any notion of attacks, proving once again the most ruthless path was the best. Cowed enemies either shied far away or did as commanded. So for two long weeks Johan swayed in his sedan chair upon the shoulders of four brutish barbarians. The master mage again wore his drab monk's disguise. Dozing, lapsing into trances, the tyrant mulled plans about how best to conquer Jamuraa, and how he might exploit this much-heralded mage Shauku.

Finally Johan's party reached a shallow valley and jerked to a halt. Framed by pine trunks in the middle distance, their destination glowed in late afternoon sun.

Johan's captain of guards barked, "It's a ruin!"

Though he kept silent, Johan's calm demeanor vanished. For a moment he saw only red. Furious, he felt like killing his entourage and immolating the forest.

It was true. The palace barely existed.

From what they saw past pine trunks and descending tree-tops, the castle had once commanded a wide shallow valley that in centuries past must have boasted prosperous farms and vineyards. At the valley's center reared a low hill, and atop a castle surrounded by a high wall, or bailey. Nowadays the fortification resembled a landslide and pine forest had reclaimed the vale. From this distance, Johan could see only half the castle's face and mere outlines of towers. Curiously, smoke trickled from fissures all around the crumbled hill. That smoke had been their first sign of human habitation in this benighted forest.

"I-is that the place?" Johan's lesser mage was the squat woman known as The Glass Mountain, supposedly because she couldn't be conquered. "Could we have wandered amiss? Perhaps Lady Shauku departed and no one knew. But those trees are decades old. Perhaps her grace dwells in another plane. Or the castle might be disguised, or shifted in time. If we cross the threshold, mayhaps we'll find it alive and . . ."

"Be silent," grated Johan.

Down the wooded slope, the huntsman waved the party on. Johan's captain looked at his master with trepidation.

Johan rubbed his bony chin. With such a powerful magician as Shauku was rumored to be, anything was possible. But the likeliest explanation was that he'd been gulled. If so, he would flay the woman alive. Howsoever, Johan mustn't look fuddled before inferiors.

Waving a lank hand, he commanded, "March."

Up close, Shauku's castle got worse. Passing a column of wood-scented smoke issuing from a hole in the hill, they found a child could have mounted the rubble of the outer curtain, which was half-buried in vines turned brown by autumn frosts. Of the stout wooden gates, all that remained were heaps of sawdust reduced by ants. The courtyard sported a young forest of red pines, birches, and aspen trees, and gardens of briars. Undermined by roots, flagstones bulged every which way. The keep proper slumped like a sandcastle in a tide. Three towers had collapsed into heaps, and the fourth lacked a roof. The castle walls still standing were smothered in vines and, curiously, thousands of red and white roses. The central archway was closed by the rusty skeleton of an iron-strapped portcullis. Beyond, they saw that trees grew within some palace wings, for most of the slate roofs had collapsed, leaving only slanted beams. Evening burned the western sky to a glowing orange streaked with purple. The many columns of smoke righted themselves as the day breeze died. The only sound was a whip-poor-will piping in nearby brush.

Sitting his sedan chair in the overgrown courtyard, Johan felt anger boil in this throat like bile fit to choke. Shauku's fabulous library was a sham. He'd journeyed all this way, seeking knowledge to conquer all Jamuraa, and found a ruin that rats would eschew. Someone would die in agony.

"Milord!" The huntsman called from beyond the east tower. "An entryway!"

Still glaring, Johan waved a hand as if expecting this news. The barbarian bearers threaded trees. Johan's captain pointed with his pike at something the mage had missed.

"A path, milord. Someone lives above ground, at least."

The eastern tower was intact, if roofless. Rounding the tower, Johan saw weathered stone bound with rotten mortar. Vines had been yanked away from a low entryway, a tiny sally port once reinforced with double doors. The beaten path crossed the threshold. The passageway should have been black but instead glowed softly with gray twilight since the roof was gone.

Silhouetted at the passageway's end stood a guard, or a statue.

The entourage trudged to a halt, weary from a day's long march. Barbarians waited for orders, dumb and patient as oxen. Cursing inwardly, Johan ordered his chair lowered.

Stepping to canted cobblestones, Johan let fall his monk's disguise. Like a candle flickering to life, he took on color and substance. Skin glowed vivid red laced with black tattoos, a horn jutted from his bony chin, two more horns downcurved from his temples to frame his raddled face. A robe of purple lizard skin hugged his gaunt form like a living parasite. His hands and bare feet and chest were also red and tattooed. This was Johan's true face, stamped by sorcery, fearful and alien, commanding and cruel. The myriad tattoos were his own doing, designed to intimidate and draw attention to his face. Other features, such as blood-red skin and horns, were accidental by-products of dabbling in black arts. Yet any well-versed mage would see immediately that Johan had juggled arcane and mystic mana and survived, so he would command respect. Inspiring awe and fear was all the wizard cared about. Now, shrugging his purple robes about his shoulders, he would mystify Shauku—if she were here. If not, he'd level this wreck once and for all.

"I'll go alone." None of his party dared question, so stood mute.

On bare feet, Johan padded down the dark passage toward the eerie silent guardian. Up close, he recognized the garb: black reptilian armor overhung with a yellow

gypon emblazoned with a startling red sun. A black helmet
bore only a slit exposing cold eyes and painted yellow vees
suggesting bumblebee stripes. The man stood with a lean
sword unsheathed and propped before a shield like a black
kite. An Akron Legionnaire, Johan knew, elite troopers
recruited from Corondor. Expensive to maintain as a flotilla
of ships or a stable of fine racehorses. Johan wondered idly if
the soldiers stoked the underground fires that dribbled
smoke.

The guard issued no challenge, and for a second Johan
thought he was ensorcelled, but the man's chest rose and fell.
Since the guard showed no surprise at his arrival, Johan calculated, the soldiers must have spotted the party from the
battlements or even in the forest. Johan would flog his huntsman half-dead for failing to spy lookouts.

Imperious, Johan announced, "I would see your master,
Lady Shauku."

"You are?" rapped the guard.

"Johan, Tyrant of Tirras and Emperor of the Northern
Realms."

The legionnaire lifted his sword to his eye slit in a salute,
as if diplomatic visits to this wilderness occurred daily. Turning smartly, the guard called in some foreign tongue. From a
distance marched an identical man who beckoned Johan to
follow.

The castle's indoors was same as outdoors. Walls rose sheer
for three stories, but the roof wore only seven arching beams
against a sunset sky. Pines and aspen trees grew high as the
walls. Broken flagstones were jumbled with broken roof slates
under a carpet of leaves. Rusted iron hooks still held gray
poles where war banners had rotted away. At each end
yawned vast fireplaces big enough to roast an ox, though
bricks had fallen. At one end, square doors led to the kitchen.
In corners, windblown dirt let thrive more roses and briars
and weeds. Johan saw swallows zip in a window, circle once,

and flit out again. Once this mead hall housed some lord's family, a home lively with drink and dance and music and laughter. Now it housed insects and birds.

And one occupant.

At the far end stood an immense dining table, once grand, now cracked and water stained. Behind the table on a wide stool sat the most beautiful woman Johan had ever seen.

Black hair was glossy with sunset highlights. A golden face with pointed chin featured sky-blue slanted eyes wide and innocent. She wore a simple layered gown of satin so blue it appeared black, unadorned. Before her sat a plate with only grape stems and seeds and a silver goblet of spring water.

The legionnaire stamped to a halt, saluted elaborately with sword to visor, and announced the visitor. The lady smiled dimly, interested but uncurious.

Flummoxed but refusing to show it, Johan pretended all was normal. Clearing his throat, he asked, "Lady Shauku?"

"Yes." Soft and musical. "Emperor Johan. Welcome. I'm so glad you came."

Johan wasn't. But he nodded, face frozen in a polite smile. Something was very wrong.

* * * * *

Adira Strongheart revived because she was freezing.

Wind sucked and slobbered at her wet hair and chilled her lax body. Every gust set her teeth chattering, but she couldn't move to get warm. People carped to hold still until she wanted to lash out and thump someone. Gradually words filtered through the fog infesting her brain.

"Not much seaway, so b-bear down! H-help me h-hold her, she's prickly as a s-s-sea robin! J-Jedit, will you?"

Adira was mashed by a sopping wet arm big as a rolled carpet. Spray stung her face, a salt chill. All this water, she fretted. Surely the ship must be sinking. Then she recalled and her eyes flew open.

"Wh-where are we?" Her lips could barely move, she was so cold. Her hand throbbed too, as if a shark gnawed it.

"M-marooned," chattered Wilemina.

"S-soon to d-die," added Simone.

Even awake, Adira couldn't see. The night sky was streaks of dark and darker gray. Wind howled all around. Spume from breaking waves spattered them like rain. Adira tried to turn, but couldn't.

Simone the Siren rasped, "Damn your eyes, Dira, stay put! There's barely room enough without you jigging like a lobster in a pot!"

Groping and floundering, Adira was pulled up half-sitting almost in Jedit's sopping lap. She croaked her feeble question again. Song of the Sea King, but she was thirsty! And the night so black!

"We're cast away, Adira." Jedit's voice was a shuddery purr. "On a rock barely big as a oxcart. Nine of us. Simone and Wilemina and Whistledove, and you and I, and four from Buzzard's Bay."

"What? How?" Adira peered at darkness. The only luminosity was the clash of sea foam on breakers. She couldn't even make out her companions. "Why not swim for shore?"

"It's three or four miles, Adira." Simone could barely speak for shivering. "We'd never make it."

"Nor can we tell direction in the dark," whimpered Wilemina. "The tide changes and the surf runs every which way. And my arm is broken!"

"We can't anchor here!" Adira's reason and strength were returning, though every time she moved her head, it throbbed as if kicked by a horse. Nor could her right hand function. "We'll shrivel from exposure!"

No one answered.

"Maybe with the dawn . . ." purred Jedit.

The crew huddled like puppies, packed so tightly one's shuddering shook the next. Jedit radiated heat like a sheet-iron stove compared to the fish-cold humans. The tiger seemed not to suffer in his coat of fur. Adira thanked her lucky stars and foresight for buying her crew the thick sweaters, for oily wool kept a body warm even when wet. Still, their predicament was dire.

"Maybe you should shove off, Jedit." Spray slapped Adira's face, and she almost raged at the sea. "You can swim like a squid. And those sharp ears must pick out breakers on the beach. You could fetch help!"

By appointment and nature, Adira took command and gave orders but knew they were useless. True, the tiger might reach the shore, but it was likely sheer cliff with no beach. He'd be bashed to death against stone. And the Goat's Walk was barren and unsettled. There'd be no rescue boats, ropes or volunteers.

"The tide rises," said Simone. "We need Jedit's help just to cling to this rock. Every rogue wave threatens to sweep us off."

"At least in drowning," said Wilemina, "one feels warm. Or so they say."

"I can't believe my own Circle would give up the ghost!" groused Adira. Despite her throbbing head, she grew angry at the sea, the fates, and her wastrel crew. "You blatherskites will just sit quietly and die?"

"Some are dead," whispered Wilemina. "This woman beside me grows cold. I poke her but can't rouse her."

"If she's dead," said the oft-callous Simone, "shove her off. We need the room."

"What of the others?" Adira cast about, but the world was thrashing darkness and spinning spume. She might have struck her skin alight, her favorite trick spell, but she was too addled and exhausted. And chilled. Early autumn in northern latitudes meant frosty nights. Adira was astonished they'd survived this long. Dawn would see their corpses sheathed in rime ice.

"Where's Virgil, and Murdoch, and Peregrine? And Heath? Surely he can't be gone!"

"Murdoch's nearby," said Simone. "We shouted until our voices gave out. Murdoch answered, but only he. Peregrine couldn't swim. Virgil sank. He was badly bashed by that tiller. It broke his ribs or guts. He claimed to be all right, but spit blood at every breath. He refused help when we jumped from the wreck."

"I see." Hot tears spilled down Adira's chapped cheeks, the only touch of warmth she'd ever felt in her life, it seemed. Cold gripped her like an iceberg.

"It's only hours till dawn," panted Wilemina through chattering teeth. "Maybe a fishing boat will see us."

"It's two hours still till the tide turns," countered Simone. "We'll be knee-deep in water soon and too stiff to stand."

"Where's the *Conch*?" asked Adira. "If it fetched on rocks we could climb aboard."

"Five fathoms deep," said Simone. "We only chucked loose a few hatches and lost those when we broached these rocks."

"I wish Lady Caleria would open the skies and pour sunshine upon us," whispered Sister Wilemina.

"Keep wishing," sniped Simone.

Screaming wind whipped away words, so silence fell. The sailors knew soon would come the silence of the grave, for their body heat ebbed even as the water sloshed around their legs and buttocks. People tried to scoot closer to the center but lacked room.

Adira croaked, "Jedit, shove off."

The tiger didn't answer.

In stubborn silence, with teeth chattering, Adira said, "Cub, you moor here only for our sake. You alone can survive this trap. Swim to shore and explore that cliff. Find a way up. Atop is forest. Build a fire or burrow in the mold. We can't, but you can. Go, swim. We need deck room. Go, damn your eyes!"

Rocking, stiff as a stone statue, Adira shoved with two hands and knocked Jedit off the rock. The tiger flopped with a great splash unheard above wind and surf. Exhausted and dizzy from her head wound, Adira crumpled again. People scooched together for warmth, none speaking.

Time passed. An eternity of cold. Simone, Wilemina, the tiny brownie Whistledove, Adira, and the bay sailors pondered death, and cold, and the unfairness of losing one's life on a windswept rock, their thoughts jumbled as the angry waves. No one spoke as water washed the rock.

From the wet darkness, a throaty purring call startled them. "Adira Strongheart!"

Dully Adira opened her eyes to surging blackness. Frozen, barely able to move her jaw, she gargled, "J-Jedit, I or-ordered you—"

"Leave, yes." Water gurgled and slopped, and suddenly they all felt the great tiger surface like a leviathan alongside the rock. With only clawed paws clutching the rock, Jedit spewed water like a fountain. Something in his voice suggested humor, and instantly buoyed their hopes.

"You ordered I go, and I did. But I fetched friends."

"F-Friends?" gibbered Adira. "Who?"

A gasp echoed around the group as lights flickered below the black water. Paired orbs glowed soft green like undersea fireflies. As the doomed mariners watched, the lights rose all around, and for a second some thought of a sea monster with a hundred glowing eyes and a gaping mouth. Narrow heads with seaweed hair broke the surface, illuminated by green eyes shining like bullseye lanterns.

"Merfolk!" chirped Wilemina.

"Do not re-mem-ber us, do you?" A woman with a hatchet face sported rippling gills at her neck. Her voice piped and squeaked like a dolphin's. "Not very friend-ly, we call that."

It was a toss-up which notion stunned the humans more:

that someone familiar rose from the sea, or that they teased as if meeting over beer. Beckoner, shaman of the Born of the Beck tribe of the Lulurian Clan, had never been known to joke.

"I-impossible!" stammered Adira. Scores of doubly glowing heads popped from the water smiling. To the merfolk, the autumn storm was as gentle as a summer breeze. "You can't . . . How did . . . I don't . . ."

"Adira," rumbled Jedit, just as sopping as the scaly water-dwellers. "Please accept their aid. The merfolk can swim us ashore. I'll go ahead to build that fire."

Shocked speechless, Adira nodded numbly. Beckoner caught the pirate queen's arm. "Tell your peo-ple we mean no harm. Some may think we drown them."

"Oh, y-yes. Sail me 'round to the others."

Beckoner nodded. Two merfolk latched onto Adira and gently drew her into the surf. It was near freezing, but Adira was too numb to feel. Keeping her chin above water, the swimmers deftly maneuvered her from one tiny rock to another. Murdoch she found alone, shivering, as terrified of drowning as of the ominous green lights. Breathless, Adira explained he'd be towed ashore by friends. Towed on, she passed word to more of Edsen's sailors, Heath, some corsairs, and Jasmine.

Hands like coral branches bore Adira toward the beach through the chop. Waves smacked her face. A flicker of yellow light beckoned. Before Adira realized her danger, she was plunged headlong into pounding breakers that sucked and tugged and tried to drown her, then she was yanked free of the water's clutch by the agile merfolk. Propped on a rock festooned with seaweed, the quaking pirate discovered the light was fire. Though the cliffs were sheer as a castle wall, portions had fractured and tumbled. Here a deep cleft formed a shelf jammed with driftwood. Grass and seagrapes and other bracken hung down from the forest floor above. Jedit had cleared a spot and kindled a fire. Adira had never seen so blessed a sight in her life.

With his keen vision, Jedit spotted the pirate queen and jumped to her aid. As frigid hands propped her from below, Jedit snagged her arms and hauled. Adira tried to crawl toward the fire, but collapsed, too stiff to move. Gently, Jedit persisted. Within minutes Adira was naked as a baby bird, propped against dry bracken and warm stone, with her wet clothes hung as a screen against the wind. Soaking in the wondrous warmth of the campfire, Adira cried unashamedly, grateful to be alive. Jedit bounded back and forth, fetching people and feeding the flames. Soon Adira's reduced body-guard and fourteen Buzzard's Baymen were huddled around a fire so close they risked scorching bare feet.

Once more Jedit returned with his arms full, this time with a huge tail-flapping tuna. The tiger broke its neck, sliced flesh with his black claws, and speared white steaks on spits to sizzle.

That done, Jedit loomed over Adira, amber-green eyes glowing. "Beckoner lingers to speak with you, Captain. She can't approach the flames."

"Oh, y-yes." Shuddering to quit the fire for frosty air, Adira nonetheless borrowed Heath's drying shirt and minced on swollen feet to the edge of the stone shelf.

Beckoner and her court perched on icy rocks, calm as cormorants. Adira could see them now, skinny as pikes, the women flat-chested, all naked but for scales wrapping their torsos almost to the armpits. With dead-white skin tinged green and gills fanning at their necks, they looked like drowned corpses returned to haunt whoever slashed their throats. As shaman, Beckoner wore the tribe's treasure, necklaces and bangles of coral beads, bronze trinkets, and wire-wrapped rubies and sapphires.

"Thank you for saving our skins," stammered Adira. "Again. After you banished the river at Palmyra, Johan's army was beached, and we defeated them in the desert. Barely."

"Is no-thing." Beckoner waved a lank hand, a gesture adopted from humans. "A pact struck with our clan lasts as long as the sea, and car-ries to our child-ren's child-ren's spawn. Glad we could save you. Merfolk have no friends a-mong land-walk-ers."

"You have friends forever," said Adira, feeling gushy and solemn and foolish. "The river creeps back to Palmyra slowly. Anything you need, any help, just mount the docks and ask. We'll grant it, I and all my citizens. So I swear. But, please, tell me. How did you find us? How did you reach us so quickly? We last saw your tribe frolicking in the Bay of Pearls on the Sea of Serenity. How got you here, five hundred leagues or more?"

"We heard cat man thrash in waves," squeaked Beckoner, again waving a hand. "Sound like no-thing else, e-ven far off. We swam through wa-ter weir."

"Water weir?" asked Adira. "A fish trap?"

"Eh? No. Pipe? Tun-nel?" The narrow face frowned seeking the right word. "All the world's wa-ters are one. To swim in one o-cean is to swim in all. To cross wa-ter, we swim down and twist, and find selves far a-way. See you?"

"No," admitted Adira.

"Odd." Beckoner was truly puzzled. "All merfolk know it. Else how cross long stret-ches of wa-ter that is emp-ty?"

"I wish I knew," marveled the pirate. "If I could twist my tail in the water and naturally shift to some spot a thousand leagues distant, I'd be the fattest merchant in Dominaria!"

Beckoner tilted her head, still unsure, but dismissed it. "We go. We shall vi-sit your docks once char-fish spawn a-gain. Un-til then, fare-well."

"Fare—" But Adira waved at nothing. Like a school of salmon, the merfolk dove as one into the frigid booming surf. Shuddering, Adira scampered back to the circle of life-giving fire.

* * * * *

The first thing Johan noticed was the library was well lit. Too well lit.

Plodding up circular stone stairs, he cursed both Shauku and himself. But silently, for the sorceress climbed behind, her blue skirts sweeping the steps with a silken rustle.

The harsh light in the tower's top room came not only from four tall windows, but also through the roof. A jagged hole big as a tabletop let in sunshine, fresh air, and whiffs of wood smoke. Johan saw swallows' nests wedged under roof boards.

Like the rest of Shauku's palace, the library was ruined. Rain, snow, and bird droppings had wreaked havoc. Directly under the roof hole stood a shelf of antique books. Despairing, raging, near weeping for the first time in centuries, Johan crunched across rotten wood, dry leaves, and broken roof slates. The first book he touched wore a red leather binding with gold letters. As Johan plucked the book from the shelf, the pages fell out in a mildewed heap that splatted on the floor. Silver insects scurried from the light.

"Please pardon the mess." Shauku's lyrical apology seemed genuine. "I inherited the library in this state and fear it's beyond my powers to preserve."

Steaming, Johan's red-black hands flexed to strangle the woman. Black eyes bulging, horns quivering, he gargled, "Near three hundred volumes? An untold fortune in antique lore? Likely most one of a kind? You their guardian, and you couldn't even patch the roof, nor shutter the windows, nor exterminate mice nor silverfish?"

"I am sorry." Slim and lithe, Shauku held up her skirts with one hand lest they be sullied by debris. "It's hard to keep up a castle, a woman alone."

Silence reigned as Johan fumed, then gradually calmed.

Lady Shauku seemed so helpless and frail, he couldn't bring himself to strike her. Yet part of his mind suspected everyone. Surely she concealed some fact.

"What was it you desired?" The sorceress peered about the ravaged room. "Knowledge of cat warriors?"

"Yes!" The word leaped from Johan's throat. Unwilling to show weakness, he hedged, "That is, I've discovered a small enclave that might aid a minor campaign."

"I remember." Lady Shauku touched a finger to her lips. "They were integral to the prophecy of None, One, and Two! Of course, how silly I am. Let me see."

Wanting to scream, Johan waited while his host traced a delicate golden hand along a tilted shelf. Plucking forth a slim volume, she offered it with a smile. Johan started. The book was bound in tiger skin.

Hands trembling, Johan flipped open the book, eyes devouring the pages. In careful but crude sketches, tiger-warriors lurked amid tea trees, walked on two legs and all fours, and worshipped at the altar of a brazen big-mouthed god.

Johan gibbered, "This is the source! These secrets I need, but—I can't read the runes!"

Unknown characters seemed to taunt the mage. None he'd ever seen, and he'd learned dozens in centuries of study. Hurriedly he muttered one spell, then another. If the runes were magically scrambled against casual viewing, the counterspells should decipher the mystic mask. But the crabbed text remained stubbornly illegible.

"So close! So close!"

"Perhaps I can help, if you'll allow it." Delicate in all her movements, the sorceress took a bottle from a shelf, cracked the stopper, and dabbed her slim finger in an oily ink. Poised, she waited. Johan nodded shortly.

Murmuring, or humming, Shauku painted the purple lizard-skin at Johan's breast with a glyph. Stepping a circle round her guest, she daubed more squiggles in a chain across

his chest, shoulders, and back. Johan tilted his horned chin
The glyphs were simple up- and downstrokes with curlicued
cross-bars. The ink was vitriol dissolved in linseed oil. Noth
ing looked sinister.

Yet, Johan recognized that the spell encircled his chest
heart, and head. What might it be? Enslavement? A deluding
spell? A withering curse? A brand marking him for sacrifice
An oath of undying fealty or allegiance to Shauku? Johan fel
like a steer paraded at the stockyards for auction and slaugh
ter. Worse perhaps, for while a steer would only be eaten, a
fool who bargained with a fiend might die a thousand painfu
deaths.

Still, the tyrant wasn't worried. In centuries of delving in
black arts, he'd learned precautions. He was charmed against
most curses, dosed immune to common poisons, warded
against mind-control, and even had eyes tattooed on his back
lest he be watched in secret. When needed, an impenetrable
shield of mana sprang forth to protect him, and gems in his
pockets would shriek in alarm if spell-struck. So any clumsy
sorcery Shauku might ply would fail.

"There!" Shauku raised a stained finger and gestured at the
book. "Does that signify?"

Johan opened the tiger-skin volume and caught his breath
The page read, "Tigers survive the Sukurvia in oases that
extend across the desert. Four tribes dwell within: the Efravans
Hooraree, Khyyiani, and Sulaki. Each tribe boasts nine clans
Most worship a human-shaped god named Terrent Amese
but one tribe pays homage to his rival Ergerborg. . . ."

"I've found it! Found it!" Intrigued, oblivious to his sur
roundings and host, Johan carefully turned the yellowed page
and read.

Smiling, Lady Shauku swished away, down the tower steps

Chapter 15

Whistledove Kithkin pelted hell-for-leather through the forest, red hair flying back in a wedge, little legs churning, making no effort to hide.

"Heath's taken! Men in black leather captured him!"

"Murdoch! Jedit!" ordered Adira. "Get after—"

The tiger flashed past his chief in long loping strides, sometimes on two legs, sometimes on four, bounding through the forest as others struggled to keep up. This patch of forest was a maze of boulders and brush. The break in the unending pine canopy was nice, for they could glimpse the overcast sky. On the other hand, it was perfect country for ambush.

Adira Strongheart, Simone the Siren, Sister Wilemina, Whistledove Kithkin, Sergeant Murdoch, and Jasmine Boreal trotted behind their captain. Adira limped from blistered toes. Like her crew, she was hungry, tired, aching, and unprepared for battles in the wilderness. Having survived the shipwreck, the sailors and corsairs from Buzzard's Bay had simply walked away, north toward home. Adira had forged on with their mission, marching into the dark pine forest with pirates and one tiger reluctantly tagging along. Now came ambush in unfamiliar territory by an unknown foe, and they had only a few blades and tiger claws. Adira prayed that, if anyone must be killed, let it be her for foolish pigheadedness.

A tiger's roar split the air. Between the towering pines four men carried Heath like a sack of potatoes. Queer looking enemies, thought Adira, like giant wingless wasps clad in leather armor, black and shiny from boots to pate. A hood let only a slit of eyes show, and even the faces behind had been blackened with soot. The four carried only naked slim swords and twists of black rope. Heath was bound by such a sinister thong. Why, Adira wondered, would wasplike soldiers kidnap folk? To be taken to the castle of Shauku?

Then Jedit struck, and the four soldiers got the fight of their lives.

Despite the frightening sight of an upright tiger charging, the soldiers kept their heads. Two shielded their prize captive while two fell elbow to elbow and raised their swords, one even switching to his left hand, so the blades could swing freely. The pair timed their strike perfectly—but missed.

Even running like a raging bull, Jedit was canny enough to plant his feet and skip in place. Skittering backward, the swords skimmed his belly fur. In the half-second the blades crossed, the tiger-warrior struck. Claws slashed the men's arms from shoulder to elbow. Black leather sheared, white skin parted, and red blood spurted. Jedit coiled stumpy clawed fingers around the men's elbows and yanked. Twin pops, sickening and loud, resounded as arms were yanked out of joint. The hooded men went down in a bloody tangle as Jedit vaulted over them.

One wasp-man stuck to his mission by shouldering the unconscious Heath and jogging off through the forest, naked blade pumping in one hand. The other fought a delaying tactic. Squatting with legs spread wide, the soldier cocked his sword overhead, blade flat, hand outstretched. Watching, Adira was impressed at the graceful and unassailable stance. Even the tiger was wary.

Doing the unexpected, Jedit let his feet slip to half-crash on his haunches. Pine needles were so thick he slid almost past the crouching soldier. Not wasting an opportunity, the assassin swept the sword like a scythe. Its tip would brush the carpet of needles and cut everything in its path. Yet Jedit again eschewed common sense. The tiger snap-rolled onto his belly and slapped both paws flat to lunge.

Mighty fanged jaws snapped shut on the soldier's black boot, cutting leather, tearing flesh, crushing bone. Slapping both paws again hard, Jedit jumped to his feet. Clamped in his jaws, the assassin dangled like a mouse. The man gargled as broken bones ground together, but nonetheless he swiped with his blade to slash his foe. With both arms free, Jedit walloped the man's spine with a fist like an anvil, then snagged the man's sword arm in two hands and twisted. The wrist tore free like a roast chicken wing. Jedit tossed the clenched fist and sword a dozen feet, then dropped the crippled mercenary to bleed to death.

Still running toward the fight, for the three-fold slaughter was over in seconds, even Adira Strongheart was stunned by the tiger's ferocity. But no matter.

Dashing past, she shouted, "Stop larking! Have you forgotten Heath? He's—Oh!"

Ahead, the path was crowded by tall people in leathers and furs. At their feet lay a black-clad warrior shot full of arrows as a porcupine. Lying nearby was Heath, woozy but whole. Yet perhaps a prisoner.

For a while, the pirates just stared at the natives. Many goggled at Jedit Ojanen. In the light of late afternoon, he loomed huge and terrifying as some primitive forest god. Both paws were bloody to the wrists, as was his muzzle, and he licked blood off his whiskers with a broad pink tongue.

For time to think, and because her blisters tortured, Adira plunked on her bottom and yanked off her boots. She hissed massaging all ten toes. Her good seaboots had been ruined by soaking and drying by fires. It was little things, she thought, that make or break you.

Like ghosts in a graveyard, with the patience of hunters, the foresting men and women waited. They looked so well-fed and well-armed that Adira instinctively resented them. Thin, tall, tanned, and dressed in hides and furs decorated with feathers, their faces were long and lean with slanted eyes that suggested wolves. Knotted arms looked capable of swinging their iron-headed knouts, axes, spears, and mallets. The Circle of Seven stood very still with hands in sight.

Still rubbing her toes, Adira said to Jedit, "I suppose it's too late to keep one wasp-man alive for questions."

"Legionnaires die but never surrender," quoted the woods-folk leader. More quiet. Adira was reminded of the pause between lightning and thunder.

Weary, Adira Strongheart didn't even rise, but sat with arms folded across her knees and wiggled her aching toes. "What will you have? You can keep Heath. Any scout that gets kidnapped deserves to be boiled in oil. He couldn't track a bleeding bull through a baron's ball, obviously." Heath blinked in dismay.

A woman shifted a spike to the crook of her elbow. The hardwood shaft was painted red and topped by an iron head like a whale's tooth. Her dark hair was braided tight to her head and stuck with white feathers. She wore a long oyster-white shirt with a wide belt, a mantle of silver fox, and boots wrapped with elkhide. A cased bow and quiver hung over one shoulder. She spoke in a odd low-pitched whisper.

"We are the people of the pines, and this is our land. You intrude. We demand to know where you go."

Aggravated, Adira could only think how elegant and proud the pine dwellers looked, and how she must look like a drowned muskrat. Her party had almost nothing. Adira had her twin daggers, Simone a cutlass, and the rest weapon-knives. No bows nor quivers, no canteens, no blankets, no cloaks, no pots or kettles. Not even cloaks or coats, just their sweaters and jerkins. Further, they were dirty and hungry. True, Jedit had knocked down deer, wild boar, and partridges, which they'd cooked without utensils or salt. Still, Adira's crew was ill-equipped to mount an expedition, and it showed to the natives.

Perhaps facing an addlepate, the spokeswoman tried again, still husking low, "We are the people of the pines, and we demand—"

"Yes, yes, we heard. Talk until your tongues turn blue. We have no idea where we go."

"Nor why," put in Simone.

Adira tugged on her boots with a grunt. She was being a balky bitch, she knew, but her feet hurt, and she disliked the leader's lofty tone. Adira pointed with her thumb. "Who are these black devils, and why do they capture strangers?"

"Akron Legionnaires." The leader spat the name. "They bring victims to Shauku. What she does with them we don't know, for none ever return."

Adira kept a poker face but secretly congratulated herself. Her bullheaded never-retreat forge-onward foolhardiness had brought her crew to their goal: striking distance of Shauku's castle, and hopefully, Johan. Swinging her left hand behind her, for her right was slashed and sore from the shipwreck, she accepted a sword from Simone. Like its master, the legionnaire's sword had a black leather haft and balanced blade slim as a wasp sting. Sword in hand, Adira hoped she looked more confident than she felt.

"The truth is, we hunt Shauku's castle to find an enemy. Nothing will stop us." The sword bobbed in her hand as if thirsty for blood.

Stunned silence dragged. Then came a rumbling purr in an antique accent. Natives goggled to hear a tiger talk. "The truth is, if our enemy shelters with your enemy, we have much in common. Furthermore, we heard of you folk in Buzzard's

Bay. You trade furs and timber fairly, so are unlikely to harm travelers without cause. The murdering warlord we hunt is Johan, who seeks to conquer or lay waste all of Jamuraa. He passed this way and goes, we are sure, to the castle. If we all run him down, we all benefit. May we count on your help?"

The spokeswoman husked, "A red man with black stripes who wields deadly magics?"

"That's he," said Adira.

"He wrought havoc on our scouting party. Please be our guests."

"We thank you," said Adira. "Lead on. I want to get off my fins."

With a collective sigh, the pirates stripped the black bodies of ropes and swords and, luckily for Adira, a new pair of shiny black boots. In diplomatic silence, the natives fell in front of and behind the newcomers. Walking no path, but simply between trees.

Murdoch asked low, "That's it? No fight?"

"No," said Adira Strongheart. "We've got a new pack leader. Jedit Silver-Tongue Ojanen, Harbinger of Peace and Master of the Soothing Balm. Who'd have thought such a fearsome warrior would prove an artist at diplomacy?"

Clearly chagrined by backhanded praise, the tiger quirked his muzzle, so one fang shone. Everyone laughed.

* * * * *

"Where is your camp?" asked Adira.

"Here," husked Magfire, the warchief. "And nowhere."

Adira blinked at a patch of pine forest like any other. Jedit further piqued her by purring, "Clever."

Heath stepped to one side and reached out a hand. Seeming to grope at thin air, the part-elf caught a film light as spider web. Adira saw some near-invisible cloth or webbing was strung between three trees to cover a bedroll, woven packbaskets, and some cordwood. Adira caught the gossamer. Even held against the dusky sky, the fabric took on the mixed-gray tone of overcast.

"Don't bother to ask," whispered Magfire. "We shan't share its secret."

Heath positively bubbled, a strange sight to his crewmates. "Anything! I'll give anything for a swatch of that fabric! Just enough to cover myself in full!"

"Anything?" The tall chief smiled as might a black widow spider, thought Adira. Magfire's whisper exuded sex. "To promise anything is rash, my friend. You might live to regret it."

Puzzled, Heath wrinkled his brow while his shipmates laughed. Jedit Ojanen had meanwhile moved on. The forest seemed untouched, as if humans had never existed, yet he stopped at a shallow depression littered with pine needles and tipped up another nigh-invisible cloak that covered a black-ened firepit.

Magfire whisked off the gossamer, rolled it into a ball, and tucked it in her belt. "Without our camouflage cloaks we'd be extinct."

"How do these soldiers snare your crew?" asked Jasmine. "Black leather is ill-fitted for a forest, while your people are born to the trees."

"They have traps and magics that deceive." Magfire gath-ered charcoal and tinder and struck a flint on her steel knife. "By the time we learn one peril and counter it, the legion-naires spring another."

"It's true." Heath was still sheepish about being gulled. "I detected no sign, smelt nor heard nothing. Just a blow upon the head."

"Verily," said Magfire. "Legionnaires have no smell. It's masked magically. They can see in the dark too. Detect strangers behind them, or above in trees, or screened by brush. They know each other's whereabouts at all times, so to assault one brings many running. They nab our hunters and pickets. Sometimes even trailblazers and trackers."

"What's the difference?" asked Heath. Everything this tribe did intrigued him.

"Trailblazers explore and trackers hunt. But their ranks mean more than that." Magfire fed a crackling pyre. "Either requires senses more animal than human that are honed by years of study under a master. Such blessings cannot be learned but are bestowed by the gods, born in the bone, then refined."

The Robaran Mercenaries marveled as—as if popping from the ground like mushrooms—more people of the pines filtered from the lowering dusk. Clad in leather and furs, with many cowled by the heads of animals, the gathering seemed like herds of ghost animals. The eerie picture was compounded because the woods dwellers trod silently and conversed in whispers. The pirates had to lean close whenever a pinesman spoke. Up close they exhaled a blend of pine sap, tannin, sweat, and juniper. Low voices and earthy spice gave an air of intimacy that was dizzying.

Over fifty natives and guests congregating made the gloomy woods almost homey. Hunters had fetched three deer on poles, as well as a bundle of grouse, fat raccoons, and opossums. Others brought beechnuts, walnuts, mushrooms, and other scomber. A cheery fire crackled in the firepit as night settled, though the flames were kept low.

"Won't Shauku's soldiers spot your fire by night?"

"Legionnaires never venture out by night. They're not that good. And we move camp often," explained Magfire.

"Good idea," said Adira. "I saw them fight Jedit. They're top-notch soldiers, all right. Practiced killers. They'd cut us to pieces going toe-to-toe."

"Something we avoid," admitted Magfire.

Warchief and pirate captain sat side by side on cloaks to eat. The pirates devoured anything handed to them. Afterward the natives passed around some fiery liquor in gourds. Even Sergeant Murdoch and Adira Strongheart lost their breath at a long pull. Yet no one got rowdy, for the natives never spoke above a whisper, even tipsy, and shushed any pirate noise.

"Where are you from?" asked Adira.

"The heights of the southern forest." Magfire accepted a gourd and sucked down a draught that made her wheeze. "This was our land decades ago. But a great disaster drove us out. Too, a monster haunted the forest."

"Monster?" Adira jolted, unsure she'd heard right. "What sort of monster?"

"What?" Magfire lost the topic and found another. "Then an old man in our village in the south began to speak. He'd been mute and senile for years. Now he talked incessantly about reclaiming our heritage, our lost homeland. The time of prophecy neared, the time of None, One, and Two."

"Song of the Sea King!" Adira swayed on the cloak and almost tipped over. "Not that again! Hazezon uncorked that bottle! It's mackerel tripe! I don't know why I married him!.."

"We swore an oath upon the war post in our village." Magfire slurred on. "Painted it red with our own blood! But when we got here, we found Shauku infested the ruins. That's where the disaster sprang from, you see. Long ago . . . Curse them all! No legionnaires will push us from our land! We will drive her and them out, on my honor!"

Both blabbed, drinking steadily. Then a voice by Adira's elbow asked, "So you venture farther afield than just Buzzard's Bay?"

"Uh, beg your pardon?" Muzzy, Adira turned toward the new speaker, who'd sat for hours without saying a word. He had a lean face and neat brown beard, and wore a homespun tan shirt, leather kilt and leggings, a hood and cowl thrown back, and on his chest, a neatly stitched wolf's head.

"My brother, Taurion," slurred Magfire. "He finds our forest confining, though it stretches a thousand leagues."

Taurion waited quietly for an answer. Addled by liquor, Adira babbled to the brother, "Uh, yes, we sail the Sea of Serenity and beyond. Past the Onyx Bridge thrice, south of Albatross Alley, and uh, elsewhere. Anywhere water will run under our keel! Why do you—"

A distraction intruded. A flash of white caught Adira's eye. Squinting across rippling firelight, she realized it was Murdoch's bare belly. A woodswoman tossed his shirt to the night, then flopped on his chest to smother him with kisses. Simone the Siren laughed amid a circle of admiring men and one woman who stroked her limbs. Jasmine Boreal whispered in Heath's ear, or else chewed on it, while a pine-dwelling woman slid her hands under his shirt. Whistledove Kithkin rode a man's shoulders, giggling. Murdoch hoisted over his head a laughing lithe woman and bellowed like a bull, but was hushed by passionate kisses. Even Jedit Ojanen received affection, lying alongside the fire while four woman rubbed his belly. Many woodsfolk had slipped away in pairs.

"But we just met." The thought struck Adira funny. She giggled and couldn't stop. Suddenly a black shape eclipsed the campfire. Under her butchered blonde mop, Sister Wilemina was white-faced and sweating. The archer had borrowed a bow, though her right arm was still cradled in a sling.

"A-adira, I v-volunteer to st-stand guard!" Then she bolted into the night. Taurion had also departed in silence.

"What distresses the girl?" mumbled Magfire.

"She's a—what do you call it—a virgin, dedicated to some goddess. I forget who." Adira took another pull of the scorching liquor. "You certainly are friendly people! What *is* this stuff?"

"Pulque from a highland cactus," Magfire gabbled. "And herbs. Lobelia and verbena to excite passion, ginger to make women fertile, zigiberis to make men virile."

"Love philters! That explains it!" Waving a hand, Adira slopped drink down her ample cleavage.

"Allow me." Magfire twisted and planted her face in Adira's bosom, lapping up liquor.

"Whoa!" Squawking, the pirate queen sprawled backward in pine needles. Magfire followed. The woman's hair was stippled with white feathers, giving her a bizarre birdlike intensity. Chuckling, she smothered Adira with a burning, throaty, drunken kiss. Gasping, snorting for air, Adira at first gave in. But as Magfire's tongue intruded into her mouth, the pirate queen bucked and tossed the chief aside.

In her husky whisper, lips inches from Adira's, Magfire said, "I should have warned you. Our tribe is too closely related to interbreed. We count on outsiders for our blanket-wrestling."

"This outsider isn't breeding with anyone!" Shaking her wobbly head, shedding pine needles, Adira Strongheart tried to clamber to her feet. Five men helped her rise, hands floating everywhere. Adira's traitorous loins tingled and itched with lust—whether the feeling was magical or natural seemed beside the point. She mumbled, "Ship your oars, you octopuses! I don't—"

"Alarm! Rouse! Alarm! Someone's killed!"

Wilemina's shouting electrified the camp. Men and women scrambled upright, some only half-dressed but all clutching weapons.

Panting, the archer pointed west with her borrowed bow. "Two folks are dead, eaten alive! They're covered with a furry moss such as I've never seen!"

"Spuzzem." Magfire shrugged aright her belt and silver fox mantle, and picked up her iron spike. "It's too late, but show me."

"Drag your anchor!" Adira grabbed the black-hilted sword of the legionnaires, which she had to carry naked for lack of a scabbard, and in her left hand. "What was that word? Spuzzem?"

Without answering, Magfire trotted after Wilemina. Jedit Ojanen launched after on all fours, silent on pine needles.

Adira Strongheart jogged too, though her brain throbbed and stomach churned. Running helped sweat out the poisons, and gradually she felt better. Fighting suited her better than loving, she thought bitterly.

Sister Wilemina stopped at two mossy logs. Jedit snuffled the air and curdled his muzzle. Magfire bent over the forms but did not touch. Adira approached and gagged.

Not mossy logs, but the remains of two lovers who'd slipped away from the party. They might have lain here for years. Covered in a fuzzy gray moss or mold, their mouths hung open in horror, teeth and tongues sprouting velvet. The pair looked like something dredged from the sea. Their bellies and loins were gaping cavities.

"The spuzzem." Magfire tapped the red-hafted spike against her hand. "It eats guts and leaves the rest. These two wandered too far from the fire."

"What is it?" rumbled Jedit. "This spuzzem?"

"No one knows." Magfire scanned the dark woods. "It's haunted our forest since the disaster. It preys on elk and other animals. And us. It has no head."

"No head?" asked Adira.

"None. It comes and goes like fog, and we cannot track it. Some think it can't be killed at all, that it's an avatar of the forest. It can't be killed by spears or arrows, we know, for heroes have hurled missiles into it in times past. Too, anyone who comes too close writhes in terror. The pixies say—"

"Pixies?" chirped half a dozen.

The warchief scratched her braided scalp where small white feathers jutted, then changed the subject. "We'll break camp. You need to see the castle."

Turning abruptly, Magfire strode back toward camp. Pirates jogged to catch up. Adira nodded over her shoulder. "What about those two?"

Magfire said only, "You live, you die, you feed the forest,

you're reborn, you do it all over again. Such is life in Arboria."

Without further ado, they quit the camp. Fires were snuffed and watered, and pine needles raked back. All other traces were smoothed over.

The pirates were armed. The people of the pines had generously shared supplies. Adira, Simone, Murdoch, and Wilemina had the captured legionnaires' swords. Raw deer hide made scabbards and baldrics tied with the black slave ropes. Heath and Wilemina, despite her broken arm, were given bows and precious hand-made arrows, for which the archers were slavishly grateful until they realized they were property of the dead souls lying eaten in darkness. Whistledove, too tall for a sword, borrowed one of Adira's matched daggers. Jasmine Boreal accepted a bronze knife and magic oddments from the tribe's shaman. Too, they were given wool blankets traded from Buzzard's Bay, water gourds, food satchels woven from hemp, and other small effects, but none received the gossamer camouflage cloaks. Only Jedit received nothing, for he needed nothing. Armed and outfitted, the pirates felt ready for anything.

Yet in packing to go, Adira missed Virgil and Peregrine. For the first time, Adira wondered if Virgil had family, a mother, brothers and sisters. For that matter, she knew little about all her Circle. There was never enough time, it seemed, to become friends. Lately her life raced helter-skelter like a skiff before a typhoon.

* * * * *

"It's the bearers, milord. They're afraid."

Johan only glared at his captain of bodyguards. For the first time, the Tyrant of Tirras gave thought to his entourage and the discomforts they endured. The castle was drear. The Akron Legionnaires shunned the Tirran soldiers as inferiors and warned that any peasants who set foot in the great hall would be cut down without mercy. So Johan's porters, bodyguards, seer, lesser mage, barbarian bearers and others camped in the moldy cellar of a decrepit tower without windows or proper chimney. Only the huntsman and two porters had permission to leave the castle grounds to hunt food, and the cook and helper to fetch firewood. Thus the entourage kept a house cramped and cold and miserable. In nine days the Tirrans had grown haggard and haunted. Not that Johan cared about their comfort, but sick troops and porters would hinder his efforts to leave when he wished.

"I fear the barbarians might bolt by night, Your Grace," said the Tirran captain. "If they desert, you'd be stranded."

"Ah." That interested the emperor.

As night fell, the two stood before the empty doorway of the crumbling tower. Johan had found almost two dozen volumes intact, and he studied daily. Arcane lore swirled in his mind like dust devils. He'd read so many spells and remedies and potions and histories that the real world was becoming a blur. Yet so much seemed familiar. Finding information on the cat warriors had thrilled him at first, but the more he read, the less he seemed to know. How could that be? Such confusion felt queer.

Just as odd as dining with Lady Shauku last evening. A gracious host, the liege lord invited him to sup each night. The emperor was not much for social graces, preferring the company of his own mind, yet he conceded to keep his privileges in Shauku's fabulous library. Every night the two wizards sat under the stars in the ruin of the great hall and talked of magical lore, though they ate barely enough to keep a pigeon alive. Johan found the conversations bland and unhelpful, but he suffered in silence. Even last night, when both had sat in an ugly slanting rain tinged with sleet, both pretending the weather was delightful. Worrisome, Johan reflected. *He* was not mad. . . .

"Milord?"

Jedit

Frustrated and disturbed, Johan forced himself to attend his captain's wishes. "Summon the bearers."

Rounding the tower, the captain drove the barbarians before Johan with blows and curses. The sullen hulks stood slack-armed and loose-jawed. Short tusks glowed yellow in fading light. Dumbly they awaited orders.

Johan frowned. Like all his minions, the barbarians were dressed in the imperial uniform, a linen tunic painted with the four-pointed star that represented Johan's skull. Yet each northman had added new designs to the sigils, so one bore a yellow glyph, one a white, one red, and one green.

"Who ordered those devices painted?" demanded the tyrant.

"Milord?" The Tirran captain squinted at the uniforms. "Uh, you did, milord."

"Of course I did," snapped Johan, "but I recollect no additional devices be painted atop my star. They are not provosts nor zephyr captains nor any other elite force."

"Of course not, milord." Stupefied, the captain fell back on simple agreement.

Johan frowned deeper. Why this insolence? He shook his horned head, promising to address it later. Bad enough Johan himself was painted with Shauku's weird glyphs in a chain around his shoulders.

Raising a lank hand, Johan waved the barbarians to the tumbledown gates of Shauku's castle. Both gatehouses were mere heaps of rocks rife with weeds and briars. Bidding the men stop, Johan reached out with deceptive gentleness and touched each on a tusk, fuddling the brutes mightily. Touching his own teeth, Johan duckwalked while his charmed hand sketched a line in the grass and weeds where once had stood iron-barred gates.

Rising, Johan gestured to the outside world. "Leave. If you dare."

The four men grunted, flummoxed, but too looked at

freedom hungrily. Finally, snorting through thick nostrils, one stepped forward.

And, crossing the invisible line, immediately collapsed.

Howling, shrieking, the barbarian thrashed amid briars in unspeakable agony. His mates stared goggle-eyed as the interloper curled in a ball from pain. The victim seemed distorted. His fingers knotted and splayed, his arms dislocated, his legs contorted as if he suffered rickets and crippling arthritis. Sobbing, begging for mercy, the northman tossed like a child in nightmare. Johan ordered the remaining three to grab their companion. As they did, their fingers twisted and knotted, so they howled until they'd pulled their comrade over the invisible line, where all quieted.

Touching a tooth, Johan explained, "One's teeth are the only visible part of one's skeleton. I touched your tusks, each one, and laid a curse. Step over the line, and every bone in your body will curve and flex until it snaps. You'll not leave the castle grounds until I allow it. Do you understand? Good."

Leaving them to sweat and squirm, Johan turned to his captain. Again he frowned. Standing alongside the officer was a greyhound. Holding onto the dog's collar sat a white monkey with luminous golden eyes.

"Whose pets?" demanded the master. "Do they belong to the legionnaires? Or Lady Shauku?"

"Pets, milord?"

"Yes!" snarled Johan. "Are you deaf as well as blind? This dog—"

The mage blinked. Dog and monkey were gone.

Johan watched the captain's face swell like an overripe melon. The man's eyes bulged. Red veins throbbed in his forehead. Abruptly, both eyes popped from their sockets like corks from a bottle. The ghastly orbs hung by their nerves down the man's cheeks, yet the captain seemed oblivious.

"Captain . . ." For the first time in ages, Johan felt a faint stirring of terror. "Captain, your eyes . . ."

"Eyes, milord?" The man's dangling eyeballs bounced as the man's lips moved. Still swelling, the orbs exploded into gobs of white-red goo. Yet the captain never flinched. "Wh-what about them, Your Grace?"

Without answering, Johan reached with a cold hand. He touched warm cheeks dappled by sweat, not ichor. Two healthy blue eyes stared back. Johan glanced at the bearers. The colored glyphs painted on their breasts had disappeared.

Sipping air through his regal eagle's nose, Johan pondered. He remembered the sigils now. He'd seen them in a book. Too, he remembered a domination spell illustrated with a saluki, a greyhound. And a potency spell sporting a white monkey. And a spell to blind a foe at a distance.

Why hallucinations?

Then, a jarring thought: perhaps he *was* mad.

Gingerly Johan touched the glyphs painted on his lizard-skin robe. Rather than the paint flaking off, it had etched the purple hide stark as a cattle brand. A badge of servitude, a yoke. Affecting his mind, altering his very thoughts, inducing bizarre daymares.

Shauku's doing. As tyrant, Johan had enthralled enough servants to see the pattern. Now was too late to prevent it. Fear knotted his stomach. Would he only be enslaved or be reduced to a drooling moron, the castle fool, the village idiot?

Time, Johan thought, to learn more about his mysterious host, and gain a hold upon *her*.

Chapter 16

Come late evening, in the privacy of the ravaged library, Johan uttered a spell to render himself invisible.

More than invisible, actually—intangible. He uttered another spell while swiping his hands down his body to mask his smell, the sound of his breathing, the rustling of robes, even any footprints he might make. Padding down the stairs and entering the passage to the great hall, Johan knew he'd succeeded when the Akron Legionnaire didn't even stir.

Behind Lady Shauku's open-air great hall, Johan discovered the kitchen roof intact, in fact cozy with a low roof and working fireplace, though the walls were stained and a window overgrown by vines. Two yellow-skinned boys in yellow tunics without emblems, no doubt cadets, polished boots by the fire. The walls were hung with soldierly gear, and off the kitchen, in what had been a pantry or larder, Johan saw bunks and heard snores.

Passing through the kitchen, the emperor descended a flight of circular stairs that must sink to the wine cellar. That, Johan reasoned, was the only place Lady Shauku could live. Down, around, and down he sank in absolute silence. Everywhere were signs of rot: mildew, water stains, crumbled mortar, and dust. A putrid smell of rotted flesh and offal assailed Johan's nostrils, though he was rarely fussy. How could Lady Shauku endure the odor?

At the bottom of the stairs, he found two stone-lined rooms. One room was black and reeked of an ancient sweet-sour smell of spilled wine even above the reek of death. The other chamber was small and illuminated by a single candle. Empty barrels stood or lay about. One had staves cut low on one side to fashion a chair. In the chair slept the lovely Lady Shauku, wrapped in a tattered robe that seemed faded to no color at all. She looked as out of place as a rare flower in a garbage heap.

Searching, Johan found a barrel with the top stove in and a bunghole in one side. Carefully he climbed inside and sat—and waited. After centuries of study and scheming and waiting for long-term plans to come to fruition, Johan had patience in abundance. He could easily wait all night and day, if necessary, to learn Shauku's secrets.

The invisibility spell faded, though Johan sat in darkness.

Time passed. Eventually a rustling like a snake over autumn leaves bespoke Shauku stirring. Peering through the bunghole, Johan watched the lady drop her hard-to-see sleeping robe and glide out the door. Where to?

Slipping over the barrel's edge, Johan started to follow, then recalled the queer color-shifting robe. It lay on the floor. In pale candle light, Johan could barely see it, thinking it gray. But as he picked it up, for a second it burned black. The fold in his hand took the color of his red-black skin. The tail of the robe looked like wood and stone. When Johan draped it against his lizard-skin robe, it shone pale purple. A curious and handy rag. Why would the sorceress sleep in this robe? To hide? From what? Or for some other reason?

Knowledge came with risks, the sorcerer knew. Wrapping the robe about his shoulders, he sat in the barrel throne to see what happened.

Nothing.

The cellar remained silent. The robe smelled of dust and mold and a snaky musk. Waiting, the minutes dragging, Johan dozed.

And dreamed.

Darkness was shot with a million stars. Lights pinwheeled to describe slow spirals. Stars shone white, blue, red, yellow, orange, infinitesimally small against the black fabric of night. Shooting stars sizzled like single-minded fireflies. Dust motes and boulders pinged on a crowded plateau. Monsters crouched, jammed together, thick as grasses on a prairie, until not an inch of soil remained uncovered, until not one single beast could send a quivering tendril in any direction but upward. Noise bubbled. Roars and hoots and squawls and bellows rose to the heavens in a cacophonous chorus that never ceased. Everywhere pressed a crushing bruising shivering desire to be free, separate, alone, unbound. Then a lurching explosion erupted into the sky.

Startling awake, Johan jumped from the barrel throne and shed the robe. Sweat ran down his face and ribs for the first time in centuries. A dream coat, he realized. But what mad realm of Dominaria did it portray, if a real world at all? And what did Lady Shauku glean from it?

Shaking, Johan quit the chamber. The opposite room was pitchy. Shauku had not ascended the stairs so must have passed within. Uttering a short spell, Johan adjusted his vision to see in darkness. Four wooden tuns big as hayricks were cradled in a frame against the wall. Johan thumped the ends, but all proved hollow. A few minutes' probing and prodding sprung the latch hidden on the last tun. The end swung inward on a wooden hinge. Steep stairs led down to a cave mouth. Immediately Johan was washed by the unmistakable stink of rotten flesh.

For a moment the emperor hesitated. But knowledge was the key to power. Girding his loins, Johan descended.

* * * * *

Not far away . . .

A faint moan and a demented gibbering wafted up from a different cave. The explorers stopped cold in their tracks.

Pirates and pine folk were shielded from sight by a jumble of rocks and scruffy birches and brush. Before them, a vertical slit of cave infiltrated the hill under Shauku's castle. As from many such fissures, smoke trickled out and rose into a light evening rain.

"These are the Caverns of Despair, I tell you. They're haunted. We shouldn't venture within." Magfire shifted her red-hafted spike from hand to hand. Her brother Taurion, the quick-handed Kyenou, and four more woods warriors were just as shaky.

"The Akron Legionnaires pass within," countered Adira. "You said they cut trees and haul them down into the caves on the far side of this hill. The smoke speaks of fires, for whatever purpose. But if the soldiers can enter—"

"They enjoy protection from the sorceress," said Magfire. "We don't."

"Then leave." Adira and Magfire hadn't gotten along ever since Magfire's burning kiss both aroused and disturbed Adira. Both bullheaded and used to command, the two leaders chafed like ship and shore. Adira faced the cave mouth and stroked her hands alight with a firefly glow.

"*Ah-shist!* Ghosts can't make me weigh anchor. Harmless as jellyfish. They're not even there, just echoes of the past. And Magfire, recall the bulk of your fighters should be pinking the legionnaires as a diversion. You can't leave them hung out to dry. Circle of Seven, follow in my wake."

Sniffing, Adira Strongheart entered the cave with her cold blue light. Four others bore torches. Despite their leader's brave words, the pirates were also spooked. Jasmine Boreal,

Heath, Sergeant Murdoch, Simone the Siren, Whistledove, and Sister Wilemina clustered like children in a graveyard as they scuffled in darkness. Only Jedit Ojanen strode tall and aloof, sniffing at the dim depths.

Voice low, he rumbled, "Something dwells below besides ghosts. I smell dead flesh, and wood smoke, but too a queer metallic tang. A great amount of it."

"I've a question." Jasmine was never one to knuckle to authority, but she whispered. "Where do we hope to arrive?"

"Somewhere under the castle," hissed Adira over her shoulder. Darkness and quiet pressed all around. Their boots crunched old leaves and pebbles in a slow descent. "Somewhere a passage must lead upward. If so, we'll root out Johan and kill him. This passage is unguarded."

"By the living," squeaked Wilemina.

"You cowards!" Adira whirled to face her followers. "You crawfishing eels! Dare call yourself pirates? I've never seen such a white-livered gutless bunch of backsliding bone-headed bream in all my years at sea. . . . What are you gawking at?"

The party just goggled at the vision past Adira's shoulder. Slowly she turned. In torchlight and magic illumination hung a rag of black curtain suspended on nothing. As the invaders watched, the spectral rag opened a jagged mouth and gave a long strangled sigh.

Adira couldn't jump quick enough to catch her crew. Pirates whirled and smacked into foresters, then all the heroes bolted headlong up the tunnel. Not until they clattered out under the dripping sky did they stop running, though all were canny enough to keep down and quiet.

Even Adira was puffing and rattled. Things undead that cried in her face were a new experience.

"Forget it, Dira!" gasped Murdoch. "We'll fight anything alive, but the dead are too eager for company!"

"It's ill luck!" squeaked Jasmine. "To look upon the face of death invites one's own!"

"We can find some other way inside the castle!" pleaded Sister Wilemina. "We can scale the walls or skulk in by night. We needn't crawl through an unquiet graveyard!"

"It's Johan we're after," cautioned Heath. "Mayhaps we could lure him outside the walls!"

"I'll clear the way," purred Jedit.

"Eh?" Even Adira was taken aback. "Why you?"

"Human ghosts don't frighten me." The cat's amber-green eyes glowed like emeralds.

"Oh, no?" snipped Adira. Rain spotted her nose and she swiped with a filthy hand. "Or is this your chance to seize command?"

"Dira, I have no ambitions upon your position." The tiger remained calm. "I just aid as I might. As when I rescued you from the shipwreck."

That fact had no answer, so Jedit added, "I'll call when I think it safe."

"Take your time," murmured Murdoch. "A week. A month."

"Shut up, soldier," snarled Adira. To Jedit, "Carry on. Don't just seek ghosts. Anything could lurk within. Beware things with paws and teeth."

The tiger passed into the dark depths. Pirates and pinefolk took a much-needed rest amid wet brush.

The tunnel twisted between fractured rocks, and many stones had tumbled and had to be climbed, but the tiger sensed someone had cleared the path in years past. Jedit clambered on two or all fours easily as a mountain goat. Several times he paused, for the darkness was so perfect even his cat eyes had trouble seeing. More than once Jedit felt a damp chill on his muzzle as he blundered through a ghost. Farther along, the feeling became more distinct, as if he waded through mist. When cold enveloped him like a shroud, he stopped and perched on a rock, tail crooked around his ankle, and waited to see what happened.

So many shades gathering in one spot brought their own

luminosity until the chill air twinkled with a twilight glow. Gradually the cat made out five, then nine, then too many floating shapes to count. Sitting unmoving, Jedit Ojanen watched ghosts hover like a flock of fireflies. He felt no terror, only a great sadness emanating from them. Some ghosts looked fresh, almost healthy, as if only dead a week, and Jedit guessed they were foresters. Some were hideous with broken necks, smashed ribs, or missing heads altogether. Others were withered as mummies or parched to skeletons. Still others, infinitely ancient, had disincorporated into black rags. Some of the dead wore clothes and some went naked. None wore shrouds that would denote a proper funeral. These disinherited souls, or victims, had died by murder. Helpless, they lingered in this world hoping for justice, restless and angry, refusing the notion of eternal death.

Having lived once, the shades could communicate, if one could bear to listen. Stone-still, Jedit tuned his ears. The ghosts voiced their sorrow in low gibberings or shrill keens or strangled moans. Many muttered the same angry phrases over and over.

". . . revenge. Give us revenge. Give us . . ."

" . . . Shauku. Shauku. Shauku. . . ."

"Shauku killed you all?" asked Jedit abruptly.

Like slamming a door, the windy whispering stopped.

Jedit weighed his words. The man-tiger knew nothing of the castle's lord except her name, but clearly she had many cruel deeds to answer for.

"Friends," he addressed the hovering mob, "we march against Johan, who marches against all Jamuraa. Johan is a guest of Shauku, and that fact alone condemns her, as does your presence. Friends, I promise you—and no one swears lightly a pact with the dead—if you let us pass in quietude, we'll do our best to punish Shauku."

He waited for an answer. None came. Except the eldritch

light of the shades faded. Jedit squinted into blackness, strained his ears in silence. Finally the tiger pushed off from his rock and padded silently up the twisted tunnel.

Pirates and woodsfolk had neither retreated nor progressed an inch. They sat bug-eyed and jumpy, staring at the dark cave. The tiger scuffed his claws to not alarm them.

Adira lifted her chin. "Well?"

"I negotiated," drawled the tiger. "The shades suffered at Shauku's hands. They'll withdraw if we exact vengeance upon her."

Rather than grow angry, Adira sighed. "That's a hell of a posture for pirates and mercenaries. If we set out to unseat every despot in Dominaria, we'll never have a day's rest and will chew through crews like spotted plague."

"If necessary," purred Jedit. "I'll enact revenge myself, for t'was I who swore the oath."

"No, no. We're shipmates." Adira rose and waved a glowing hand. "Proceed, Master Diplomat. We follow you."

"Hold," said Magfire. Everyone turned, squinting in rain, breath steaming. The warchief said, "If this is the big push, it's time to call in *all* our warriors."

Digging in a pouch, Magfire produced a thin bone whistle, then faced the forest and blew a triplet piping. People waited, puzzled. Then Jasmine gasped.

Winging from the trees, flying jerky as drunken bats, came two pixies. They perched on a birch tree, clinging to the bark with a hand and bare foot like sailors on a ratline. Their wings pulsed slowly as if puffed by invisible winds. Adira and her crew goggled and dared not move lest the tiny creatures spook. They were tall as a man's forearm with pale skin and green-blond hair yanked back and tied. They wore mole and rabbit skins. Tiny bangles or else tattoos decorated their arms and bare legs. Most startling were their intelligent, luminous green eyes that reminded the pirates of merfolk.

Magfire talked low in an unknown tongue to the fairies, who stared big-eyed without speaking. One asked a question in a high-pitched squeak like a bat's, waggling a hand the size of a dandelion blossom. Tribeswoman and pixies came to some agreement, and the two made to fly.

Whistledove Kithkin surprised everyone by asking a question in the same squeaking tones. Magfire looked peeved. One pixie spilled a long half-singing speech like bird song. Whistledove smiled and nodded.

"What did you ask?" asked Adira.

Shy, the redheaded brownie blushed. "I just asked if they knew someone I know."

"Have they names?" breathed Jasmine. The druid couldn't take her eyes off the pixies.

"Oh, yes. The smaller one is Sacred Tree, the larger Peaceflower."

"Let's get on." Magfire thumped her red-hafted spike in one hand.

Trooping silently, following buzzing pixies, the party trekked deep into the hill. They saw no ghosts. Wary of horrors, most missed the change.

Heath was first to notice. "Does it grow hotter?"

Everyone stopped. Jedit sniffed, "Fire ahead."

"Wood fires," said Adira. "For whatever our murderous sorceress cooks."

Farther on the tunnel fractured into four or five paths. Adira asked the way and Jedit pointed unerringly. Abruptly a questing pixie swooped over some boulders, chattering and pointing. Instinct primitive as a kitten's made Jedit pounce before he even recognized prey. Arching twelve feet in the red-lit tunnel, he landed with a slam behind the boulders. Something squeaked and bleated like mice. Jedit leaped, swiped, nabbed, stamped and came up holding by the ankles three creatures who punched and shrilled.

Jabbering, kicking, whining, shrieking captives the size of

half-grown children had gray-purple skin, big noses, bald heads, and short fangs. They wore rags and squabbled incessantly. The tiger bounced them on the boulders. Half-stunned, they subsided.

Magfire and her foresters gawked. "What are those?"

"Paint me pink!" snorted Sergeant Murdoch. "Kobolds!"

"Yes, kobolds!" blared a toothy shrimp. "We rule these caves, lords of all life, terrors to any who venture into our domain! We're the most feared of the fiercest tribes that range from the Blue Mountains to the Sukurvia!"

"So," added another kobold, "seeing as how we're feared and all, could you hold us heads up? My nose is stuffing up!"

"Do you have any food?" asked the third.

"Hush, you boobies." Adira pulled a dagger and tapped a bony head. "How many kobolds live under this hill?"

"Um . . ." Still upside-down, one held up eight fingers, all he had. "This many."

"He's lying," said Murdoch.

"How do you know?" asked the pirate queen.

"He's a kobold," replied the ex-sergeant. "I once tried to drill some. An insane plan of some shah. We finally prodded the beggars over to the enemy. You can't get a straight answer without a threat. Cut one's ear off to start."

"*Waak!*" All three kobolds waggled fingers in the air. "This many! No, this many! No, he's a liar!"

"How live you under this hill?" put in Magfire. "My tribe lived in this region for generations, and we never saw any kobolds."

"We don't like the sun!" gabbled one. They looked much alike, skin so muddy gray-purple they seemed bruised from head to toe. In firelight they squinted with deep piggy eyes past huge warty noses.

"What are your names?" asked Taurion.

"Dog Ears!"

"Pink Eye!"

"Biscuit Tooth!"

"You're not Biscuit Tooth!" carped the first kobold.

"Am so!"

With a long arm, Jedit swung the kobolds in a screaming circle to get their attention. He growled, "Answer truthfully or else."

"Or else what?" squawked the most fidgety one.

The tiger grabbed a scrawny neck, opened a mouth full of fearsome fangs, and shoved the unfortunate's head in.

Voice muffled, the captive shrieked, "All right, all right! We'll answer!" Jedit spat out the troublemaker's head.

"If we do," asked a second captive, "will you let us go?"

"Do I look like a fool?" growled the tiger. "We owe you no mercy. You inhabit the domain of our enemy. Answer right, or I'll gnaw a leg off each of you."

"Hang on," said Magfire. "They didn't answer my question. How came you to these caves?"

"We were fetched here," said the middle quibbler. "By magic."

"We didn't want to come," said the third. "We're peaceable. We love our enemies! All of them!"

"If you live here," asked Taurion, "what do you eat?"

"Pig!"

"Cattle!"

"Rats! I mean, pumpkins," they chorused.

"Who fetched you here?" insisted Magfire. "And why?"

"Mistress," answered the first.

"Who's that?" asked the second.

"Yellow Lady, you stupid picknose!" One kobold slapped another and sparked a flurry of smacks and curses. It ended as Jedit spun them in another sweeping circle.

"Lady Shauku?" asked Magfire. "Why call her the Yellow Lady?"

"She's yellow."

Silence.

Taurion rubbed his beard. "You, what's your name?"

"Prince."

That hadn't been one of the original names, but Taurion let it go. "You never leave the caves. So what do you eat?"

More silence. Hanging inverted, kobolds stared at the walls and floor like naughty children.

Magfire raged, "Kill them!"

"What?" asked Adira. "Why?"

"They eat our dead!"

"How do you know? Wait!"

The warchief swung her iron spike in a vicious arc. Kobolds screamed and covered their heads. Jedit swung them aside as Adira blocked Magfire and Taurion snagged his sister's arm. Vainly he tried to shush her.

"Our scouts and warriors disappear into the castle!" shouted Magfire. In flickering torchlight her face was strained and ugly. "They never return, none of them! Their corpses are never found! So these little wretches—"

"Belay!" Adira Strongheart still blocked Magfire. "We're not finished asking questions!"

"All you'll get is lies!" Magfire's bosom heaved under her long wool shirt, seething with anger. "We should stave in their skulls and throw their carcasses into Shauku's courtyard."

"Fine idea!" retorted Adira. "Tell the enemy we've penetrated under her castle! Would you pipe down and think? It's bally lucky your tribesmen have survived this long, if you go bulling headlong into every fracas."

Abruptly Magfire rammed her palm against Adira's breastbone, nearly toppling the pirate. Only Taurion, trapping her arm, kept Adira from being smitten with lethal iron.

Magfire rasped, "You criticize my leadership? I'll kill you in single combat!"

"You pigheaded pelican!" retorted Adira. "Save it for Shauku."

Pirates and woodsfolk stirred, some hands drifting to

weapons. Still clutching the kobolds, Jedit Ojanen wedged his bulk between the two women. Silence crackled and spat like the finicky birch-bark torches.

"Sister." Taurion was surprisingly mild. "Before we proceed, may I ask a few more questions of our prisoners? Any knowledge we gain aids our quest to oust Shauku."

Miraculously, the fiery Magfire backed off before her brother. Huffing and glaring, she stuffed her iron-headed spike in her belt and plunked on a boulder. Adira's mercenaries marveled at Taurion's diplomacy. The trailblazer only scratched his chest above his wolf-mask and concentrated on interrogating the enemy.

Calm and persistent, listening intently with a dash of sympathy, Taurion actually elicited some useful answers. The kobolds had lived in these caves for several of their generations, though they were short-lived and couldn't express the time in years. Lady Shauku, an archmage, had magically summoned the kobolds to tend fires. Sometimes, the trio said, when they behaved, kobolds were shifted home and exchanged for brethren. They had no idea where lay the Blue Mountains, had no concept of being near the western coast of Jamuraa. That these caves were warm and offered food contented them. Taurion gently steered around their ghoulish cannibalism. The kobolds told the truth because it was easier, and they weren't punished. They were simple as untutored children but capable of viciousness if let off the leash.

Taurion asked, "Why do you maintain the fires?"

"We're guards," piped all three.

"Talk about pitiful defenses," muttered Murdoch.

"What do you guard?" asked Taurion patiently.

"The crying horror."

The adventurers pricked their ears.

"It's big and ugly and chopped up," said a prisoner.

"It fell from the sky."

"It cries all the time. Not out loud. In your head."

Pirates and pinefolk goggled. Taurion asked for details, but the kobolds couldn't explain.

"I'm more confused than ever," said Murdoch. "What kind of a thing falls from the sky?"

"I don't know," said Adira, "but we'll find out. You three. Show us."

* * * * *

Johan's journey into the caves beneath Shauku's castle showed at once his personal bravery and his thirst for knowledge, for both were sorely tested as he descended short wooden stairs within the sham wine tun.

His first warning was a smell so awful it made his nostrils cringe and his head ache. The air was already ripe with eye-watering wood smoke, but worse was a stench that carried like a slaughterhouse, the corruption of carrion.

Below the wine cellar ran a dim catacombs, no more than a craggy rambling tunnel. Bolted to two walls were chains with manacles but no prisoners.

A shriek welled up from the darkness beyond.

A victim? Of Lady Shauku?

Chiding himself for squeamishness, Johan girded his loins and took another step in his bare feet. He had to see Shauku's secret source of knowledge, learn more of whatever she glimpsed when donning the dream coat. It lay ahead, Johan guessed, or hoped. He had to go on. Still invisible, almost intangible, Johan crept forward toward a dim flickering light.

As he crept along, one hand brushed the dusty walls. Odd walls, he found, that grew stranger with each step. So queer was the substance, Johan stopped to investigate where two walls intersected at a shallow angle. With a flint-hard fingernail he shaved silver-gray stuff from a doorway. It wasn't stone but was soft as chestnut wood. Holding it to his eye, Johan saw the sliver was veined like skin with a delicate webbing.

Surely, thought the mage, that couldn't be right. The veins had to be tracks of old vines or water stains, even cracks of metallic flaking. Stepping to another oddly-angled wall, he scraped another sliver. The same. Marveling, Johan drilled a thumb through the porous not-stone. Not soapstone, not wood, not glass, so what was it? Shaking his head, the mage realized he was truly puzzled for the first time in decades.

All the walls were made of this not-stone material. Whence had they come?

That answer, at least, was simple. The ruined castle was built atop even more ancient ruins of . . . ?

Shaking his head, Johan passed on.

Finally, where smoke billowed along the ceiling of the angular catacombs, Johan reached his destination. He stopped in shock.

A chamber big as a mead hall was lit by a ring of fire. At first glance, the archmage thought of a giant nest occupied by some ugly baby bird. Yet the reality was far stranger.

Covering the floor of the cave were fractured crystals of amber. Even broken, their gorgeous golden luster, reflected a million times in firelight, gave the room a scintillating homey glow.

As if by contrast, wedged in the center of the room was the ugliest creature Johan had ever beheld.

Big as a house, a gray mound of fetid flesh sprouted toothy mouths, bulging eyeballs, whiplashing tentacles, and questing tongues. The thing stank abominably, like sewage and sulfur and gangrenous flesh. Gaping in shock, Johan thought it some alchemist's wild experiment gone awry, as if some dastard had herded together elephants, then hacked the poor beasts to pieces, then mashed and fused the pieces together. Yet this mess still lived and suffered every second. For there was no doubt in Johan's mind that the being, or thrust-together beings, was fully conscious and in enormous pain. Never still, the giant thing quivered like a jelly. Mouths champed, fangs clashed, tongues waggled, tentacles whipped, eyes bulged fit to explode. One source of the monster's pain was clear, for it was surrounded by a trench filled with burning charcoal and chunks of freshly stoked wood. The ring of fire hemmed the creature so close the heat licked its tortured flesh like a burning tongue.

"Impossible!" Johan shook his horned head, doubting his eyes. He'd seen so many hideous hallucinations lately, this must be another. "But I smell it! And the noise!" Johan didn't know what to think. If he did imagine this giant freak, surely his sanity had teetered into the abyss.

Someone came into sight. Feeling like a child stealing apples rather than an emperor, Johan ducked behind a boulder and peeked, heart pounding, throat dry.

Mincing inside the ring of fire, oblivious of heat, came another being, more hideous because it was closer to human form. Tiny, bald as a baby, pointy-eared, sleepy-eyed, with skin sallow as if jaundiced, it wore only a rotting robe of faded gray that smoked from the steady wood-fire heat. The hideous keeper ignored lashing tentacles and fanged mouths. Indeed, the wizened one looked almost gentle as it caressed the corrugated flesh of the giant. Johan actually saw the mangled monster recoil at its touch, though it was rooted as a tree. The archmage watched the keeper produce a small knife and diligently saw off tiny buds that had sprouted. The captive giant thrashed and writhed, but the sallow keeper paid no mind as it snipped and cut. Stubs dripped slimy goo in greasy gray-white runnels.

A commotion came from another dark tunnel, and Johan recalled the bloodcurdling scream heard earlier. In came three people. Two brawny legionnaires in black leather and yellow tunics manhandled a struggling young woman, thin and tanned, dressed in leather and fur, obviously a member of the pine tribe. The scrappy woman kicked and cursed her captors, but her arms were bound behind by black rope. The soldiers pushed her to her knees amid fractured amber crystals.

Johan watched in fascination as the sallow invalid by the monster's side stepped barefoot into the ring of burning coals, one jaundiced hand holding its hem high, though the rag smoked and had to be stamped out. The woodswoman struggled anew, bucking and jumping so hard the legionnaires used four arms to pin her down.

Approaching the kneeling prisoner, the sickly keeper extended a single yellow finger with a pointed nail and touched the woman's ear. Instantly she stilled as if paralyzed. Gently, like an aged grandmother holding a newborn baby, the fiend stroked the prisoner's tawny hair. Slowly the invalid bent its head as if to kiss the woman's neck. Opening a withered mouth exposed fangs like white needles—which sank into the victim's tanned throat.

Chapter 17

Vampire!

Even the Tyrant of Tirras, with many black deeds writ against his name, was appalled by the frightening site. A vampire infested this palace like a monstrous rat within its walls. And he'd lived here for days and not known! Could have been drained like a chicken as he napped!

A long while the vampire fed like a leech from the victim's throat. Unable to move, the woodswoman gibbered in fright. Her mouth and tongue quivered as she uttered some prayer. Two trickles of red ran down her neck as the vampire sucked her heart's blood. The two legionnaires stood stock still, backs straight, eyes fixed on the chamber's smoky ceiling. Gradually the victim stopped shaking and wilted, drained white as a mushroom. Wiping a red mouth delicately with a finger, the vampire signaled the legionnaires to remove the corpse. Grabbing the dead weight, they hustled it away into a tunnel.

Hunkered behind the stones, with only one eye showing, Johan broke a cold sweat. Then he trembled as the wizened fiend called in a raspy voice, "I know you are there, Emperor Johan. I expected you to follow eventually. You came seeking wisdom, after all. You shall have it. Come. Come out."

Terror gripped Johan. His only thought was to flee. Yet he could not. Feet, hands, head, even his jaw and eyeballs were fixed fast, frozen in place where he knelt behind boulders. Paralyzed, he saw the wizened vampire shuffle to his side. Sallow skin, wrinkled bare skull, even red veins outlined in pointed ears and thin eyelids were all visible in the guttering light of the ring of fire. The musky snake odor of the vampire mingled with the curdled whale-meat stench of the giant horror, odors so rank Johan wanted to gag.

Gently the vampire reached out a thin fingernail that curled like a fishhook, just as sharp. The finger caught the outer rim of Johan's ear and tugged. Split, the ear bled, so Johan felt warm drops splash on his neck.

Stepping around to face the mage, the shriveled fiend smiled, a ghastly sight given dry lips and needle teeth. Then the smile reddened. The vampire grew taller. Sprouted dark hair. Gained a curved form. Lost its sallow pallor to a golden glow.

Facing Johan was Lady Shauku, austere, blue-eyed, glossy-haired, and beautiful.

Gently the lady touched a finger to Johan's ear, then touched his blood to her moist lips. "Tasty. But I have better plans for you, my dear Emperor. You see, I have ambition too. Schemes far too vast for your petty mind to encompass.

"Such a fool." The beautiful vampire chuckled, a sound like branches scraping in the wind. "All those days spent studying, and what did you learn? Nothing, I'll wager."

Johan's eyes bugged. Yes, his studies had definitely gone awry, but he never grasped how or why. For one, the wild hallucinations had distracted him, making him doubt everything he saw. Yet no matter how much he read, it still seemed familiar!

Seeming to read his thoughts, the vampire said, "Poor deluded Johan. The more you read, the less you learned. Wonder why? Those books contain nothing, Johan. Many are blank, bought and sold to be scratched with a quill. Some are shop or city ledgers, some dreary family histories. The last lord of this castle was illiterate but wished to appear well-read, so collected trash to fill a library. And you, dear Johan, pored over each empty or useless volume as if to unlock the secrets of creation!"

Despite his frozen state, the wizard shivered with rage and shame. How could he be so completely deluded?

More chuckling from the beautiful, evil creature. "Don't blame me, my dear Emperor. You gulled yourself. You wished to read of cat warriors, so I offered you a book, and a string of arcana painted across your shoulders, and a dose of hellbore. That tome had a plain calf cover, but you, pitifully eager, imagined it was bound in tiger hide. Daily you pored over page after blank page, imagining you sopped up great stores of knowledge, when really you only mulled facts already planted in your own mind. Oh, how I laughed each evening to hear you spout enlightened babble and gawk like a rustic at hallucinations. Oh, such amusement!"

Stepping back, Lady Shauku tilted her pretty head, then pointed to the writhing horror. "And now, dear guest, you finally discover a source of new knowledge—no hallucination—yet you can't comprehend it. How sad. Let me explain. That celestial being came from beyond the stars. I own it. From it I leech unworldly secrets such as no wizard on Dominaria ever conceived!

"So shall I treat you, Johan. You'll stay here alongside the horror while I whittle away your mind. Thanks to these deluding glyphs, you are long down the path of becoming my thrall. One day soon I shall release you into the world to become Emperor of all Jamuraa, my brainless puppet. Then shall *I* rule as the real empress!"

Chuckling like a saw biting wood, the vampire plucked up a fragment of amber crystal. Gently Shauku pressed the broken shell against the wizard's back. "Much have I learned from yon creature, good Johan, spells you'll never know. Here's a sample."

Pinned on his knees, helpless, Johan shuddered as the very air flushed amber.

* * * * *

"Spirits of sea and sky!" bleated Adira Strongheart.

Led by three reluctant kobolds, pirates and pine warriors emerged from a cleft in a wall to see the hideous "crying horror" writhing in eternal torment. Eyes bulged and rolled, tentacles lashed, mouths full of jagged teeth champed and clashed, tongues lolled. A gigantic cobbled-together mistake, it was rooted like a tree stump amid golden shattered crystals and a ring of coals that gave a dim red glow.

"Blood of the martyrs," breathed Murdoch. "Where does it start and end?"

"It's not a horse, sergeant," said Adira, "but it's obviously a living thing."

"So's a turnip," said Simone. "Does that thing think?"

Adira just shook her head. "Who could say?"

"Even if it could," put in Jasmine, "Shauku's torture may have driven it mad."

"Good for us," returned the practical ex-soldier. "Hurt breeds hate. That thing must loathe Shauku. We need all the allies we can scrape up."

"Good luck enlisting it," said Simone the Siren.

"But what *is* it?" Like most, Whistledove felt a combined pity and disgust. "Why the ring of fire?"

"To mask the stink?" asked Simone. Everyone's eyes were bloodshot and irritated by the pall of smoke wafting along the ceiling.

"So it can't grow," said a kobold.

"Grow how?" asked Adira.

"Like a plant. It makes little sprouts, but Shauku saws them off." People shuddered.

"So the fire keeps the roots from spreading," mused Heath.

Even as they watched, another quartet of kobolds dragged a log into the chamber, dumped it in the fiery trench, then went away. No other people were evident. "How big would the beast grow, given free rein?"

"Big," said a kobold.

Adira Strongheart's reduced Circle of Seven crouched in darkness and stared, pondering how to proceed. As did Magfire, her brother Taurion, the scout Kyenou, and four other woods warriors. The three kobolds were restrained by ropes around their necks lest they dash off and alert legionnaires or Lady Shauku herself. The two pixies Sacred Tree and Peaceflower perched on rocks, wary of queer newcomers.

Nearing the huge cavern, the party had been joined by five fire sprites. Long as a man's hand, naked and yellow with glaring black eyes, the fairies rode the air on wings of pure flame, hot as coals from a forge. One in passing frizzled Adira's chestnut curls. The sprites didn't whistle or sing like their wood brethren but simply tagged along like fireflies. The kobold Dog Ears or Prince explained that fire sprites were common in the Blue Mountains, and a pack of fire sprites had been shifted here along with the kobolds. They cast a pleasant yellow glow, so the adventurers ignored them, aside from watching their hats and hair.

As sudden as a thunderclap, a tiger's roar shook the walls and jarred human ears. The crying horror snapped and flailed helplessly. Pixies and fire sprites vaulted into the air to hover near the smoky ceiling.

"That's Jedit!" snapped Adira. "Where the hell—Where did he go?"

No one had seen the tiger slink off. One of the pixies flittered and jabbered. Hurriedly, lurking behind jumbled rocks where possible, the party skirted the hazy cavern. Magfire designated pickets while the pirates split to circle the trapped monster. Then stopped cold in their tracks.

Whereas so far they'd seen only broken fragments of amber

glass, now they beheld a giant crystal intact, six-sided, half as tall as a man. The tiger Jedit Ojanen wrestled the crystal as if mad, making the thing rock like a ship at sea. Black claws skittered and screeked over the glasslike surface, unable to score it. What mostly stunned the adventurers was the shadow tumbling inside the crystal.

"Strike me blind!" piped Adira. "Johan!"

Trapped within the amber cube crouched Johan, Tyrant of Tirras, Emperor of the Northern Realms, and prisoner of Lady Shauku. Onlookers gawked. Jedit Ojanen, raging, bunched his mighty thighs and slammed into the crystal as if to tear it open. Talons skittered off harmlessly. Still the tiger hammered, mindless with fury.

"Heath! Hit him! With your bow!" barked Adira. When the part-elf balked, the pirate chief snatched away the thick bow, wound up with two hands, and whacked Jedit hard across the muzzle. Stunned, the tiger backpedaled and made to leap. Adira had drawn her black sword. "Stand fast, Stripes, or I'll fillet you like a hake! I may anyway! What's the idea of caterwauling like a banshee? Would you bring Shauku and every last legionnaire in these hills down on our heads?"

"I'll kill him!" Frothing at the mouth, Jedit had barely regained his senses. Rubbing his nose, he growled, "I'll crack this egg and suck the meat! This despot killed my father! I'll render him dead and rotten with his bones scattered for vultures!"

"Belay that bilge!" Adira didn't lower her sword. "This poxy bastard owes me half a crew and a tenth the population of Palmyra! We've all suffered at his bloody hands! Now settle down, or I'll lop off a limb and you can limp three-legged the rest of your misbegotten life!"

Throughout the show, Johan sat with arms around his knees, for he was cramped inside the crystal. He watched the clustered comrades coolly as a basilisk. In a pause, his voice came faint and tinny as if piped through a keyhole.

"Children, control your impulses. I'm safe. You can't crack this crystal any more than I."

"We'll see," snapped Adira. "Murdoch, strike."

"Aye, milady." Black sword in hand, the ex-soldier wound up two-handed, slung his blade high, and crashed it atop the crystal. The sword bounced off and almost wrenched from Murdoch's hand.

"As expected," tisked Adira, "but we must essay everything, and simplest things first. Johan, tell us how to free you, so we can kill you."

"Gladly," called the archmage in a fine bout of sarcasm. "If only I knew."

Simone the Siren snorted. "We finally find our archenemy helpless as a hung goose, and we can't lay a hand on him!"

"Speaking of confinement." Murdoch was used to keeping his head in dangerous country. "If Jedit's cry does summon Shauku, we might all get smothered by amber."

"Too true," said Adira. Magfire had put out pickets, but now the pirate chief sent Heath and Murdoch to explore for more boltholes. The pirate queen sheathed her black sword. "What now? Can we roll this blighter through the tunnels and crack him out later? Will it even fit?"

"Why free him at all?" asked Jasmine Boreal. "Wouldn't it better serve the world to find a deep cleft and roll him into it?"

"So does a simple mind squander a valuable resource for spite," sneered the mage inside his amber cage.

"Who's simple?" retorted the druid. "Who's painted 'round with runes of enslavement?"

"Stifle your blather," chided the prisoner. "However loathsome, it's best we work together to stop Shauku."

Adira Strongheart waved a hand. "Shauku is nothing to us."

"Beg to differ!" bristled Magfire. "My people seek to unseat and punish Shauku! Don't count on our aid unless you also fight Shauku!"

Adira Strongheart didn't argue. Idly she drew a dagger and picked at a joint in the crystal. The keen blade left no mark. "How do you breathe in there?"

"I have no idea."

"How did she trap you? Do these crystals unlatch like bird cages, or did she shove you inside like a finger into a soap bubble?"

Johan shook his horned head. "I know not. I was spell-bound."

"Spellbound? The master of deceit, overthrown by a greater liar?" Idly Adira tapped the crystal. "I wonder if this surface would take paint or pitch. We could black this crystal all over, smear it with dirt, then roll it into a dark corner for a hundred years."

The pirate queen was rewarded as Johan's eyes widened. Rapidly he said, "Did you know Shauku is a vampire?"

Consternation struck the heroes of Palmyra and Arboria. Magfire swore bitter oaths. Adira and the rest listened raptly as Johan described how Shauku shed her disguise and bled a woodswoman. Then Johan pressed his case.

"Clearly Shauku is the greater danger. But I have a suggestion to undermine her power."

"And free yourself?" asked Adira.

"Hush," demanded Magfire. "Let him talk. He's not my enemy, though I agree he's a rat. Shauku preys upon my people like a giant leech. I want her head on a pike. Johan is your problem."

"This is how you aid allies?" snarled Adira. "I pity your enemies."

"Gentle women," soothed Taurion, "surely we can find middle ground where both Johan and Shauku are rendered dead or impotent."

"Yes, stop spatting!" chided Jasmine Boreal, large violet

eyes aflame. "You quibble like two lovers on a honeymoon! It profits nothing and grates on the ear! Punish those who deserve it!"

Chastised, Adira and Magfire settled for glaring. Taurion prompted Johan, "Go on."

Confined, Johan squirmed on his rump. "This patchwork monster possesses great and unknown magics, for it fell from the stars. Shauku found the beast and taps its knowledge and spells. No surprise. Some wizards in Dominaria spend all their time accumulating new sources of magic to tap. To pin it in one place, Shauku rooted it here. The monster grows like a plant, you see, propagating by sending out shoots that take root. Thus Shauku orders the kobolds to maintain the ring of fire to confine it. Now, see the amber crystals scattered about? These crystals are like eggs."

"Eggs?" asked several people.

"Exactly. An egg contains both the substance of a bird, the yolk, and the food it needs to grow, the white. The crystals are the same. Inside is a jot of meat or wood that becomes a beast, and the amber fluid to sustain it. There's more. The monster is somewhat like a plant, but too a hive beast like a colony of bees, where separate minds and bodies cooperate to survive."

"How know you this?" asked Magfire.

Silent a moment, Johan finally confessed, "I saw its dreams."

"*What?*"

"Shauku communes with the monster by wrapping in a robe and napping," explained the mage. "Her dream coat lets the wearer absorb errant thoughts. I donned the coat and dreamt of the beast's foreign world in the sky."

"That can backfire," put in Jasmine. "Even insane, the monster might still possess unimaginable magics to fry your brain like an egg, or do worse."

"World in the sky?" Magfire, down-to-earth and edgy,

hissed in exasperation. "Do you claim this ugly twitchy blotch fell from the Glitter Moon?"

"Never mind its origins! We waste time!" Adira was aware the vampire might arrive any time. "Why speak of all this?"

"The beast has no food," said Johan simply. "It starves."

"Sad," said Adira, "but so what?"

"If you extinguish the fires and give the beast food, it might regain its strength. Then *it,* not *we,* could lash out and punish Shauku!"

Adira and Magfire looked blank. Taurion, Heath, and Jasmine squinted.

"Think!" admonished Johan. "Any plan Shauku pursues discommodes us! To scotch her plans can only help your cause! Or will you fight Shauku and her legionnaires with your ragtag misfits?"

"We might fight the horror too!" retorted Adira. "Who knows what happens if it's loose? It might kill Shauku. It might kill all of us, or turn us into jellyfish, or pull the mountain down on our heads!"

Yet Adira Strongheart looked at her battered crew. She'd lost Virgil and Peregrine. Sister Wilemina had a broken arm. And none of them, she guessed, despite their bravery, could win against a single schooled and skillful Akron Legionnaire, let alone fifty.

Finally Adira said, "I hate to agree, but Johan's course makes sense. As Murdoch said, we need allies. Best we set this massive monster free to strike at its enemy. We'll have enough fighting to satisfy, I judge. Very well, Johan, how?"

"Look around," said the trapped wizard. "At the walls. Disregard the rubble. See how the walls join at odd angles? See the hints of six-sided tunnels, same as these crystals? These walls are made of no material found in Dominaria."

"So what?" asked Adira.

"I see it." Taurion's brown eyes went wide. He pointed through the haze at facets stippled along the walls, six-sided edges like a gigantic honeycomb. Until now, the adventurers had been too busy to notice.

"Exactly," said Johan with a tone of triumph. "When the monster fell from the stars, it crashed *right on this spot*."

* * * * *

"It makes sense." Magfire crept down a tilted tunnel with six sides. "Our tribe fled this place because of a great disaster three-score years ago. These queer tunnels . . ."

"The ruins built atop this hill are more than sixty years old!" countered Adira. Her hands and face were lit with her cold blue glow, giving her a ghostly pallor.

"I know that!" snapped Magfire. "The castle dates to shortly after the glaciers receded. It was obviously built on a crater. What I say is, sixty years ago the lord living in the castle must have delved into the ruins and unleashed the ancient horror that drove him from the castle and my people from the forest!"

"Could be," conceded Taurion. "I look forward to putting the question to our tribal historians."

Adira wanted to spit, tired of crotchety forestfolk and their moldy traditions. She stroked a hand along a wall that felt smooth as marble but warm as wood. By matching Johan's observations to the kobolds, the freedom fighters had learned that six-sided tunnels honeycombed the hill deep under the sky-monster's chamber. The kobolds had pointed out one descent, but just in case, Jedit led two kobolds by leashes like war dogs.

The explorers were the pirates Jedit, Adira, Simone, Murdoch, Heath, and Jasmine, and the pine warriors Magfire, Taurion, Kyenou, and three others. The tunnels were a fractured jumble canted at a bizarre angle, as if a large apartment house had been picked up and dumped on end. Skidding and sliding down the tunnels, the adventurers found their leg muscles trembling in protest.

Adira said, "I still don't understand. Do you claim these tunnels once flew through the sky?"

"Fell from the sky," corrected Taurion. "Yes. The crying horror or its eggs were in a sky-ship that sailed through the heavens and wrecked here, same as your sea-ship beached on rocks."

Adira conceded, "Anything is possible. It explains why these passages are so dreadfully canted. I thought they'd suffered a groundquake. But why six sided? Who builds a giant honeycomb but giant bees?"

"The crying horror bears features of both animal and plant," said Taurion. "Why not the habits of an insect?"

"The spuzzem!" Adira halted with one black boot braced on the edge of a portal. "Recall how it layers moss on its victims? Perhaps it's some spider webbing! Perhaps it's a giant insect too, let loose from these ruins!"

The thought jolted them, but they pressed on. Time was short.

Jasmine said, "This place reminds me of the stone sarcophagi of the ancients. In northern climes, frost heaves push them upward and out of the soil. Country folk think underground demons seek elbow room."

"That's it," muttered Simone. "Tell us a jolly bedtime story to soothe our nerves. But how could glass crystals survive such a crash?"

Taurion peered everywhere by the light of a torch as they took one fork after another. "Recall how tough the crystals are. Neither tiger claws nor a steel blade could sunder them. So it's possible some are intact."

Adira blinked. "How do we crack them to feed the horror?"

A voice squeaked, "Water."

Everyone looked at the kobold on Jedit's leash. The gray-purple cad looked sheepish. "Sometimes we fetch big golden boxes for Yellow Lady. She shoos us away. She thinks we don't know, but we do. Water makes them break."

"Water." Taurion rubbed his beard, nodding. "Yes. If the sky-ship crashes like a shooting star, anything alive must die. But the crystals can't be shattered, so they'd lie in the ground intact. Forever, unless something intervened. The first rainfall would make the crystals crack, so the horror could grow freely."

"Like cactuses that sit for years inert," said Jasmine, "then flourish on a handful of rain."

"Grow how much?" asked Jedit.

No one knew. In the lead, Taurion came to a triple fork and hesitated. Jedit braced both paws across a tunnel, gave a mighty sniff, and announced, "The spuzzem passed this way not long ago."

"Ohhh!" said half a dozen. Yet with a collective shrug, and no other choice, they passed on.

The tiger crept along comfortably on two feet or all fours as needed. The humans stumbled behind, heads bowed, ankles and calves throbbing from the treacherous tilted footing. Gray-stone tunnels intersected at odd angles, as if the original inhabitants had crawled on every surface like ants. Not every passage was tunnels. They found several six-sided rooms full of nothing identifiable. One room held miles of spun floss like spider webbing. Another sported gadgets like lead water pipes all jumbled and crumbling. One held big empty vats oddly spaced. One held hundreds of cells, each big enough to hold a man. In a few holes they found desiccated husks like cocoons. Every room only confused them further.

"Tar and blisters," muttered Adira. "This building has more holes than a sponge and holds just as little! If we don't find— *Ulp!*"

Jedit halted so suddenly that Adira trod on his tail. In garish torchlight, the tiger's eyes glowed, and his whiskers twitched. Signaling to wait, the man-beast crept ahead without a sound. Adira and others watched his striped back slither over a threshold where the passage forked and angled down.

In a moment he returned, striped face peeking over the edge, curled claws beckoning.

This room was larger, fifty feet across, but still six-sided, with each wall broken into facets like a fly's eye and several holes leading to more tunnels. More gadgets and junk projected from the walls: crumbling pipes, a stonelike trough big enough to bathe in, a bed of points like stalactites. Yet what took the explorers' breath away were amber crystals that sparkled in torchlight like jewels—thirty or more as big as bushel baskets.

"Right then!" Adira broke the spell. "Everyone fetch a jewel, or crystal, and let's breeze out of—"

"Adira . . ." Jasmine swayed on her feet. "I . . . feel . . ."

The woods mage pitched on her face as if shot by an arrow. In the gaping hole behind her, a ghastly green headless body loomed from darkness.

"The spuzzem!" bleated Magfire. "Kill it!"

Yet the alien monster had already attacked, invisibly and silently. Victims dropped like tenpins. The two kobolds crumpled first. Jedit Ojanen took a flying leap but crashed on his belly, out cold. Heath wavered and crumpled to his knees, pitching his torch away lest he burn himself. Others staggered and succumbed.

Succumbed to what? wondered Adira. Sleep? Fighting panic, she studied the approaching enemy wildly for a clue on how to assault it.

The green beast walked with a stiff up-and-down motion like an upright insect. The limbs were smooth as plant stems. The feet and truncated arms bore backward hooves. A tail with veins like a maple leaf jutted behind. Most alarming, the thing had no head, just a rounded dome atop its moss-green body. Lack of a head made it seem a slimy headless corpse seeking revenge on the living.

Adira Strongheart got fresh worries as the spuzzem's queer backward hooves shot streams of cobweb. Magfire squawled as gunk struck her hair and face. Clawing only tied their hands with gummy strands. Adira dodged but was slapped by a ropy cobweb. Repelled, she swiped at it. The stuff tore easily but stuck like honey. As Adira wrenched glop from her chin, she stumbled, clumsy as a cow, and went to one knee, struggling to keep her torch high.

Panic swelled in her bosom until Adira felt as if she were a sparrow trapped by a hawk. Why clumsy? Struggling with gummy strands by spitting firelight, she misjudged the floor and flopped on her bottom. Weakly she cursed and resisted the urge to cry.

Clumsy. Fearful. Dizzy. Despairing. Why?

Adira's head swam as if drunk. Her brain felt muzzy as the cobwebs in her hair. Part of her wanted to lie down and nap. Yet horrid images swirled in her skull. Ghastly visions of desiccated corpses gutted and hung in cocoons from the ceiling. Bodies dried like peat, eyes sunken into black pits, cheeks drawn so tight teeth showed through skin, ribs and breastbones jutting starkly, hair fallen out or reduced to stringy fuzz. Adira saw herself worse than dead, swaddled in a cocoon, unable to move, barely able to breath, knowing she was food stored for the nightmarish—

Spuzzem. A fiend that attacked with strands of webbing, but something fiercer, a gnawing assault on the mind.

Weak as a blind kitten, Adira felt more slimy rope slap her ear. The pirate queen didn't bother to mop it off, just struggled to think. She was still awake and fighting while others had collapsed. Jasmine, closest to the fiend, had dropped right away. Heath had staggered and dropped his torch. Murdoch had flopped. Simone had almost stayed on her feet.

Shaking her head, trying to claw back to full consciousness, Adira went over details again. Why did some of her crew collapse but others only wobbled? Sleepy, sinking, Adira knew she'd collapse and set her hair on—

"Fire!" snorted the pirate queen. Cranking her eyes open,

Adira confirmed her suspicion. No one had been touched, but people without torches had collapsed immediately. People with torches only staggered, unless they dropped their fire, whereupon they blacked out. And hadn't the spuzzem killed those lovers in the dark?

"Fire keeps off . . . poisonous vapors . . . like those that suffocate dwarves in mines! Magfire . . . uhh! Simone . . . Wave your torch before your face!"

Heedless of igniting her wild curls, Adira lifted her torch and almost singed her eyebrows. Breathing smoke, sniffling and coughing, Adira found her head cleared. Through rippling flames she saw the spuzzem stump toward Simone, who crawled blind as a mole.

Adira jiggled her torch to make it flare. Fire was life here, same as if they still froze on those cruel wave-swept rocks. Shouting to encourage her crew, Adira scurried across the tilted floor to Simone. Jamming her head against Simone's black curls, Adira sheltered both behind the protecting flames. Woozy, Simone fought against stupor.

"Simone!" Adira shouted across five inches. "Wake up! We'll die if we don't attack!"

"Kyenou! Ply fire! Get up! Stay together!" From another side, Magfire goaded her scout. Magfire squatted over one woodsman and tore off shreds of his woolen shirt, then wadded the shreds around Kyenou's odd double-ended spear. Igniting the rags, she and Kyenou advanced on trembling legs against a lifelong terror.

From their side, Adira and Simone attacked. The lieutenant's face shone from the heat of the torch, but her eyes bulged with anger. Stepping carefully, Simone tore off Jasmine's blue skirt and spiked it on her black sword blade. Together Adira and Simone crabbed four-legged toward the spuzzem.

The creature swiveled slowly as four desperate people advanced with fire. Adira laughed grimly as the spuzzem back-stepped on plant-stem legs.

She barked, "Stick it!"

Magfire and Simone rammed spear and sword into the spuzzem's torso, easy as puncturing a cactus. Fire scorched, stinking like burned cabbage. The spuzzem's body proved no denser than a flower. Simone and Kyenou sliced away a flap like green leather with an inner core of white cottony threads.

"Fire its insides!" called Adira and Magfire together. Makeshift torches were shoved into the body cavity. White threads sizzled and charred black. Smoke spewed from the spuzzem's vegetable body. The women punished the monster with steel and fire. The spuzzem's supple arms thrashed weakly. Chitinous hooves drummed on the floor.

"That's deuced odd!" Adira twisted her black sword from the monster's body. "It's changing?"

Indeed. Rather than grow weaker, the spuzzem kicked and flailed with more animation, as if feeling pain for the first time. Knees grew supple. Arms elongated and sprouted hands, then fingers. The green body deepened to brown. From the smooth hump of charred torso popped a head with black curly hair.

Kyenou and Simone jumped back, their attack forgotten. Adira felt queasy and knew her face blanched.

In killing a monster, they'd killed a man.

A naked brown-skinned man wore tight black curls. Blue tattoos swirled across his chest and shoulders and thighs. His nose was flat, his teeth strong and white, his eyes dark and fierce. All four women knew they faced a warrior.

A dying warrior. His belly was torn open. Hideous burned gashes leaked a red river. He bit his tongue in agony, yet his face was oddly stoic.

Choking on blood, the brown man stared straight at his killers, or saviors, and gasped a warning in old-fashioned words. "Never . . . eat . . . food . . . crying gods . . ."

A death rattle escaped his red-smeared mouth, and the man sagged.

The four warrior women stood with bloodstained hands and dripping weapons, wondering what they'd done.

"I don't understand," mewed Simone the Siren. "He was the spuzzem?"

"An Old One." Magfire's voice rang hollow in the underground chamber. "Ancient people from legend who inhabited this forest when it was jungle. He lived a lifetime under the sun, it's plain, and went without clothes because it was hot. But that's *thousands* of generations."

"Cursed," Adira whispered. "By the crying god. To live forever as a spuzzem."

Groans broke their reverie as Jedit, Heath, and others roused. Slowly they shuffled up to stare at the time-lost warrior. Jedit Ojanen, not even human, gave the most profound lament.

"Imagine what he could have taught us."

Adira Strongheart mopped tears and sweat and cobwebs from her face with filthy hands. "So the wind blows. Magfire, your forest is rid of the spuzzem. Now let's hoist these crystals and take our fight to Shauku. And Johan."

Chapter 18

"Set them down here. *Ugh!*"

Adira Strongheart yanked off her headband and mopped sweat from a dirty face. She plunked down on an amber crystal and sighed, "I'd give ten years off my life for a hot bath!"

The explorers half-collapsed on broken shells and dusty stone. They wheezed and coughed in grimy smoke. Each of the twelve pinefolk and pirates had lugged one awkward and heavy crystal seeming miles up twisted slippery six-sided tunnels. They'd found the cavern the same, with the crazed cosmic horror still lashing its tongue and tentacles, and Sister Wilemina and two foresters guarding Johan in his golden prison. The air was still rank with sweat and wood smoke. The pixies had refused to descend any deeper and had departed, same as the fire sprites.

"What time is it?" asked Adira. "What part of the day? I've lost track."

"We entered these accursed caves as evening fell," said Magfire, eyes red as anyone's. "My warriors were to stage a sham attack to keep the legionnaires busy. Likely it's past dawn and mid-morn now."

"I hope they're still at it," said Murdoch. "I couldn't wrestle a kitten."

"I feel we've crawled through caves forever," said Simone. "Maybe we're dead in some pocket of hell."

"Hist!" warned Jasmine. "Such talk is jinxy!"

"Enough rest." Adira pushed herself erect. "Let's see if the kobolds lied or not. Give me your gourd, Murdoch. Mine is dry. And help me lug this thing."

The two hefted a golden crystal the size of a bushel basket and crab-walked toward the ring of fire. Under Adira's orders, the kobolds had ceased to stoke the fire. The trench was less than a pace wide, but heat from hot coals and stone was still withering.

Together, counting, Adira and Murdoch lobbed the crystal over the ring, so it thudded against the scarred gray trunk of the goggle-eyed tooth-gnashing terror. Clamping down her stomach, Adira skipped over the fire to stand beside the monster out of reach of whiplashing tentacles. The footing was all intertwined roots. Between smoke and the monster stinking like a rotting whale, Adira almost gagged but pressed on.

The crystal was full of translucent amber liquid. Deep inside hung a fist-sized knot like a tree root, which must be a young horror. Holding her breath, Adira pulled the stopper of the gourd and trickled water over the topmost joints.

Results were immediate.

Adira jumped as cracks raced around the facets of the crystal. The crystalline egg fell apart so quickly that her boots were splashed. Facets like panes of glass clanked. Sweet-smelling golden sap gushed and vanished amid a million cracks of the horror's roots.

Adira sipped air, as did her crew outside the circle of fire. Atop fallen facets lay the fist-sized knot. It quivered and curled and rolled. A single bulging eye flicked open, making Wilemina chirp. A tiny tongue lapped at spilled nectar.

"Kill it! Kill it!" shouted Murdoch, panicked all out of size by the minute menace.

"No!" yelled Jasmine. "It's a living thing!"

"It's evil!" said Kyenou, for once charged with emotion.

"We don't know that," countered Taurion. "Lady Shauku tormented this beast for years. It may be harmless as any other animal."

Adira Strongheart watched the tiny creature wriggle like a tadpole. It wedged its whiskery tail amid the roots of its gigantic parent, then curled upright. For a moment the pirate chief considering stamping on it like a cockroach, but she didn't have the heart.

She told her crew, "Hush. Let it be. Heft those other crystals."

"The spuzzem!" Taurion interrupted with a cry. "The ancient warrior who became the spuzzem! He warned not to eat the food of the gods! That must be this nectar! It smells sweet! Lapping it must have transformed him into a plant-beast, the spuzzem!"

"Oh!" Adira looked in dismay at her spattered boots, then quickly hopped across the ring of fire. Scooping ashes with her toes, she smeared her boots dry and crusty.

"Behold the monster!" breathed Jasmine.

Where they'd spilled the nectar, the monster's gray hide had flushed green. As if painted by invisible hands, color rose from the soil six feet or more. Where touched by life-giving green, the bulging eyes retracted, the tongues ceased to loll, and tentacles quit thrashing. Indeed, one tentacle sprouted a thousand roots like hair and elongated.

Adira hissed, "I'll be keelhauled! It works. The thing grows!" Despite earlier revulsion, the pirate queen felt a thrill to feed a starving creature, no matter how alien. Somehow, she knew in her bosom, this strange star-lost brute must feel gratitude.

Cheered, Adira turned to her soot-smeared comrades. "Shift those other crystals and crack them open! We'll see if the creature thanks us or eats us!"

Heartened by success, pirates and pine warriors grappled the eleven remaining crystals across the ring of fire, then splashed on handfuls of water. All the crystals split and the precious fluid soaked in. The monster looked healthy and happy as a summer cornstalk.

"Adira! Johan wishes to speak!" Wilemina, with her arm in a sling, stood guard.

Adira walked to Johan's side. Framed in golden glass, the triply horned red-black emperor looked like a djinn trapped in a bottle.

The emperor piped, "Will you renege your word and refuse to free me?"

Adira snorted and kicked the crystal. "I never promised to free you, Hornhead. Dare not accuse me of crawfishing on a pledge. I can name two hundred Palmyrans who died because you were discontent in your rocky homeland. We'll lug you home in your box. For now, don't go away." Tapping a finger on the smooth top, the pirate queen turned to go.

But with the crystals sundered, Adira's pirates and Magfire's foresters gathered for the next step. Jedit Ojanen loomed over the amber trap like a primitive god.

Rumbling like distant thunder, the tiger said, "I've a question, Johan. What of the prophecy of None, One, and Two?"

"Here?" The devil-bedecked emperor glowered behind glass walls. "I know somewhat. Shauku blithered about her cleverness. The people of the pines were told by a gibbering seer the time of prophecy had come, were they not? That they must reclaim their ancestral lands and heritage?"

"Yes!" said Magfire. "The prophecy foretold—"

"A sham," interrupted Johan. "Shauku visited your seer with a vision, same as she gulled me in the Western Wastes with visions of her palace. Nonsense about history and ancestral pride was mere pap to lure you north within her grasp. You were herded here like cattle for slaughter."

While the foresters digested this shocking news, the pensive

Heath asked, "Why did Shauku imprison you? What was her intent?"

"I remember you." Johan's black eyes narrowed. "You shot an arrow into my breast on the lake at Palmyra."

"Had I known it would prove ineffectual," said the archer coldly, "I would have poisoned it with venom of pit scorpions."

"You'll regret . . . regret . . ." Suddenly distracted, Johan shook his horned head. The heroes of Palmyra and Arboria stared, for never before had the tyrant shown befuddlement or hesitation. Johan mashed his hands against his eyes. Clearly his skull throbbed. Adira wondered if the emperor had run out of fresh air. If so, was she obligated to liberate him now and punish him later?

A piercing whistle cut the smoky air. Down a murky passage raced one of Magfire's pickets. "Shauku comes with legionnaires! Not a hundred yards behind!"

* * * * *

Pandemonium.

Adira Strongheart bawled, "Stick together! Heath, find us two boltholes where we can fight clear! Any direction will do! Jedit, scoot Johan's prison behind those boulders! Partner up!" Between tunnels and the littered cavern floor, a thousand hiding places beckoned, but they would give advantage to legionnaires as much as pirates. As Adira orchestrated a line of defense, teams of black-clad terrors charged from the haze. Battle was on.

Eschewing any partner, Jedit Ojanen leaped to meet black-hilted swords with wicked black claws. Leaping at a pair of Akron Legionnaires, Jedit swiped left and right to force one or the other back, lest one gut him while the other was distracted. The soldiers were trained to stand their ground and work in pairs, yet the quick ferocity of the man-killing tiger knocked one man against a boulder, so he skidded and fell. Immediately, Jedit Ojanen whirled to kill the other.

Looming like a behemoth, Jedit shot both paws like clusters of knives. The soldier's back slammed a boulder, but he kept his feet. Perhaps too well. Claws punctured leather and ripped long tears that half-undressed the man and raked his skin with stripes of blood. Still the soldier gamely rammed gloved fists and sword hilt to crash under Jedit's jaw. The tiger's teeth clacked, and he bit his tongue. Another brutal slam actually shoved Jedit back, so he momentarily lost track of his foe. He paid a double price as a painful jolt crashed on one eye and an ice-cold slice behind slashed his upper thigh.

Enraged, Jedit scooched and leaped to escape the returning sword swipe. As he landed, he didn't hesitate, for that invited attack. Squatting like a bullfrog, Jedit lunged and tackled the wounded man before him. The legionnaire hammered his sword's diamond-shaped skull-popper on Jedit's head with both hands. The blows stung so hard Jedit saw stars. Still, straddling him, Jedit Ojanen knew where every squirming limb must be. Opening a jaw full of razor fangs, the tiger bit savagely into the soldier's left biceps, slapped one paw on the man's chest for leverage, then humped his powerful neck and wrenched backward. With a gruesome grinding and snapping, the tiger ripped the man's arm from the shoulder.

Again Jedit paid a price for his single-minded attack. From his left, the surviving legionnaire whacked him across fur and skin and muscle, and almost creased his spine. Spitting out the arm, Jedit ducked, whipped a half-circle, and cannoned into the legionnaire. The soldier was bashed so hard against another boulder he lost his breath and almost his sword. The tiger warrior gave him no chance to recover. Scooping both hands under the man's crotch, Jedit slammed him headfirst into the rock so hard his neck and spine snapped in a dozen places.

Similar fights boiled all around. Salted amid the brawl ran a perpetual argument.

"We must pull out!" hissed Magfire, swinging her spike left. "I told you these caverns are unlucky!"

"We can't retreat with a job half done!" snarled Adira Strongheart, slashing right. "Johan's still alive!"

"Legionnaires know each other's whereabouts!" reminded Magfire in her husky whisper. "Killing one will fetch down all fifty! We'll be massacred!"

"Shut up and fight the enemy!"

*   *   *   *   *

Completely forgotten, the cosmic horror bubbled with new life. Freshened and strengthened by luscious nectar, the monster fought for its own freedom in its alien, half-mad fashion.

Nearby, Johan suffered inside his crystalline prison. Having once read the dreams of the star-lost beast, Johan now found his skull throbbing and reeling as the alien marshaled its thoughts. Other-worldly ideas and laments and pleas and phrases surged through his mind like seawater through a sinking ship. An apt analogy, for Johan felt his sanity ebbing as a thousand incomprehensible images blared in his brain.

Then, one stark truth shone like a beacon.

A shooting star.

Johan fixated on the picture. A rock. Falling through an infinite black void. With nothing to compare against, the wizard could not guess its size. It might have been a pebble, or a boulder, or larger. Straining to understand, Johan watched the pebble glow from dark dusky gray to a warm orange. Then a fiery red. Then white-blue. Then pure white, so bright and sparkling it was painful to see.

White hot?

Trapped in the crystal with the throbbing thoughts of the cosmic horror, Johan fought to think. How could a rock become hot? Ah! The rock had become a falling star!

Falling where? wondered Johan. And in the same instant he knew the answer. The monster was trapped and could never win free. Overwhelming despair wracked Johan. This landing place had proven hostile. The monster was imprisoned by painful fire. It would rather die than be a prisoner. So, with a tiny reserve of strength, it sought oblivion.

By reaching for a star. A shooting star.

With a jolt, Johan threw back his head and stared through amber glass at the cavern ceiling.

* * * * *

The clang of sword on sword rang throughout the cavern with an earsplitting clatter. Pirates and pinefolk defended a jumble of boulders as a makeshift fort while legionnaires swarmed from all sides. Hacking furiously, Adira Strongheart felt her belly grow cold as ice. Very bad, thought she. Her pirates were canny swordsmen who could board or brawl, but these legionnaires were diehard professionals, and she couldn't even lift her head to count their numbers. The only outcome was slaughter.

Heath and Taurion and a woodswoman tried in vain to kill a single swordsman who met all their thrusts and hacks and paid them back. Taurion was felled with a slashed arm and the woodswoman was clipped above the hip. Before Taurion could defend, the same sword whacked him alongside the neck, and he fell.

Behind Adira, Magfire jabbed at two soldiers while a forester and Murdoch ganged another and Jedit grappled still more.

"We don't have luck in caves!" With one broken arm, Sister Wilemina had to hang back and feebly jab with her bow. "The last time we ventured underground merfolk drowned Treetop and nearly ate us hoof and hide!"

Adira cast back and forth, trying to decide who needed aid, and spotted Simone the Siren, who suffered attacks from two men. Her cutlass flashed wildly just to fend the blades aside, never mind return a thrust. Trapped in the midst of a scrap with no way to help, Adira shouted for her lieutenant to watch her footing, for the floor was lumpy.

A fatal misstep. Simone ducked a thrust that was actually a feint. While she lurched off-balance, the assassin dipped his shoulder and lunged. Two feet of red-smeared steel jutted out Simone's back. Not wasting a motion, the killer twisted the blade and ripped in another direction. Adira screamed as Simone was gutted like a fish.

"Simone! No!" Too late, the pirate queen drove to kill. Furious, but keeping a clear head, she lashed straight and hard in an overhand arc that split a legionnaire's throat. Blood spouted in a crimson fountain that painted the ceiling. "Heath, help me reach Simone!"

Heath was busy. Lamed, he skittered between a legionnaire's legs, dumping him backward. Heath aimed his sword like a dagger and rammed steel in the man's belly. The part-elf twisted the blade as if to pry the man's soul from his bowels. It took Jedit Ojanen to clear the way by killing a half-dozen foes with bare, blood-soaked paws.

Combat rang like temple bells, yet Adira heard none of it. Scuttling on hands and knees, she dragged Simone to her bosom, soaking herself in blood. Even clamping both hands front and back couldn't stanch the grievous wound.

"Simone! Simone! Please, don't go! Not you! I couldn't bear it!"

Simone's face waxed gray. Her black curls hung limp as petals on a dying flower. Blood trickled from her mouth. Weakly she tried to focus.

"Di-ra? I can't—Scarzam's Dragon, it hurts."

"Potion!" Magfire scrambled over rocks to reach Adira. Dropping her bloody war club, she yanked at the wooden stopper sealed with beeswax in a stoneware crock. "Alabaster potion'll save anyone! Pour it down her—"

"Magfire!" Kyenou, the scout in deer hide and ermine tails, snagged her leader's arm. "Taurion's neck is split open!"

"Brother!" Cramped amid rocks and corpses, Magfire crabbed back around. Everyone shouted, calling, scrabbling, moving. She called to Kyenou, "Wind of the West, help us! Is he alive?"

"He's dying!" The cool-headed Kyenou was crying.

"Give it here!" Adira slapped at Magfire's sleeve, bloodying her silver fox mantle, groping down her arm in the dim light to grab the crock without spilling its precious contents. "Give me some potion! Simone dies too! Then you can dose Taurion."

"No!" Magfire hugged the potion to her chest. "It's only potent in one dose! It can't be shared!"

"Give it to me!" Still with Simone's head cradled in her lap, Adira Strongheart grabbed the war chief by the mantle, flipped her bodily over her dying comrade, and slammed a fist into her jaw twice.

Iron-handed from a lifetime of warfare, Magfire refused to surrender the bottle. Spittle made bloody froth on her battered lips, and fire blazed in her eyes. Her free hand shot at Adira's face, four fingers spread, and would have blinded the pirate queen if she hadn't ducked. Snagging Adira's chestnut locks, Magfire twisted and almost popped her foe's neck.

The forester hissed, "One of mine or one of yours is no choice, outlander!"

"By the Sea-King's Crook!" Grabbing Magfire's wrist to stall the wrenching of her hair, Adira groped wildly for her black sword. "I'll gut you and every one of your benighted woods rats."

"No!"

Adira jumped as a cold hand clutched hers. Simone dragged down her friend's fingers as if disciplining a child. Her beautiful dulcet voice, that once had caroled from the crow's nest and carried miles across the sea, was faint as a whisper through a winter cave.

"I'm too far gone. . . . Torn up . . . Give it away. Oh, kiss me, Adira. . . . It's dark."

"Simone! Oh, Simone!" Shaking off Magfire's slackening grip, Adira held her friend's dark head and sobbed and sobbed as killing raged around her.

Confusion reigned as Magfire jumped over living and dead to reach her fallen brother. Tilting back his lolling head, she poured the alabaster potion between her fingers into his mouth. So potent was the mana-charged fluid that a pale white glow washed over Taurion's skin. The gaping wound at his neck sealed from both ends as if pinched by invisible hands. Flesh knit into a nasty white scar wide as a finger. Within a minute the near-dead man flushed pink and healthy.

Opening his eyes, he gasped, "Why aren't I dead?"

"Because a strong heart breeds strong friends." Magfire couldn't explain to her confused sibling, for she broke down crying.

"Listen!" called Heath.

Orders barked in a foreign tongue. The nearest legionnaires dropped back in the haze.

New to combat, Jasmine croaked, "Did we win?"

"Reinforcements must've arrived," explained Murdoch. "They'll switch and come at us again with fresh troops."

In the odd lull, pirates and foresters saw only glimpses of the enemy through the pall of smoke and dust. Veterans checked their blades, straightened tackle, sipped water, awaited orders, and talked of small things to banish fear. For soon they would die.

Murdoch bobbed his looted black sword in the air. "I wish I had my shield. That's how we trained in Yerkoy's Royal Army, sword and shield together, attack and defend. This one-handed steel-slinging is for high-faluting mercenaries or fog-headed fools."

"You're a mercenary yourself," said Sister Wilemina. Even with one arm in a sling, she checked her bowstring for frays. "Thanks to me. I recommended Adira adopt you back in Palmyra. I wish I were there now."

"I wish I had my own arrows. Pheasant feathers don't compare to good goose quills." Heath bound up his bleeding knee, his bow and quiver near at hand. "I can sink a shaft in a crow's eye at a mile with my own handwork. These arrows are sticks glued with eiderdown. Still, it was kind of Magfire's people to give us them. I wish I'd thanked them all properly."

"I wish I knew a spell so frightening it would scare even me." Jasmine Boreal fidgeted with her antique bronze knife. "But without my oddments this far underground, who knows what works? May the Virgin, Mother, and Crone pity me. I wish I'd paid them more fealty."

"Wishes are regrets glimpsed in yesterday's mirror," quoted Heath obscurely. "One of you women rouse Adira, will you? Time speeds."

Whistledove Kithkin was as tall standing as was Adira kneeling over her dead lieutenant. The brownie touched her chief's shoulder gently.

"Adira? We're sorry about Simone, but we need you. The legionnaires regroup. We've got to gird and break through their line, or we'll never leave this cavern alive."

"Aye, aye." Hovering over dead Simone, Adira tried to think of a benediction, but failed. As leader, she could only succor the living. Planting a final kiss on Simone's cold brow, Adira swabbed blood off her black blade with her sash.

Ducking low among boulders, treading yellow-clad corpses strewn mostly by Jedit, Adira positioned her mercenaries and Magfire's foresters, then summoned Jedit. Measuring the odds and comparing her resources, Adira fell into old patterns as if Simone had never existed.

In less than a minute Adira formed a loose phalanx with right- and left-handed swordbearers spaced apart and spear-wielders ranged behind. It gave her a bitter satisfaction that this two-tier rank had been used by Johan to raid Bryce and Palmyra. Such a formation just might break through the legionnaires' line and escape into the tunnels. Once in the twisting corridors, they could run hell-for-leather while guarding their rear. They didn't have to destroy the legionnaires, after all, only outrun them.

She finished, "Jedit, you take point."

"Yes, captain." The tiger looked a nightmare. Blood and dust matted his fur in clumps. His broad breast was more red than white. One ear was slit, his whiskers were splintered, gore dripped from lacerations on his long arms, and he listed to port from a ferocious leg wound hastily bound with rags. Yet, Adira noted, when she needed unquestioning loyalty, he gave it. Much like Simone.

For a second Adira felt her throat seize up, then nodded. "When you're ready, go."

Without a word Jedit Ojanen spun in place, tail flying like a bullwhip, and bounded over a boulder toward the still-forming enemy. Pirates and pine warriors ran just to keep up.

Ahead through haze and dust waited a long yellow-black line of Akron Legionnaires, as if Jedit charged a hornet's nest. This suicidal charge into slaughter would make a fine heroic saga, thought the cat warrior. How sad no tigers would ever sing it. Briefly, in the never-ending seconds hanging before combat, Jedit thought of his homeland Efrava, of his mother Musata, of Hestia and her affectionate teasing, of his doughty opponent Ruko, of all the tigers he'd abandoned for a life of adventure and a desire to follow in his father's footsteps. And of his father, Jaeger, who'd pursued Johan and never been seen again. Despite his predicament, the battle-mad brute grinned so fangs winked below his striped muzzle.

Jedit murmured aloud, "Promises to keep, hurts to mend, wounds to avenge. Best I not be killed so far from home. Too many people need harassing."

There was no sign of the vampire Shauku, but her body-guards were ready. Time to strike. Sucking wind into his belly, Jedit extended claws on all four limbs, gave a bloodcurdling roar like a volcano exploding, and entered the fight of his life.

Twin claws snagged two black leather hoods and raked faces to bone. Blinded, spitting and drowning in blood, the legionnaires barely blubbered and screamed before they crashed to earth and died. With waspy blades whisking all around, Jedit's huge head butted three men flat. His claws slashed from high to low to cripple the greatest number the quickest. The tiger bit a man in the belly, shearing through his yellow tunic and leather armor, disemboweling the victim with a wrench of his thick neck. To the right he clawed a man's neck so bright frothy blood geysered, then slashed another's arm, so his sword clanged on stone, then ripped a third across the kidneys, so he spun against his comrades. And on and on, an orgy of destruction.

Shouting vile oaths and the names of gods, Adira and Magfire's troops charged in Jedit's wake like a school of sharks.

Heath shot away all his and Wilemina's arrows, then threw his bow to his left hand, so fast did he need his sword. Stabbing straight, he tunked a wooden shield, then flipped his blade sideways to harass the enemy's face. But two legionnaires tackled him as a team. Even as one shied from Heath's scything blade, the other knocked it high. The archer tried to block the partner's jab, but his ebony bow only skidded down keen steel. Heath gasped as his side was pierced, but rather than give ground and invite attack, he bit down on pain and hacked. Quick reflexes and an archer's iron forearms saved his life, for he beat back the legionnaire who'd pinked him and swatted the other off-stride. Still, the two soldiers bounced back and lunged, twin blades flickering like adders' tongues.

Scenting death on the wind, Heath caroled, "Ye dryads and naiads, prepare your bowers!"

Murdoch slung his borrowed blade against scaly black leather backed by wood, for some legionnaires plied shields. The ex-sergeant sidestepped to avoid being impaled and to make a smaller target, then he actually crowded behind the thrusting legionnaire's shield, so the man was temporarily blockaded. Slinging his left elbow, Murdoch slammed the man's jaw and hacked small. His slim blade slashed the legionnaire's elbow to sever tendons and grate on bone. As the arm fell slack, Murdoch stripped the leather straps from the man's forearm and stole his shield.

Spitting at his enemies, Murdoch crowed, "Step up to the sergeant, you slackarse sluggards! I'll teach you how to spell slaughter!"

Wilemina, Jasmine, and Whistledove clung together, hoping their collective strength would offset weaknesses. Falling rump to rump to shoulder, they were instantly bracketed by legionnaires bearing naked steel.

Holding her bow and sword in her good left hand, Sister Wilemina shrieked, "For Lady Caleria!" and stabbed straight. Her sword was clipped by a shield, knocked upward and away. But the archer's bow functioned like a part of her arm. Heedless of his blade, Wilemina banged the ornate bow atop of the man's shield and jabbed at the leather hood's eye slit with the horn tip. The legionnaire hooked his head back to save his eyes. In that second, Whistledove scooted low as a cockroach and stabbed high. Her dagger point slid under the man's kneecap. Writhing, he jerked the leg and kicked the brownie, but Wilemina sent her bow singing in a long arc that whacked his temple and laid him out cold.

The other swordsman stamped and pranced to pin Jasmine. The druid skipped back, then clapped both hands. A blue cloud flashed in the man's face and set him sneezing uncontrollably. Whistledove flitted like a hummingbird, circled, and sliced. Steel bit the legionnaire's inner thigh, sliced leather and flesh, and spilled blood in a torrent.

One-armed, Wilemina grappled with the second attacker, clinging close to spoil his aim even as she prayed aloud to Lady Caleria. Jasmine hammered the man's head with a rock, then dropped it as a sword creased her back. Only by pitching forward past the toppling man did she save her life, but more swordsmen trotted up, and death sang seconds away.

The toughest veteran of them all, Adira Strongheart jumped into battle with little regard for safety, as if life had lost its meaning. Even as she was overrun by diehard killers, her thoughts were of her friends and companions. This fracas, she marveled, might be the last stand of the Circle of Seven. Oddly enough, what pained her was the idea that her ex-husband Hazezon Tamar, whom she professed to loathe, would never learn their fate, but would wonder what befell them the rest of his days.

She shouted at the yellow-black horde, "Brace up, you jackstaff backsliders! Mark on your tally sheet t'was Adira Strongheart sent you to hell!"

A whirlwind swept past Adira's red-misted battle fury. Orange, black, and white filled her vision as yellow and black were scattered. A helping hand strong as an ox pull steered her across boulders and pools of blood. As quickly as battle was joined, it was stopped. Adira and her Circle, every one wounded, cast about. The Akron Legionnaires had withdrawn to a side tunnel. Jedit Ojanen stood tall, drenched in blood, awaiting orders.

"Tiger," puffed Heath, nursing a bleeding side, "you saved . . . our lives . . . again!"

"No." Even the tiger's chest heaved from exertion. "The legionnaires pulled back. I don't know why."

"They fear us!" croaked Murdoch, trying to joke.

"Who knows?" panted Adira. "We might get out of this mess with our guts intact. But we can't leave Johan alive! Shauku would find him too handy a tool!"

Slashed on a buttock and thigh and forearm, Adira gasped

as she tottered to Johan's golden prison. Her sword dripped blood.

"Make ready, Whistledove! You splash water on the crystal, and I'll drive home my blade before he can escape."

"Stand fast, mortals!" Like an echo from a tomb, the voice came from nowhere. Then a clammy mist swirled in Adira's face like the breath of a frost giant. The pirate queen couldn't shift her feet, and her arms stiffened as if frozen. Equally rooted, Whistledove chirped in fright.

From within the amber crystal, Johan blurted, "Beware Shauku!"

Like a face escaping pea-soup fog, a sallow visage took shape. The vampire formed from the scalp down, so her shriveled yellow head with pointed ears and needle fangs hung suspended a moment, then were joined by her ragged robe and small clawed feet.

Yet Adira was not nicknamed "Strongheart" for nothing. The petrifying spell had yet to seize up her good sword arm. With a grunt of effort, the Sovereign of the Sea of Serenity rammed her wasp-sting blade straight and true. Black steel split Shauku's bitter heart before the misty body had fully formed.

Alas, to no effect. Once Shauku ceased to shimmer, she glanced down at the blade stuck in her chest, curled a clawed hand around Adira's clenched fist and, easily as disarming a child, withdrew the blade. The withered hand was corpse-cold but inhumanly strong. Shauku cocked Adira's wrist and almost splintered the pirate's arm, forcing her to drop her steel. Shauku smiled, the most frightening sight Adira had ever beheld. Behind, she knew her Circle of Seven must likewise be frozen, else they'd have already attacked. At least they knew why the legionnaires fell back.

The rusty-hinge voice croaked, "A worthy fight your cohorts give, but it ends now, for other plans run apace."

Adira tried to answer but only squeaked. Her mind

screamed with terror, more for her crew than herself. Vaguely she supposed the vampire smothered them with some scare spell, for Adira's guts felt watery, her heart raced fit to burst, her hair prickled, and sweat coursed in rivers. Paralyzed, the pirate queen tried to stare the vampire down, but her bravado failed. The undead eyes were black and blank as a shark's.

"Adira!" Johan's trapped voice rang tinny inside the amber shell. "Free me! I can fight Shauku! Match her spell for spell!"

With a dry chuckle, Shauku reeled in Adira as a python might constrict a mouse in its coils. The vampire's free hand touched Adira's wrist with black claws, then slowly pressed. Adira watched her blood ooze from twin punctures that burned and itched. To her everlasting horror, she watched the vampire bring lips to wrist and begin to suck her blood.

Drained, thought the paralyzed pirate. I'll be sucked dry and left a husk, or else rendered a night fiend myself. And I can't move a muscle. Hazezon, where are you?

"Release her!" hissed a tiny voice.

Barely able to avert her eyes, Adira saw Whistledove Kithkin draw her borrowed dagger. Somehow, perhaps because of her small size, or her mystic heritage, the brownie had escaped the petrifying spell. Fast and feisty as a rat-killing terrier, Whistledove's rapier sang, slashing Shauku from neck to elbow, white steel furrowing sallow skin.

The attack netted nothing. Though slit to bone, the undead fiend couldn't bleed. From lips dripping ruby droplets, Shauku commanded, "Die!"

Without a word, Whistledove rolled up brown eyes and pitched face-first on the stone floor with a sickening clonk.

We're finished, thought Adira. All my fault.

Yet they were not, entirely.

Frozen and forgotten was Jasmine Boreal, a witch of nature, who plied not a sword or bow but the essences of the earth, so held a knife not of steel but of bronze, an alloy of brass and tin. The druid in sky-blue knew she was lost, out of her element, not in a cozy forest rich with magically charged greenery, but rather in a dingy cave where even the air was eye-smarting and foul. Still, many forces of nature awaited her beck and call, and a vast friendly forest lay almost overhead. Improvising as best she could while paralyzed, Jasmine Boreal pictured soaring timber, lush pine-scented foliage, and the unending carpet of intertwined roots. Wishing she might sprinkle iron filings and pine shavings, the druid pried open her hand to let fall the bronze knife.

Druidical magic usually brought small results, but with earth elements a little charming went a long way. Swollen by magic, the knife's ping on the cavern floor was amplified a hundred times, then a thousand. In an eye blink, the floor of the chamber jumped less than an inch. Yet that minor groundquake bucked the earth as if snatching a rug from under everyone's feet.

Adira, straining backward from Shauku, was flipped head over heels to *whang* her skull so hard she saw fiery spots. Shauku shivered into misty droplets, temporarily ethereal. Jedit Ojanen was jolted and dumped to all fours, where he clutched stone with battle-blunted claws. Murdoch was pitched forward onto his stolen shield. Heath, Sister Wilemina, and Magfire's foresters spilled like nine pins. Even Jasmine Boreal jiggled like a jelly, amazed at the ruckus she'd caused. The groundquake flung dust and ashes in the air that set many sneezing and weeping.

Adira Strongheart had crashed alongside Johan's crystal cage. Temporarily stunned, or still partly paralyzed by the vampire's curse, Adira fumbled to roll over and gain her feet. All the time Johan shouted from two feet away, though his voice was as muffled as if buried alive.

"Loose me, Adira! I can fight Shauku! I have the magical prowess! Get me free, and I swear on my sacred honor I'll combat her! Adira! Can you hear? Let me loose!"

Groggy, the pirate queen gazed at Johan, Tyrant of Tirras,

not seeming to recognize the red-black face framed by horns. Of more concern was the vampire Shauku reforming from fog. Close by lay Whistledove Kithkin, like a child overcome by sleep, except her eyes bore the thousand-league stare only the dead achieve.

"Dead." Adira struggled to think. "We'll all be dead. Unless . . . What?"

"Let me out!" bellowed Johan through a glass wall.

"Never!" Groggy as a hammered ox, Adira levered against Johan's crystalline prison to rise. Her left hand dripped blood from the vampire's punctures. "Nay tyrant! You're bad as—"

Blood, of course, is made of water.

Adira lurched as, in a wink, the seams of Johan's prison opened. Amber plates like glass clattered on stone. Free, Johan surged to his feet. For a second or two, again dumped on her rump, Adira goggled at the looming monarch. With his purple robes and red-black tattoos and double devils' horns, he *looked* like a master of men. Yet the illusion shattered as Johan lifted his skirts and scampered away on bare feet.

"Like a rat." The pirate queen didn't even rage, only lay in dust and blood, infinitely tired. She'd made so many mistakes, caused so many deaths. Virgil. Peregrine. Whistledove, valiant as a wildcat. Simone, her boon companion and faithful lieutenant, always jolly and never complaining. Adira missed her friends as if her heart had been cut out. All gone for nothing.

No. Dimly Adira corrected herself. Her comrades gave their lives to stop the depredations of Johan and Shauku. To give up the fight was to sully their sacrifices. Shaking her aching head, the woman called Strongheart groped for her fallen sword.

"Very well. I'll *not* die. I'll kill this bloodsucker myself, if only to get Johan's throat between my fingers to strangle him slowly."

The Circle of Seven and the woodsfolk likewise struggled to their feet. Bruised and shaken, some watched the misty form of Shauku regain shape. Others staggered to aid their leader, who crawled aimless as a baby. The unkillable Jedit Ojanen reached her side first, as always.

"Dira," rumbled the tiger. "Let me help."

"Don't call me Dira, damn you," gasped the pirate chief. Awkwardly she rose. "Only Simone could call me that! And Hazezon, damn his white whiskers. And most especially I damn Johan."

Even addled, Adira blinked. Johan had never run away before. Always he stole opportunities from the crisis at hand. What secret knowledge sent him pelting helter-skelter for the upper air?

"Haahhh!" A cobra's hiss startled everyone. Like a ghost from the mist, or smoke issuing from a fissure in the ground, Shauku rematerialized. The vampire grinned with needle teeth and peered with black eyes like burn holes in her yellow parchment skull. Withered hands crooked in the air. "Stand fast, ye humans!"

Indeed, pirates and pinefolk again felt their limbs stiffen, and this time Adira knew they wouldn't escape. Nothing could save them.

In one long stride, Jedit Ojanen slung a balled paw far behind his shoulder, wound up with all his massive weight, and punched the vampire square in the brisket. Shauku was plucked off her feet as if hurled from a catapult. She struck a stone wall thirty feet away with a bone-breaking crunch, then flopped on her shriveled face out of sight amid boulders.

Adira grunted. "How did you do that? That curse petrifies people in their tracks!"

"This time she commanded humans, not mortals." Jedit grinned so long white fangs winked below his muzzle. "Nor tigers."

"The legionnaires?" Magfire peered through a haze of smoke and dust. The tattered soldiers fell into a ragged encircling rank as an officer rapped orders in a foreign tongue. "They ring us still."

With the vampire temporarily out of the way, Adira had bigger worries. Not far off, the green-flushed cosmic horror peered upward with bulging eyes. Even the hideous tongues and tentacles were turned upward as if awaiting deliverance from the sky. And Johan, Adira recalled dimly, had quit this chamber running.

"Never mind the legionnaires! They're not the threat! Grab Whistledove." Adira squatted where the brownie lay as if asleep, hoping against sense for a breath of life. But one clasp of a cold hand made Adira let go. "Oh, for pity and cruelty! Leave her! Make ready to run!"

"Run how?" asked someone. "Adira, wait!"

Adira Strongheart pushed past her crew and Magfire's to stand not twenty feet from the nearest legionnaires.

Pointing with her sword, she called, "Hear me! The cosmic horror wakes and works celestial magic! The mage we fought read the beast's dreams and now flees as if his skirts were afire! I don't know what portends, but best we all flee without further foolishness!"

Legionnaires turned hooded heads to hear orders. Some officer, in garb indistinguishable from the rest, hesitated a moment. Not seeing Shauku, he decided. With a curt bark in a foreign tongue, the legionnaires faced left and double-timed in two ranks to the nearest tunnel.

"Who'd believe that?" marveled Magfire.

Adira jolted her with a smart shove. "Run! All of you! Just run!"

Her crew and some foresters called questions. The pirate only shouted to keep running, pushing shoulders and prodding kidneys. Johan's desertion and Adira's panic proved infectious. Soon everyone saved their breath to run.

"Keep up!" called Adira. She scooped the wounded Heath under the armpit to hurry him along. "All of you! Don't dally! Whatever set Johan running must be bigger than any threat of vampire or soldiers!"

Racing into a dark tunnel, far ahead they heard a hollow boom.

Panting, Wilemina asked, "Whatever can that be?"

"At a guess," gasped Adira Strongheart, "it's the entire mountain crashing down on our heads! *Run!*"

Chapter 19

The race up twisting tunnels was an unending nightmare.

Jasmine Boreal's groundquake had splintered stone in a thousand places. Gaps as wide as three feet threatened to engulf the heroes every dozen yards. Thrice they had to skirt or scramble over fallen rocks that blocked the passageway. Murdoch and Magfire had rescued some torches, but dust boiled thick. Jedit's cat eyes led the way, but everyone's eyes and noses streamed. Coughing tore at throats.

Booms and crashes sounded hither and yon, some percussions so hard they shook the ground. That the mountain might collapse and entomb them spurred the adventurers on.

After what seemed hours, Jedit called that roots snaked underfoot. Coughing, wheezing, half-blind from smoke and dust, holding each others' shirt tails, the heroes blundered past fallen rock—

—and miraculously found themselves outside in an overcast noon.

Finally clear of the cursed castle and caverns, people lagged, sobbing for air. Adira let no one rest. Slapping, cursing, batting, she bullied them like balky sheep away from the ruins, into the forest, and up the valley's gentle slope until their feet slipped on pine needles. Exhausted, some dropped weapons or tackle, but Adira urged them on.

"Must we . . . run . . . clear to Buzzard's Bay?" rasped Murdoch. His breath frosted in crisp autumn air.

"We're . . . free of the haunts!" gasped Wilemina. "May we . . . Oh, my!"

A keening whistle rose to a harsh scream that drowned out words. Everyone cast their eyes to the sky. A black jot marred the overcast like a hole punched in cloud cover. But in seconds the jot loomed big as a moon, then bigger.

When the meteor struck the ground, the roaring impact flicked the onlookers off their feet. As they stiffly clambered upright, they spotted a new hole in the valley floor. Fifty feet across, the crater showed black loam and yellow sand pitched out in windrows like wheat. Heath pointed to other fresh holes scattered about, a half dozen or more.

"Those booms we heard!"

"More stones fall!" Kyenou pointed straight up.

Another meteor sizzled from the sky, growing larger in fractions of seconds. This time no one gawked. They ran uphill, astonished they'd ever felt winded.

Twice more the heroes were tossed off the ground like ants flipped off a stalk of grass. Each time they surged onward, up the shallow valley dominated by Shauku's castle. Holding hands, urging each other on, dodging loose boulders and broken trees, they trotted doggedly with aching legs and lungs.

Came a whistle so fierce their ears rang and heads felt swollen to bursting. Adira screamed to dive for cover. No one heard, but pirates and pinefolk flung themselves flat on the forest floor.

The howling ended with a noise like the end of the world. A crash and smash resounded so vast their minds couldn't encompass it but shut down and left them deafened and stunned. The world shook like a bog, so hard that pebbles and sticks pinged upon them where they clutched hands over ears and heads.

A long, long time the heroes lay, stunned, half-blind, and as numb as if struck with sledgehammers. Gradually, as the sun pierced the cloud cover and warmed their chilled and filthy heads, one, then two, could rise to their feet. Gently they helped others up.

The ruined castle and hill were gone.

* * * * *

"Let them go."

"Magfire!" Adira Strongheart snorted. "The world has truly turned topsy-turvy if you let enemies escape unharried!"

"They quit the field. We hold it," said Magfire. "To fight for revenge is foolish."

Magfire and Adira stood atop a tree toppled like a bridge. As the sun set, the two chiefs watched a line of yellow and black trickle out of the valley. Some thirty-odd Akron Legionnaires had survived the onslaught of the shooting star. Tired soldiers and cadets shouldered pack baskets and blanket rolls and trudged east of north, presumably bound for Buzzard's Bay and a voyage home. Magfire spat after them.

"I hope Shauku's truly dead." Adira stared at the vast crater where the castle had stood. "At the least she's buried beneath a mountain's worth of stone. Along with that poor cosmic horror, and Simone, and Whistledove."

A laugh welled up to pierce Adira's gloomy thoughts. Below their wooden span, and despite the autumnal chill, pirates and pine folk splashed beside a stream that meandered through the forest in a rocky mossy bed. Filthy as outhouse rats, looking the sorriest of ragpickers, men and women stripped to sop off grime and blood, and modesty be damned. They guzzled water until their bellies sloshed. Safe, with good water and some rest, they were happy. Adira envied them.

Adira Strongheart hopped from the tree trunk and padded silently over pine needles. She breathed deeply, only now appreciating the wonder and glory of just being alive. Kicking off her seaboots and shucking her ratty sweater and shirt, she sluiced frigid water over her chestnut curls and ample breasts.

"I don't ken it all." Murdoch sat back and admired his chief's form, blatantly staring. "Did that sky-monster pull down a shooting star to commit suicide? Why didn't it do that sooner?"

"We'll never know." Shivering, Adira donned her sweater and finger combed her hair. "You'll have to ask Johan. He gleaned its thoughts."

"There's no trace of him?" Wilemina hissed as, one-handed, she bathed a sword cut on her hip. "Surely he can't get clean away? Where's the justice?"

"Justice weighs differently on tyrants." Adira let the argument drop. She was weary to her bones from weeks of warfare and worry. Frankly, she didn't care what the cosmic horror or Johan had done. No amount of talking would change the past. "But don't fret. A blight like Johan will surely pop up again."

"A weed that needs uprooting." Jedit Ojanen padded up silently. "I circled the vale twice but failed to sniff any trace. Nothing even of his entourage. Perhaps my nose is still stuffed full of dirt. *Ach!* Caves are for bears, not tigers!"

Without warning, the tiger leaped in the air like a swan taking flight, then splashed in a great gout of flying water. The humans on the banks chirped and yelled, but all in fun, for all were glad to be alive. Grinning with wicked fangs, impervious to cold, Jedit sloshed on his back and blew a waterspout.

Sitting the stream bank, Adira sopped her shirt on rocks and rung it out. Washing done, she counted noses and found a dismally low number.

Sergeant Murdoch, his naked torso sporting a dozen old scars and several new lacerations. Sister Wilemina, skinny as a skinned rabbit with arms and shoulders taut as bowstrings.

Jasmine Boreal, soaking a cloud of strawberry hair. Heath, gazing into the distance, dreaming wide awake. And Jedit, who stained the stream pink from an uncountable number of cuts and scrapes.

Adira's throat tightened fit to choke her. In her wake bobbed corpses as from a slave ship. Virgil, Simone, Peregrine, Whistledove. Why had she embarked on a life of adventure that brought so few rewards and so much destruction to so many?

She murmured aloud, "Because I know no other life. Shall I sit in a corner and spin my days away?"

"Beg pardon?" Magfire had doffed her silver fox mantle and loom-woven shirt. Revealed was a woman broad as a door across shoulders and hips with more scars than even Murdoch could boast. She bit her lips as she bathed a dozen nicks and dings.

"Nothing." Adira Strongheart used a handful of sopping grass to scrub her seaboots. "I wish we'd been friends."

"I also," conceded the war chief. "But when thunderheads butt, lightning flashes. I'm sorry your friend died but not sorry my brother lived."

"Nor am I." Adira sighed and resumed scrubbing. "Any road, you'll be shed of us soon. We must hie back to Palmyra, though we'll sail from Buzzard's Bay rather than trek overland. Walking's for horses."

The women were quiet, for once sharing time without quarreling. People fussed to clean clothes and tackle, glad for small tasks. A whistle piped through the trees. Magfire whistled back. Hunters from Magfire's tribe trickled in as the sun set. They carried partridges and rabbits and two barren does. Murdoch laughed for happiness.

"What more bonny sight can a hungry soldier see than food hung on the spit!"

The adventurers rested while Magfire's hunters kindled a pit fire and chopped roasts. Jedit Ojanen crawled from the water and sprawled on his back. For once Wilemina gave in to temptation and rubbed his furry white belly.

As the fire crackled and savory smells filled the night, Jasmine Boreal broke the silence. "With your permission, Adira, or without, I wish to remain with Magfire's tribe, if they'll have me. I'm not cut out for pirating, it seems. I've no use for a sword, so no worth to you. Better I spend my time sharing spells with the tribe shamans. Magfire, may I?"

Magfire nodded. Adira Strongheart only shrugged. The druid had proven prickly and aloof and would not be missed.

"If that's the case . . ." Taurion, the doughty trailblazer and thinker, blushed to find every eye upon him. "If you w-wouldn't mind, Adira, I'd like to join your Circle. I wish to see the world. Too, I feel an obligation. Simone's sacrifice gave me life. I would repay that debt."

"With your life?" Adira turned serious. "I fear to recruit anyone these days. My crew only learns new ways to be killed."

An uncomfortable silence fell. Magfire nudged Adira's elbow, a silent request on her brother's behalf. Adira waved a hand.

"Yes, Taurion, you're welcome."

"And me?" Kyenou, in her long leather shirt dotted with ermine tails, waggled her double-ended spear.

Adira blinked, for the female scout hadn't said ten words so far. "Uh, if Magfire will release your oath of fealty."

"I enlist only volunteers," said Magfire. "Like you, Adira. Then when the going gets hard, they've only themselves to blame. It cuts down the bellyaching."

"Well put." But the pirate queen's mind drifted, already charting their next course. She wondered what transpired in Palmyra and Bryce, and what Hazezon Tamar did.

She mused aloud, "Say your good-byes while you may. We shan't linger long."

Sighing, Adira clapped Magfire's knee. "Some good comes

of this suffering. It's lucky we met the people of the pines. Luckier we became allies. With Johan loose, all of Jamuraa will be engulfed in his madness before long. That's my prophecy."

Strength sagging, Adira laid back on pine needles and watched stars wink on in a perfect autumn night. Worry later, she decided. She had work still.

Sitting up, Adira announced, "Jedit Ojanen, I appoint you lieutenant of the Robaran Mercenaries."

"Me?" The dozing tiger crooked his neck, looking so puzzled that everyone laughed.

"It's your own fault." Adira kept a straight face, but her eyes twinkled. "You've proven capable in combat and even at taking command when needed. You've saved every life here a dozen times. What d'ya say?"

"I say . . ." Jedit coiled upright. In evening firelight, his amber-green eyes sparkled like emeralds. "Thank you. I'm sure my father would be proud."

"He would. All your homeland shall be. You'll see." Adira cleared her throat. Damn sentimentality, she thought. "For the rest of you moss-back turtle-thumpers, while we wait on supper, drag out your blades and hone a fine edge. Wherever we go, we'll need three things for certain. Good beef, good ale, and sharp steel!"

MAGIC: The Gathering®
Tales from the world of Magic

Dragons of Magic
ED. J. ROBERT KING

From the time of the Primevals to the darkest hours of the Phyrexian Invasion, dragons have filled Dominaria. Few of their stories have been told—until now. Learn the secrets of the most powerful dragons in the multiverse!

The Myths of Magic
ED. JESS LEBOW

Stories and legends, folktales and tall tales. These are the myths of Dominaria, stories captured on the cards of the original trading card game. Stories from J. Robert King, Francis Lebaron, and others.

The Colors of Magic
ED. JESS LEBOW

Argoth is decimated. Tidal waves have turned canyons into rivers. Earthquakes have leveled the cities. Dominaria is in ruins. Now the struggle is to survive. Tales from such authors as Jeff Grubb, J. Robert King, Paul Thompson, and Francis Lebaron.

Rath and Storm
ED. PETER ARCHER

The flying ship *Weatherlight* enters the dark, sinister plane of Rath to rescue its kidnapped captain. But, as the stories in this anthology show, more is at stake than Sisay's freedom.

A world begins anew...

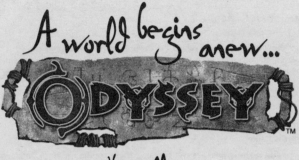

Vance Moore

**A hundred years has passed since the invasion.
Dominaria is still in ruins.**

**Only the strongest manage to survive in this
brutal post-apocalyptic world. Experience the glory and
agony of champion pit fighters as they enter the arena
to do combat for treasure.**

In September 2001,
begin a journey into the depths of this reborn
and frighteningly hostile world.

The tales that started it all...

New editions from **DRAGONLANCE**® creators
Margaret Weis & Tracy Hickman

The great modern fantasy epic – now available in paperback!

THE ANNOTATED CHRONICLES

Margaret Weis & Tracy Hickman
return to the Chronicles,
adding notes and commentary
in this annotated edition of the
three books that began
the epic saga.

SEPTEMBER 2001

THE LEGENDS TRILOGY

Now with stunning cover art by award-winning fantasy artist Matt Stawicki,
these new versions of the beloved trilogy will be treasured for years to come.

Time of the Twins • War of the Twins • Test of the Twins

FEBRUARY 2001